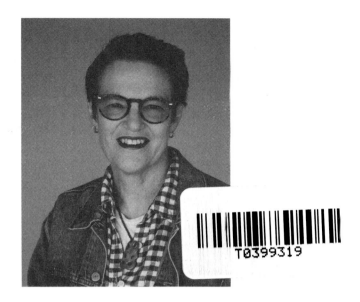

Joanne Drayton is an acclaimed New Zealand author whose output is globally recognised. Her book *Hudson & Halls: The Food of Love* was the winner of the Royal Society Te Apārangi Award for General Non-Fiction at the Ockham New Zealand Book Awards in May 2019, and was a cover story for the *NZ Listener* in October 2018.

Joanne's *The Search for Anne Perry* was numbered in the top 10 non-fiction books on the *New York Times* bestseller list. It was a finalist in the New Zealand Book Awards in August 2013, the subject of a *60 Minutes* programme and a cover story for the *NZ Listener*. It is an 'important' and 'beguiling' read that has received excellent reviews. Both *The Search for Anne Perry* and *Hudson & Halls: The Food of Love* have been optioned for feature films.

Her critically acclaimed *Ngaio Marsh: Her Life in Crime* (2008) was a Christmas pick of the *Independent* newspaper when it was released in the UK in 2009. Her other biographies of expatriate painters include *Frances Hodgkins: A Private Viewing* (Random House, 2005); *Rhona Haszard: An Experimental Expatriate New Zealand Artist* (CUP, 2002); and *Edith Collier: Her Life and Work* (CUP, 1999). She has curated exhibitions and publishes in art history, theory and biography. In 2007, she was awarded a National Library Fellowship, in 2017 the prestigious Logan Fellowship at the Carey Institute in upstate New York, and in 2019 and 2020, the Michael King Writers Centre and Stout Scholar residencies.

Joanne is a research associate at the University of Auckland and an English teacher at Avondale College. She lives in Auckland, New Zealand, with her partner and three cats.

the Queen's Wife

Joanne Drayton

PENGUIN

UK | USA | Canada | Ireland | Australia
India | New Zealand | South Africa | China

Penguin is an imprint of the Penguin Random House group of companies, whose addresses can be found at global.penguinrandomhouse.com.

First published by Penguin Random House New Zealand, 2023

1 3 5 7 9 10 8 6 4 2

Text © Joanne Drayton, 2023

The moral right of the author has been asserted.

All rights reserved. Without limiting the rights under copyright reserved above, no part of this publication may be reproduced, stored in or introduced into a retrieval system, or transmitted, in any form or by any means (electronic, mechanical, photocopying, recording or otherwise), without the prior written permission of both the copyright owner and the above publisher of this book.

Design by Cat Taylor © Penguin Random House New Zealand
Illustrations by Joanne Drayton and Suzanne Vincent Marshall, unless otherwise indicated
Cover artworks: red queen Hinepau and white queen Gunnhildr, by Joanne Drayton, photographed by Neil Finlay
Poem on page 5 used with kind permission of Patti Gurekian
Author photograph by Fiona Quinn
Prepress by Soar Communications Group
Printed and bound in Australia by Griffin Press, an Accredited ISO AS/NZS 14001 Environmental Management Systems Printer

A catalogue record for this book is available from the National Library of New Zealand.

ISBN 978-0-14-377677-2
eISBN 978-0-14-377678-9

The assistance of Creative New Zealand towards the production of this book is gratefully acknowledged by the publisher.

penguin.co.nz

It talks and sings to me,
It follows on walks with me,
It preys and sticks to me
With all of its power and might,

Even though

I did not ask for this,
This need for a voice,
This need to write.

Patti Gurekian

—

For my soulmate
Sue

For Katherine, Jeremy, Jason
and my brother Guy

For my mentors,
Harriet, Fr John and Rebecca

And in memory of my mother
Pat Drayton (1935–2022)

'I may be criticized for applying the term vikings to the Polynesian ancestors, but the term has come to mean bold, intrepid mariners and so is not the monopoly of the hardy Norsemen of the North Atlantic. To the Polynesians, the sunset symbolized death and the spirit land to which they returned, but the sunrise was the symbol of life, hope, and new lands that awaited discovery.'

Sir Peter Buck (Te Rangi Hīroa), *Vikings of the Sunrise*, 1938

Frantisek Riha-Scott

CONTENTS

PREFACE 13

PRELUDE 15

CHAPTER ONE: **Escape to Whanganui** 19

CHAPTER TWO: **The Beginning of the Affair** 38

CHAPTER THREE: **Canterbury University and Cleaning Carpets** 44
I: The Lewis Chess Pieces 50

CHAPTER FOUR: **My Freudian Slip** 56
I: Whakapapa: Sue's Ancestry 62

CHAPTER FIVE: **A Stolen Kiss** 67
II: The Lewis Chess Pieces 74

CHAPTER SIX: **Roped Together** 79
II: Whakapapa: Sue's Ancestry 85

CHAPTER SEVEN: **A Fire Sale in Christchurch** 88
    III: The Lewis Chess Pieces 94

CHAPTER EIGHT: **Moaning and Groaning** 98
    III: Whakapapa: Sue's Ancestry 106

CHAPTER NINE: **Millie and Billie from Chile** 109
    IV: The Lewis Chess Pieces 117

CHAPTER TEN: **A Diet of Worms** 121
    IV: Whakapapa: Sue's Ancestry 128

CHAPTER ELEVEN: **Dovedale Avenue was Paradise** 134
    V: The Lewis Chess Pieces 141

CHAPTER TWELVE: **Things You Love** 145
    V: Whakapapa: Sue's Ancestry 151

CHAPTER THIRTEEN: **Barbara and Ringley** 154
    VI: The Lewis Chess Pieces 167

CHAPTER FOURTEEN: **An Amputation** 172
    VI: Whakapapa: Sue's Ancestry 183

CHAPTER FIFTEEN: **Whanganui, a City Divided** 185
    VII: The Lewis Chess Pieces 197

CHAPTER SIXTEEN: **Whanganui and the Family Court** 200
    VII: Whakapapa: Sue's Ancestry 211

CHAPTER SEVENTEEN: **The Vengeful Victory** 216
    VIII: The Lewis Chess Pieces 231

CHAPTER EIGHTEEN: **Life's Strange Little Detours** 235
    VIII: Whakapapa: Sue's Ancestry 248

CHAPTER NINETEEN: **A Clean Start in Auckland** 252
    IX: The Lewis Chess Pieces 261

CHAPTER TWENTY: **Around-the-World Ticket** 264
  IX: Whakapapa: Sue's Ancestry 277

CHAPTER TWENTY-ONE: **The Spirit of My Ancestors** 281
  X: The Lewis Chess Pieces 296

CHAPTER TWENTY-TWO: **Alexandria, Egypt** 298
  X: Whakapapa: Sue's Ancestry 303

CHAPTER TWENTY-THREE: **A Tower and a Death** 306

CHAPTER TWENTY-FOUR: **Rhona Haszard's Daughter** 317

POSTSCRIPT 322

AUTHOR'S NOTE 326

KEY TEXTS 328

ACKNOWLEDGEMENTS 330

INDEX 332

PREFACE

Not many people want an ordinary life, but mention the word 'normal' and there's a stampede. I think of my life as ordinary, but I do believe some extraordinary things have happened. How to tell you about them? The problem is there's so much stuff. Biographer Lytton Strachey had a strategy. In his preface to *Eminent Victorians*, he suggested this: that the biographer should 'row out over that great ocean of material, and lower down into it, here and there, a little bucket, which will bring up to the light of day some characteristic specimen, from those far depths, to be examined with a careful curiosity'*. The following is a collection of memories brought up in buckets filled from the far depths of my life for your careful curiosity.

Some buckets contain the stories of objects. Museum curators call them artefacts, but for me they are carriers of magic. They sing songs to the dead and herald the future. They live in the present, but are voyagers on a journey without end. The marvel of treasured objects is that their stories are layered. There is the meaning embedded by their maker. A message fashioned in the past and made material. So often objects are a mix of practicality and enchantment. Of application to a purpose or task, and mysticism. Then there are the stories of their creators, the act of creation itself and the life of these time-travellers. Whole histories are told by a shaped bone or a notch carved

---

* Lytton Strachey, *Eminent Victorians*, London, Penguin, p 9.

in wood, by paint on canvas or marks chiselled into stone. Finally, there are the layers added to objects after their creation: how they were bought and sold, perhaps stolen or reshaped; the different values placed on them and the varying interpretations they accrue. Objects tell us who we were and what we might become.

There are buckets that relate to the search for our tribes. For my partner, Sue, they relate to the exploration of her Māori heritage and whakapapa; for me, the chronicling of a hoard of Viking chess pieces found in the Outer Hebrides, on the Isle of Lewis. Sue's journey is a peeling back of family stories, objects and relationships to reveal her bloodline. My quest is enmeshed in the sagas, annals and runestones of Scandinavia. These peoples are my ancestors, and their prized objects, my treasures. The treasures that called out to me.

In the game of chess, so full of controversy and intrigue for its early Scandinavian players, I saw the moves we make in life to win; but mostly just to survive. And in the taking of chess pieces, the parts of ourselves that are lost. Fragments of heart and soul taken by our opponents as trophies. Removed from the board. Lined up along its edge. Gaming pieces that are forever observers. Spectators of an epic struggle that in Sue's and my situation involved the ugly break-up of two marriages, chaos for our precious young children, a custody case, a lesbian love affair — moves, counter-moves, victories and defeats. For me the game of chess is an apt metaphor for our existence.

Many of these buckets tell stories that are intimate and deeply personal. They map our love, and greatest joys, and recall events that are redolent with regret. They contain accounts that are challenging to remember, difficult to tell, and that touch on the lives of others. Because of this, and to preserve the privacy of others, a few names have been changed. I fully acknowledge this book is how I experienced these events; those involved might well have viewed them differently.

The stories written in the alternating chapters in a different typeface belong to my imaginings, grounded on facts and speculation from researchers on the Lewis chessmen. And on facts and family stories from Sue in the other chapters. The rest are fragile and imperfect memories, remembered in fragments, as episodes and events, put together to shape the story I am about to tell.

PRELUDE

1960s

You probably know that Māori believe objects carry magic powers...
    I didn't learn this fact; I inhaled it. My family home was a bone-yard of objects. Mother dusted her fossil collection like other mothers tend their Lladró. Normal was a moa's leg strung with string, bone on bone, in the entrance hall. There were countless other objects: a musket; cannon balls; a rusty prospector's pan, pick and shovel; a wooden swingletree, or crossbar between horse teams, and a harness; a legion of coloured-glass and ceramic bottles, to say nothing of the Natural History section. All objects were on display. My childhood was not so much lived as curated. Home was a cabinet of curiosities, and that by no means excluded the humans.
    If they had met, my mother and modernist Mies van der Rohe would have murdered each other. 'Less was less', in Mother's opinion, 'and more was simply better'.
    This maxim did not so much define my growing up as disfigure it with clutter. There were objects everywhere: freestanding, fixed to the wall, in cabinets, on shelves, hanging from the roof. Even our toilet was a rotating installation.
    But not all objects were equal in my household. Each had a story and a

place in the march of time, but only a few were enchanted. Growing up, I knew which objects were special, and which were not. The charmed were in a lockable cabinet — the finest, on cotton wool. They had mysterious powers and the cachet of being rare. These artefacts were the proud outcome of countless family expeditions to an ancient Māori pā site at Purau, on Banks Peninsula. Thinking back today, those trips make me cringe. I can't believe we thought it was okay to unearth these artefacts and keep them. But back then my parents believed fervently in the culture and heritage of Māori, and felt they were honouring their finds by giving them a special place in their cabinet of treasures.*

My father took us to Purau in a dowdy old grey Singer motorcar, which was notoriously unreliable. Inside the car was an ocean of dark red upholstery. Red was the colour we saw when my younger brother and I fought like feral cats in the back. My mother, for whom the journey was a pilgrimage, would flail an arm in our direction, hitting the closest object — usually me. Sly looks and sulky tears were followed by a solemn lecture. Dad just drove the car.

Perhaps it's the way children collect memories, but I never remember any of those daytrips without blue skies. I have pictures in my mind of threatening weather rolling in across the sea, and lengthening shadows as we packed up to go home. But the abiding colour is blue.

Trips there were dangerous. The shingle road off the main highway was treacherously steep and one-way in the most perilous places. My parents belonged to an amateur archaeological society that had permission to dig on private land. We parked our car in a farmer's paddock, loaded ourselves up like pack animals, and followed a disused farm track down a wind-blasted valley to the sea.

The society's founder, a kaumātua named Selwyn Te Moananui Hovell, was usually there to greet us. He stayed overnight, sometimes in a makeshift shack composed of driftwood and odd bits of wreckage washed up on the shore. Close by, the sea spat spume through jagged volcanic rocks. The sea was never calm there. Archaeological trenches ran parallel to the shoreline like a battleground marked out for war.

It's the meticulousness I remember. Instead of a spade or a trowel, I was handed a brush. Not a decent-sized brush, but one fine enough to paint the missing eyebrows on the Mona Lisa. I looked incredulously between my

---

* In the 1960s my mother learned te reo Māori at night classes from Sir Paul Reeves. Before much of Aotearoa understood the importance of tikanga Māori, she was being schooled in it. The preciousness of Māoritanga is now enshrined in the Ministry of Culture and Heritage's strict guidelines for Māori finds. See AGS7 Finding of Artefacts, which is available as a pdf on the Ministry's website.

brush and the excavation site, which was half the size of a football field, and lost my hunger for hidden treasure. Every teaspoonful of dirt was sifted; every bone brushed and washed to look for chisel marks; every discarded shell or burnt rock examined. Even the worms got a working over by the seagulls, who couldn't believe their good luck.

My parents were the proud excavators of the pā's rubbish dump, which unsurprisingly contained mostly waste. They took over the partially excavated site, not realising it had been abandoned by the previous occupants for good reasons.

One of the few objects from the dump to find its next resting place in our lockable cabinet at home was a pendant in the shape of a fish. The hole where the cord went was the eye. It was made of pounamu, burned pale green in a long-ago fire. The piece was small, elegant and broken. It would have been an object cherished by its owner, a taonga. The Māori believed that these treasures carried a trace of their ancestors' wairua, or spirit. Wearing or using them called back the dead to be among the living. So, the mystery remained. How did this beautiful object end up in a mix of black midden soil, shell and refuse?

One of Selwyn Hovell's theories was that the pā had been the site of a fierce battle. He felt it. The unquiet souls of the dead were not free to make the trip to Cape Rēinga and on home to their ancestral birthplace of Hawaiki. We were believers because things at the dig site had gone wrong. There were accidents, missing implements, and the sound of wailing on the wind when people stayed overnight. Selwyn went through the process of taking the tapu off numerous times, but things continued to happen.

To a child like me who leapt metres each night to avoid the hand under the bed, these stories were chilling.

The explanation seemed to come one day when Selwyn, working steadily at the soil face, revealed a flat area of aged bone. As he continued with his soft sable brush and a trowel shaped like a palette knife, the skulls and complete skeletons of a woman and young child were uncovered. Selwyn believed the woman's presence explained our misfortunes. Her skull was smashed near the crown. It seemed she and the child buried in her arms had met with a violent end. Until her spirit and that of the child were properly released, they would stay among us.

Selwyn conducted a ceremony over the bones. We bowed our heads, and he chanted the woman and child away to Hawaiki. Their remains were interred in an unmarked grave well away from where we worked. The wailing stopped, the camp items ceased to move, we had fewer accidents.

But I never quite trusted that they were gone.

Under the soil was the footprint of a community, complete with building posts, cooking areas and signs of cultivation, but there were few human remains. When the village had been ransacked, those who could had fled. Only the woman and child remained.

Our rubbish dump never delivered a great hoard. Perhaps that was a good thing. There was an eardrop pendant, a broken flint adze and a few fishhooks carved from bone. Artefacts made from bone change colour when worn or handled, honeyed by the skin's oils. They absorb the wearer's physical as well as spiritual presence, which are then passed on to subsequent generations. For me the energy of the artefacts in our cabinet was palpable. I had met their owners. They lived. Even as a child I felt these simple objects carried the thread of memory that connected the living to the dead.

Perhaps that's why my mother never locked the cabinet door.

CHAPTER ONE

Escape to Whanganui

Life is a game of chess. You should try playing it with two queens. People usually see two queens — and no king — as game over. The laws of contest are embedded in its structures, and with a king and a queen on the board heterosexuality reigns supreme. While the queen is arguably the most dangerous piece on the board, protecting the inadequate king is what the game is all about. He moves just one square at a time. Not enough to save himself unless a clever queen, bishop, knight, rook or pawn has his back. Having two queens in courtly love on the board changes everything. The laws of nature are defied. The rules of engagement are tipped upside-down, and each move is uncharted.

I was naïve when I believed I could play on with a queen as a mate as if it made no difference. In fact, the game for me would never be the same again, and no move I made unaffected by this pairing. In the end, life — like chess — is a contest of strategic cruelty, of pieces won and lost, of sacrifices made to survive. This book is the story of a game with two queens, of two women in love, battling to stay together on the board . . .

Visiting the British Museum during a research trip to the United Kingdom in June 1996 felt like being at home for me. Dark, full of treasure: a repository of the world's wonders. There were things there I had only ever seen as images in books before. The Elgin marbles, the Rosetta Stone, the Anglo-Saxon Sutton Hoo treasure, and cabinets full of Egyptian mummies. What a complex death, I remember thinking. A body preserved for thousands of years in a swathe of bandages, guided to the afterlife by a book of spells, and an entourage of dead people.

But it wasn't marbles or magnificent mummified death that transfixed me. It was a weird collection of tiny Romanesque figures called, when I looked down to read the label, the Lewis Chessmen.

They were displayed on a simple chessboard, as if their owners had gone for a moment but would be back soon to resume play. Unlike any chess pieces I had ever seen before, they were Lilliputian-sized human figures, except for the pawns, which were shaped like miniature tombstones. It was the detailing of the faces and costumes that captivated me. This was a medieval world in miniature. In fact, it could have been almost any world — Māori even — where power resided in the hands of the rangatira and the foot soldiers were tribal warriors. The complete spectrum of society was represented from the majestic king and queen to the simple foot soldier.

Thinking back now, I was searching for my own backstory. Digging around in this world-class collection of curiosities as I did as a child in the excavations at Purau, I wanted to discover signs of my ancient past. And I wondered. Did a trace of my Scandinavian ancestors remain in these objects as they did for Māori, connecting the living and the dead? Linking past and present through legend and belief. I felt instinctively that I had found something related to me. Many years later I would have a DNA test and discover that some of my ancestors were Scandinavian. This would confirm what I had already suspected after developing Dupuytren's contracture — a syndrome known as the 'curse of the Vikings'.

But in that moment my sense of connection with these objects was visceral. Something that wailed, called and sang songs, that stopped me in my tracks. I wanted to pick them up, to examine them, to unravel their story. But how long can you circle a display cabinet looking with such intensity before you appear odd, or menacing? I glanced around to see if the security guard was watching, and then moved on.

Haunting thoughts of the chess pieces receded after we arrived back in Christchurch, New Zealand. My partner, Sue, and I were moving house. Less than a week after returning from our research trip retracing the footsteps of the New Zealand modernist painter Edith Collier in the United Kingdom, I was shifting to a job in Whanganui. Through our family counsellor, Sue had made a difficult, but we hoped workable, settlement with her ex-husband over custody arrangements for their children. My ex-husband, however, was intractable.

In the four years since we had separated, he had remarried, had another child and I thought moved on from his battle with me. But as we sat in the waiting room of the family counsellor's office, on the fifth floor of a building later demolished after the devastating 2011 earthquake, I realised this was far from the truth.

It was a bitter July, and ours was the last appointment on a stormy Friday evening. The rain threw itself against the enormous plate-glass windows in sheets; below, the city was a sparkle of watery diamonds in the blackness. I knew Richard was rattled, as he sat apparently calmly reading a *Where's Wally?* book from the children's area — upside-down. We were ushered into the counsellor's office like opponents on either side of the chessboard, and we matched each other, move after move, for over an hour.

But Richard would give me nothing. No custody of our children, not ever. The atmosphere became increasingly icy. We exchanged threats. It was a stalemate, and, caving into the pressure of the impasse, Trish, the counsellor, abruptly concluded the session and fled the room at high speed with Richard and me in pursuit. I guess we both hoped this finely built, fashionable woman would horsewhip the other into submission.

Outside, the waiting room was silent. The receptionist had gone home. Sue, waiting, looked up at me for any sign of hope.

'Let's get home quick,' I urged her, under my breath. I was terrified that Richard might uplift my two boys and take them back to his place.

I was so relieved when we arrived home and all four children were still there: my boys, Alex and Jeremy, and Sue's children, Jason and Katherine.

That night and the next day, Sue and I pored over the possibilities. Many variations of our future custody arrangements had already taken shape in my mind and been discussed with my ex-husband. Obviously, shared custody could only work while he and I lived in the same town. Unless some new arrangement could be made, if I left Christchurch, custody of the children automatically reverted to Richard. Now that no agreement had been reached, it seemed only the most drastic options were left. But if I took my children with me I was breaking the law. I was due to start work in Whanganui on the Monday morning. Now it was Saturday, already. I had no tickets booked, no arrangements made except a car passage on the Interislander ferry. Naïvely, I had believed there would be a resolution.

Sue's children seemed resigned to their future. While we would see him in the holidays, Jason was to stay with his father, and Katherine would join Sue and me in Whanganui in October. Alex, my elder son, was adamant about staying in Christchurch with his father, but Jeremy, who was ten, was torn between my ex-husband and me. He cried in bed at night over our separation. I was completely conflicted. I couldn't stay in Christchurch. We were desperately short of money and this might be my last shot at a proper job.

'Why don't you ring the lawyer?' Sue suggested. We had her home phone number. She had become something of a friend over the months of custody negotiation. I agreed. That was the thing to do.

Our phone conversation was ominous from the beginning.

'If you want to see your son again,' she told me, 'don't leave him behind. The law takes a dim view of parents who take their children, but an even dimmer view of those who abandon them.

'These things take months to settle in the Family Court. You'll have Jeremy with you for 18 months, or so,' she explained. 'If the decision goes against you, then at least you've had that time.'

But it would be expensive, she promised me, and Sue and I were broke. My three years as a doctoral student at university had left us depleted. Years as a clergy wife in the Anglican Church before that meant I had no reserves. 'The only thing I got from the Church was holey underwear,' I used to joke to Sue. But financially this was pretty well true.

Eager to share the responsibility of my decision, I asked the lawyer, finally: 'So, what do you think I should do?'

'I can't answer that. In fact, we shouldn't even be discussing this.' I'd crossed a line.

'Okay. So, don't give me legal advice. Tell me as a friend. What would you do?'

'I'd take him.'

Our conversation ended there. I didn't tell her I would abscond with Jeremy, and she didn't tell me what would happen if I did.

I find peace in motion, so I paced the floor endlessly, getting nowhere. It was Sue who took charge.

'Why don't you take Jeremy with you on a red-eye flight to Wellington?

You can catch a bus there and disappear for the day. I'll drive the car to Picton and take it across on the ferry.'

'I'm just too stressed,' I said, paralysed by fear and indecision.

It was early evening when Sue sat down on our bed and began ringing around making arrangements, and jotting down flight and bus times, and costs, on a piece of scrap paper. She booked us under her surname, Marshall, so that Jeremy and I could make our illicit escape to Whanganui. My ex-husband, now no longer a Church minister, used private investigators at his new job at the Accident Compensation Corporation (ACC), and I knew he was on friendly terms with a number of them. It was possible he had the house under surveillance: my imagination boiled. Had he guessed that I might try and escape with Jeremy? Were they watching us now? Would he try and stop us?

That evening when we said 'good night' to the children, it was actually 'goodbye'. My children both believed they would be staying in Christchurch with their father. Jeremy cried himself to sleep.

Once they were asleep, we packed. I had earlier secretly filled a suitcase full of Jeremy's clothes and some favourite toys. I now packed my things, and Sue packed hers. Then we tied a giant trunk full of my books and folders of notes on the roof of our Ford Telstar. The car had belonged to Sue's parents. Her father had been tragically killed, and her mother had died 18 months later. This was one of the few possessions from their estate that became hers.

As I flung the rope under and over the trunk, winding it around and pulling it tighter each time, I thought about things. If this had been my legacy, I would have policed it more fiercely. But Sue had a different way of holding on to things. From almost the first time we met she told me she was Māori. It was part of the family myth. But to look at her this seemed preposterous. Three generations of Māori women marrying British-born men had given her grey eyes and sandy-blonde hair. But beneath her fine-textured olive skin beat the heart of a Māori. Tall, statuesque, she was a woman who walked lightly through the world.

The finishing touches to packing the car were the big, bulky gas heater and cylinder, and my 1989 SE Mac computer, which contained every bad or sublime thought I'd had since the beginning of my PhD.

We went to bed to grab an hour or so of sleep, but there was no sleep for me. Every terrible possibility ran through my mind.

I had gone to bed half-dressed, and didn't need an alarm clock to wake me, even though I had set one.

'Sue . . . Sue . . . get up,' I whispered. 'It's time to go.' We were quickly out of bed. I finished dressing in the dark and slipped downstairs to open the door to Barry, a brave friend of ours who had offered to be there when the children awoke, and when our ex-husbands arrived later in the day to pick up the children.

Sue left first. We opened the doors to the internal garage by hand, and almost soundlessly the car slipped out and down the short asphalt drive to the street.

I scanned the darkness to see if anyone was there. The street was empty of cars. Our duplex was on a slight rise, not far from a corner street-lamp, so it was a handy vantage point. I couldn't see anything suspicious.

Soon after Sue left, the taxi arrived to take me and Jeremy to the airport. My heart pounded. This was another moment of vulnerability.

I handed the taxi driver our suitcases, and he shut the car door behind me.

'Now take this and whatever you do, don't lose it,' Sue had said as she handed me a scrap of notepaper with all our travel details on it. I didn't have tickets, just a flight time and a booking number. Now I scrambled around in my backpack, going from pocket to pocket, searching for the piece of paper with mounting desperation. Just before we reached the airport, I found it. I helped Jeremy out of the car, paid the taxi driver, and grabbed our bags.

As the woman behind the counter handed over our boarding passes, I remember thinking that my anxiety must be manifest. But the exchange went ahead as usual.

We were early, so I took Jeremy to the cafeteria, which was just opening up.

'Have anything you like,' I said, feeling that this was a moment for mild celebration.

Jeremy chose a large meat pie. Within seconds the pie was being generously covered in sauce spluttering out of a large red plastic tomato. I helped myself to a piece of ginger crunch from the cabinet. But my appetite had vanished. I trimmed off a corner of the slice with a knife and ate it distractedly, all the time watching Jeremy tuck into his pie. His large, chubby hands wielded his knife and fork with awkward determination.

Everything about Jeremy was big for his age. The paediatrician skimming through the wards at Christchurch Women's Hospital had been stopped in her tracks at the sight of him as a baby.

'This child will be a giant,' she pronounced after the briefest look.

'How can you possibly tell?' I asked, amazed.

'Look at the hands, the feet, his length! I've seen lots of babies,' she said as she turned to go, 'but he's going to be huge.' Initially, I was sceptical, but her prediction began to come true. Jeremy shot exponentially off his Plunket chart. Holding his hand crossing the road was like holding an adult's hand. When Jeremy came to play, mothers padlocked their refrigerators. But he was sweet, and gentle, and mine — for now.

From the moment I woke him that morning, he seemed relieved. Like some difficult decision had been made for him.

'Are you sure you want to go with me?' I had asked him in his bedroom as he dressed and then again at the airport. I knew this was unfair. But for some reason, asking salved some of my conscience.

Jeremy was finishing his pie as the announcement to board came over the loudspeaker.

'Let's go, Jeremy,' I said, picking up a small brown paper bag from the counter and dropping my piece of ginger crunch into it.

My heart pounded again as the woman took our boarding passes, but she just smiled at Jeremy.

The sun rose on our flight to Wellington. It was a magnificent sky of reds, hot pinks, and oranges. I breathed deeply for the first time as the heavenly furnace turned green, then a gorgeous eggshell blue.

When I looked down at Jeremy, he was smiling. This was an adventure for him. Deep down I think he liked the idea that he had been taken: chosen. But he was ever the diplomat.

'Dad will be okay, won't he, Mum? He's got Alex and you've got me, and I'll stay with him in the holidays.'

'Yes, Jeremy, that's right.' And it did seem right to me. But I knew his father would never see it that way. Although it sounds terrible, in reality in custody disputes children are pawns on the board. On one hand they are moved and manipulated; on the other, as François-André Danican Philidor has said, 'pawns are the soul of the game'.

Wellington was glorious. No wind. No one to stop us as we disembarked. We collected our bags from the baggage claim and went outside. The sky was cloudless, but out of the sun it was freezing cold. There had been a heavy frost. The puddles were still icy, and in the shade the ground was white.

I looked around, still fearing we might be spotted.

We will hide at the zoo, I thought, as I scanned a list of Wellington attractions. I found the bus number on a route map, then checked the timetable. We waited just a short time before the bus arrived. Jeremy leaned on the back of the seat in front, excited by the prospect of going to the zoo.

Once there, he ran from cage to cage in delight.

'Mum, Mum, look at the polar bear!'

Then: 'What are those?'

'Meerkats,' I said with authority, surreptitiously double-checking the signage to make sure I was right. This was an encounter of equals: we stood looking at the meerkats as inquisitively as they looked back.

I bought myself a coffee and an orange drink for Jeremy, but felt more comfortable sitting away from the crowds of people out enjoying the day.

I checked my watch repeatedly. Our bus was the last of the day to Whanganui. With time to spare, we caught a connection from outside the zoo to the bus terminus at the railway station from where our intercity bus departed.

The afternoon shadows were deepening, and a bitter wind had picked up as the bus driver checked his clipboard for our names.

'One adult, one child, for Marshall,' he called, scanning the list.

'Yes, that's right.' We were on the list. What a relief. I still looked at him anxiously to see if I could detect a flicker of recognition. But all he did was stow our bags into the luggage locker, and turn to the next passenger.

Jeremy and I found a seat towards the back of the bus. It was warm and comfortable. As Jeremy nestled into the window seat and began playing death games with his two plastic Ninja Turtles, I reached up to my bag above our heads and retrieved the papers I had been sent by the lecturer I was replacing in Whanganui.

This was my next jeopardy. I had taken the job assuring my new boss that I could teach anything. On Tuesday I had my first class, and I wasn't entirely sure of the subject, let alone how to teach it.

Critical theory? I thought. Sounds dry. I was, however, about to embark on a crash course. Work seemed trivial after the day's events, but I knew in the scheme of things my job was crucial.

The gentle rocking of the bus and the engine's hum carried Jeremy off to sleep first. I picked up my papers and began reading. It was not long before the words of some post-modern theorist began to swim on the page . . .

After what seemed like seconds, but must have been several hours, we were jolted awake by the intercom. I caught the final words.

'. . . If you're not back onboard by six-thirty, the bus will depart without you.'

We rose stiffly and got off. Within seconds of entering the bus station,

Jeremy was prowling the food cabinet, looking expectantly between me and the biggest sausage roll I'd ever seen. I had insisted on no guns, and until he was three years old Jeremy's favourite toy was a Barbie doll, which impressed my feminist friends. But the battle over healthy eating was still being waged.

'How about one of these nice club sandwiches? Look, there's ham, and cheese and lettuce.'

'You have that, Mum,' said Jeremy. 'Can I have a sausage roll, please?'

It was a hard logic to argue with.

I carefully lifted Jeremy's enormous sausage roll out of the warmer with the tongs and put it onto a plate, followed by a piece of chocolate cake from the cabinet. The virtuous club sandwich went on my plate. At our table I got out my piece of ginger crunch from the morning and we feasted.

Back on board, we watched as the last stragglers left the brilliantly lit cafeteria for the bus, its engine already running in the darkness. Jeremy slept again. This was a shorter leg. I stayed awake. My mind shifted to our arrival in Whanganui.

Barbara had promised to meet us at the bus station. She was the niece of my PhD subject, Edith Collier. Medieval sculpture had captured my imagination at university, but it was early New Zealand painting that seemed the practical thing to do for my post-graduate study. I found a clever simplicity in the best of Whanganui artist Edith Collier's painting that kept me entranced for almost a decade. She lived in London for nine years, from 1913 to 1922.

Barbara had inherited the Collier family homestead, with everything in it, including all of Edith's magnificent paintings. I had stayed with Barbara numerous times since starting my PhD. When she learned that I had a job in Whanganui, she invited me to stay in the flat attached to her house until I found permanent accommodation. She had accepted the fact that my marriage had ended, and the fact that I lived with a woman friend, but beyond that it was a case of 'ask no questions, tell no lies'. Instinctively, I understood the revelation of my sexuality would take me off the board. Barbara would never allow me access to her aunt's material if she knew I was a lesbian. This would finish my PhD and any future prospects of an academic job.

She was an astute, but largely uneducated woman, who had been schooled on rough-and-ready farms, and later in the ways of well-to-do rural 'spinsterdom'. Barbara was an odd mixture. She had lived a frustrated life of comfortable martyrdom: aging parents and relations — she had nursed them, in turn, to the grave — never living life for herself. At the end of all the sacrifice there had been a pot of gold, but not enough youth left to enjoy it.

Barbara could have made a killing when she inherited Ringley and all its contents. Instead, she gave the most valuable of Edith's work to the Sarjeant Gallery. I liked Barbara from the moment I met her, but her house, a rambling villa on St John's Hill, scared me to death.

Fearful thoughts swirled around in my head. Barbara knew we were coming, but was she ready for the fall-out from an abduction? I told myself it wasn't 'an abduction'; but knew most people would see it that way.

Jeremy slumped against me, snoring. He had snored for as long as I could remember. His snoring had the volume and timbre of an overweight middle-aged man. People gaped at his pram when he was a baby, as it jolted *Exorcist*-style on its wheels with each intake of breath. I parked it slightly around the corner when we visited the doctor's surgery to avoid the flabbergasted stares.

I shook him gently as the bus pulled into the station.

'Wake up Jeremy, we're here.'

I could see Barbara illuminated by the light above a sign. *Welcome Intercity Bus Passengers to Wanganui*, it announced.

At the time Barbara was about 60 years old, but her face was very lined, as if she had done all her aging at once. She was short and rotund, with large hands — 'the hands of a sculptor' Edith had called them — and short blonde-grey hair, and dazzling blue eyes. They twinkled eerily like cut glass in the light, until one day she had revealed the mystery, admitting the lenses were artificial.

'Fantastic to see you, Barbara,' I said, stooping to give her a hug. 'This is Jeremy.'

'I've heard a lot about you, Jeremy,' she responded, looking at him almost eye-to-eye.

'How was your trip?' she asked.

'Quite a drama,' I said, knowing this was the understatement of my life.

'Great,' she said, searching through her handbag for her car keys. 'Ah! Found them . . . You can tell me all about it over dinner. I've got a big lamb roast waiting in the oven at home with lots of vegetables, gravy and mint sauce. Hope you're hungry.'

Jeremy and I shot each other a horrified look. Even he was green at the prospect of a second dinner.

We drove to Ringley in Barbara's white charger of a Holden station wagon that required a booster seat of cushions for her to see over the dashboard. Henry Collier, the family's founding patriarch, had built Ringley originally as a relatively modest family home, but it was added to with each prosperous business venture, until there were nine bedrooms for nine children. There was also an extensive formal dining room and lounge with a gloriously embossed Victorian tin ceiling, large reception areas, halls, and a huge country kitchen that Barbara had created by knocking the galley kitchen and pantry into one room.

The park-sized lawn and formal gardens were in blackness as we drove down the long, curving drive.

Barbara pulled into the garage, and in the light of the security lamp triggered by our arrival, we unloaded our suitcases. As Barbara opened the front door her hyper-charged Jack Russell, Sam, came bounding out, jumping and licking wildly. We later discovered that Sam had a foot fetish and a penchant for eating cat pooh. He would lurk around our cats' dirt-box, licking his lips. Waiting.

'This looks yummy,' Jeremy said, as he sat down to dinner number two. I shot him a stunned look, but caught just a hint of defeat in his expression.

'Not too much for me, Barbara,' I announced.

'Are you sure you haven't had dinner?' she challenged.

'No. No. We've had nothing much. Just a light snack,' I lied.

We were interrupted by a ringing sound; Barbara's property was heavily alarmed. At the gate was a sensor that was tripped by cars that passed through it. It was so sensitive that a trail of ants walking across the beam had set it off intermittently for days on end until the culprits were discovered and duly sprayed. The alarm rang loudly in the house.

'Who would that be at this time of night?' Barbara asked, startled.

'That'll be Sue,' I replied, praying that it was.

We waited a few minutes, then heard the sound of gravel crunching under the weight of car tyres, and saw the security lights go on. To my enormous relief it was Sue and not the police.

Fortunately she was hungry after her trip, and she and Barbara did justice to the meal.

Later that evening the terrible phone call came through. It was my ex-husband, Richard, on the end of the line, cold and withdrawn. He had worked out where we were and rung Barbara's number.

This was the voice of war. Our contest had begun in earnest.

It was three years before this, almost to the day, when I first visited Barbara at Ringley. Her welcoming generosity was in full force back then as well.

I had contacted her to ask permission to look at her aunt's archive at the Sarjeant Gallery, and in true country-style she invited me to stay the night.

The Sarjeant Gallery is a white, domed, neo-classical building that sits up on a hill. From its front steps, there are vistas of the city of Whanganui. At its rear on a clear day, the distant cone of Mount Ruapehu is visible. In its bowels are the gallery's collections and its archive. I was given full access to Edith Collier's work, which was stacked haphazardly in corners, on shelves, with the bigger framed paintings being kept in something that reminded me of a wooden bicycle rack. I loved the challenge of piecing together Collier's life with her art.

It was love at first sight. Some of the work was dangerously modern, and her nudes were breath-taking. Studies in charcoal pencil with so much life they almost stepped off the page; quiet oils, a girl sitting naked on a bed in a London attic flat; dancing Matisse-like figures in gouache and water colour; and the enigmatic *Lady of Kent* sitting starkers in a landscape of oast houses.

But Edith's words as much as anything opened up her world to me. There were boxes with the letters she wrote home from England immediately before and after the First World War.

Celia Thompson, the gallery registrar, had stacked up a pile of file boxes for me, titled *Edith Collier Papers,* numbered one to eight along the spine, and more grey conservation boxes full of memorabilia. The little office where I sat was a dingy corner of the 'dungeon', the name the gallery staff called the basement. A spotlight above my head lit the desk where I read, like a restaurant scene at night in an Edward Hopper painting.

I opened the first box, and on top was a letter, handwritten in ink on a small piece of textured notepaper. It was specially conserved in a sleeve of clear ultraviolet-proof plastic. I picked it off the pile and attempted to decipher the words. It was difficult. Some were easy to read, and others were like filling in a crossword. I had to find the word that fitted the space. With perseverance things became clear.

It was a letter from the early New Zealand modernist painter Frances Hodgkins, written to Edith after her return home in 1922. Towards the bottom of the page were these words: 'I am certain your fate will bring you back to England, as mine did . . . don't mind the buffets or knocks. They are inseperable [sic] from the artist's life. Its [sic] an uphill tug all the way & its [sic] only the stout hearted who win through.'*

Sadly, Edith would never return to England.

---

* Collier, E. Papers. MS. Sarjeant Gallery, Whanganui.

I continued reading and taking notes, lost in these fragments of Edith's story.

'I'm afraid we're going to have to ask you to leave. We're closing now.' It was Celia, the registrar, again.

I stood up, groggy with concentration, packed my notepad and pen away in my backpack, and left.

Outside it was dark and gusting to gale force. In the car I turned on the overhead light and studied the map, trying to get my bearings. I went past Barbara's gate twice before I found it. As I drove up the long, looping driveway, large, splattering drops of rain began to hit the windscreen. By the time I reached the homestead with Barbara waiting at the back door, the rain was gathering momentum.

'Park your car in the garage,' she called to me, gesturing to turn in. 'I've cleared a space.'

I pulled into a large double garage filled to bursting with a ride-on mower, wheelbarrow, garden implements, workshop tools, redundant furniture, stacked winter wood, and boxes piled on top of boxes. I got out of the car as Barbara stepped forward to greet me, her eyes glinting in the light.

'Come in quick, you'll get soaked. It's going to pour down any minute.'

Walking into Ringley was like stepping through a portal in time. A musty smell permeated everything. It was ambient, like strains of incidental music. The swirling-patterned carpet was worn in doorways, and mottled and chewed along skirting boards by damp and insects. Embossed wallpapers, worn bare of pattern around light switches, hung tired and sagging on their scrim. The rooms were cavernous, festooned with giant lengths of sun-scorched nets and faded curtains.

'I'm doing it up,' Barbara announced. 'The aunts,' she said, dropping her voice, 'they let it go.'

As we approached the kitchen, over the pervasive smell of mustiness came the enticing aroma of cooking. I stood at the doorway, while Barbara moved around the dingy space with familiarity. She pulled a roast chicken out of the oven and put it on a platter.

'Can I do anything to help you? Carry these, perhaps,' I said, pointing to the serving tureens into which she had just tipped the vegetables.

'Yes, please. We're eating through there in the dining room. I've had the gas heater on all day.'

I carried the dishes through into the next room. At the end of a large expanse was a table lit with candles, and set with sparkling crystal and glinting silver. It reminded me of a nativity scene blasted by starlight.

'Where would you like me to sit, Barbara?' I called out.

'Either one,' she replied from the kitchen.

'Do you drink wine?' she asked.

'Yes,' I said, trying not to sound too enthusiastic.

'Red or white?'

'If you've got both: white, thanks.'

I heard a cork pop, and soon afterwards Barbara appeared with an open bottle of Chardonnay and a dish of minted baby peas. She poured a generous glass of wine for each of us, and my glass was nearly empty before the tension in my neck from reading letters all day left me.

We talked about Edith and her eight younger siblings, especially her sisters Dorothy and Thea, Barbara's aunts, who had left Barbara the property. But she focused on Dorothy, the most eccentric of the three sisters, who had a notable run-in with council surveyors staking out a piece of land. The sisters had donated a chunk of their property for the erection of an old folks' home, and Dorothy believed the surveyors had placed the pegs incorrectly. Instead of going down to discuss it with them, she discharged a round of shot-gun pellets over their heads.

Unexpected and disconcerting outbursts were a trademark of Dorothy's. In the middle of family meals she had the odd habit of leaping up and rushing out to flush the toilet. The action of flushing would often be repeated three or four times over the course of a meal. On special occasions, when visitors came for dinner, she was also known to go into the pantry and salt the food. Particularly when it was one of her sister Thea's famous desserts. 'After that, they couldn't even feed it to the pigs,' said Barbara in disgust.

By this time we were both well through our third glass. Quite unexpectedly, Barbara leaned across the table and, with a confidential air, said: 'Now promise you won't put this in your . . . what do you call it?'

'PhD,' I said.

'Yes, that's right: PhD,' she echoed, with emphasis.

'I promise,' I said, wondering what earth-shattering scoop would now be missing from its pages.

'She's still here.'

'Who's still here?'

'Dorothy. Dorothy's still here. She died in 1983, but she never left the place. I've seen her. Wearing the clothes she wore when she was alive. A red floral dress. She loved to wear floral dresses. Would you like another glass?' she asked, lifting the wine bottle to pour it.

'No, thank you, Barbara. I think I've had enough.' Technically, I'd stopped believing in ghosts, but I still wanted my wits about me. 'It must be a bit unsettling being here on your own, with no other houses around and so far from the road. I wouldn't cope.'

'I do worry. There's a lot of rough types around here. But I've installed plenty of security, the perimeter fence is electrified, and the entrance is alarmed.'

'What about Dorothy? Doesn't she disturb you?'

Barbara shrugged her shoulders.

'Not really.'

'Why do you think she's still here?'

'She had a bent brain,' Barbara said. 'Dorothy had the most brilliant mind of the three sisters, and she never got to use it. Frustration, and the envy she felt for her sisters, Edith and Thea: it twisted her mind. There was a lot going on at Ringley, then,' she said mysteriously, standing up to clear the plates. 'Can I get you some dessert? I've baked a cheesecake.'

'That would be lovely, thanks. You shouldn't have gone to all this trouble.'

Over dessert we chatted about more benign subjects. Then I helped her clear the table, and dried while she washed the dishes.

'I've got your bed made up. The electric blanket's been on since mid-afternoon. Let me show you your room. It was Edith's.' Was Edith on the roster of spectral visitors? I couldn't help wondering, as we left the kitchen.

'I'm in the process of doing this part of the house up,' my hostess continued as she led me down the long, dim passageway. Suddenly, my heart lurched. In the distance stood the figure of a woman. I froze.

'Oh, don't worry about that,' Barbara laughed, seeing my reaction. 'I should have told you: that's my mannequin. Come and have a look.'

Near the end of the hallway was a fully dressed, female figure, as stiff as a board. She had the sophisticated air of a Parisian shopper, with a synthetic bouffant wig, handbag over her arm and silk scarf wound frivolously around her neck.

'She's part of the security system,' Barbara explained, still amused at my obvious discomfort. 'You can see her from the driveway. So it always looks like there's someone at home. At a quick glance she looks real.'

You got that right, I thought, wondering whether fright could kill you. 'I'm just glad it wasn't Dorothy!' I responded.

At the door to my room I noticed a hook-and-eye latch like the ones they use to lock outside toilet doors, but the reach on this one was much longer. This meant my room could be locked from the outside with me in it. As I looked along the hallway I noticed each room had one. I wasn't game to ask

Barbara why, in case the explanation was too disturbing. We said good night and parted.

There was no overhead light in my room. This was part of the renovations. But the lamps on the dresser and by my bed glowed warmly.

Despite a deep mattress, soft flannel sheets and a warm duvet, I didn't sleep well. There was the noise of the wind, and rain battering against the roof and windows, and the sound of footsteps in the corridor. Barbara had told me she took a bath at about midnight, and so if I heard anything, not to worry.

But the thing that disturbed me the most that night was the fear of being locked in.

'Now, have you got everything you need?' asked Barbara as Jeremy, Sue and I followed her down the passageway, past Edith's room on the right.

'Barbara has a mannequin to scare burglars,' I had warned Jeremy.

As we approached Barbara's hapless shopper, Jeremy chuckled to himself, which was not the reaction I'd expected. Clearly he was already at home with the oddities of Ringley.

'Don't tell Katie,' he whispered to me with an arch look on his face as he contemplated the impending arrival of Sue's daughter. 'Let's give her a fright.'

'Do you think that's a good idea?'

'Of course it is,' he said, confused by my reservations.

Past the mannequin was the part of the house that Barbara rented out. It was largely unfurnished. There was a tiny kitchenette, an enormous lounge, and two large double bedrooms opposite each other, across a hallway. The ceiling stud was more than 13 feet high. Jeremy's room had a little camp stretcher in the corner, made up with sheets and blankets, and ours had two single beds with matching orange candlewick bedspreads.

'This was Dorothy's old bedroom,' Barbara informed us as we stood in the doorway of our room. My heart sank. Great, I thought, Dorothy and the mannequin can take turns watching us.

'I put your electric blankets on before you got here, but Jeremy, would you like a hot-water bottle?'

'Yes, please.'

'Well, come with me then,' said Barbara, and they wandered off together down the corridor like two old comrades-at-arms, chatting.

Monday was orientation for me at the Quay School of the Arts at Whanganui Polytechnic. Tuesday, the court papers were served. The bailiff waited outside the theatre at the museum, where I was giving my first lecture.

'Are you Joanne Drayton?' he asked, as he stepped forward to hand me the envelope. It had happened. Richard had made his first major move.

We settled comfortably into our new life at Ringley. We paid a nominal rent like tenants, and Barbara treated us like family. She often invited the three of us for dinner. We would sit in her newly renovated kitchen, along her deep-cushioned beige sofa, and watch television. When the telly was turned off, we were a captive audience for her tales of the house and her three maiden aunts.

Ringley was full of stuff. The Colliers were collectors like my mother. There were cabinets of precious ornaments and china. Every surface was laden with objects. Figurines cast in silver and bronze, set in porcelain or carved in wood. Chandeliers hung from the ceilings, and rare and valuable books sat on shelves. It was an expensive but ad hoc collection gathered on some European tour, or brought out from England by their founding father, Henry Collier.

For many an hour I sat in Barbara's old study, which never seemed to get done up, waiting for faxes from the lawyers. It was full of her aunts' treasures. Diaries, photograph albums, programmes from stage shows in London in the 1910s and 1920s. I would sit there on tenterhooks, waiting for my latest message from the lawyer among the remnants of the aunts' lives.

Sue's daughter, Katherine, arrived at the airport in Whanganui on 26 October: my birthday. She was nine years old and a ballet girl. Tall for her age, and skinny, she wore her blonde hair in a ballet bun. She was sweet and sour. Brought up in relative luxury, she had a warrior's resilience — which would be tested — and an undying affection for her mother.

'Hi, Katie!' Jeremy shouted with malevolent delight as she ran past him in the arrivals area to hug Sue. For nearly three months Sue had waited patiently for Katherine to come, never entirely sure that her ex-husband would comply with their agreement and send her. With no children at all I would have been distraught. But Sue didn't believe in desperation or in clinging on to things. Perhaps that was why she never had to.

The addition of one more to the line-up on Barbara's couch meant I got relegated to the padded footstool at the end. Barbara insisted we had a meal with her at least once a week. We brought the wine, nibbles and dessert, while she cooked the roast.

The backdrop to our daily lives was the acrimony of the custody case, and my research on Edith for my PhD.

'It's for you,' Barbara announced to me one day when we were lined up watching telly.

'Do you want to take it in the study?' she suggested. 'It's quieter in there.'

'Who is it?' I asked as we stepped into the hall and I shut the kitchen door behind me.

'I think it's the psychologist or maybe the counsel for the child. I'm not sure. I didn't catch his name.' These were people Barbara would never have come across had our worlds not so incongruously collided.

I picked up the receiver of the fax phone, as Barbara put hers down in the kitchen. It was the counsel for the child. He was bent on returning Jeremy to his father in Christchurch, and the phone call was to persuade me that this was in Jeremy's best interests — and mine. He threatened me with a prolonged and ugly legal battle, which he predicted would probably not go my way in the end, anyway. When he realised I would not be moved, he switched the focus to Alex. Alex did not want to join us for Christmas at my parents' place in Golden Bay, I was informed.

'That can't be right,' I said, dumbfounded.

'Yes, it is,' he assured me.

'Well, you're going to have to talk him into coming,' I said. 'How is it that we have an order instructing us to return Jeremy to his father at holidays, and Alex is free at 12 years old to do what he likes?' I had the distinct impression that it made a difference to the counsel that we were two queens together on the board. He was condescending and clearly fighting on Richard's side. I should have realised the contest would be skewed by a bias so intrinsic to the game that it would be invisible to everyone else but us.

'I'm afraid that's the law,' he replied. 'Alex's custody is not in question, and he's older. At his age we listen to the child. It's up to him to make the decision.'

He would talk to my elder son, he promised me, but he didn't like my chances of meeting Alex in the foreseeable future.

This was catastrophic. I put the phone down and sat there amongst the clutter, fighting my emotions. How could he deliver this devastating news in such a matter-of-fact manner, as if I deserved to be punished? It would appear that he felt my parenting was contaminated, second-best to Richard's. I couldn't go back to the kitchen straight away. The children would see that

I had been crying. I'd wait. Calm down a bit. There had been enough sudden see-saw dips without them witnessing another.

Tragically for me, that phone call was a foretaste of what was to come. There would be months, which would turn into years, of negotiation over Alex. All the time I wondered whether I would ever see him again. I cried and I fretted, experiencing feelings of loss and despair like I had never known before. Often I thought of that Māori mother and child in the ground at Purau on Banks Peninsula. I felt for them both, left behind, not at peace. In the years since, I have come to know what it is to have your love for a child buried alive in an unmarked grave.

CHAPTER TWO

The Beginning of the Affair

B ut this story began in 1989, when Sue and I first met . . .

N either of us returned to university to begin an affair. That wasn't what we intended. On the other hand, I think we did revisit study because there was something missing in each of our lives. I had been home with young children for more than six years. At that point in my life, I would have talked to a brick wall if I thought there was any adult conversation to be had.

In the time I had been at home my chances of getting another job had atrophied. My mother used to talk of things being as rare as hen's teeth. Well, teaching positions in Christchurch were scarcer. A bright, shining-new qualification seemed the only way to get back into the job market. Something no one could argue with: a Master's or a PhD degree.

University had been my sanctuary. I wouldn't say I was a bookish person, but among the history books and the storybooks my imagination took flight.

During my three years there, the first time around, I became an A student. Coming from a rough, co-educational school, I was ill-prepared for university. Footnotes, I thought, were a line of shoes from Dowsons, and bibliographies were a complete mystery to me. I was exploring new territory for my family, an academic Marco Polo. While other students commenced their journey halfway there because of their parents' educational backgrounds, my start was from the beginning.

So it was with huge pride that, at the end of my third year, I received an invitation to enter the Master's programme in History. Now they sell you a place, but in the days before fees you had to earn one.

But by then I had met Richard. And young women of my generation were expected to sacrifice their own progress to that of their husbands. I don't think I ever questioned it, nor was ever encouraged to think I should question it. This was part of the marriage package.

It wasn't until much later that I began to see my folly. Perhaps it was the grind of my high-school teaching, when Richard was mucking around at theological college, or maybe the mindless moments of motherhood? I'm not exactly sure, but somewhere along the way I realised I wanted more for myself.

Alex was born in 1983, and Jeremy in 1985. By the time Jeremy was four years old, and off to kindergarten, I was making plans to return to university.

Sue found her way there via her own circuitous route. She had completed a three-year design diploma at Wellington Polytechnic, and then worked for nearly a decade in the design department at TVNZ in Auckland. Her portfolio included variety shows, telethons and *Play School*, before she settled for a long stint with the six o'clock news and current affairs. But eventually the writing was on the wall. As television began to computerise, and the reckless days of long lunches and limitless budgets came to an end, she moved on. She went to teachers' training college, then, after a few months in a plum teaching job at Epsom Girls' Grammar, moved with her husband to Christchurch. It was there that Sue had her two children, Jason and Katherine, in 1983 and 1986.

In 1989, she was lured back to university to do a Fine Arts degree, and we met in Art History classes. I was about 10 years older than most of the students in the class by that time, and Sue even older. So I guess we just connected. I was looking for friendship and a place to escape the drudgery of my life; she was looking for inspiration and the discipline to work. What we found was each other.

One day, a few weeks into the term, I noticed that the exercise book she was clutching as she filed out at the end of the lecture was covered in children's scribble. By then we had had a couple of lectures, and I hadn't spoken more than a few words to anyone. The students seemed younger than I had expected. This day, Sue sat a couple of seats down from me in the same row.

She was attractive and smartly dressed, or at least smarter than me. What aroused my interest most, though, was the scribble. Did she have young children now? I wondered. Or was the scrawl historic? The lecture finally over, I waited until the people between us had left, and caught up with her.

'Excuse me. Do you have young children?' I blurted out. As the words left my mouth, things in my mind lurched to a sudden stop. Instantaneously I thought: perhaps she was their maiden aunt. Worse still: maybe she couldn't have children. But before I had the chance to torture myself further—

'Yes,' she replied, looking mystified. 'How do you know?'

Relieved, I said, 'I saw the crayon scribble on the front of your notebook. I wondered if you had children because so do I.'

It wasn't long before we realised our children were pretty much the same age. On our way to the library, we discovered we had more and more in common. It seemed extraordinary at the time, but those sorts of coincidences happen in life and they don't often enmesh peoples' futures as they would ours.

Usually, Sue left her young children playing with their toys outside the lecture theatre. This astonished me. I had left mine at home for five minutes once, and came back to find Alex chasing Jeremy down the middle of the road with a wad of toilet paper in his hand. He was trying to wipe his brother's bottom. Even with his pants down around his ankles, Jeremy was tough competition. My children were runners. If I took my eye off them for a minute, they were gone. Not like Sue's, who waited demurely in one spot for her lecture to end.

However, on the day we first met, her children were with a friend. She was getting books out of the library for an essay, and I walked all the way there with her, chatting excitedly. It was only when we were standing on the steps that I remembered I had to get home urgently.

That's the one thing love does that's universal. It telescopes time. An hour becomes a moment, and there are never enough of them. Love is an addiction that makes you hungrier and hungrier for time with that person. For me, the addiction didn't begin then, but a profound connection did. As the sun set on this April evening, I scurried back to my car, thinking: I've found a friend at last.

But we almost didn't connect. This was a strange time for me. Richard had recently left the Anglican Church and taken a position with the Accident Compensation Corporation. My standard joke was that he had swapped one type of life insurance for another. The reasons why he left the Church were complex and more than a little scandalous.

By the end of the 1980s the Church was retrenching: a generation of young people was missing from the pews. The older age groups were moving from fixed incomes to walking frames. If the Anglican Church kept spending at the current rate, it would be bankrupt. The Canterbury diocese, where we were based, was also becoming increasingly evangelical in orientation. My ex was an Anglo-Catholic, which put him out of step. The wick in the powder keg, however, was the vicar where Richard did his final curacy.

The vicar, Blair, was gay, which might have gone largely unnoticed if he hadn't been apprehended in the 1970s for soliciting around the public toilets in Invercargill. This was a major problem for him, and for his wife and two young children, but an even bigger problem for the Church, whose natural instinct was to sweep it under the altar. Blair received treatment for his homosexuality and was 'cured' according to the Church. But Richard saw Blair's not-so-cured homosexuality as an opportunity to topple him, and did more than a little stirring in the parish.

The explosive mix of diocesan budget cuts, clerical biases, cliquey dog-collared boys' clubs and the agitation over Blair blew up in our faces. Although Richard had behaved badly, I felt sorry for him; to a certain extent he was collateral damage. His demise was part of a bigger fiscal picture, as well as a new theological agenda. I had compassion for Blair, too, but I also saw him as a hypocrite. I was in the high-minded position, I believed, of thinking I might be bisexual, but choosing not to cheat on my husband. Although I had already thought about leaving Richard, after his departure from the Church I didn't feel I could.

So when I met Sue, and she began asking me over for dinner, my life straddled two worlds. Although there was no future for Richard and me in the Church, we were not completely out of the round of its activities. This meant that each time Sue mentioned a date to get together, I had a clash. A couple of times I even had to cancel on her.

She told me later that she had decided to give me one more chance, and, as fate would have it, the date worked and it was a great success. The children got on so well that it wasn't long before she had our family for dinner at their beautiful split-level, three-storey home close to the summit of Mount Pleasant. We kept in touch over our course-work, had occasional coffees together, and enjoyed the family get-togethers at their house.

Reciprocating was the problem. Our house was a dump. When we left the Church, we departed with almost nothing. I had a little money saved from my teacher-training allowance at university, which I had invested in an empty section at Diamond Harbour. We had to sell that property in order to renovate a catastrophic villa we had purchased with almost no deposit. Alex was three years old, and Jeremy just over one year old when we bought it.

On the corner of Canon and Bishop streets sat our money-pit: a mammoth house almost visibly sinking into its unstable peat soils. It had a heavy terracotta-tile roof and massive double chimneys, the weight of which drilled down, opening up sinkholes under the floor. The frame of the house was banana-shaped, and the floors so twisted and uneven that vacuuming made me seasick.

Behind was an eyesore of disintegrating outhouses. The doors and windows that could open were those which the previous owner, a notorious miser, had shaved bits off, leaving drafty gaps when they were shut. The only thing he had added to the interior in the 35 years he had lived there was a thick layer of tar-coloured nicotine. The walls, and also presumably his lungs, were blackened. For months we didn't even realise there was a pattern on the wallpaper.

Ironically, the house was next to the one where my mother grew up. My Victorian grandmother used to talk disparagingly to my mum about the mean old miser next door, who tortured his wife with his frugality. My ex-husband purchased it while my parents were away, knowing they would try to stop him if they were around. It should, however, have been me who stopped him, but I was as captivated by the dream as he was. We had seen more suitable places, but this was the grandest, with its magnificent leadlights, bay window, spacious rooms and decorative plaster ceilings. It had once been an imposing villa, a fine home for the upper-middle class.

My mother was horrified when she found out. I assured her quite sincerely that Richard would do it up in no time. This had been the sole condition of the purchase for me. I said to him many times: 'You realise that I have two very young children to look after and I'm not going to be able to give you much help?'

'Yes,' he said, each time I raised the matter. 'I realise that, and I am going to do the work myself.'

'Are you absolutely sure?'

'Absolutely,' he would reassure me. And I believed him.

When my mother came around for the first time, I was showing her the filthy galley kitchen painted in hideous end-of-line blue and orange, when I opened the bread bin and a mouse jumped out. Without visibly touching anything, it flew across the room and up the chimney.

'Didn't you look at anything else?' she asked, as we peered into the bin at the mouse's dead mate rotting at the bottom.

'Yes,' I said defensively, 'but this is the one we wanted.'

A neighbour told me that the place had been the refuge of a soldier-deserter during the First World War. The story went that his spinster sister hid him there for years. His figure was glimpsed silhouetted against curtains and at the window's edge looking out. At the end of the war, he disappeared. People in the neighbourhood knew he had been there, but no one could ever prove it.

So it was a house with a turbulent past, and I never felt at home there. If I had, I probably would have felt more like inviting people over. When Sue and her family finally did get an invitation, the place looked shambolic. There was certainly no escaping the yards of tarpaulin, which covered the monumental-sized holes in the walls where the chimneys had been taken out to level the floors. But even this demolition site was progress, and had been achieved at enormous cost. Each night, almost all night, Richard and I had worked to remove the chimneys. The filth that spewed out, and unrelenting grit from between the bricks, went through everything. Just before dawn we would grab a couple of hours' sleep, before the children woke up and Richard had to go to work. During the boys' afternoon nap, I cleaned and stacked the bricks. As soon as the boys were in bed after dinner and a bath, our nocturnal labours began again. Once the chimneys were gone, the holes that were left went up into the roof and down through the floorboards to the earth below.

In the five awful winters we had there, we could never heat those spaces properly. We huddled together at the back of the house in a room that connected to the kitchen.

The cold weather had not begun in earnest when Sue and her family visited. I was acutely aware of how terrible things looked. Especially to Sue and her husband, who were designers. I remembered how much discussion there had been at her place over what sort of lampshade they would hang over their dining-room table. In the end they chose something that looked like the Star Ship Enterprise. But why not? They married young and had their children late. They had the money to buy it.

But, in spite of my many misgivings, it was a good night when they came for dinner, and our friendship coasted comfortably along after their visit.

CHAPTER THREE

Canterbury University and Cleaning Carpets

I loved being at university again. There was my new friend Sue for company, and a campus that was a clean, warm place to go as winter set in. During 1989, my first year back at university, it became apparent that our money would never fund the vast amount of renovation required at Bishop Street. When we discovered that the sewer pipes and the drains emptied out directly under the house, we borrowed the then vast sum of $10,000 from my parents to pay for new drains, waste pipes and a bathroom renovation.

In order to pay them back, I got a job working a night shift at ACC. So my days and nights were split like Jekyll and Hyde. During the day I was a mother and, when I could fit it in around the routine of school and kindergarten, a university student. At night I was a claims-handler and data in-putter. I saw less and less of Richard. When he arrived home, he handed me the car keys and I was off. Sometimes, we had time to say a few words. Often it was little more than a grunt of recognition on both our parts. We grew apart at that time, not helped by the six weeks' separation when the bathroom was unusable and I lived with the children at my parents' place.

In the background, Sue and I met up, wrote essays and studied for slide tests and exams together. Our friendship was casual, but fun: a relief from my dour life of dirt and despair.

Richard was a spender. This wouldn't have been so much of a problem if there hadn't been so little to spend in the first place. Towards the end of our second year in the house at Bishop Street, Christmas was approaching and I thought I would begin buying the children's presents. So I went to the bank to cash a $20 cheque, which in my world represented a tidy sum.

'I'm sorry, madam,' said the woman behind the counter at the Trust Bank, 'I can't cash that cheque for you.'

'But why?' I asked, dumbfounded.

'Because your account is overdrawn.'

'What do you mean, "overdrawn"? It can't be.'

'I'm afraid it is, madam. Here, let me show you,' and she tilted the screen so I could see it.

I was thunderstruck. We were hundreds of dollars in the red, and it was November. There was no way we could make it up before Christmas.

'This has to be a mistake. How could it possibly get this overdrawn?'

'Well, if *you* haven't spent the money, madam, then I suggest you discuss it with the other account-holder.'

'Don't worry — I'll be doing that!' I said, fuming. Things were not happy in our house that night.

'What do you mean you bought the equipment and the paint to finish the interior of the house? Now we've got nothing left in the bank to buy the children's Christmas presents, and anyone else's for that matter. How will we pay for the petrol for our trip to Golden Bay? That's our holiday plans down the drain as well.' (My parents had us to stay over the Christmas holidays each year. It was the only way we could afford a break.)

'But the paint was half-price,' he said. 'And I had to buy that much to get the discount.'

'Are you insane? We don't even need to do it yet. And what about all the rollers, and the brushes . . . ? What about all the extras you've bought?'

'They were on special, too.'

'This is unbelievably irresponsible of you. You can't just go spending whatever you like, whenever you like. You know it's nearly Christmas. Didn't you look at the account to see if we had enough money to cover it?'

From there the conversation, which was already heated, accelerated into a flaming row. I went to work that night feeling almost homicidal. I was furious.

I stewed on it. How to make that kind of money quickly? What could I sell? When I returned home, I walked past the window and saw the pile of bricks stacked outside. 'Fifty cents a brick,' someone had told me. 'You want to sell those bricks.' There was the solution. I was thrilled. We had such an enormous stack, it was like having a brick mausoleum in the backyard.

I was so proud of my idea that it shocked me almost senseless when Richard rubbished it that night. I couldn't believe it. He had got us in this predicament, but wasn't prepared to do anything to get us out of it. He was vehement.

'Exactly how do you think that's going to look?' he shouted. 'What are people going to say when they realise it's *us* advertising? They'll think we are poor, that we can't manage on our income.'

'And they'd be right!' I shouted back.

By this stage I was so wild I was dribbling. It must be the most primitive of instincts, to be so mad that you salivate. Maybe it's something animals do before they attack and eat something. All I know is, I was rabid.

'You have to put an advertisement in the newspaper. Fifty cents a brick! We may not sell any, but we have to give it a try.'

He would not do it. He completely refused. So the argument continued full-force, getting nastier and nastier.

Finally, I said: 'Okay. If you refuse to do it, I'll do it myself.' I wasn't sure how I was going to pay for the ad, because we obviously had no money in the bank, but I told him I'd borrow it from my parents. It was at that point that he begrudgingly said he would put one in the newspaper: for that weekend.

The bricks that I had already stacked had only been roughly cleaned. To sell them they would have to be pristine. So I spent all my remaining spare time with a hammer, chisel and wire brush, cleaning them. It was the perfect job to get rid of all my pent-up anger.

We were woken early Saturday morning by the first punter, keen to buy a trailer-load of orange bricks. I was amazed. It was like selling the crown jewels at a knockdown price. The calls kept coming long after we had sold out. Miraculously we made up the deficit in our account, and had enough left over to pay for Christmas. The venture was a fantastic success.

The hardship we endured because of our lack of money and horrendous house felt oddly out of kilter with our actual situation. Richard was the heir to a considerable fortune. Three distant cousins of Richard's mother had died childless. The two sisters and a brother had lived together all their lives on a huge landholding at Mangatangi. In a publicly heralded gesture, they gave one thousand acres of native bush back to the government. What was left was still worth a fortune.

There were seven heirs to the estate, and 14 years to wait until the youngest was 21 years old and the farm could be sold. The cousins' will stipulated that until the 14 years were up, the estate was to be held in trust and worked by a manager. We had been married three and a half years when we learned of Richard's inheritance. When the last distant cousin died, the executors got in touch to say the farm couldn't be sold yet, but its contents were up for grabs.

Going to the farmhouse to divide up the chattels was an unsettling experience for me. I felt sorry for this family of elderly siblings, whose only heirs were people they hardly knew. The dividing up of their possessions was a personal process handled by relative strangers. There was evidence there, still, of a life of cultured grandeur, long neglected as age, illness and death overwhelmed them one by one. Their precious things were laid out in lots and we bid for them. Each heir had a single bid. The young children were represented by their parents. It all felt a bit sordid to me. But how else do you divide up the effects of an estate fairly?

The elderly cousins had been collectors. One of the rooms, the study from memory, had so many stuffed creatures, both native and exotic, that they could have populated the animal parade of a natural history museum. The house was full of dusty and decaying antiques, and mysterious objects with narratives that would never be revealed to us. Their stories belonged to the cousins, and this auction was the end. Possessions that had been cherished, kept, cared for, traded, stolen — their histories extinguished death by death, and buried by time.

Out the back, a large kitchen garden and orchard were overrun with weeds and creeping vines. The fruit trees were ancient flavoursome strains of plants that had long since evolved into tastelessness in our supermarkets. It could have been a secret garden if there had been anyone around who loved it. But we were merely hovering for a brief time over that world. Vultures. There to pick the bones clean and fly home.

My life in those days was a beautiful irony wedged between two unrealities. We were neither rich nor poor, but travellers like Dickens's Pip through a no-man's-land of great expectation. The money was always there on the horizon: a distant dream to mock our daily grind. There was also the temptation because it became possible for each person to cash in their share of the farm. The pay-out would be approximately a seventh of the current valuation, but Richard was determined to wait it out.

This made it hard because, with toddlers who were constantly sick, it seemed cruel to live in squalor and deprivation. Our children were lurgy-magnets and, like homing pigeons, every virus in circulation went to their throats, heads, chests or ears. While they looked big and robust, they were actually walking medicine cabinets.

Richard and I had both been sickly children, so what could we expect? According to my mother, I was the youngest person in New Zealand to have my tonsils and adenoids removed. This was probably true because my most vivid memory of that visit to hospital was taking the Signal toothpaste tube out of my toilet bag and piping it like icing around the lip of the potty the nurses had given me. My previous experience of toothpaste was that it was white. The red stripe seemed a spectacular addition that I thought was completely wasted in the tube.

My poor mother. Now I realised how excruciating these childhood illnesses could be for a parent.

It was impossible to keep our house dry and warm. Even the boys' bedroom was a challenge. After their evening bath when we made the dash from the bathroom along the long central hallway to their bedroom, you could see your breath. It was freezing. In the front room, where a big double fireplace had been taken out, the room was the same temperature on winter nights inside as it was out.

The winters in that house were the bleakest of my life. I got sick myself, as you do with young children. Long, rumbling illnesses that never went away, and would occasionally erupt into something worse. One time, after the third bout of a bug that had an evil modus operandi, I sat in the doctor's surgery and cried. I was desperate for an end to this epidemic of ill health.

The doctor sent me home with another prescription for antibiotics.

M omentous events. You remember them, don't you? Where you were when President Kennedy was shot, or when Elvis Presley or Princess Diana died? Well, I was vacuuming when it struck me.

The floors were as straight as they would ever be after the house had been re-piled, and were covered along the hall and in the living area with a salmon-coloured synthetic carpet. While the carpet was easy to wash, everything stuck to it. The house was still in renovation chaos, but somehow the obsessive-compulsive in me came out over the newly laid carpet. It was the one small territory in my universe I could control. White lint was not so much of a problem, even though I knew it was there. It was cat hair that proved the biggest nuisance. We had two cats then, Morris and Ethel. Morris was black, and it was his fur that I was struggling to remove this particular morning.

Vacuuming a statically charged synthetic carpet is not unlike spreading butter. It is less about sucking it up and more about distributing the fur into creative new configurations until finally the static attraction gives way and it shoots up the hose.

It was one of Christchurch's beautiful June mornings, when the sky is clear and the sun low and golden. Shafts of light were filtering through the deep sash windows and hitting the section of carpet that I was cleaning. Just as I was concentrating on a particularly recalcitrant wad of Morris fur the epiphany hit me . . . I had fallen out of love. My marriage was over.

I

I love objects. Things made to carry with you through life. Totems, talismans, mascots, amulets, heirlooms, objects of beauty as well as magic charms. This response was an instinct from my childhood and steeped in my training as an art historian. The idea that I could hold an object and see the hand of the maker and unlock its meaning has always fascinated me.

Objects are also time-travellers, their presence in the world often affecting the lives of people long after their creators are dead. Such artefacts have been handed to you by the past. That is how I felt when I encountered the Lewis chess pieces in the British Museum. They stopped me. They called to me. I felt a connection to them. As if their story was my story and they carried the spirit of my Scandinavian ancestors.

It intrigued me that all kinds of human events had happened around these pieces, and that they might have helped shape the most tumultuous ones. For they are alive in their own way, becoming animate when they move across the chessboard and through time. I wanted to know more about them. To go back to their beginning. To discover where, how, why they were created, and to know what journey they had taken to arrive in a museum vitrine. Whether this imperative came from the desire to discover myself, to build a new identity, or was a latent need, just waiting to be triggered, I will never know. What I can testify to is that it would become completely compelling.

Over years of research in museum archives and libraries, the history of the Lewis chess set would unfold for me. There emerged a number of theories about what its journey had been. Fascinating alleyways of possibility involving pirate ships, murder, hangings, Viking long-boats, treacherous sea journeys and storms. These mute objects would tell their story in the shapes carved and the lines incised in their creamy surface, and in anecdote and myth. But they would also hold on to their mysteries and keep some of their secrets forever. My investigations would begin with the writings of Frederic Madden, Assistant Keeper of Manuscripts at the British Museum in the 1830s.

As he sat researching his article on the chess pieces for publication in the journal *Archaeologia*, Frederic Madden was a man racked with grief. Born in Portsmouth at the very beginning of the nineteenth century, Madden was the son of a captain in the Royal Marines. Rather than securing a scholarship to go to Oxford or Cambridge, he studied the wonders of his father's library. It was full of books, antiquities and curiosities gathered from his adventures around the world. Like me, he grew up with cabinets of objects that told enchanting stories.

Madden met and fell in love with his sweetheart, Mary, when he was just 18 years old. They waited a decade until his appointment as Assistant Keeper of Manuscripts at the British Museum meant they could afford to marry. They wed in April 1829, but Madden's beloved wife was dead just 11 months later. Mary lived for five days after the birth of their son. At first she seemed alright. The doctor told him she would recover. But then by a tragic twist of fate she died, and the baby lived as a sad reminder of her sacrifice. It broke his heart. For six weeks Madden couldn't make an entry in the diary he had kept every day for the 10 years of their courtship and brief marriage.

A year later, on the anniversary of Mary's death, he was still grief-stricken. 'My own blindness not to know the dear innocent was on the brink of the grave!' he wrote in his diary. 'Oh horrible retrospect! Oh fearful future! The tomb, the old cheerless silent tomb! And those sweet laughing eyes, those roseate lips, to touch which was to me a heaven — what are they now? Oh shame, shame — sin & sorrow! Oh God have I lived to witness this, and still live. — I could not rest.'

Madden was still missing his wife terribly when the Lewis chess pieces arrived on his desk at the British Museum. They came in the possession of a shabby, rather sly antiquities dealer.

There is more to say about the shady character that flogged the pieces off. But on the afternoon of 17 October 1831, Madden was sitting in his study at the British Museum. On a velvet cloth in front of him lay an amazing collection of 77 chess pieces. He had already detected differences in style between groups of the figures. Even though not one of these groups represented a whole chess set, his supplier had guaranteed that this was all that had been found.

Madden waited. An important visitor was due to arrive. As he sat behind his large dark-oak desk, he picked up a queen seated on an elaborately carved medieval throne. Beside him was his magnifying glass, which he needed to see the detail.

He was struck by the queen's mortified expression. She sat squarely on her throne with her hand raised to her face, like a person with toothache. The hand gesture, he thought, was probably intended to remind chess players of the Virgin Mary overwhelmed by grief at the death of her son. He had seen echoes of that expression in pained pictures of the Madonna at the foot of the cross.

Madden was a great lover of chess, and he knew its ancient heritage. It had originated in India before AD500. In the eighth century, Arab historian al-Mus'udi recorded instances of Indians so caught up in gambling on games of chess that not only did they lose all their money and property, but they would go on to wager their bodies. When a board was set up for a new game, a pot of ointment would be put on to boil at the same time. Al-Mus'udi explained that 'if the man who wagered one of his fingers loses, he cuts off the finger with a dagger, and then plunges his hand in the ointment and cauterizes the wound . . . sometimes a man who continues to lose will cut off in succession all his fingers, his hand, his forearm, his elbow, and other parts of his body'. Eventually this addictive game would spread around the globe.

When Madden held his magnifying glass closer to the queen, he could still see the remnants of sand and, on some of the 'black' pieces, what he believed to be traces of blood-red dye that he had been told was much darker and stronger in colour when the sets had first been unearthed. This was proof, he thought, of the chess pieces' fragile state. He was hoping Sir Walter Scott, the well-known poet and writer, would bolster his case with the acquisition board of the British Museum for their purchase.

At this point his musings were interrupted by a knock at the door.

'Come in,' called Madden as he returned the chess piece to its place on the velvet cloth. When he looked up again, he was shocked by the apparition coming towards him with a hand extended.

'I sh[oul]d have instantly known him, from portraits,' Madden would write in his diary that night, 'but it is impossible to convey by the pencil, an idea of the uncouthness of his appearance and figure.' Square-shouldered and boxy-chested, Scott lurched towards Madden like a character out of one of his own gothic novels. 'His hair almost white,' Madden noted. 'His large grey unexpressive eyes — a red-sandy complexion and straggling whiskers,' plus, he wrote, a 'slow thick manner of speaking — and broad Scotch accent.' To this picture of gaucheness was added black-and-white checkered trousers and a badly cut coat. Scott, who limped heavily, supported himself on an immense stick.

Madden shook his hand.

'Please, sit down,' he said, indicating to a chair on the other side of his desk.

Scott wheezed as he lowered himself into the seat.

'So they were thrown up by the sea,' said Scott, as he looked with fascination at the hoard. 'This is quite a treasure. May I pick one up?' he asked.

'Certainly,' Madden responded. Leaning forward with some difficulty, Scott reached over and picked up a king, turning it in his hand, examining it, entranced.

'These are extraordinary,' he said, looking intensely at the intricate detailed carving on the back of the throne. 'Tell me, how were they discovered?'

Madden shifted in his chair, settling himself for what he knew would be quite a story.

'They were discovered in the Outer Hebrides on the Isle of Lewis. More precisely,' he said, wanting to get the detail right, 'a wide bay that runs east to west, known to the local inhabitants as the Bay of Uig.'

Scott chuckled to himself. Madden regarded him coolly.

'Did I say something that amused you?'

'Och, no, not at all. It's just that Uig means "solitary place" in Gaelic, and that western coastline must be one of the remotest places in the world,' he said, repatriating the king, and picking up a bishop, which he subjected to similar scrutiny. 'So, tell me, how were they found?'

'Well, the account I have,' replied Madden, 'is that they were found hidden in a sandbank.'

'But who would dig in such an isolated spot?'

'Not dig exactly,' Madden corrected him. 'The story I have from a number of sources is that an earthenware container holding all the pieces was uncovered by a cow.'

'By a cow?' Scott repeated in disbelief.

'Yes. As I said: a cow. It was part of a herd feeding on the tussock grass in the sand dunes.'

'Remarkable,' Scott said, as he picked up another bishop, looking between the pair and comparing them. Both had a bishop's mitre, and crook, but it was the differences that intrigued him. One wore a cope and the other a chasuble, and one was standing, and the other seated on a throne, like the king and queen. The throne was covered in swirling mythological animals, which were chewing and clawing each other. The virtuosity of the carver amazed him.

'But these pieces must be about 500 years old,' he said, confounded.

'Yes, that's what makes this treasure so valuable. I believe they are Viking pieces, produced in one of the medieval carving workshops in Trondheim.'

'But how could they have survived that long so close to the sea?'

'That is something of a mystery. The herder who reportedly made the find was so terrified when he opened up the container to see an army of tiny faces staring back that he fled in horror, believing that he had unearthed a circle of pygmy sprites and gnomes. As you know, such wee folk are part of local Celtic folklore. It was his wife who told him off, and sent him back, still quivering, with a spade to finish digging. The chamber that housed them was quite dry, and on the floor were what appeared to be ashes. Perhaps the remnants of something burnt long ago in the stone oven, or the material of a leather bag that had once kept the pieces together. I imagine we will never know.'

'How do you think they got there? Surely they didn't just wash up on the beach?'

'It's perplexing, indeed,' agreed Madden, exhaling with a sigh. He was not a man who liked loose ends. 'There was rumoured to have been, many, many years ago,' he said, 'a convent of Black Nuns close to the site where they were found. Celibate nuns could live a forgotten existence there, hidden from depravity and worldliness. A life punctuated by wild storms, and the occasional game of chess.'

'Och,' exclaimed Scott in disbelief, interrupting him, 'No! The inhabitants of a nunnery would never have played chess. It was a game for aristocrats and romantics, but never the Church.'

'Yes. You are right in principle, of course, but I have the transcript of an eleventh-century letter written by Damiano, the Cardinal Bishop of Ostia, punishing the Bishop of Florence for playing chess.'

Scott interjected with a bellicose laugh, 'If the Catholic Church was as capable of controlling chess-playing as it has been its other excesses, we can assume the playing of the game was rife.'

'Regardless of your cynicism, Sir Walter, it seems only a select few indulged in this dangerous pursuit.'

'Hmm, I imagine that's what they would have posterity believe. Still, a convent of Black Nuns playing this seemingly disreputable game could perhaps explain why the pieces were hidden in this oven-type structure.'

'Yes, that is one of the most curious aspects of their story,' Madden conceded, 'and it explains why they survived so well in such brutal conditions. See these tiny channels cut randomly across the surface of the figures? Here, use my magnifying glass.'

He passed Scott the ebony-handled lens.

'Yes, I see them,' said Scott, as he squinted into the glass. 'They remind me of holes created by worms burrowing into wood, shell and stones washed up on the beach. What do you think caused them?'

'I have solicited the opinion of our Natural History section, and so far the verdict is that they were made by worms, as you call them; tiny termites, to be precise. Or, possibly, the fine roots of marram grasses. Whichever it is, I am sure they didn't roll around long in the pounding seas.'

'Do you believe that they were the property of an abbess at the Black Nunnery, or maybe some visiting bishop, and secreted to avoid discovery? Or perhaps they were hidden from marauders?'

'At the present time, we can't be sure,' Madden replied. 'The only thing we know is that someone with immense foresight and an acute sense of the value of these pieces put them there for safekeeping, and that they may have sat in that chamber for as long as 600 years.'

'Aye,' said Scott with his eyes set on some far-away place. 'But why didn't the owner ever come back to retrieve them? Surely if they were a treasure worthy of all manner of effort to hide, then when things were safe, it would have been obvious to anyone that they should be retrieved.'

'Exactly. Something must have happened for the owner to have abandoned them for so long. And given that this was the time of the Vikings, the reason was probably not a happy one.'

'Indeed. And now,' Scott said, becoming more serious, 'shouldn't such an important collection be held not here at the British Museum, but in the Museum in Edinburgh?'

Stiffening, Madden responded, 'It seems to me highly unlikely that the Royal Museum will come up with the necessary money to fund such an acquisition. It is imperative that the purchase is made now. If we delay, I fear the hoard will be broken up and sold off separately. Besides, there is the fact that the offer has been made to us.' Madden stood, as a signal to Scott that their interview had ended. 'I don't think there is anything more I can add with any certainty at this point, so thank you for coming in. I appreciate your comments and will make sure I pass them on to the Board of Acquisition.'

With that, Scott rose awkwardly to his feet, gathered up his heavy stick and made for the door.

CHAPTER FOUR

My Freudian Slip

My carpet-cleaning epiphany in Christchurch was more amorphous than the word 'epiphany' suggests. It didn't come as a fully fledged plan for exiting my marriage, but as a bolt of self-awareness like the heavenly shard that pierced the heart of Gian Bernini's *The Ecstasy of St Teresa*. That sculpture has always astonished me. St Teresa with an arrow through her heart; lying prostrate; legs and lips parted in ecstasy; her eyes rolled back as if she were on the verge of an orgasm. *La petite mort,* for Christ. How could the Church fathers have missed it?

But my epiphany was neither sexual nor divine. It was just that simple realisation that I was vacuuming the wrong carpet. There was an initial sense of euphoria. Like I was acknowledging something at last.

I turned the vacuum cleaner off. Propped the hose against the white-painted wooden frame of the door, and went through to the kitchen. Grabbing a damp cloth from the sink, I came back and wiped up Morris's hair. The synthetic pink carpet had been out-manoeuvred at last.

If I had been as relentless at sorting out my sexuality as I am at cleaning carpets, I wouldn't be in this mess, I thought, as I slumped down onto the beige vinyl sofa nearby and began to cry. It was a mix of emotions. The agony and the ecstasy that make you sob like a child. Body shaking, heart-rending intakes of breath. The admission. The grief. The GUILT. Why had it taken me so long to admit this to myself?

'Sue, I've got something important to tell you after our lecture.' This sounded more tantalising than I had intended, but I was worried she might slip out after the class and I would miss her.

'Okay,' she said, her interest piqued, 'let's go to the cafeteria for a quick cup of coffee afterwards. I've got half an hour before I have to pick up Katie from kindergarten.'

'Great, let's do that.'

I didn't hear a word the lecturer said. At the end I glanced down at my meagre page of notes and struggled to recall any of the slides she'd shown us. Sue would be the first person I'd tell. I was anxious about how it would change our friendship. My confession was a risk. I knew that. But I felt I couldn't go on without telling someone, and she was a person I felt I could trust.

'What did you think of the lecture?' she asked me as we filed out of the front row at the end. (I hated the front row but she insisted on sitting there.)

'It was...' and I was just about to say 'great', when I had to admit to myself that I hadn't even registered the topic. 'I was a bit distracted,' I confessed, instead.

'Oh,' Sue responded, looking concerned. 'So, what was it that you wanted to tell me?' By this time, we were standing in the central vestibule outside the lecture theatre, where the mass of students mingled. The seething crowd had not yet dissipated. It wasn't the right place to make a momentous admission, but I had stewed on it for so long, I believed it was better out than in.

'You can't tell a soul,' I began, as we pushed our way through the main entrance and along the asphalt path to the cafeteria. I glanced around to check we couldn't be overheard.

'Not anyone, at all,' I repeated, 'but... I think I might be a *lesbian*.' This wasn't a word I found easy to say, so the effort to get it out was huge. In fact, it had taken me 33 years to get it out. I was the same age as Christ was when he was crucified: a fact that resonated with me then.

Instead of recoiling in horror as I thought she might do, Sue laughed out loud. When she managed to control herself, she said: 'That's impossible. You're just imagining it. It's a phase, it'll pass.' For a moment I believed maybe she was right. I experienced a surge of relief, which was followed almost as quickly by a cold wave of despair. I wanted to believe her, but I knew I couldn't.

'I'm afraid it's true,' I said after a long pause. 'I don't think it's just a phase. I mean, I wish it was but, but I doubt it.'

'Why do you doubt it? What makes you so sure, suddenly? How long have you been married?'

'Ten years.'

'Well, surely you must know by now. Have you ever slept with a woman?' she asked, shifting to interrogation mode.

'No, never,' I answered.

'*Never*,' she repeated in disbelief.

'No,' I responded, again, 'never.'

'How on earth would you know that you're a lesbian, then?'

Her logic was flawless, but I was still unconvinced.

'It's hard to explain. I guess I could be wrong, but for some reason marriage hasn't worked for me. Maybe marriage to someone else would have been better, but I have tried hard to make it work and now it's time to try something new.'

'So can lesbians get AIDS, then?' she asked. 'If they can, I'd be careful.'

'I'm not planning to rush out and go to bed with the first woman I meet,' I retorted. 'Just because I'm a lesbian, it doesn't make me a nymphomaniac.'

'I was just wondering,' she replied, 'I'm only thinking of you — Oh my goodness, look at the time! If I don't hurry up, I'll be late to pick up Katie. Let's keep in touch, okay?'

With that she was gone.

I was alone, and suddenly aware of my environment. Of the clattering and clanging of cutlery, trays and dishes: of the loud buzz of student voices punctuated by raucous laughter. It is strange how lonely you can feel in a crowd. I had been in their place once, full of optimism and plans. Like them I had visualised a future life, and now a decade on I was about to destroy it. I felt sick, diseased — *wrong*. If homosexuality was normal, then why wasn't everyone doing it? In that moment I hated myself.

I thought of suicide, and eternal nothingness where I wouldn't have to tell anyone. Not my husband, parents, children or friends. Perhaps it was the hum of hope and life in that cacophonous room that turned me around. I felt disconnected. I realised I needed to find a community. If that turned out to be a disappointment, I would kill myself, then.

I began going occasionally to the women's bar when my night shift ended.

I went with a neighbourhood friend, ostensibly to dance, which I loved. Initially, I thought I had come to the wrong place because in the dim, mood lighting with its flashing strobe almost everyone looked as if they were male. It was a foreign world to me, but one which for some inexplicable reason felt right. I wasn't there to cruise, but to reassure myself I wasn't the only person in the world who felt the way I did. Like a leper who covers their deformity, I hid my secret. Things carried on normally on the outside, but inside me there was just turmoil. Change was inevitable, but please not now.

'So, you don't think I'm sick, then?' I asked Sue, the next time I caught up with her at university. I was anxious that she might have changed her mind in the meantime. 'You are still happy being friends?'

'Of course I'm happy being friends. But you're the first lesbian I've ever known. How does it work, exactly? Do you just . . . sort of . . . fancy women?'

'Um, yes, I guess that covers it. I'm not really the best person to ask, having only slept with my husband. I don't think that qualifies me as any expert on lesbianism.'

'*Seriously?* You mean to say you've only ever slept with your husband and nobody else? No uncontrolled urges that led to bed? Didn't you at least . . . you know . . . try it out before you got married?'

'No,' I said. 'I know it makes me look like a dinosaur, and my friends did think I was a bit odd—'

'They'd be right there,' Sue cut in, 'I mean, weren't you ever . . . you know . . . carried away by your hormones?'

'No.' This line of enquiry was almost a welcome relief. Suddenly it was not my sexuality but my libido that was under the microscope.

There was no bell to signal the beginning of lectures at Canterbury University, but, like a herd of cows waiting for milking, the assembled students began flooding into the lecture theatre and I was saved any further scrutiny.

The year roared on. With university during the day, shift work at night, and two young children to taxi around to primary school, kindergarten, violin lessons and karate, I had almost no spare time. I went to the occasional bar, but even this got less frequent as exams loomed and study became more important. I finished my last exam with a sigh of relief.

I guess it was inevitable that once the term ended I might have to face a few things. Over the months since my confession, Sue had become more and more of a confidante. For years I had managed to find someone special to confide in. It was only ever platonic, but there was always a woman on my psychological radar. Sue had declared herself heterosexual as had most of my women friends. This time, though, I was determined not to get caught up in that frustrating web of unrequited love.

So, as the warm early summer weather settled and the days lengthened, I resumed my habit of having a drink at the bar after work on a Friday. Not every week and not with much peace of mind. I felt guilty because I was leaving Richard at home with the children, and also because of the contempt. When the lesbians at the bar discovered I was married and still living with my husband, there was a lot of pressure for me to 'come out'. My ideal community, the haven for my bleeding soul, was a lot of hard work. The struggle inside went on, and, if anything, it escalated — and the only person I felt I could discuss it with was Sue.

We went on long walks together. Walks where we never stopped talking. When we had discussed a problem, it gave me peace of mind. Spending time with Sue was like plunging into a cool pool after a hot, turbulent day. She was the balm that took away the burn. But I'm not sure I had worked that out then. I just knew I felt better when she was around.

Our most adventurous walk was a hike from the Sign of the Takahe (which is an incongruous medieval-style castle) to the old staging post and now a café called the Sign of the Kiwi, at the summit of the volcanic cone which stretches out to become Banks Peninsula. The route we took went up through Victoria Park, then out of the park following a narrow track above the road that wended its way up to the summit. It was the beginning of a hot day. Dawn's clouds had long since burned off and the sky was a breathless blue vault.

We had arranged to meet at the Sign of the Takahe, just after 10am. Although I was there first, I didn't have to wait long until Sue pulled up in her Ford Telstar. This felt deliciously transgressive because up until now every second of my day had been committed. For the first time all year there was a gap: the children were at kindergarten and school; no essay to write; no exam to sit.

Sue looked gorgeous and fresh in her white t-shirt, long denim shorts and white leather trainers. We were elated to see each other, which did worry me because I was still adamant that I didn't want to fall in love with a straight woman and endure any more heterosexual heartache.

As we climbed out of the fringe of houses around the lower reaches of the

Port Hills we talked about our lives. I told her about the pressure I was under at the bar to 'come out', and my deep, unfathomable fears over what would happen if I did; and she told me about her marriage. We had talked about it before, especially about the difficulties she was having, and the amount of time she was left at home on her own. Sue's marriage seemed less ideal than I had imagined.

I didn't see this as an opportunity, but more as if we were kindred spirits in limbo. Not comfortable with where we were, but unable to move on. We were tied by history and commitment to our husbands and the love we felt for our children. The issues were complex, and we were lost in them like two people in a desert who discover their own footprints and realise they have walked in a circle, without finding the way out. But it was pleasurable, and we were unperturbed because our friendship was about the journey.

Until I made one fatal mistake. I patted Sue's bottom the way I'd seen sportswomen do on the netball court, but of course we weren't playing netball. I regretted it as soon as I did it, and started to agonise. What would she think: that I was some sleaze trying to exploit the loneliness of a remote path? If I could have cut my hand off at that point I would have. Mortified, I waited to see if she would react. Nothing. Thank goodness. Either she had genuinely not noticed, or she was prepared to let my Freudian slip go unchallenged. For the rest of the walk to the summit I flagellated myself. I deserved a straitjacket. At least that would stop me from ever making the same mistake again.

I

Sue's self-assurance unnerved me. She was a contradiction of bridling self-confidence and true humility. Sue was a tōtara with a rootedness that I often envied.

'I'm a Māori princess,' she said one day, as if it were an announcement on the six o'clock news. This proclamation caught me off guard, inspiring an immediate mental audit of all the offensive things I might have said. Next, though, my imagination soared. That is, after I got over my 'I believe you, but thousands wouldn't' initial doubts.

'So, how do you know?' I asked, wanting some concrete evidence. A tiara, maybe.

'I just do. My cousin Terry Kendall, the golf pro, researched our family tree. He discovered that we were related to Te Wherowhero, the first Māori King.'

'Wow! You mean to say, we've known each other this long and you haven't told me?' I demanded, feeling a little betrayed and deprived of months of bragging opportunities.

'Well . . . I haven't said anything because not all of my family believe it. My Aunty Ted (Zelma) said, "You don't want to believe that stuff." But I took notes from Terry's research.'

These jottings had disappeared long ago under a pile of family calamity, beginning with the tragic death of Sue's father in Palmerston North at the hands of a 16-year-old learner-driver. Vince was hit crossing the road close to a roundabout. He wasn't wearing his contact lenses after a cataract operation. He died at the scene. The family, who had already gathered from around the country to celebrate Vince and his wife Norma's fortieth wedding anniversary, attended his funeral instead.

Jason, Sue's first-born, was a toddler when Vince was killed. Sue miscarried twins, then Katherine arrived three-and-a-half years after Jason. She was 11 months old when Norma passed away. Sue always maintained her grief-stricken mother died of a broken heart. Norma had been unwell, but didn't complain. She was a dignified spirit whose quiet confidence spoke for her.

Births and deaths dominated Sue's existence, until, rubbed raw, the facts of her family history were only dimly traced in her memory. This was on top of other erasures: the generational shame of being Māori; the silences of language and culture that over time had left her whakapapa mute.

'Children were punished for speaking Māori at school,' Sue often reminded me. 'Nana was brought up on Māori land at Hopuhopu near Ngāruawāhia. She grew up in a family that spoke Māori, yet I never heard her use a word of it.'

The instinct to curtsey quickly left me, but my new-found respect for Sue's heritage did not. For years, I would drop this thrilling piece of information into conversations, and Sue remained a princess without provenance until she could bear it no longer. Digging through the sands of silence to unearth her genealogy was a birthing: the beginning of a deeper, richer understanding of identity. This was her journey, one that she carried me along on, that she enthused to me about, but was her own exploration of whānau.

It started many years after we first met, with the chance discovery of Russell Bishop's essay in a book on the whakapapa of Irihapeti Te Paea, in the research library of the Auckland War Memorial Museum.

'See, I told you I was a princess!' Sue shouted across the room, to the astonishment of the library's hushed readers. 'Irihapeti Te Paea is my great-great-grandmother and she was the daughter of King Te Wherowhero. I knew it! Everything Terry said was true!' she exclaimed. Sue had scanned through Russell's introductory essay, then found herself named among the lengthy list of relatives. This was confirmation. A eureka moment. The beginning of her odyssey.

'So, is that 50 cents a copy?' I called over to the librarian at the desk, as I held the book down on the photocopier and the lightbar sped across underneath, while at the same time groping in my shoulder bag for my purse. The lightbar had made many trips and I was worried about our capacity to pay. I had to hunt down every stray coin.

Sue stacked her trophies on-end, evening up the photocopied pages before she put them carefully away in a clear file. The library was open for only a half-day on Saturdays, and our eviction was imminent. Reading the essay properly would have to wait until we were home. Sue would ultimately learn that this book on Irihapeti Te Paea and her whakapapa was the centrepiece of a family reunion in 1994 at Port Waikato, where Irihapeti and her husband, John Horton Mackay, raised their 12 children.

Having a whakapapa is more than having a family tree. The names of tīpuna, the events, the places, the mountains and rivers locate and anchor Māori on the timeline of their heritage. It provides a connection to the physical and spiritual, to history and mythology. It grounds those who are in it within Māori custom and philosophy. It is a taonga, and like an artefact is resonant with stories.

If Sue's illustrious whakapapa meant she was a Māori princess, then the essay's author, academic Russell Bishop, and his brother, writer-illustrator Gavin Bishop — both descendants of Irihapeti — were princes with their own quest. Their grandfather Benjamin McKay buried his clue to their identities in their mother's middle names. Her first name was Doris; her Māori middle names were Irihapeti and Hinepau. 'Everything you need to know is in the names I have given to Doris,' Benjamin McKay had said.

This is the miracle of whakapapa: when ancestors whisper secrets to their mokopuna. The way the shame of one age can become the pride of the next. The earliest stories come from waiata passed on from Sue's ancestors, and this is the one she has chosen:

They sing of a beach. Of an emerald-blue sea rolling in across yellow sand. A swell of white foam running, reaching its tide mark, then drawing back in a sparkling rush of sound. The day is breathless, hot and humid. A day when beads of glistening sweat stand proud on your skin. The beach is fringed with palms and tropical trees of iridescent greens. While the beach shimmers in a scorching haze of heat, on the horizon, grey convectional clouds stack themselves high and close together like kuia at a kōrero. There was something old and wise about this gathering of clouds. As if they have been meeting to discuss the mysteries of the Earth forever.

The canoe is ready. The great waka, *Tainui*, has been carved from a single tree. This giant of the forest was fed by sacred soils, planted on the burial site of the chiefly child, Tainui. As it grew tall then towering, rituals were performed. Its journey from tiny seed to colossal tree has been sanctified. During *Tainui*'s carving, prayers and incantations were chanted. On one side of the enormous waka is an outrigger named *Takere-aotea*, which offers stability and shelter from the waves. Two other grand canoes, similarly blessed, one called *Mātaatua* and the other *Te Arawa*, will join *Tainui* in its epic quest.

Generations have lived and died in expectation of this day. Waka are sacred vessels. Their histories from earliest days navigate the dangerous waters between humans and the gods. Especially, Tāwhirimātea, god of the winds, and Tangaroa, god of the sea. Carvings along the sides and at the prow and stern of these waka are a conversation with the spirit world, placating the gods, and pointing to past tīpuna and to future iwi who will anchor their bloodline to the migration of these canoes.

Travellers, Toi and Kupe, voyagers who crossed the ocean, have told of cooler territories to the south. Great expansive lands they called Aotearoa. Huge islands that sat on the horizon like a white cloud waiting to be discovered. The gods have been called on to see the waka safely to landfall. They have been supplicated and appeased.

The celebrated chief, Ngātoroirangi, has been chosen to command the *Tainui* waka on this perilous expedition.* He is an experienced navigator. Ngātoroirangi can read the stars, and the sun and the moon. He observes the migratory movements of birds. He understands the winds, the clouds, the currents, the sea and the seaweed it carries. Ngātoroirangi is a lodestar, a guide who knows the rhythms of the universe.

Ngātoroirangi steadies the waka as it sits solidly in the surf. He can feel the warm, salty water cool as it deepens, rising around his waist. His powerful arms lift his wet body effortlessly up as he clambers onboard the canoe with his men, who grab their paddles. Their collective downward thrust into the dazzling sea sends the waka forward with the cutting power of black volcanic glass.

'Will the gods sanction *Tainui*'s departure?' Ngātoroirangi wonders in trepidation as his vessel speeds towards the reef, which shelters the island of Ra'iatea from the turbulent depths of the ocean. He does not fear the gods when they are still, but their wrath when they are aroused is terrifying.

Ngātoroirangi has already seen some frightening signs. The amassing clouds

---

* According to the source I consulted (Marie Nixon, 'Credibility and Validation through Syntheses of Customary and Contemporary Knowledge', PhD thesis, Massey University, Wellington, 2007); however, there are a number of versions of this story.

are moving closer, covering the sun. Before he even has a chance to raise the triangular sail, a lightning bolt slices the sky in two, unleashing rain in torrents. The deafening thunder-clap that follows rolls on in a petrifying rumble. The winds are summoned; giant waves rise up, as if they are enemies and this is war. They throw themselves over the waka, pushing it landward. Ngātoroirangi knows not to fight this battle, for he and the great waka *Tainui* will be defeated. So Ngātoroirangi turns around, not beaten, still resolute to clear the reef.

He will chant an ancient karakia, then try again, and must try once more before he and his waka reach the ocean. Liberated at last, the lessons Ngātoroirangi and his people learn from the gods are ones of courage in adversity and above all persistence. Ngātoroirangi knows it will take every bit of both of these qualities to survive. This ever-changing expanse of unfathomable blue is an unpredictable host.

There will be starvation and death on this long, long journey. But, in spite of the suffering and the storms, Ngātoroirangi will find his way across the oceans. He reads the skies, the sea and the birds. The canoe will land near Cape Runaway in the Bay of Plenty. Ultimately Ngātoroirangi and his waka will travel as far north as Whangaparāoa and the Waitematā Harbour, and explore the tributaries of the Waikato and Waipā Rivers. Its passage will end on the east coast at Kāwhia. Two limestone pillars at Maketū Bay mark the end of its voyage, and the beginning of a new life for its people.

CHAPTER FIVE
A Stolen Kiss

For the rest of our Port Hills walk, I punished myself for patting Sue's bottom. It was not until I experienced the full force of the panoramic views, across the Hills, down into the bays and out over the distant city of Christchurch, that I put my woes into perspective. At the far-flung harbour heads, you could see where the ocean had lapped at the volcanic cone, washing it away and flooding the enormous crater. The bones of the volcanic landscape were now covered in warm, honey-coloured tussock, with the occasional slate-grey rock projecting through, or a stand of Prussian blue-black pine, set against the jade seas of the harbour and an aquamarine sky. The distance shimmered with heat. Sue and I sat down on a bench, looking out at the view, and ate. My poor effort at a packed lunch was jettisoned in favour of Sue's feast of Asian-style chicken drumsticks and fruit.

The trek back down the hill was shrill with cicadas and unrelentingly hot. Before we disappeared into the plantation of pines along the edge of Victoria Park, we stopped to capture a last look at the heat-hazed city. For me, Victoria Park meant one thing: the Parker–Hulme murder. This had been the backdrop to my childhood. My mother went to high school with the girls, two teenagers who formed a friendship so intense and misguided that they brought one of the girls' mothers up to the park and killed her. If that wasn't the cure-all for unnaturally intense same-sex relationships, then the jail terms they served, one in Mount Eden, a gruesome Victorian prison, and the other at Arohata, certainly were. The story that had disturbed my days growing up, now only added to my misery. Payback, perhaps, would come many years later when I researched and wrote my book on Juliet Hulme, who became bestselling crime novelist Anne Perry.

Sue and I said goodbye when we returned to our cars. Our parting made me aware of my loneliness. Even after I had picked Alex and Jeremy up noisy from school, there was a silence inside me.

At home, I vividly remember the phone, mounted on the wall in the hall, ringing. It jolted me out of my thoughts as I sat on the beige vinyl sofa. I jumped at the noise, then raced down the long hall to answer it.

As I picked up the receiver, I could hear our television blaring in the background. The boys were glued to the children's programmes.

'Hello, Jo speaking,' I said into the receiver.

'Hi, it's Sue here.' I knew her voice, but wasn't expecting to hear from her again so soon.

'Oh. Hi, nice to hear from you. Did you manage to get to school in time to pick up the kids?'

'Yes, I just made it.' There was an awkward silence. 'Look,' she continued, 'I just wanted to clarify what happened today.'

'What . . . what do you mean, "what happened"?' As I said this, I was slipping down the wall, my back against it, knees buckling like someone who had been shot by a firing squad.

'You know what I mean. When you touched my backside. Are you interested in me?'

I breathed in and out slowly, trying to compose myself. It had finally happened.

'No, not in that way.' I was lying again. 'Well . . . not if you don't want me to be. Look, if it makes you uncomfortable, I'll make sure it never happens again. I promise.'

'We need to talk. I don't know how I feel, but it didn't make me feel uncomfortable.'

'Really?' I asked, shocked. 'You mean it didn't send shivers of revulsion down your spine?'

'No. Why? Did you expect it to?'

'I'm . . . I'm not sure. I guess I did.'

'When can we meet?'

'How about Friday night at the bar after work? That's the only time I've got. I could be there about 10.30pm, but not much before. We could have a drink and discuss things.'

'Okay,' she said, 'I can probably get away from the house for a while. Let's make it Friday night, then.'

'You can't miss the bar: it's on the corner of St Asaph and Madras streets, diagonally across from the Christchurch Polytechnic.'

'Great,' she said; then: 'I'd better go and get the dinner on now. Bye.' With a click she was gone, leaving the hollowness of an empty line. It was a weird conversation. One that felt dangerous. But I had fallen too far down the rabbit hole to pull myself out.

It was agony waiting until Friday. That evening at work went by like individual grains of sand slipping through an hourglass. It wasn't riveting work at the best of times, handling low-level Accident Compensation Corporation claims, but that night it was more arduous than usual. The shift was broken up by a 10-minute tea break. I sat in the sterile tea room waiting even for those happy moments to slip away.

When the shift ended, I raced downstairs and out into the car park. That day we'd had one of Canterbury's infamous nor'westers, but the warm night air was now gentle and still, as it always is before the rain. I fumbled to find my keys in the dark, already nervous that I wouldn't make it to the bar in time. The car door opened and I was hit by a rush of hot air. I would have to take my jacket off. The office was air-conditioned, but my car wasn't.

As I turned the key in the ignition, beads of perspiration were beginning to form on my skin and run down my back. My anxiety accelerated in the heat. It wasn't far from my work to the bar, but finding a car park this late on a Friday night would be a challenge. I circled the block, navigating the one-way street system with mounting frustration. Trying to drive as well as scour the line of parked cars for a space was difficult. Finally, I spotted one and, throwing the car into reverse, I managed to park it in the smallest gap possible. I was 10 minutes late already.

With a sense of relief, I got out, locked the car door and headed towards the bar, which, as I approached it, seemed unnaturally quiet. My heart sank. The bar was closed, and on a tiny scrap of paper stuck to the door, already curled at the edges and faded, was the new address. This was in the days before mobile phones, so I couldn't contact Sue. Had she come and gone? If she hadn't arrived yet, should I wait for her, just in case she missed the tiny notice? I stood there in despair, not knowing what to do. The disaster dragged me towards the bar door; then back towards the car; then to the closed clubroom, again. It was an awful dilemma.

Eventually a plan emerged. I would wait for 20 minutes or so on the street corner. If Sue turned up, I could explain. She may well have come and gone, and could even be waiting at the new bar already. There was no way of knowing.

I positioned myself strategically on the street corner near a lamp, so I could see her if she came around the block searching for a park. I looked into each car in case it was her. Nothing. Then there was a flood of cars, none of them white. I noticed there was one passing my corner for a second time. The window was down, and as the driver got close to my curb he shouted out: 'Fancy a shag, sweetheart?' I waved him off, shaking my head. 'Just waiting for a friend,' I called back.

It dawned on me that I was in the town's red-light district. I would have enjoyed the joke more if I hadn't felt so downcast. The wind had turned southerly while I was standing there, and with it came a chill edge that began to cut through my thin top. I was propositioned and tooted at several more times before I finally abandoned my post. I considered going home. The whole thing had been a disaster. I weighed up my options, however, and decided drowning my sorrows was the best one.

On my way back to the car, I paused at the notice to see if I had remembered the address correctly. The new bar was in an even sleazier area than the last. I found a car park opposite it, and was across the road and ordering a drink in no time. Even as I did so I scanned the room, hoping I might see Sue's face. She wasn't there.

In fact, there was only one person I recognised, and she was playing pool. The previous pub had character, but the single interest in this room was the pool table, which I moved over to. My mind was running its reel of regret (Why hadn't I checked that the bar was still at the same address? Couldn't I have got there quicker? . . .). Then I glanced up from the game, and she was there. Sue. Looking gorgeous in her denim shirt and tight stonewashed jeans. I was elated and couldn't deny it anymore. I found her sexy, and I wanted her more than I had wanted anyone else.

'My God, you're here!' I said, rushing across the room and embracing her. 'I'm so sorry: I had no idea the bar had moved. I should have asked someone. How on earth did you find it?'

'I was running late,' she admitted. 'When I arrived at the bar there was no one there. I spotted the note on the door, but had no idea where the address was. I found a phone box and rang a friend, who looked it up on a map and gave me instructions.'

I was overjoyed. That we managed to find each other seemed miraculous.

'Can I get you a drink?'

'You don't have to do that. I can pay for my own.'

'No, honestly, I'd like to.'

'A white wine would be good, then. Not too dry.'

Reluctantly, I relinquished the few moments it took to get us drinks. The evening was late, and I knew we would have to make our separate ways home soon.

I ordered two glasses of house wine, which generally tasted like paint-stripper. But now Sue had arrived everything was perfect, including our parting. Heavy drops of rain began to thud down as I walked Sue to her car. We kissed, a soft, silky, bristle-less kiss that did not satiate, but rather inflamed, my desire. We agreed to meet again on the following Sunday morning. Sue and I would be on our own with our children. They loved being together and would be off playing immediately.

My first encounter with Sue after our kiss was not what I expected. I had thought of nothing else. But she seemed strangely distanced from me again. I could tell she'd been having second thoughts. It was natural. Even I was having nightmares about what a same-sex relationship would unleash. I could only call it same-sex because Sue was adamant she was heterosexual, and I myself hadn't got used to using the word 'lesbian' yet.

We sat awkwardly over our lattes made with Sue's mother-in-law's coffee machine. It was a Christmas gift. Sue was the only person I knew who had an 'espresso coffee maker'. She talked about her husband and the dangers of taking our relationship further. I agreed. I was facing the same dilemma. We talked things around in circles, and at one heart-rending point I thought it was over.

'So, you want to leave things?' I asked, believing that was her conclusion.

'No, not exactly. I think we can continue.'

'Do you mean it?' I asked, still trying to grasp the gist of what she was thinking.

'Yes, but I want you to know the implications of this, and what we are putting in danger. There are two husbands and four children involved. It's not like we're unattached. If this goes wrong, we stand to lose everything. We need to go into this with our eyes open. It's a huge risk.'

'I know, but I'm prepared to take it — in fact, I have to take it.' I paused for a while, then said: 'Let's try things out . . . Shall we go to bed?' I waited again, to let the idea sink in. 'Let's make a time.'

'Make a *time*? To go to bed?'

'Yes,' I answered, as persuasively as I could. 'If we don't make a time, it'll never happen.' Clearly an appointment to make love was not something Sue had ever done before. However, what it lacked in spontaneity would be made up for in the soundness of the plan. I needed to close the deal. 'So, how about after 9.30am on Monday?'

'No. Not Monday. We can't possibly go to bed on Monday. That's my shopping day; I buy my groceries on Monday.' This wasn't a good start. Going to bed with me came after grocery shopping. Although deflated, I was still keen to see things through. Whatever the end might be, I was determined to get there.

'If Monday's out, how about Tuesday after 9.30am?' I waited for the next excuse. Perhaps that was the day she washed her hair.

'Yes, that sounds okay. I don't think I've got anything else on.'

'That's great. Let's make it Tuesday, then.' It wasn't long after that that I left. Taking two reluctant children home with me. Jason and Alex had been down the back of the property playing a super-hero game, while Katie and Jeremy were in the bedroom stirring mud cakes and serving them to her dolls. Jeremy was approaching the end of his Barbie-doll phase, but was not averse to serving slices of mud pie or pouring out a pretend cup of tea.

On Monday morning, I thought of Sue doing her grocery shopping. I wondered where she went to do it, and what other mysteries there were in her life. Was this a big mistake for both of us? Sue had been married 16 years and I, 10. Were we not better to leave things as they were? Heterosexuality was so much easier. At least, superficially. But, in truth, it hadn't been for me. And I remembered Blair, the homosexual minister with a wife and children. His denial of his sexuality was hypocrisy. Surely, I should be better than that? The battle raged on in my mind. The dishonesty to myself was pitted against the betrayal of my husband and the impact it would have on our children.

For once I was grateful to go to work, a welcome distraction from the conflict playing out inside me. By the time Tuesday morning came, I was resolved. After all the turmoil, I had made a decision. My mind was calm now. I dropped the children off at school and drove back home on autopilot. I let myself in the back door. The rambling outhouses were still there with the musty odour of rotting wood, but the L-shaped kitchen and living room that I entered were a sign that at least a part of this enormous beast had been tamed.

I looked at my watch. 9.15am. I'm in good time, I thought. I sat down on the sofa. My calm decisiveness began to evaporate. With each minute my anxiety mounted. I got up and walked about aimlessly, trying to settle my nerves. 9.30am came and went, then 10am. I prowled the bay window at the front of the house, hoping to catch a glimpse of her white car. Nothing.

II

The story of how the Lewis chess pieces were found was a fascinating one that Frederic Madden first heard from Mr Forrest, the sly antiquities dealer who had brought the ivories to him to sell to the British Museum. The tale involved the escapades of a cattle herder living on the Isle of Lewis. He was Malcolm Macleod of Penny Donald, also known as Calum nan Sprot, who danced a jig with his wife, Mary, around the kitchen table when he arrived home with his hoard of gaming pieces excavated from the sandbank.

'You've done it now, Malcolm: we'll be rich. But we must keep this a secret,' his wife said after a pause. 'We mustn't tell anyone, until we find a dealer who can sell 'em for the best price. Swear to me, Malcolm. You'll nay tell a livin' soul?'

Malcolm stopped his jubilations and assumed a more serious disposition. 'I swear,' he replied, solemnly raising his hand. 'I swear on my honour.'

It's not that Malcolm wasn't an honourable man, it's just that he was partial to a drop or two of the tongue-loosening evil of drink. So on his trip to town the next day to get supplies, it was little surprise that he went first to the tavern, rather than to the general store.

'You look very pleased with yourself. You come in ta money?' asked one of the local fishermen, as Malcolm placed a jug of ale on the heavy wooden table for a rare round of drinks on him.

'Someone died?'

'Nay,' chuckled Malcolm. 'Somethin' much better 'an that.'

'What is it, then, Malcolm? Tell us.'

'I couldn't possibly do tha'. I've sworn on my honour to the wife nay ta tell a livin' soul.' At that there was an explosion of mirth and jeering amongst the company.

Malcolm was affronted.

'I'll have you know, my wife can be a very difficult woman.'

There was more laughter.

Just these few, he thought. Telling just these few couldna do any harm. He was dying to tell someone. 'Well, then, I'll tell you if you swear nay to breathe a word of it beyond these walls.' And then, rather self-importantly, he began detailing his discovery.

'There's still an uncanny strangeness about them,' he confessed as he came to the end of his tale. As if the telling had taken a toll, he picked up his mug and downed the contents in one mouthful, swaying slightly as he took his seat.

'Are you going to sell them, Malcolm?' asked a solemn individual sitting at a table nearby. He was better dressed than most, in a well-cut dress coat and top hat. An Edinburgh merchant doing business in Stornoway, no doubt, Malcolm thought.

'Because, if it's getting rid of the pieces you want, then perhaps I can help you. There may be good money to be made,' the stranger continued. 'Let's take the table over there,' he said, gesturing to a secluded spot.

The thought of money was like a splash of cold water in Malcolm's face.

'If I were you, I'd make a quick trip home,' the merchant counselled as they conferred in a corner of the tavern. 'Hide the treasure forthwith, and lock yourself in until such time as you can put the hoard in the hands of a dealer. The sooner you pass them over, the safer you'll be.'

'Thank you, sir. I would be most grateful ta make the acquaintance of someone in'erested in purchasin' them.'

'Of course I'll have to see them first to authenticate them and ascertain their value.'

Malcolm made a pact with the merchant. He would hide his finds as quickly as he could, and the next day the merchant, who went by the name Captain Roderick Ryrie, would visit him at his cottage with the intention of taking the collection away with him.

They parted with a handshake. Malcolm looking furtively around the now-crowded tavern to see if anyone was watching. He had come into town for supplies, but they would have to wait.

It was dusk by the time he stepped out of the tavern. As he stood on the narrow, cobbled street he could smell peat fires being stoked into life for the long, wintry evening. Malcolm looked both ways. Having reassured himself that there was no one waiting and watching, he began to run homeward.

Behind him, he heard the voices of men leaving the alehouse. Were they after him already? He fled as fast as he could, stopping from time to time to catch his breath, which he drew in with difficulty. He knew the road well and had followed it on many occasions in far more compromised conditions than now. But this time he was alert to every sound. Every rustle in the growing blackness was a person in pursuit, every moan of the wind a voice calling after him.

When he finally reached his cottage, he was exhausted and sweating heavily. His wife was suspicious. Her husband's excesses expressed themselves in many ways, but exertion was never one of them.

'What have you been up to, Malcolm?' she demanded.

'Nothing,' he retorted, as he stood on the doorstep.

'You look like the hounds a Hell ha' been after you.'

'Out of my way,' he said, as he pushed past her. Once inside the cottage, he shut the door behind them, slamming the bolt across. He checked the shutters, rattling each one of them to make sure it was secure.

'You've told them lot in the tavern, haven't you?' his wife accused him.

Malcolm looked sheepish: his face had always been an open book.

'You'll be the death a me, Malcolm!' she shouted. 'In fact, you'll be the death a both of us.'

'Stupid woman. Can't stop yourself from making more a things than there is.' At the same time, he shot a worried glance at the table where the rows of chess pieces stood. 'I . . . I . . . think we should hide these.'

'Fool,' said his wife between her teeth. 'You've put us both in mortal danger.'

But there was nothing to be done now but hide the chess pieces and try to limit any consequences.

'There's the sack over there,' she said. 'Let's fill it quickly and get them out of sight. I know a place where we can hide them not far from the cottage.'

'Are you sure we should leave the cottage? We're safe in here. Out there anything could happen.'

'You should have thought of that before you opened your big mouth, Malcolm,' she fired back. 'I'll carry the lamp. You take the sack — and hurry up.'

The herder hesitated on the doorstep, steeling his nerve before he dived into the frozen darkness. Even though the sweat-soaked shirt still stuck to his back, the temperature outside was frigid.

'Over here,' his wife called, gesturing with the lamp.

For a second, Malcolm thought he heard something breathing and the sound of a footfall in the heather around the cottage. Fear propelled him towards his wife and the lamp.

'Wait for me, Mary!' he called.

The hiding place was not much further on. Mary raised the lamp to show him where to deposit the hoard. As he pushed aside the surrounding vegetation, a cleft in the rock was revealed. This was the ideal place to put the pieces for now.

That night Malcolm slept fitfully, stirring himself with his blood-filled dreams. Each time he woke, he heard the rhythmic breathing punctuated by the gurgling snores of his wife. He was up before dawn.

While Mary went about her usual tasks for the day, Malcolm paced the cottage floor. Mid-morning, he saw his Armageddon arriving. Along the track to his cottage a group of dishevelled men were approaching. He recognised a number of them from the tavern the day before.

As the men came closer, a ringleader stepped forward and called out: 'We've come ta see the wee men, Malcolm!'

The cottage door opened and Mary appeared on the step.

'Donna be soft, Malcolm. They're nay ta be trusted. They'll have the hoard 'n' cut your throa'.'

'Rubbish, woman!' their leader exploded. 'Our intentions are honourable. We just want ta see the wee people.'

The man's plea seemed so genuine.

'Do you swear on the Bible that you're nay up ta no good?' she called back.

'I swear, Mam.'

'Malcolm, go and bring us back an armful of the figures.'

When he returned, the crofters had moved closer to the cottage, and he could see the look of amazement on their faces when they saw his selection of pieces.

"T'is a treasure indeed,' exclaimed their spokesman. 'Will you take some of ma meagre property in exchange for a wee man from this marvellous collection?'

No one knows how many of the set were exchanged that day, or how 11 of them came to be separated from the hoard and kept in Scotland. Captain Ryrie arrived later that afternoon, and, in exchange for a letter of receipt from the merchant, Malcolm swore on his honour that these were all the pieces he had found. But this was untrue.

Malcolm was paid the colossal sum of £30 for his find.

'Not a bad rate for a day's diggin',' he said to his wife as they danced again around the kitchen table together.

On 11 April 1831, the 82 pieces Ryrie had purchased went on show at the Society of Antiquities of Scotland, at Edinburgh. They had passed from Captain Ryrie to the antiquities dealer, Mr Forrest. His hope was that the chessmen would find a home in the Royal Museum in Edinburgh, but no backer was found. So Mr Forrest took the ivories south to London, where he negotiated with Frederic Madden at the British Museum. Madden's desire was always to keep the treasure together. Little did he know that this hope was, already, an impossibility.

CHAPTER SIX

Roped Together

Despair. I was still waiting for Sue to arrive. Now I knew how deep despair went. Then, almost as if it were a figment of a tortured brain, I thought I saw a flash of white disappearing around the corner of the bay window. My view was interrupted by the fence. I raced down the hall to the back door, which was the one we used most often. As I put my hand on the handle there was a knock. I threw it open, hoping that it was Sue.

'I'm sorry I'm late. I was held up in traffic.'

'No problems at all,' I lied, and, to be honest, it didn't seem like there were any now she was there.

'Come in. Can I get you a cup of coffee? I've only got instant. Is that alright?'

'Yes, that's fine.'

So, we sat nervously on the beige sofa looking at each other over our steaming mugs of Nescafé.

'I'm not sure,' Sue said, finally draining her cup, 'where we go from here. I've never done this sort of thing before.' She looked at me as if she were expecting me to be the experienced one, to make the first move. It didn't seem the right time to remind her that it was a new frontier for me, too.

'Well, let's give it a go. I'm sure it will be great,' I said, as if we were two climbers, roped together and about to scale Mount Everest. 'In here,' I added ushering Sue into the bedroom.

It was the softness of making love with a woman that struck me first. Her gentle enveloping flesh held me suspended like water. This was my baptism, my ecstasy, and I knew I wanted more. While I felt like I floundered, Sue took to love-making like an Olympic swimmer. Sassy, sexy, passionate — she was a natural. I was in awe. Still waters did indeed run deep. At the end of it was the moment of reckoning.

'Did you come . . . you know . . . properly? Do you think you will want to go to bed again? Did you enjoy it?' I didn't want it to sound like I was conducting a customer survey, but I needed to know how she felt.

'Yes, of course I enjoyed it, and I would like to go to bed again, but this can't break our marriages up. There's too much at stake here. We have to be discreet. We won't be able to see much of each other from now on. It's nearly Christmas. The children will be off school. There won't be many opportunities to meet on our own.'

'Yes, I know,' I admitted. This reality-check was a blow. It seemed that I finally had what I wanted and it was already evaporating.

We didn't manage to see much of each other as Christmas approached. What time we did get was precious. While my conscience troubled me, and will never be silent on the matter of my betrayal, physically I felt relaxed, at peace, and the love-making got better.

Our last meeting before we went off on our separate family holidays was difficult. It would be a break in the momentum, a time of re-evaluation for both of us. Whether we arrived back from our month-long break in the same place was anyone's guess. I already felt committed. My epiphany had ended my emotional ties to my marriage, but Sue had not experienced the same transfiguration. This was new for her and would have to be processed.

After we separated, it surprised me how much my life lost its colour. How flat and mundane things became. Nothing would ever be the same again. I had been alone: I realised that now. A part made whole by the joining of us both. I was complete in her, I felt — but was she complete in me?

Our Christmas break with my parents at their house in Parapara Beach in Golden Bay was joyless. It culminated in a row that began as a squall with my brother and ended in a perfect storm with Dad. I was testy and distracted; my brother his usual challenging self; and Dad, who could always be difficult, was suffering from undiagnosed shingles. Richard sat back and let me be savaged. After this catastrophic conflict, I crossed the days off until I was back in Christchurch. Richard and I returned mid-January to begin work at the Accident Compensation Corporation, him to his day job, and me to my night shifts.

My first phone call to Sue was made with trepidation. I wondered how the holiday had changed her.

'Hi, Jody,' she said, greeting me with the nickname she had given me. We chatted for a while, until she asked me: 'So how was your holiday?' She had been so enthusiastic it felt sacrilegious to admit that it had been such a spectacular failure.

'Good and bad,' I replied, which nailed it. 'How about yours?'

'Just wonderful,' she gushed. And then she proceeded to unpack the whole family event: the in-laws they visited; the Christmas meal they shared with a crowd of friends and relations; the presents given and received. It sounded superb. Why in the world does she need me? I thought. It didn't make sense. When she got to the end of her warm family fuzzies, I asked her straight.

'So what about us? Are we still together?'

'Yes,' she responded, 'we are.' My world was radiant again.

I had never had an affair before, and I never want to again, but it was a singular experience. One that taught me more about myself than I ever dreamed possible. I am not a risk-taker, but I discovered that I was prepared to take risks, and even learned to enjoy them. If love is a drug supplied, according to Shakespeare's Mercutio, by 'Queen Mab', then affairs are her heroin. It gave me the highest highs and the most tormented lows. The craving gnawed away until it became an obsession, and the more I got, the more I wanted. Everyone experiences love differently, like we process drugs according to our metabolism; but however you experience it, love brings out *who* you are, at the core.

With one exception, 'love' before had left me complacent, and a little disturbed by my coolness. Not sociopathic, exactly, but it was affection through a filter of rationality that I knew I shouldn't have. With Sue I fell headlong in love. There was no slowing myself: no foothold, not even any friction at the edges of my descent. I was consumed. I asked Sue often if it was the same for her. She said it was, and in her own more reserved, quiet way, I believe she was equally as lost.

We continued to meet. None of our rendezvous felt as constrained as the first one. But time to spend together was difficult to find. My parents upgraded and gave Richard and me their second-hand bed. I moved our old one into the spare room and this became ours. Each time we made love we ran the risk of being discovered. The peril of being revealed didn't give me a thrill like it might some people, but it did charge our love-making with an adrenaline that it would not have had normally. After a time, I wondered whether our relationship would be as electric if it wasn't charged with fear. If things were ordinary, would we feel ordinary about each other? The testing of the hypothesis felt a long way off.

But the possibility came a little closer to reality one day in the bitter grind of late winter. It was 13 August to be precise. This was the anniversary of the death of Sue's dad and the day she miscarried her twins six years before. Perhaps we should have sensed the day's ominous vibe and changed our plans. Too late, I heard Sue's knock at the door, and raced down the corridor, eager to see her. As I let her in, I noticed the sky outside was leaden, portentous, the light filtered in through a wash of grey.

'Come in, quick, it's freezing.'

'Yeah, the wind cuts right through you,' she responded as I closed the door on its savagery. 'I've got a load of washing on the line. Hope it doesn't start raining before I get home to take it in.'

'Fancy a coffee, or would you rather have a cup of tea?' I called over my shoulder as I moved automatically to the kitchen bench to fill the electric jug.

'I think I'd better skip a drink for now. Maybe I'll have one before I go.'

'Okay,' I replied, replacing the jug on the bench.

I rounded the corner to see Sue sitting on the sofa hugging the gas heater. Apart from the boys' room, this was the only space we heated, and the high ceilings sent most of the heat up to the roof.

'Are you sure you won't have a cup? It'll warm you up.'

'No. Honestly, I'm fine.'

We passed along the arctic passageway to the spare room, which I also used as an office. The books and papers from my latest essay were strewn across the floor by my makeshift desk. I'd been working there when I heard Sue's knock.

'Shall I bring the gas heater down?'

'No, it'll be fine. We'll warm up,' she replied, giggling. I laughed, too, knowing she was right. I threw my clothes off as quickly as I could. Leaping between the freezing sheets was like plunging into an icy pool. How our ardour survived the splash was unfathomable to me even then. But we clung to each other with an intensity that generated its own heat. It was frictionless, smooth and glorious. Floating . . . floating . . . then lost, beside, above, falling into one's self again in a shuddering climax.

It was only seconds after that, that I heard a knocking at the back door.

'Shit, shit!' I exclaimed in horror, sitting bolt-upright. 'Quick, quick, get dressed. Hurry!'

'Where are my clothes?' whispered Sue, as she stood naked, already out of bed.

'I think this is your bra,' I said, throwing it to her. I had already wasted crucial time putting it on before realising the cups looked like a couple of deflated parachutes strapped to me. Whoever was at the door had come inside.

'Oh my God, I forgot to lock the back door!' I had to slow the person down.

'Just a minute,' I shouted, 'I'll be with you soon.' Bugger my own bra, I thought, pulling up my trousers and buttoning my shirt. There was no knowing who it was until I heard my father's voice answer back. This was not a relief, but I knew it could have been much worse.

'I'm on my way,' I called out again. 'You stay here,' I whispered to Sue. 'Let me handle this.'

I left the room, walking quickly. There was no way I wanted Dad to get as far as the bedroom.

'Coming,' I called again, almost at the end of the hall. I had stopped him.

'Hi, Dad,' I said casually as I walked into the kitchen-living room where he was waiting for me. As soon as our eyes met I realised an explanation was essential. We were one of those families that bickered and bitched at each other, but when your back was against the wall we rallied. That day I tested the maxim to the maximum. With my father I couldn't keep up the charade. I told him everything. Starting with my epiphany over the vacuum cleaner and ending with how right it felt in bed. It was one of the most cathartic experiences of my life.

I cried; I confessed my guilt; I begged him not to lob an incendiary device into the middle of things.

'I need more time to sort things out,' I told him. 'I know this is wrong, but sometimes you have to do wrong things to get the right result. If this blows up it will impact the lives of so many people. Please, please keep it to yourself. Just a bit longer.'

Asking my father to keep quiet about an affair was dangerous territory, I knew. My mother had always prefaced her good advice with 'Do as I say, not as I do.' That was her indemnity clause for her vices, especially smoking and drinking. My father's favourite saying, on the other hand, was 'You're only as good as your word', which he pretty much stuck to. He was from a long line of Oxford Terrace Baptists in Christchurch, who like Dad had probably found their own unique ways to stray. Buried in my father was a core of old-fashioned Christian values, and I was not being as good as my word to my husband, and we both knew it.

When I went out to the car after a troubled shift at work that night, there was a note under my windscreen wiper. It was from Sue. While I had been talking to Dad in the kitchen-living room, she had let herself out the front door. The front door was entered via a magnificent lead-lit sun porch that had long since buckled and twisted into disuse as the house sank into the peat. The cracked pathway and mangled steps to the porch, which once would have been rather marvellous, were now seldom mounted, offering a surreptitious escape route.

Sue left knowing we had been exposed. Her message simply said *Ring me*.

'Thanks for your note, sweetheart,' I said when I rang, revealing more of my agony than I intended. My angst was less about whether my father would shop us, and more about Sue getting freaked out and giving up. I didn't know how I would cope if she did.

'I just wanted to find out what happened. What did your father say?'

'You won't believe it, but he took the lesbian thing pretty much in his stride. Maybe he suspected something.'

'But what about us?' she responded. 'How did he handle that?'

'Quite well. He thinks we need to say something. Not leave it too long.'

'But in the meantime, will he keep quiet?'

'Yes, I think so. He realises the implications of blowing things apart.'

'That's a relief,' she said, relaxing. 'But I'm prepared to tell the guys if you want to,' she added, leaving me to make the tough decision.

'No,' I said, 'I'm not ready. I don't think either of us are. Do you?' I needed her to accept some responsibility.

'You're right,' she agreed, 'I don't think it's time yet.'

So that's how we left it. Relying on our flawed abilities to keep our relationship secret, and my father to keep his word better than I had kept mine to Richard.

II

In waiata that sing of Ngātoroirangi, who navigated the seas to bring his people safely to land, Sue learned of her great-great-great-grandfather's beginning in Aotearoa. For he belonged to Ngāti Mahuta, a tribe whose songs echo back to the waka of *Tainui* and *Te Arawa*. The waiata of Sue's great-great-great-grandmother's people, however, tell of another beach and a different journey. There are various versions of what happened. This is the one Sue was drawn to.

Near the town of Whakatāne, which in ancient times was known as Kakahoroa, there is a stretch of pure white sand. In the bay that it fringes, even before the presence of people, was Whakaari, a great ivory-coloured island with a heart of spuming fire. Over centuries, pumice from Whakaari gifted the beach at Kakahoroa with its mantle of alabaster sand. On fine days when its god was at peace, the sight of Whakaari from the beach was of a blue-grey cone rising up from the sea: the sky above it a billowing cloud of soft whites and blues.

Whakaari is at peace the day a young woman named Kurawhakaata is standing on the beach looking across at the steaming volcano. But in that moment, she sees something else: an enormous canoe with a triangular-shaped sail heading towards the shore. As the waka gets closer, she can see the pierced carvings on the prow are not of that area. She knows how to read the crafting on the waka: its size and the intricacy of decoration suggest this could be a war canoe.

Kurawhakaata, the daughter of the celebrated chief Tamakihikurangi, composes herself. She will not be afraid. Kurawhakaata has been taught that fear is undignified, but caution is a good guide. She hails the waka as it approaches.

'You are welcome here, visitors, if you come without weapons or warfare in mind.' The magnificent waka is named *Aratāwhao*, and aboard are two chiefs, Hoaki and Taukata. The visitors greet Kurawhakaata with respect and assure her that their journey is one of exploration and discovery, not conflict or war.

When the canoe is pulled up beyond the high tide, Kurawhakaata takes her chiefly voyagers to her father Tamakihikurangi's fortified pā of Kaputerangi on ground high above the beach. Hoaki, Taukata and the people of the *Aratāwhao* are greeted as honoured travellers.

From pits dug deep in the ground, steamed on hot firestones, kai is provided: mamaku (black tree fern), aruhe (fern root), pikopiko (young fern shoots), kiore (rat), manu (bird) and ika (fish). This is Tamakihikurangi's finest food, a feast to welcome his hungry guests.

The chiefs Hoaki and Taukata respond to Tamakihikurangi's generosity with a koha of treasured food they have carried with them. From their girdles they draw dried kūmara, the last of the store prepared for their trip. The people of the stronghold of Kaputerangi are overwhelmed. This is a gloriously satisfying food, with a flavour they have never tasted before. Hoaki and Taukata explain that kūmara are the fruit of the soils of Hawaiki.

So intense is the desire to have this food that the great chief Tamakihikurangi sails with Hoaki and Taukata to Hawaiki aboard the *Aratāwhoa*, to bring back the kūmara to his people. *Aratāwhoa* lands at a place in Hawaiki where the soils are rich and kūmara grow in abundance. That night they feast on this precious crop. There are many more banquets and celebrations between chief Tamakihikurangi and the people of Hawaiki before the waka *Mātaatua* is built, carved and readied for their return to Aotearoa.

Two chiefs, both brothers, are chosen by Tamakihikurangi to carry the kūmara back to the people of Kaputerangi near the Island of Whakaari. Toroa is to be the navigator, and Tāneatua the canoe's tohunga. Tamakihikurangi tells the two young men to beach their waka where they see a cave in a hill, a waterfall and a rock known as Irakewa. This sacred site is where they are to plant the kūmara.

Blessed by the gods, their journey across the ocean is without incident.

When the men see the cave, waterfall and rock, and reach the shallows, they leap over the sides in their excitement.

The canoe, still with its women onboard, drifts in the bay for a time. Then the current grabs its prow like a hand clutches a paddle and begins to pull the canoe through the water and out to sea. The women of the waka are frightened, for they are forbidden to take hold of the paddles, even to save themselves. Across the cries and wails of despair, Wairaka, Toroa's daughter, picks up a paddle, holds it in the air and cries 'Kia Whakatāne au i ahau!' — 'I will act as a man!' — and she plunges the paddle into the sea and the women with her do the same, taking the vessel back to the safety of the shore. Her decisive action saves the waka and everyone aboard. The bravery and self-determination of this event is preserved in the soul of the waiata and in the place name, Whakatāne.

The kūmara is planted along with the sacred red soils of Hawaiki, at a place named Matirerau. The mokopuna or progeny of Toroa and his daughter will become rangatira of great mana. Among their descendants will be the fearsome warrior Pūkeko whose courageous name will be given to the warrior tribe Ngāti Pūkeko of Whakatāne.*

---

* Informed by Bradford Haami's essay, 'Mataatua and Ngati Pukeko' in: *The whanau of Irihapeti Te Paea (Hahau): the McKay and Joy (Joyce) families* (compiled by Rex and Adriene Evans). Auckland: Evagean Publishing, c. 1994.

CHAPTER SEVEN

A Fire Sale in Christchurch

For three years each spring and summer Richard and I put our house in Christchurch on the market. It was a fire sale. The process began with a team of real-estate agents walking through the property, moving from room to room, sizing it up. Trying at the same time to diminish the sellers' expectations.

'So, you've taken out the chimneys, I see. Interesting that the old timber frame still retains its banana shape.' . . . 'I see the previous owner shaved off the bottom of all the doors and windows, and now that it's straighter there are big gaps.' . . . 'I'm sure there's someone, somewhere, keen to take on a "project" like this.' He didn't add the words 'in some far-off galaxy' because he didn't have to. It was obvious.

They would leave me demoralised, on the verge of putting a sign out the front 'free to a good home', but since it already was a home that seemed redundant. Each season we had a few tyre-kickers through. Usually developers, who sighed, and whistled through their teeth, and left shaking their heads. It felt like we were trying to flog off the *Titanic* as it was sinking.

'We'll have to be a bit cautious,' I said to Sue, after the house had been listed for its annual stint on the market. 'I don't think they just turn up, but the agency has a key. Surely they'd ring Richard or me first?'

As it turned out they had rung, and the very afternoon Sue and I managed to find some time to go to bed the real-estate road-show arrived for its annual viewing. We had just stripped off and were under the bedcovers when I heard a key turn in the lock.

'Holy shit!' I said, leaping out of bed and almost running on the spot with anxiety, wondering what to grab first. My clothes were all over the place. 'Someone's opened the front door.' Just as I said this, I heard their voices.

'Get dressed, quick,' I urged Sue in as low a whisper as I could.

'I can't find my underpants,' she cried, frantically searching.

'We haven't got time to worry about your underpants.' Already the voices were getting closer. The sales team had finished in the kitchen-living room area, and was on its way up the hall.

'Quick, pull the sheets together then get under the bed.'

'But I don't think I'll fit.'

'Try!' I hissed. By now I was dressed after a fashion. 'I'll delay them.' They were already in the boys' room. Their next stop was the spare room — and us! I stepped out into the hallway.

'Hello,' I called out, 'I'm sorry, I didn't realise you were coming.'

When I reached the boys' room, I was greeted by two overdressed and overly made-up females and three suited men.

'My apologies,' the alpha agent said, stepping forward to shake my hand. 'I'm Brian. How do you do?'

'Nice to meet you Brian, I'm Jo.' Then we did the round of introductions, the names passing over my head in a blur. I was still shaking with the shock.

'Were you not expecting us?' Brian ventured, picking up some of my vibe. 'I'm sure it was today that we agreed to.' He was thumbing through the paperwork on his clipboard. It was my turn to apologise.

'Yes, I remember now.' I had made the arrangement over the phone weeks ago. 'I'm sorry, I completely forgot. Can I offer you people a cup of tea?' I had gathered my wits about me sufficiently to formulate a delaying tactic.

'No, thank you,' said Brian. 'We have a number of houses to go through this afternoon, and this is the first on the list. But thank you very much for asking.' Our pleasantries had taken just a few minutes: that was all the time I could delay the procession.

'Now, the next room along the hall is the spare room and the master is on the left. Is that right?' he said, turning to me.

'Yes,' I replied, 'but it's a bit messy. Maybe it might be best if you skipped it this time.'

'I've seen it all,' replied Brian, chuckling. 'There's nothing fazes us.' I wouldn't be so sure about that, I thought, picturing Sue naked as she hurriedly pulled the bedclothes together. Before I could say anything more, Brian was out of the boys' room, his entourage following like sheep.

'In here is the spare room,' I heard him announce. By the time I was in the hall again he already had his hand on the door handle. The next thing, he turned the handle and pushed. My heart thumped; my mouth was dry.

'Just look at the magnificent leadlight windows,' he called over his shoulder as his minions filed in behind him. I was down the corridor and standing outside the room as fast as I could. Looking in myself, seconds later, I saw— *Nothing*. Thank God. No sign of Sue at all, just Brian prattling on. Whatever he was saying was drowned by the sound of thumping in my ears. There had to be a better way.

Our diagnostics over a cup of coffee later were decisive. We realised we couldn't go on.

'Good on you for getting under the bed,' I exclaimed, staring traumatised over my mug of coffee.

'Thanks. I didn't think I was going to squeeze myself under it. Have you seen how low it is?'

'No,' I admitted, thinking that I had never considered whether a person could fit underneath that bed before. 'But we can't keep doing this, can we? I feel wrong about it. We shouldn't be meeting here at home.'

We both sat despondently over our coffees, until Sue said: 'I've got it. Let's rent somewhere.'

'But how can we afford to do that?'

'Just a room, like a studio; some of the other students on my course have them . . . you know, away from the university. I was thinking of getting one, anyway.'

It was sublimely simple, yet brilliant. Why hadn't I thought of it?

'Gosh, that's a great idea. But can we get one cheap enough?'

'I think so,' she replied, after a brief hesitation. 'I'll go through the To Let column in the newspaper and see what I can find.'

Sue rang me a few days later with a list.

'No, no,' I said to each one as she went through the list, 'too expensive.'

'The cheapest one is a shop in the Sydenham Mall.'

'How cheap?' She quoted the rate, and we decided that between us we could easily meet the weekly rent.

'Ring up and make an appointment to see it,' I told her. 'I hope it hasn't gone — at that price it's a bargain.' I could have saved myself the worry, because as it turned out this was not a property about to fly off the shelves.

Sydenham Mall was on the wrong side of the railway tracks, and perhaps that helped explain what happened to it financially. Some enterprising person built the mall, fitting out the stores in olde-worlde English style. The store-fronts downstairs were made of a heavy rustic wood that resembled oak. I vaguely remember its heyday, walking through when the children were very young, and wondering at its cleverness.

The covered mall ran through from Colombo Street to a large car park at the rear. On that visit, the two shop-fronts on Colombo Street were deliciously enticing. On one side was a magnificent antique shop with treasures that could have been saved from Miss Havisham's house fire. Dazzling crystal and silverware; gorgeous Georgian writing desks; heavy mahogany tables with inlaid tops; large leather-bound books; a pitch-black perambulator with narrow iron-rimmed wheels; and a giant amber-coloured rocking horse, with a real horse-hair tail. It was a spectacle of Victorian upper-class elegance, its bounty shoe-horned in so you could hardly reach the counter.

The shop on the other side of the entrance to the mall made its own confectionery, and the smell of drizzled chocolate, roasted nuts and nougat was enough to raise the dead. A world of temptation: its shoppe-ness was defined by the rows of large Victorian glass jars full of extravagantly coloured sweets and the antiquated scales that weighed out every lime-drop or liquorice allsort sold. 'They're all handmade,' the proprietor told me. My mouth watered when he described the old sweet recipes he had resurrected. The last time I visited the store was before Easter, when it was festooned with piped-icing eggs and chocolate bunnies big enough to have been on steroids.

Coming back to it now was a shock. Stopping the engine, I looked around the car park in search of Sue. My heart always pounded more heavily during these 'waitings'. I felt sometimes like I lived my life on a precipice. I wasn't parked there long, however, before I saw her car pull into a space a couple of rows over. My heart flipped; each meeting was like the first, only better. I locked the car door then bounded over to where she was parked.

'Hi, sweetheart.' That would have to do, as we never kissed in public. She smiled broadly and squeezed my hand. Then we got down to business.

'According to the person I spoke to on the phone, we pick up the key from the antique dealer.' Sue grabbed her purse from the front passenger seat and locked the car.

Entering the mall through the back entrance, we were confronted by a run-down clutter of objects. Mostly, I imagined, from deceased estates: old bits of shelving, miscellaneous door-knobs, drops of faded curtains, rusty bikes with wicker-baskets up front and bells on the handlebars. I was waiting for the good stuff to begin, but the junk continued on from shop to shop like a cancerous blight. Hand-painted signs announcing wool, home-crafts and embroidery 'shoppes' were still there executed in an old English font as a cruel irony.

'Wow, this isn't how I remember it. What a shame, it's gone downhill.'

'I guess that's why the rent's so cheap.'

I couldn't help but feel a pang of pity for the people who were trying to make it work.

'The person we need to speak to is in the front shop.' The business in the front shop was more marvellous, and a number of the items mixed among its bric-à-brac could claim an antique pedigree. But the shop opposite, where the confectioner had been, was now just a dairy.

'Gee, this is so different,' I said to Sue. By this time we were standing outside the antique shop looking in. The antique dealer was a short, rotund, balding Italian-looking man in his mid-fifties. The shop was as crowded as its predecessor, so it amazed me how he moved around the clutter with such precision.

'You go in,' I said to Sue, pushing her forward. 'You made the phone call.' That was me, through and through, always reluctant to break the ice with people and make the first approach. 'I'll wait out here.'

'Okay,' said Sue, entering without hesitation. I watched the proprietor's unhealthy delight when he spotted her. Was it that she was a potential customer, or did he fancy her? I kicked myself for being so standoffish. Sue soon emerged, not with the key, but with the ebullient antique dealer gesturing and flapping his arms expressively like a territorial rooster.

'Let me show you where it is,' he said with gusto. 'Is this your friend? Are you both renting the shop?' he asked.

'Yes, we are,' I replied.

'Follow me then,' he said, gesturing ahead.

He locked up his shop and led us about halfway down the mall to where a large stairway swept up in a curving movement to the second floor, which was a mezzanine.

'So what are you planning to use the room for? Are you opening a shop? There's not much foot traffic up there now.' I hadn't prepared myself for a grilling, so I shot an anguished look at Sue.

'I am using it as a painting studio, and my friend here will be using it as an office to write,' she said. By this time we had passed a series of little shop-fronts, now either empty or used for storage.

'You've got one of the bigger rooms,' he said, turning the key in the lock and pushing the stiff door open. 'Nobody's been in here for months,' he said, waving invisible cobwebs away and stepping over a litter of curling envelopes and yellowing newspapers that had been pushed through the letterbox slot. The shop window was a massive pane of glass that stopped about two feet from the ground. Along the window ledge was a squadron of dead blowflies. The *Closing down sale* banner, now tired and torn where it slumped on its tape, was still emblazoned across the glass, a remnant of the room's former occupants.

'I can show you something else if this doesn't suit,' he added.

'No, there's no need. We'll take it.'

The man, surprised at my apparent hastiness, looked at Sue.

'Yes,' she agreed. 'I'm happy to take it, too.'

'Very good,' he said, 'I'll inform the landlord and he can send the tenancy agreement. Where shall I tell him to send it?' he enquired.

'Could we sign it here? It would save sending it out.'

'Marvellous, let's do that,' the antique dealer said with a final flourish of his hands. He was obviously pleased to close the deal, and to have us as near-neighbours. Not next-door but, as I estimated it, directly above his shop.

'You will need to pay a bond and the first two weeks' rent into this bank account.' Digging into his trouser pocket, he retrieved a scrap of paper with a bank account number written on it.

Standing outside in the car park afterwards, Sue and I were both a bit thunderstruck by the seamless way in which we had progressed our audacious plan.

'It's a bit exposed with that massive front window. We'll have to find some way of covering it up.'

'Newspapers,' Sue announced. 'You bring them, and I'll collect together some cleaning things from home: Dettol, a bucket, and some rags.'

'I'll bring the vacuum cleaner,' I offered. 'The carpet is gross, and I don't fancy handling those dead flies. By the way, what are we going to use for a bed?'

'I think I've got one sorted, already,' Sue replied, 'and it's free.'

III

Frederic Madden discovered from his enquiries that there were two main theories for how and when the ivories came to be buried on the Isle of Lewis before Malcolm's cow discovered them. The more recent story included the horrific exploits of a herder known as the 'redheaded Gillie'; the older traced a deeper, more distant history involving Viking diaspora and their bloody seafaring empire.

The latest account, written down by Reverend Colonel A. J. MacKenzie, was one the reverend had heard told many times in the community house near the old sanctuary of Baile-na-Cille. This story commenced with the struggle for control of the Isle of Lewis, which was fought over for years by the Macleods and the MacKenzies. At the beginning of the seventeenth century the war was finally won, and the chief of the MacKenzies divided the spoils of battle between his clan. Among the clansmen was the fierce Calum Mór. To him was given Baile-na-Cille, and the bleak and bitter pasture of Ard Mhór. His farmland included the rugged hills that surrounded the bay of Uig. It was a desolate expanse, poorly serviced by rough cart tracks; the territory so remote that to tend his stock Calum Mór used hired hands.

The herder charged with caring for this distant corner was a man by the name of the Gillie Ruadh, or the redheaded Gillie. The land where he grazed his master's cattle was strewn with rocks, across the hills and almost down to the beach. He moved the herd relentlessly in search of fresh grazing. It was a subsistence existence.

Sometimes he took his herd almost to the top of Ard Mhór, which had an uninterrupted view along the beach and out to sea. This day he stopped, transfixed by a ship sailing into the bay. Its anchor was lowered, and an hour or so later he saw a small rowing boat leave its side. As the craft got closer to the shore, Red Gillie could see that the sailor was young, perhaps a cabin boy, and he had a large bag with him. Red Gillie hoped it might be treasure. The youth glanced over his shoulder often, but no one on the vessel had noticed his escape, and no one came after him.

When he reached the water's edge, the boy quickly pulled the small craft up the beach, checking once more that the alarm had not been raised. Intent on following, Red Gillie was descending the hill as the cabin boy crossed the sands, clearly searching for shelter, probably to hide from the sailors as much as to escape the freezing night that would come.

For a while the boy was lost between the rocks where the sand dunes became low hills. But then Red Gillie caught a glimpse of him up ahead, labouring under the weight of his sack. Though there was still a sense of urgency to his flight, the boy was forced to stop often. Skirting around, and moving quickly, Red Gillie met the boy face-to-face at the head of the glen.

'Good afternoon to you, boy,' he said, smiling sweetly. The boy was cautious.

'Who are you, sir?' he replied.

'I'm known in these here parts as Red Gillie. I've left ma herd grazin' the hills o' Ard Mhór. Now, more ta the point, what's a young lad like you doin' in these parts?'

'I've escaped,' he said.

'An' where would you be escapin' from?'

'From a crew a cut-throats, moored in the bay. They were so murderous I feared each night that I'd wake up dead.'

'That be a terrible thing,' the herder commiserated. 'What is it you have there in the sack?'

'It's all I could take in payment for ma wages and to keep me safe 'til I make ma way home. The sailors had one thing of value in their possession: chessmen. They would play into the early mornin', neglectin' everything except the money they gambled. Blood was spilled and lives were lost.'

'In that case, once the crew notice you gone, an' see the chessmen missing, they'll come after you with knives. I know this land as well as any livin' man. Let me help you hide in one of the caves around here.'

The boy was won over by the herder's words.

'Would you help me? All I need is shelter for the night and I'll be on my way in the mornin'.'

'Aye, in the mornin',' the herder repeated, 'but for now, come with me.'

So, they left the spot where they had met, scrambling up the incline, avoiding boulders and climbing around rough gullies. Their progress was slow until the herder offered to carry the boy's heavy load. The youth hesitated, but he was buckling under the weight. It took all his strength to lift it, let alone carry it over this taxing terrain.

'Aye,' he said, 'thank you, but you must give it back to me when we reach the cave.'

The herder threw the weight onto his back and carried it much more easily than the boy. He moved ahead quickly. The last section was steep, and in the waning light it was important not to stumble over the rocks.

'Here it is,' the herder called back as he approached a jagged-looking crevice. The entrance was narrow and hard to see, but as they clambered through the gap it opened up enough for the youth to lie down.

'Boy. Let's look inside the bag and make sure nothin' is broken.'

Although perturbed, the boy clearly decided this was the only way to be rid of the herder. As he bent down to untie the cord his sandy-coloured locks fell across his eyes.

That was the last thing he would ever know.

The shattering of his skull made a sickening thud. The boy fell forward over the bag, limp and bleeding.

The herder straightened, the bloodied weapon — a jagged rock — in his hands. He paused for a moment, not from remorse or regret, but from the silence that mocks the killer at their victim's death. For never again would the herder's nights be his own, or his dreams be free. Murder, the most intimate of acts, would bind them together, forever.

It was surprisingly hard to move the body off the bag, as if even in death the boy still clutched his hoard. When Red Gillie opened the bag, what he saw inside gave him a start. There were tiny figures with tiny faces looking at him. He could see at a glance that they were ivory: a treasure trove of rare material. But the staring faces unnerved him.

In the growing darkness, Red Gillie buried his load in the sand dunes. He lined the hole with rocks, then covered the whole thing with sand. The chessmen would be protected until he could safely return and retrieve them.

Red Gillie had left his cattle grazing, unattended. In the morning he tracked down the wanderers. Nothing, he thought, should look out of the ordinary. Once herded together, he went to tell his master he had seen a ship in the bay.

'You could gather a ban' of clansmen and take the ship by stealth. Then its bounty would be yours,' he told Calum Mór.

'What kind of a man are you, Red Gillie, that you would think a such a thing? This ship has our protection and its crew are guests of this land. Be gone with you and your savage ways.'

That wasn't the reaction Red Gillie had hoped for, so he would have to bide his time before retrieving the chessmen. However, it was not long before he fell foul of his master and was exiled to the mainland in disgrace. There, he took up a life of violence and debauchery.

After numerous brushes with the law, he was finally arrested, it is believed, for the rape and murder of a young woman. He was tried and sentenced to the gallows. Inside the stone walls of the prison, his conscience brought him to account. Visions of each of his victims visited him in his cell as a terrifying reminder of the destruction he had wrought.

In desperation, he called for a priest: for anyone who could rid him of this abomination.

'You must confess your sins,' the priest told him. 'You must bring your trespasses to God and beg His forgiveness. Kneel down, my son, and rid yourself of this terrible burden.' So, on the very spot where he stood, he knelt down, telling the priest about the sins he had committed.

The story of the fair-haired sailor boy was his last. Red Gillie told the priest that many years had passed after his banishment from the Isle of Lewis before he managed to slip aboard a ship and sail back in search of his treasure. The dunes that had concealed the herder's secret had shifted with the winds and the tides. No landmark seemed the same: no reference marked the spot.

Once he got to the place where he imagined the pieces might be, he began digging. When nothing appeared, he moved on. Not there, he thought, no, it must be here. The day proceeded and his searching got more frantic and futile. When the sun sank into the sea, he threw down his shovel and let out a tormented scream. Only the seabirds that left the beach in frightened flight heard his cry.

The herder was hanged on the day dictated by the judge. Maybe he had told one of the other prisoners, or perhaps the priest let slip his confession, no one knows, but the story escaped the cell and survived the gallows to live on in the imaginations of generations to come. Eventually, it took on the character of myth.

CHAPTER EIGHT

Moaning and Groaning

'Far out,' I said, under my breath, trying to shift my grip so I could carry the heavy, unstable weight more effectively. We had planned our move into the shop in Sydenham Mall, in Christchurch, down to the last detail. This part was to be a covert operation. Sue and I agreed that the fewer people who saw us carry a three-quarter mattress up to our room the better. We were especially anxious that the antique dealer should not see us and become suspicious. It was 1.30 in the afternoon and fiercely hot. The mall roof, two storeys up, had milky-coloured Perspex skylights that heated the interior like an oven in summer.

I was wet with sweat, my T-shirt and jeans sticking to me. The mattress swayed then slumped against the balustrade, yet again. I was just about to unleash a mouthful of expletives when the antique dealer appeared from nowhere.

'Hello, girls,' he called out. 'What are you doing with that mattress?'

I looked up, then took off my glasses, wiping the perspiration from my eyes, and answering as casually as I could.

'Just taking this mattress up for somewhere to sit.'

'I'd offer you girls a hand, but I can't leave the shop for long.' He stared at the mattress.

'Can I open the door for you?'

'No, thanks, we're fine.' I grabbed the piped cord around the mattress edge, pulled it tight, then lifted the awkward weight off the step.

'Come on, Sue, if we don't get this up there, I'm going to asphyxiate.'

'Are you sure you girls want that thing up there? The second-hand dealer has some nice cheap fold-up chairs out the back.'

'We'll have a look, thanks. But in the meantime we're happy with this.'

'What about that for bad luck?' I said to Sue when we sat on our mattress in the room recovering. 'Halfway up the stairs and Mr Twenty Questions arrives.'

'Yeah, he certainly makes everyone else's business his own.'

'That's a polite way of putting it,' I replied. 'He's a pain in the neck. Every time you turn around, he's there.' We had already made a number of quick trips to the room. He appeared on the mezzanine when we were cleaning, waving through the glass at us, then again when we were sticking up the last few sheets of newspaper.

'Just seeing how you girls are,' he called, smiling broadly through the gap in the papers.

'What do you think he's up to? Do you think he suspects something?' I asked Sue, getting up as I did so to grab the Sellotape and a spare sheet of newspaper to cover a space between the pages that was only visible from the floor. Any chink in the newspaper was an opportunity for our attentive friend, I reflected.

'I don't know,' Sue said. 'Maybe he does. He certainly turns up every opportunity he can.'

The room was fully operational after a few more additions: a small wooden chair, a table for me to write at, and an electric jug and two mugs to make coffee. It was the perfect hide-away. No one other than the antique dealer ventured onto the mezzanine, and, if we were careful about it, we could slip in the back entrance and up the stairs unobserved. I felt so much more relaxed. The room was ours. Some days Sue would sketch the disorderly piles of second-hand furniture and junk from vantage points around the mall, and I would sit and research or write my essays. Our pleasure was in being together. Other times we made love that shook and shuddered me so violently that I thought I would tear myself apart. It was sex like I had never experienced before.

For weeks we managed to evade the antique dealer, sneaking in and out undetected. Then one day he caught us.

'Hello, girls,' he called as we crept downstairs. His face was the longest I'd ever seen it. If I hadn't been so eager to get away I would have asked him what was wrong. But there was no need to ask: he was going to tell us, anyway.

'I'm very worried,' he announced.

'What's wrong?' asked Sue, more concerned about his state of mind than I was.

'I've heard things. Terrible things.'

'What?' asked Sue. 'What have you heard?'

His eyes widened as if he were remembering a nightmare.

'Strange sounds,' he said. 'Moaning and groaning. Like the place is haunted.'

'How often does it happen?' I asked, riveted. He turned to answer me.

'It's sporadic. Not every day, and at different times of the day. It sounds like someone's dying.'

I shot a glance at Sue. Her face was a mask of concern.

'Has anyone else heard it?' she enquired of him.

'Yes,' he replied, triumphant. 'The first few times I believed I might be imagining things. That it was a child calling out or a play on the radio. I observed my customers when I heard it. No reaction. The last time it happened I couldn't contain myself. "Did you hear that?" I called across the shop to a woman who was browsing. And she had. "Sounds like you've got ghosts," she said, and immediately purchased what she had in her hand and left. I went outside into the mall and even upstairs where the sound seemed to be coming from. Nothing,' he said. 'I don't even like going up there, now I know it might be haunted. I just wondered if you'd heard anything yourselves.'

'No,' we chorused.

'We're not in here that often,' I added. 'But we'll let you know if we hear anything. I'm sure there's a logical explanation for it.'

He seemed reassured by my words.

'Well, lovely to see you girls again. I'd better get back to the shop. I haven't seen you for a while, so I thought I'd let you know.'

We didn't say a word to each other until we were out of the mall and in the car park. 'Holy-moly,' I said, 'that was a close shave. I told you we should keep the noise down.'

'I can't help it,' said Sue, smiling.

'You're going to have to help it. Otherwise, the antique dealer will be organising an exorcism.'

After that we were as discreet *in* the room as we were coming and going from it. On the occasions when we did bump into the antique dealer, he looked happier.

'No more noises,' he called out one afternoon, although we never saw him upstairs again.

We continued to use the room, knowing that one day things would unravel horribly. It was a last desperate attempt to keep our lives as they were, even when we wanted something else. I'm not sure what we were waiting for. Some light to come on in our heads that would say 'This is the one relationship you must risk everything for'? But if we began thinking about that, we were soon overwhelmed and then paralysed by our dilemma. We were not brave enough to face either set of consequences: to end our affair or destroy our marriages. Therefore, we waited in a lovers' limbo, knowing we would be discovered, and that our chronic indecision would leave us powerless to determine when and how things would end.

It created a terrible trepidation, and one day in early April it came. The phone call I had dreaded.

'We have to meet. It's important.'

'What's wrong?' I asked, immediately concerned. My heart was pounding like I had rehearsed this moment before.

'I can't tell you. Not over the phone.' Sue's voice was urgent and low, like she was afraid of being overheard.

'Are you okay?' I asked, worried about her.

'Not really,' she responded. There was something distant about her reply that worried me more than her words.

'Meet me in the room at two o'clock,' she said, then hung up.

My head was a Spaghetti Junction of thoughts whizzing back and forth, cutting under and over each other. How I passed the time until two o'clock, I can't remember. I think I wandered between the cavernous rooms of our Bishop Street house, tormented by the traffic in my mind.

Arriving at the mall, I let myself into the room. Sue wasn't there; I was early. More awful waiting. But it wasn't long before I heard her key in the lock. The relief was overwhelming.

'What's happened?' I asked, knowing instinctively that it was about us.

'He knows,' she said, meaning her husband. 'He's found a card you gave me.'

'But how could he have a problem with that?' I asked, my voice shaking.

'It was a card that you'd written to me.'

I thought about it. I couldn't remember any cards that I had written that would have incriminated us. She described the card and the occasion on which I gave it, and I remembered.

'But that wasn't anything. Surely he hasn't worked anything out from that?'

'No. Not just that; but it was the card that made him confront me.'

'What did you say?'

'What could I?' she responded. 'Nothing. I wouldn't say one way or the other until I'd spoken to you. I said I'd talk to him about it tonight.'

'Holy shit, I can't believe it's finally happened.' I was thunderstruck.

'We have to make a move: it's now or never. Either we admit it and face the consequences, or we deny the whole thing and finish: here, now, today. We can't go on like this — it's wrong.'

'I'm with you, completely. Let's do it.' I wanted to seem strong for her, but inside I felt the enormity of what was in front of us. It would be huge and agonising, and I feared that our frail friendship, which had thrived on the excitement of an affair, would fail us. I was more harrowed than I had ever been about anything before.

I cried when I told Richard that evening. Howling sobs of pain and grief. Selfish from the perspective of what I had to lose, but also broken-hearted about my deceit. My justifications for conducting an affair felt fickle and self-serving in that moment, and still do. But, oddly enough, there were also no regrets. I knew that, given the same circumstances, I would do it again because the years of cowardice and self-denial had had no integrity either. I wanted Sue, and that day I would have announced it from our terracotta-tile rooftop.

Richard's grief was more passive. His winter of dark fallow fields, internal. There would be a reaction: delayed, clinical, remorseless. For a while he seemed to take it all in his stride; in truth, that day the furies were unleashed.

Mortifying situations followed one after another in a chain of hideous events. If telling Richard was hard, explaining things to my children was like plunging a sword into my stomach and tearing it open. Jeremy was nearly seven years old and Alex, nine. The one thing every parent should offer their children is a safe and stable home, and I was taking this away from them.

Jeremy cried; Alex, who was upset, too, wanted to make sure that all the things we did for him would continue. That he would still be delivered to his clubs and to his friends' places. He wanted his life to continue as it had, and, although I guaranteed that Richard and I would do everything we could to keep things in place, I knew change was inevitable. It was the hardest thing to do. My children were hurting, and I had done it to them.

Before, I was a wife and mother: benign, wholesome, good. Now I was heinous. Overnight I fell from grace. Even I had thought that my coming out might change me. I had hoped there would be some shift. Not necessarily detectable when you looked in the mirror, but a deep-down change. Disappointingly, there was just the same old me looking back. But what did shift on its axis was the way I was perceived. The dizzying fall from an ex-minister's wife to lesbian vamp would not have seemed much less quantum than Satan's own fall. That thump when you hit rock bottom in everyone's estimation is a moment of absolute clarity, when you see yourself stripped bare of all illusion.

In the end there was a single voice; a scream; a scrambling to fill the nothingness. Inside was the void and outside the nakedness. When your identity has been liquidated, you either accept your empty invisibility or you fight it. If you take on the struggle to reconstruct 'self', then it is a brutalising battle waged under the glaring white-light of absolute honesty. There are no deceptions left. Sue and I would both make this journey to reimagine our identities. It would become an unlocking and a discovery. But in the meantime the imperative was simply to survive.

For word of our unnatural liaison spread rapidly. I was the villain of everyone's story; the instigator; the perpetrator; and the true lesbian Siren who had lured two marriages onto the rocks. Social ostracism was the cruel punishment I felt I deserved. I'm not sure how Sue coped because the pressure on us both was immense.

We kept our room on for a few weeks and continued to meet. In fact, we met there the next day. The shock was new and we needed to talk. The thing we had to discuss was whether we continued with a plan for a weekend away with both families to the thermal springs at Hanmer. Now our husbands knew, how could we go ahead? The bomb was dropped on Thursday, and we were leaving the next day to stay together in a church hall.

'We can't go, surely?' I said to Sue.

But we did go, and stayed oddly amicably in the church hall that we had holidayed in on a number of occasions before. Despite all the terrible tensions and the weirdness, it was good to be with Sue on a more honest footing. The old wooden hall had a kitchen out the back and a Sunday school room, where they stacked the chairs. Richard and I and our children stayed in the little Sunday school room, while Sue, her husband and their kids took the hall. We did this out of habit.

The husbands were shell-shocked, perhaps. Restraint prevailed. There was no bonhomie between them, though if there had been they might well have defeated us. Our love felt fragile. Newly planted. Likely they believed it would all blow over. I knew Richard would never have me back, but maybe Sue's husband might. This was ceasefire: a soccer match with the enemy in no-man's-land. We were all on our best behaviour.

Sue and I seemed strangely incongruous in that hallowed hall with its foxed prints of a blond-haired, blue-eyed Christ, and Holman Hunt's *Light of the World*. The hall was on one side of the drive, and the church on the other. This was my old life, beside the new one.

We spent the days soaking and swimming with the children at the hot pools. The kids seemed to be taking it in their stride. After all, this family blending had been happening for a while now and they loved each other's company. The sun was setting as we walked back home to the hall. Hot, golden days ended now with a hint of winter in their brisk evenings. The cicadas were calling farewell to summer. There was a mystery and magic in this place.

That night Sue made a massive apple crumble. The children watched the process with anticipation. After the first course, the children sat hungrily at the table in the kitchen. Jeremy was the first to sample the treat, which was served with a huge dollop of cream. His face was a picture of horror. He spat his first mouthful back into his bowl.

'Yuck!' he screamed and rushed to the sink, running his mouth under the tap, gargling and spitting out the last of it. He was quickly followed by Jason, who elbowed him aside in his desperation to get to the water.

'What's wrong, Jeremy?' I asked.

'It tastes terrible,' he shouted, between bouts of wiping his tongue with the tea towel.

'I'm sure there's just the usual in it,' Sue responded, looking confused and grabbing a dessert spoon from the cutlery drawer under the bench. She was a little more cautious about how much she took than Jeremy and Jason had been, but the reaction was just the same.

'That's disgusting. You try it,' she said, after washing her mouth out. 'It tastes like salt.'

I was even more cautious and took the smallest piece I could.

'How could it be salt?' I asked in disbelief, joining the queue at the sink.

'I forgot to bring sugar from home, so I used the church's. I just assumed it was sugar in the jar next to the tea and coffee. I guess I was wrong, and it was salt.' As she said this, she was already sampling the contents of a screw-topped jar that she had taken from a cupboard above the bench.

'Salt,' she declared, as she looked dismally at the vast dish of delicious-looking crumble.

'Bugger, I was looking forward to some of that.' As it turned out, even the cream had been given a generous teaspoon of salt. I now had a new respect for the suffering of Lot's wife in the Bible, when she looked back at the city of Sodom and was turned to a pillar of salt. Sodom and Gomorrah, I mused as I walked past the snowy-haired Christ hanging on the hall wall. How could I make sense of my old life now? Christianity was a closed book to me. Being true to myself seemed incompatible with a religious life.

III

The descendants of Ngāti Pūkeko were the people of Sue's maternal line. Ngāti Pūkeko, renowned for raiding parties and fearsome fighting, was a hapū of the bigger Ngāti Awa, both with shared whānau relationships, living in territory around Whakatāne. This was an alliance of bloodlines and a safeguard against enemy incursions. Together, these were the people of the land, a power block of protection.

The arrival of Pākehā muskets in the 1820s brought a new kind of war to the tribes of Whakatāne. Combat no longer depended on the strategy of clever chiefs and the prowess of their warriors. Hand-to-hand combat was no longer the sole determinant of victory or loss. A fired musket ball could take down the most noble and towering combatant. The rules of the game — the ancient understandings of battle — were turned upside-down.

Power was shifting. Old vendettas between tribes and individuals ended in massacres. Scores were settled in new and tragic ways, so that the blossoming youth of an iwi lay in bloody desecration across killing fields of unforgivable conflict. There could be no peace of mind, no settling back. Defences were raised, war parties mobilised. The Pākehā musket was a paradigm shift; a journey into the darkness of the human soul.

Marriage had always been an alliance written in the blood of generations to come. This union brought peoples together so that the rangatira of one tribe might be the mokopuna of another. When one branch was attacked, the tree fought back. This was familial strength — husbands and wives, aunts and uncles, brothers and sisters — in relationships of commitment and obligation, joining hapū and tribes together to become the parts of one.

The formidable warrior chief Kihi, whose exploits of combat became the subject of waiata and stories in Whakatāne, had two sisters, Rongomaiwhiti and Hahau, who married two brothers from another branch of Ngāti Pūkeko. Taimitimiti married Hahau and the couple had a daughter they called Hinepau.

Hinepau, a puhi, or young maiden of high birth, grew up healthy and strong. The white sands where Kurawhakaata welcomed those ancient kūmara-bearing visitors from Hawaiki are her playground, as is the sea that laps its shores where she gathers kai moana. Her life has been patterned by the seasons. Hinepau has seen 12 summers come and go, and is now approaching the zenith of another. She is young, but not a child anymore. Hinepau has an adolescent energy, tempered by the dawning desires of womanhood.

Today she is accompanying a canoe from her hapū on a trip to Whakaari Island to gather muttonbirds. The day begins with a crispness in the air, but by the time the waka has been pushed beyond the breakers, the wind is gentle on her skin, made dark by long days of summer sun.

As she sits clearing the wild locks of black hair from her eyes, she sees the cone of Whakaari puffing a warning. There is no petitioning, no reasoning, no supplication that can still this fire-monster. When the volcano will fume, spew lava and rocks, and the ground shake, no one can predict, and no one will be safe.

But today their time on the island will be brief. Just long enough to hunt the tītī and get home. Whakaari is a landscape of white ash and bleached bones. Only seabirds like the tītī that take their nourishment from the ocean can survive here.

Once the canoe has been beached, Hinepau escapes the main party to hunt tītī alone. She is usually accompanied by several female attendants, but today there is only one, and when she becomes distracted for a moment, Hinepau is gone. The young girl has done this before, as she knows that the best spots to find tītī are on the far side of the island. The day passes and she has a hefty haul of birds. The gentle breeze buffets her as she clambers over the rocks in the late afternoon. The gusts are still not cold, but they are stronger now and come from the sea.

Hinepau has her head down, the basket of dead tītī on her back weighing heavily, when she sees them. Her heart races with the surprise. The shock. In front of her stands a man, a warrior not of her hapū or tribe, and behind him are more strangers. A war party. Hinepau turns to run back across the jagged, unforgiving rocks that she had previously picked her way through.

She knows her flight is futile, and even before she stumbles Hinepau is caught, and carried off to a waiting war canoe beached in the next bay. Her captors see from her dress and demeanour that she is a puhi of noble birth. In her hair are the black feathers tipped in white of the huia; on her lips and chin is a moko that speaks of her rank and hapū; and around her neck a pounamu hei tiki gifted to her by her ancestors. Hinepau's status makes her a prize. She is not a lowly slave who will be put to work, but a 'treasured virgin' eligible for aristocratic marriage.

The war canoe belongs to the turbulent tribes of the Waikato. On its way back from battles and skirmishes down south, the party has stopped on Whakaari to replenish supplies of food. Seabirds such as the tītī are plentiful. When they planned this sojourn they never imagined how bountiful the expedition would prove.

Hinepau is bound and carried back with care to the stronghold of the Ngāti Mahuta, in the Waikato, and offered to their giant chief Te Wherowhero. At first Hinepau is terrified. She has never seen a man this tall before. Long-boned and magnificent, Te Wherowhero looks like a god in his brilliant red-feathered cloak. Hinepau understands all that is woven into the weft of this garment, for the rare kahu kura is a symbol of chiefly power. It connects to the god Tāne, father of the birds, and endows the wearer with the oratorial skills of the raucous kākā, whose feathers adorn it. She knows that the kahu kura can also signify peace. Te Wherowhero is a warrior chief, who will eventually lead a confederation of tribes. But when he meets Hinepau he is simply a young man of promise: a rangatira approaching his prime.

Te Wherowhero sees their union as a chance to draw the peoples of Whakatāne and Waikato together. He sees also her youth and her beauty, and he wants her. He will sleep with her and they will have tamariki together. Te Wherowhero tells his men that 'she must not be defiled', because when she is ready he will take Hinepau as his wife.

Several summers come and go before Hinepau is big with their child. Her time of confinement finally comes, and a woman, a tohunga, is summoned to the hut away from the hapū where Hinepau is to give birth. Te Wherowhero waits, anxious to welcome his child into the world. He paces, he frets, he prays to the gods to save his precious young wife and their child. For once, his mighty strength is useless. There is nothing he can do. Te Wherowhero is in despair. Will there be no end to this terrible waiting?

CHAPTER NINE

Millie and Billie from Chile

The stay with our two families at Hanmer Springs was the calm before the storm, which broke after our return to Christchurch. I caught snatches of time with Sue to talk about the fall-out, and there was a lot of fall-out. It was a case of surviving day by day. We were nearly five months living with our husbands before our separations became final. The great gift that Richard gave me was our house. It was an act of profound generosity. It was the best of the person I had married — decent, virtuous and kind.

He came home from work one day and he told me.

'You have a few days to change the title,' he said. 'If you don't do it in that time, I'll take the offer back.' He was deathly serious. A cold, icy shutter had come down, and I didn't blame him. We were emotionally estranged now. He would swim for his survival and I for mine. But there was still the last remnant of memory left of what we'd had.

'I need a lawyer urgently,' I said to Sue when we met at university that day.

'Wait . . . So, have I got this right? Richard is going to give you the house, but you only have a few days to change the deed?'

'That's right. And he means it: he was as cold as stone. I've never known him to be so ominous.'

'That's a huge financial help.'

'Yeah, I'm really grateful. It's probably not worth much, but all of nothing is much better than half.'

'Well, I'd get a lawyer now if I were you, one who's good at conveyancing. A new one.'

As soon as I got home that afternoon I rang my cousin Philippa.

'Yes, I know a good lawyer,' she said. 'Alison McDuff — I teach her daughters at Christchurch Girls' High School. I think her area of law is conveyancing.' Philippa, who was my second cousin, had been a friend and confidante for years. I liked her a lot. She had taught me how to carve bone, and was what I believed to be a quintessential Drayton: sincere, eccentric — a bizarre combination of Baptist and Bloomsbury bohemian.

I took her advice and rang Alison's office directly. I had an appointment the next day, and Richard and I signed the papers not long after that. Something changed, then, irrevocably. My part of the bargain was that I agreed never to make any claim on his inheritance.

He asked me to be out of the house one Saturday. 'Don't come back until late,' he said. So I spent the day with Sue and the children. When I arrived home that evening, his things were missing: he was gone. When Richard left, it was like a death. We had shared a dream, a hope and a life together. Richard just wanted to escape me and the unwanted change that had enveloped his life. None of this was his fault, he felt. He could blame me: even *I* blamed me. I cried for my loss and I cried for his. There was a special emptiness to the house that night, the silence of a friend gone for good.

It was a week or so later that Sue moved in with me: 23 September. Funny, how momentous dates stay with you. There was no fanfare, no ceremony: just an amphitheatre of expectation that our facile little *ménage* would fail. We were jeered and booed and mobbed with contempt. Our old friends fell away *en masse* and there were few new supporters.

Sue's friends had coffee mornings for her in Mount Pleasant where the undisguised agenda was to convince her of the terrible mistake she was making. Once they realised it was a *fait accompli* they snubbed her — friends, family, her brother, the lot. I was given my own special serving of contempt. While Sue was seen as the victim, I was the perpetrator, the dominant deviant who influenced a weaker-willed follower. My friends and associates in the

Church were especially judgemental. We were looked through, spat at and spurned. It was like putting your life in a shredder and trying to reassemble something recognisable at the end.

Sue left her beautiful home on the hill to live with me in my hovel. She arrived with little more than her clothes and the car she had inherited. I had Alex and Jeremy one week, and Richard had them the next. Within days, Sue and her husband adopted the same shared-custody arrangement. One week he looked after Katie and Jason in their family home on Mount Pleasant, and the other week he lived with his new lover, a woman he was involved with at his work. I had my children one week, and Sue had hers the next. In the middle weekend we had all of them together. In spite of the hardships, those weekends when we were together were the most fun parenting I ever had.

In one another's company, the children raged with excitement. While Alex and Jeremy kept their old room, we renovated one of the outhouses for Jason. Sue made sparkling new curtains, and I removed the decades of dirt. Katie got the sunroom with the broken pink leadlight windows. We moved some of her toys in and used a blow-heater to soften the edge of winter.

On Saturday morning I made stacks of Aunt Jemima's buckwheat pancakes for everyone. It became a ritual.

'I feel bad,' I told Sue one Saturday morning as I lay in bed contemplating all the change the children had coped with.

'You just like feeling bad.'

'No, I mean it. I think the kids have had it really hard lately, and I'd like to do something nice. I've got an idea.'

'What kind of idea?' Sue asked.

'I want to buy them something. It won't cost much. Promise.'

'What?'

'A rat.'

'You're crazy! How do you think a rat's going to make things better?'

'Well, it's probably more of a distraction. Something to look after.'

'You've been listening to too much Michael Jackson.'

With that I burst into the lyrics from 'Ben' about not needing to look any more.

'Okay, stop!' she cried, interrupting me. 'Be it on your head . . . but remember, rats smell bad.'

'No, it's not rats that smell, it's mice. Rats are much cleaner . . . Look, I'll just make some enquiries. If it seems too difficult, I'll shelve the idea.'

So that was how I found myself standing outside an enormous pet shop in Linwood. I went inside: I love pet shops. If looking at animals were placed on the spectrum of peeping Toms, then I would be a repeat offender struggling with the urge to climb in the window. There were kittens, puppies, fish, birds, and masses of cage and aquarium hardware, drinking bowls, pet food, straw, sacks of litter — anything to do with pets, they had it. I saw the rats in a large cage in the corner, and as I approached I had to admit to myself that there was an odour that smelt vaguely like vomit coming from their direction. On the way over to look, however, I was hijacked by the sight of a massive cage, the inmates of which looked like they had come from an episode of *Lost in Space*. They had rodent faces, with ears like Mickey Mouse; a rabbit's body, fur and feet; and a squirrel's tail. They looked like Nature had put some genes in a blender and whizzed them up just to see what would happen.

'Can I help you?' asked a heavily tattooed female shop assistant, her 'sucker detector' on high alert.

'I'm actually here to buy a rat, but these are gorgeous creatures. What are they?'

'Chinchillas, madam,' said the woman. 'They're brand-new: we've just imported them from Chile.'

'Gosh,' I said, gobsmacked at their cuteness. 'They're expensive,' I added, looking at the 'big ticket' price-tag of $160.

'Yes, madam, but they're odour-free and they cost nothing to keep.'

'Nothing?' I queried.

'Just a few rabbit pellets and a raisin a day.'

I looked at the enormous bag of rabbit pellets for a few dollars that she was pointing at, and figured that even on the leanest day we could find the money for a raisin. I was almost convinced.

'But I don't have a cage yet.'

'Buy a cat cage to take it home and build one later.' She had closed the sale and she knew it.

'What would you like? A male or a female?'

'But . . . are they in a relationship? I don't want to break up a couple. You know, are they a breeding pair?'

'Not at all, madam, chinchillas find it very difficult to breed.'

Now I should have pulled on the handbrake there and backed up, but I was so sold on the idea, I questioned nothing more.

I arrived home that evening and was greeted like Jack when he presented the magic beans he had exchanged for the family cow. Sue was not amused.

'What do you mean you spent $160 on a rodent? That's outrageous.'

'But there are no overheads from now on. She just eats a few rabbit pellets and a raisin a day to keep her regular. Her name's Millie,' I announced; 'Millie from Chile.'

It wasn't long before Sue was admiring Millie from Chile having her dust bath with as many enraptured 'oohs' and 'aahs' as the children. The dust-bath powder that she rotated around and around in was an additional cost, I explained to Sue, but there would be 'no more'. For just over a week Millie lived in the cat cage, being released at night for a race around the house and her exhibition dust bath. Friends and neighbours gathered to watch her.

On the ninth day, I came home from university to find Millie clutching the bars of her cage. There was something sad and pained about the way she held them.

'I don't think Millie's well,' I called to Sue from our bedroom.

'How on earth can you tell?' Sue asked, amused. By this time I had come through from the bedroom and lifted the cage onto the kitchen table.

'Look there. What do you think that is?' There were a couple of lumps in the bottom of the cage that looked like chopped liver. 'Have the kids done something dumb like try to feed her meat?'

'No. They know better than that.'

Then, it dawned on me.

'I think she's miscarried.'

'Yeah,' Sue said, 'I think you could be right. We'd better call the vet; she certainly doesn't look comfortable.'

I grabbed the Yellow Pages and began looking through it for a vet who specialised in small animals.

'Here,' said Sue, 'let me do that . . . Here's someone,' she said after a few seconds. 'This vet specifically mentions rats, mice and birds in his ad, and he makes house calls.'

'Perfect, I hope he doesn't cost too much.'

Sue rang and arranged for him to drop in on his way home from the surgery.

The knock at the door came at about 6.30pm. I was surprised by the vet's youth. He was my age, maybe younger.

Giving miserable Millie the once-over, he pursed his lips.

'This does look serious. Not that I've ever worked on a chinchilla before,' he added. 'Can I see the material you found in the bottom of the cage?' Sure enough, Millie had miscarried. 'I think the best thing to do is for me to observe her for a while. See if there's any improvement. If she recovers, great, otherwise it will be a hysterectomy.'

'A hysterectomy!' I exploded.

'Any material that hasn't aborted will cause blood poisoning.'

Sue, the farmer's daughter, explained it all to me after the vet had departed with Millie. Apparently, it would kill her. So, we were on tenterhooks. The phone call came the next day. She would need an operation.

'I'm not even sure how well a little animal like that will come through the anaesthetic.' But it was me who needed an anaesthetic when he told me the price.

'Hell,' I exclaimed to Sue, 'I could probably get a hysterectomy myself for that amount of money.'

The operation went ahead, and Richard paid for it, which was very good of him considering things were rapidly chilling further, with his new live-in girlfriend on the scene.

We received a phone call that evening to say that the operation had been a success. The vet would keep her under observation, then deliver her back in a couple of days.

'She will look very different,' he warned us. 'I have had to make a large incision along the length of her underbelly.'

Sure enough, poor Millie from Chile arrived back with a long line of ugly black stitches running like a zip from her nether region almost to her chin. I had seen stuffed turkeys that were better stitched.

Then, to add injury to insult, he took her out of the cage and put her on our kitchen table, unrestrained, and in terror she jumped off and broke her back leg.

'There won't be any charge for this operation,' the vet said, as he placed her back in the cage and took her away again.

'I should damn well hope not,' I said to Sue after he'd left. 'What an idiot, thinking Millie would stay on the tabletop. How many brains has he got?'

The final phone call from the vet came while I was at university. One of the librarians found me amongst the shelves. 'You can take it in there,' she said, gesturing towards an empty office.

'Hello,' I said in trepidation, as no one ever rang me at university.

'I'm afraid I've got some bad news. I thought I'd better ring so you can tell the children. Millie died on the operating table this morning.' This was upsetting news. I had hoped Millie's misadventures had ended. 'Would you like me to return the body?' he asked in an 'undertaker's' tone of voice.

I am ashamed to say I snapped.

'Why would I want the body back? The only thing she's good for now is a bloody pencil case.'

'No . . .' he stuttered, 'I mean, do you want the chinchilla back in a box so the children can bury it?'

'No,' I said, 'definitely not.' The last thing I felt we all needed was a funeral. I was still raw about the fact that he let her drop off the table; however, we finished our conversation reasonably politely.

I told the children that night and we all cried, and I felt guiltier still.

A trip to the pet shop alleviated nothing. When I told the woman behind the counter that my chinchilla had been 'up the duff' on purchase, when I had specifically enquired after its marital status, she told me to 'go away'.

'But I'm only after a replacement animal, not my money back,' I assured her.

'Look, lady, you bought it. Buyer beware, now piss off,' she shouted into my face.

The atmosphere at home that night was blue. We were $280 out of pocket with no cute fluffy rodent to show for it.

The pain eased, the memories of Millie faded, and one day the tape affixing Katie's drawing of Millie to the fridge door perished, and it slipped like an autumn leaf to the floor. I picked it up. There was the chinchilla again, interpreted by our seven-year-old Katie, with a glorious fire-burst of crayon tail.

'I'm going to write to *Fair Go*,' I called out to Sue as I raced down the hall to my office. It had occurred to me that that was a forum I could appeal to. Banging away at my old word-processor, which had a tiny screen with green letters and no mouse, I outlined Millie's sad story in a letter to the programme producer. Then, as I was about to lick the envelope and add a stamp, I remembered Katie's chinchilla drawing. Just the heart-rending material we need, I thought, but I would have to negotiate with the artist. That evening I approached Katie with her drawing in my hand.

'Katie, would you mind if I sent this drawing of Millie to the TV station?' Katie looked back at me, affronted.

'It's not Millie,' she snapped, 'it's My Little Pony.'

'Oh,' I said, 'I'm sorry. Yes, My Little Pony. I can see that now.' This was an outright lie, but I didn't want to crush her aesthetic sensibilities.

'That's alright,' she said, grabbing the drawing out of my hand and racing over to the kitchen table, where Jason had been doing his homework. She picked up one coloured pencil after another, rapidly adding a few more lines to its already splendidly iridescent tail.

'There,' she said, handing it back, as if she were Jackson Pollock finishing an action painting. 'It's Millie now.'

As soon as my letter hit their desk, *Fair Go* began trying to get in touch.

'I've rung your home phone number five times today,' the producer told me when I got back from university that afternoon. 'We'd like to start filming as soon as possible.'

They filmed the first part at our home. Then they went to the pet shop to challenge them with our version of events: the crux being that I had not received pure virgin chinchilla. The pet shop refused to accept responsibility, but offered us a replacement animal. The second part of the programme was shot after the arrival of Billie from Chile, at Bishop Street.

When the show aired some weeks later, there was Katie's magnificent drawing featured in the intro, looking 100 per cent chinchilla.

Unfortunately, Billie was no fit replacement for our demure little Millie. In fact, he was probably the reason for her demise. He was a sex addict. Nothing was sacrosanct. Billie bonked miscellaneous soft toys; folded washing, especially socks; he cast amorous eyes at Morris the cat; and even attached himself to the back of our ankles while we were watching TV. At one stage he disappeared through a gap in the floorboards where the old chimney had been in the lounge. Secretly, I hoped that was the last we'd see of our Chilean Casanova. But a week later he reappeared, constipated, I imagined, and ready to resume his raisin a day.

IV

Historical accounts buried more deeply in the past that helped explain the Lewis chess pieces were found by Frederic Madden in the recited chants and storytelling of the Vikings. The Vikings collected their memories in sagas that were passed down through the generations. One of the mysteries of the Lewis hoard was why they were carved almost entirely in walrus tusk — but also in the elongated spear-shaped tooth of the narwhal whale — rather than elephant ivory. And where was this precious material found, and how was it harvested?

According to the sagas, Norsemen were in Greenland from the 980s. It was Erik the Red, during his exile for manslaughter, who first explored the area with a view to establishing a permanent settlement there. He duly built a large estate for himself, then gave away territories to his band of followers. The settlement survived by exporting furs and skins; timber; whale, seal and walrus blubber; live animals like polar bears and white falcons; and valuable walrus ivory.

The route ivory had traditionally taken to Scandinavia was from Africa. Huge elephant tusks were carried by traders across oceans to the Norse town of Trondheim, which had become a centre for ivory carving. But inexplicably the ivory had ceased to arrive. No one knew why. Merchants now no longer turned to the warm lands of the south, but to the frozen territories of the north to procure this precious material. Walrus ivory was harvested along the coastline of Norway and Greenland — or Groenland, as the Vikings called it — but much more came from places along the North Atlantic coast of North America and Labrador and Newfoundland, named Helluland, Markland and Vinland, respectively, by the Norse.

Among Erik the Red's children were Leif Erikson, believed to be the first European to land on North American soil, and Thorvald Erikson, who also sailed across the North Atlantic. It is Thorvald's story that interested me, and which offered up an alternative story for the chessmen to the others that Madden had explored.

Sea trips were treacherous. The waters that rimmed the shores of Norway and the lands of the North Atlantic boiled and pitched like they had been raised by Thor's hammer. Thorvald Erikson's boat held fast like a limpet to the coastline. Such travel was risky because the very thing that kept seafarers from vanishing forever into that vast uncharted ocean was the sight of land with its hazardous rocks. The sagas told terrifying stories of stormy nights where, when steel-grey waves met thunderous skies, the voices of the perished could be heard calling out. They were the spirits of the wandering dead, lost forever at sea.

The sub-Antarctic summer was brief. Thorvald had had to wait until the calmer weather of June to begin his journey. He would have little time to harvest the ivory before cooling temperatures and the threat of icebergs made the return trip impossible. He did not want to be trapped there through winter.

Helluland was a bounteous territory from which they gathered timber, narwhal tusks, walrus ivory and skins. Walruses were the mermaids of the sea, but on land the bulk of their flesh made them cumbersome and slow. A wary hunter with his long lance-like spear was a worthy opponent. Occasionally there was a miscalculation — a foot caught in a rocky crevice; a body crushed and ripped to shreds by the wild, slashing tusks — but this was rare. Mostly the walruses sat oblivious to the slaughter that awaited them.

As his boat nosed into the lee of the harbour, Thorvald recognised it as the bay they had sheltered in the previous year. They would set up camp there again and use it as a base. It would also serve as a trading post, if they were visited by nomadic bands of indigenous Skraeling. Thorvald detested the filthy primitives. If they hadn't had goods to trade, he would have dismissed them.

Thorvald's men brought the boat in as close as they could. The long flat-bottomed hull enabled them to manoeuvre in shallow seas and in the narrowest, lowest reaches of rivers. When the water was waist-deep, Thorvald and the other sailors leapt out, grabbing the sides to guide the boat in. They would sacrifice to Thor for their safe passage; although Thorvald's father worshipped the old gods, his mother had become a Christian, so he was free to follow either or both.

Once their boat was beyond the reach of the highest tide, he called out instructions to his men to prepare camp. It was one of those warm, sun-baked days when everything felt alive. The long winter had burst forth into life. The seas ran with fish; the grasses along the coast buzzed and hummed with insect life. Nature's bounty was unleashed.

With this in mind, Thorvald sent off a party to hunt for the deer that populated the woods fringing the beach. Fresh meat would be a feast after the dry provisions and fish they had eaten on their journey. Among the hunters was Bjorn, Thorvald's younger brother, one of their most successful hunters. It was not many hours before Bjorn and his party arrived back carrying an enormous elk on a long branch.

It was still light and would be for hours to come when Thorvald sat down to drink a fiery brew distilled from grains. He was surrounded by plenty, in front of him was the infinite sea, and he could smell the aroma of roast meat on the spit. This promised to be a lucrative trip. Ivory was in short supply, meaning he would be able to command a high price.

'Can we talk?' demanded his brother Bjorn, interrupting Thorvald's drowsy reverie.

'Of course, why not?' he said, jolting back to reality.

'I'm worried,' Bjorn told him. 'When we were tracking the elk, we saw signs of Skraeling. Through the woodland: broken branches, footprints and abandoned campsites. This is their land.'

'But you knew that when we came,' his brother retorted.

'Yes, I did, but I had no idea how much they used this coastline, or that they were such stealthy trackers.'

'What do you mean, trackers?'

'I mean just that. They tracked us almost from the beginning.'

'Through the woodland, you mean?'

'Yes. I believe they did. It's almost impossible to tell for sure. First it was a birdcall that answered another, then the crack of a twig, and a sense that we were not alone.'

'Did you see anything? Anything real, I mean.'

'No. Never.'

Thorvald began to laugh. The more he thought about his younger brother shying at the snap of a twig or the cry of a bird, the harder he laughed.

'You have forest fever, my boy,' he called, reaching over unsteadily and slapping his brother's shoulder. 'The Skraelings are savages. They roam; they tend no crops; they would not have the guile to follow you so artfully. Relax.'

They ate and drank well that night, celebrating completing the first leg of their journey, and the kill tomorrow. A dusky light stayed with them long after the flames burned down to hot embers.

There was no chill to dampen their spirits as the next day began as gloriously as the one before.

After breakfast, Thorvald divided the men into groups. A small party was left to guard the campsite, and the rest made the trip on foot to the walrus breeding grounds. The narrow track followed the beach for a distance, then disappeared into woodland. The trees became bigger and more numerous the further they got from the sea. They were moving along swiftly, when Bjorn grabbed Thorvald's arm.

'Did you hear that?' he said under his breath.

'I heard nothing at all,' Thorvald retorted at normal volume, ignoring Bjorn's caution. 'How can you hear anything at all over the noise of those insects? You are hearing things again, Bjorn. Noises, from things that do not exist.' The men behind them laughed, and this annoyed Bjorn.

'May God protect your soul if I am right, Thorvald, for there is sure to be bloodshed if this is so.'

CHAPTER TEN
A Diet of Worms

Our new life together was precarious. Sue and I sailed close to rocks that threatened to wreck everything. We lived together in my house on the corner of Canon and Bishop Streets for 18 months before we shifted to a new home close to the university. During that time, I chopped down an enormous stand of ugly trees that had grown up large and dark down the side of the house during the miser's time. There had been so much else to do that the thickened stand of poplar trunks had never been tackled. Standing high up in the treetops, I gradually worked my way down with a bow saw, until the very thickest trunk was finally taken out with a chainsaw by our friend Barry. Inside we painted and papered, and the boys helped me pull the outhouses down. All but the one Jason slept in were removed. It was hard work, but also exhilarating for me to see the changes. This was the test of our relationship I had dreaded.

I woke up Boxing Day morning after our first Christmas together to find Sue gone. The place in the bed beside me was empty. My heart surged. I felt sick. My head pounded so that it felt like it would explode. When I went to look for her there was nothing. No one. I was alone in the house. My heart broke. I had never experienced such agony. Some of her things had gone.

Her cookbooks were missing from the kitchen cupboard, and her car was missing.

The plan had been that we pick up the children later in the day and take all four of them up to Golden Bay to holiday with my parents. I was devastated, but I had to know: was she coming back? When I phoned her house at Mount Pleasant, my mouth was so dry I could hardly get any words out.

'Is Sue there?' I asked her husband.

'Yes, she is,' he replied.

'Can I speak to her, please?' He was gone.

When Sue came to the phone, it was like talking to someone else. Her manner was distant, unrecognisable.

'Are you coming back?' I asked, paralysed with anxiety.

'I don't know,' she admitted. 'I can't cope with things the way they are.'

'Please,' I begged her, 'please give it another chance.' By the end of our conversation I had extracted a tacit agreement. She would come over mid-afternoon with Jason and Katherine.

While I waited, I could think of nothing but her. I moved around the house like a soul in Purgatory, imagining Heaven and Hell, and not knowing which it would be. As it approached three o'clock, the tension became too much to bear. Finally, I stopped sneaking looks through the bay window and went out to the gate to wait. When I saw her car coming down the street it was a vision of salvation.

I had so many questions that I wanted to ask, but couldn't. She seemed to be in shock. Things were too much. My life at Bishop Street had no comfort to offer her. On top of it all was the contempt we had experienced since getting together. The stripping away of self to reveal the nothing that people now decided we were. I could see it all. It had been too much to ask. But I was so grateful to have her back.

'Are you going to stay?' I asked.

'For now,' she replied.

Things were truly in jeopardy. I knew this as I packed the car.

Our holiday with my parents in Golden Bay was idyllic for the children. On New Year's Eve, we had a massive bonfire on the beach. For hours beforehand, the children combed the sand dunes gathering driftwood. People from beach houses nearby contributed until the pile of wood was enormous. The boys were determined to see the New Year in, but Katie quietly faded away, half-conscious, head nodding as we carried her to bed.

Mum and Dad were in the lounge with friends, ready to toast in the New Year and cut a wedge of dark, fruit-laden Christmas cake. The bonfire was well ablaze by the time we got back, a beacon in the blackness to new beginnings. As we kissed, my apprehension was tinged with hope.

On a clear night you can see the light of every star ever created, there. Parapara Beach is the place from my childhood where I built my dreams. There, my imagination moved from dolls, to dances and university degrees. Like so many nights before, I heard the gentle roll and rush of the water. The moon cut its luminous path across the surface of the sea. In the darkness I held Sue's hand. Maybe a little more tightly than I should have because I didn't want anything to end. Sue and I had our own toast that night, after we tucked the boys into bed in my parents' caravan, parked so it looked out over the beach.

'To us and to the future,' I said, as our glasses touched.

'To us,' she repeated.

I wanted to believe that this was a toast to forever, but I would live for years in anxious doubt, fearing that one day Sue would not return, that she wouldn't be with me. I tormented myself imagining the silence in my days, the empty place in the bed, the vacant seat. Fear and anxiety were the worms in my head, but tonight we were together and there was *hope*.

My parents' house was high on a hill. Inside, it was extravagantly proportioned. A large staircase swept up from the front entrance to a landing, off which were two double bedrooms. Both had views that followed the coastline to Farewell Spit. On a crystal-clear day you could see the very faintest outline of the volcanic cone of Mount Taranaki. The wind often blew at Parapara Beach, but a still, shimmering day was heaven.

My mother is a conjurer: a weaver of white magic, a hoarder of objects, the curator and gatekeeper of her castle. All that festooned the walls of my childhood in Christchurch was here in Golden Bay, and more. The sumptuous velvet-draped downstairs lounge with leather couch and chairs was littered with things, from tiny porcelain and ivory ornaments to a sailing ship's piano. Every object had a story; a life with my parents, and an even older life, because mum loved old things. The fireplace surround was a fantasy of ceramic figures that Mum was making in clay, antique objects, stone and bone fossils. She made clay masks with the children, and twice a day took the kids first to the top paddock, then to the bottom field to walk the llamas. The animals were a magnet, and our kids were the envy of every child down the beach because they were living with the man and lady who owned the llamas.

My father took the children rowing, sailing and swimming. One of the highlights of the trip was sitting on the rickety old wharf that stands in the channel that connects the tidal Parapara lagoon and the sea. Dad baited hooks while the children fished on the turn of the tide. The boys' bait was ravaged by a school of fish, too small to take the hook. The rods danced up and down with the tugs. Every so often a line was optimistically reeled in, but there was nothing to take home.

My parents were very disappointed at the break-up of my marriage. Although my father guessed the day would finally come, he probably hoped it wouldn't. My mother had been so proud at the prospect of having an Anglican curate for a son-in-law that she had painted the words *The curate's mother-in-law* on the back of her Suzuki jeep.

She took some pacifying when the news broke, and it was my brother, Guy, who stepped in to give a final word in our defence. I'm not sure where things would have ended up without his assistance. When Sue and I arrived at my parents' place that summer, my father met us with his treatise. It was not unlike the Ninety-five Theses Luther nailed to the church door in Wittenberg after the Diet of Worms. Written on the unprinted inside of a flattened WeetBix packet were the rules Sue and I were to follow while we were staying with them.

'No holding hands on the beach; no kissing in public; no physical signs of affection . . .', and the list went on, all neatly numbered and handwritten. He had managed to ban things I hadn't even thought of doing. Sue was 40 and I was 35, and while it seemed like a high-handed and draconian thing to do, I urged her not to react. There was nothing to gain from doing so and everything to lose. Very few people had stood by us, so we needed to take whatever goodwill was on offer.

It was quite an undertaking selling our two houses in Christchurch to buy one together. After so many summers on the market with no bites, I was certain Bishop Street would never move. But this time I enlisted the help of Roger, a real-estate agent who was also a family friend. He was more positive about the prospect of a sale. It was his job to be optimistic.

'You just never know,' he said, as he sat at my kitchen table and ran me through the contract so I could sign the endless bits. He explained how it would be marketed, what real-estate magazines it would be advertised in.

I barely listened: I had heard it all before. His parting gesture was to erect a *For Sale* sign at the front gate.

It was completely unexpected, therefore, when I received a phone call from Roger on the first day of its official listing. He had a buyer who had already put in an offer. The news was like a rush of smelling salts.

'That's impossible!' I exclaimed. He had my full attention now.

'It certainly is possible because it's just happened,' he replied, elated. 'I've just got off the phone from him. He's made an offer and says he won't budge. "Take it or leave it," he told me. He's a property developer and he knows about hard bargaining.' The price he was offering was close to the government valuation.

'We can't just let it go like that,' I said to Roger. 'Let's try and push him up. What do you think we should make as a counter-offer?'

The next day Roger came around with the developer's offer and I countered. But our developer was true to his word: he would not pay a penny more. It annoyed me that he had deprived me of the ritual of bargaining.

'So what do we do now?' I asked Roger, irritated at the would-be buyer's arrogance.

'If it were me,' he said, 'I'd take it. It's probably the best offer you'll get. You haven't had any other enquiries about the property. This could be it.'

So I accepted.

Sue's money, which was split with her husband after the sale of their house, was already through, so on the day that my house was due to settle we arranged the purchase of one-half of a duplex in Dovedale Avenue, near the university and teachers' training college. On the settlement day, there were countless phone calls between agents, lawyers and me. As the day went by, it became increasingly clear that our developer-buyer was avoiding our calls. The money had not arrived in the bank and he was nowhere to be found. I began to panic. My money was essential for the purchase of Dovedale Avenue. If the sale didn't go through, then our purchase couldn't go through, either. It was a disaster. When Alison, my lawyer, finally got hold of the developer's lawyer, who turned out to be his wife, it seemed he still wanted the property but was scrambling to raise the cash.

'So what are our options?' I asked Alison, when I spoke to her on the phone.

'There's really only one — bridging finance — if you don't want to lose your deposit on Dovedale Avenue.'

'But where could we possibly get bridging finance from? We're just a couple of solo mothers. No one's going to lend us any money.'

'I think I can point you in the direction of someone who could help. I know a bank manager who might approve a bank loan for you two.' With that, she gave me a name and number and I jotted them down on a piece of blank paper. As soon as she rang off, I dialled the number to make an appointment for as soon as possible.

Each day that went by put things more at risk. The Dovedale Avenue owners were prepared to give us a few days' leniency at the cost of an exorbitant default penalty fee. The news that our purchaser's deposit on Bishop Street went straight into the real-estate agent's pocket and not ours sent me into a tailspin of depression. If we wanted to save our deposit, the deal had to go through.

I couldn't sleep that night for worrying about it. Sue and I went to see the bank manager together the next day.

'According to Alison, she's a member of the club,' I said with a nudge at Sue, who continued to look blank. 'You know . . . one of us.' Still no recognition. 'A lesbian,' I said, overly loudly considering we were sitting in the woman's waiting room.

'Oh, yeah, I get you. So how much good do you think that'll do?'

I shrugged my shoulders and was just about to let forth, when a young woman dressed in smart, corporate clothes opened the door to her office and ushered us in. I took one look at her and decided Alison must have made a mistake. We sat down in the two chairs she indicated on the other side of her desk.

'So, you want to borrow $160,000,' she said, getting right down to business, 'That's quite a sum. You realise you'll be paying top interest rates on that?'

Yet another thing to toss and turn about that night, I thought.

'What's your income stream?' she asked.

'We're both students on the Domestic Purposes Benefit,' I answered, 'that's about $12,000 each a year, and next year my grades might be good enough to get me a doctoral scholarship.'

'What's a doctoral scholarship worth?' she asked.

'Twelve thousand plus university fees,' I told her.

'Let me get this right: all up you two are earning $24,000, and you want to borrow more than six times that amount in bridging finance?'

'I know it looks grim,' I said, defeated. 'I'm sorry, it's just awful.'

'What's awful?' she asked.

'Coming here and asking you for money when we have no obvious way of paying it back.'

'What do you mean?' she challenged, 'You're doing a doctorate. You'll probably be earning more than me one of these days. You're two solid citizens with good earning potential. I wouldn't be sorry about asking for a loan. So, what are you doing at university?' she asked, turning to Sue.

'I'm a painting student,' Sue replied.

'But she's going to teach,' I added quickly, hoping it wouldn't weaken our chances.

After another lecture from our bank manager about our fabulous careers, we left with a colossal bank loan. We never found out whether our bank manager was a 'member of the club', but I took her words to heart. She was a shaft of light that cut through the pessimism — most of it mine. As it turned out, we only needed our emergency finance for 11 days, at the end of which, hallelujah, the developer settled and we had our house!

IV

Treasured objects or artefacts that tell us about the past become more personal when they are bound to our identity. This was the case when Sue and I visited the Auckland Art Gallery a few years ago. Our trip there brought back memories of my family pilgrimages to the dig site at Purau. This was an unearthing, a digging up of the past. But instead of blue skies, Sue and I were in the gallery lobby staring at huge digital screens flashing hypnotic images of exhibitions and upcoming events. I sat awkwardly on blazing-red furniture wondering why comfort was the one thing modernist designers almost universally decided they could do without in the 'less is more' equation.

I looked at my watch.

'It's not four o'clock yet,' Sue said, knowing I'd be worried we were late. She was semi-recumbent, I noticed when I looked around, having worked out that the weirdly designed sofa worked best when treated like a chaise longue. But I was not going to give away my rigidly perpendicular position easily. I was still squirming, trying to find a comfortable position, when Julia Waite, the curator, arrived. I knew her, and had arranged our appointment.

'Hi, Julia,' I said, leaping up, relieved to end my battle with the foyer furniture. She greeted us warmly and invited us to follow her.

Our journey with Julia to the storage area took us upstairs, through rooms and down corridors, some ambient with light, others darkened or starkly lit. I enjoyed the vicarious thrill of a swipe-card that could take you to the centre of the Earth.

Once there we met the registrar, who had retrieved the large wooden archive box that we had requested to see. Julia opened the lid, then lifted out the heavy acid-free boards until she came to George French Angas's magnificent image, painted in 1847, of Te Wherowhero's monument, reportedly to his dead daughter. I was struck by the elegance of the carved wooden structure depicted in the hand-painted lithograph. By the soft browns and sepia tones, interrupted by the occasional blaze of strong colour. A rich brown-red, unexpected in this palette of soft wood colours and gentle eggshell blue.

This is what Angas wrote about what he had painted:

> It is customary in New Zealand, when any person of rank dies, to erect a mausoleum or monument of carved and ornamented wood to the memory of the deceased. The dead body being placed in an upright position within the building, until the ceremony of lifting and depositing the bones takes place: this monument is called papatupapaku and is variously decorated according to the taste of the Tohunga. The most elaborate of these structures still remaining, is the one raised by Te Wherowhero, the head chief of the Waikato tribes, in memory of his favourite daughter, at the now deserted Pah of Raroera; the old Pah was laid under a strict 'tapu' by the chief Te Waro, and has not since been inhabited, the people leaving their arms and provisions exactly as they remained at the moment of the 'tapu' being pronounced. At the period of my visit to the decaying ruins of this once magnificent Pah, I found the monument in a tolerable state of preservation: it is about twelve or fourteen feet high, and the carving which displays exquisite skill, was entirely executed by one man, his only instrument being an old bayonet; this person is lame, and still lives at Ngahuruhuru, where I had the satisfaction of meeting him; on seeing the facsimile of his handiwork, he was so much astonished, that he at once said I was 'Ka nui Tohunga' or 'a great priest'.*

---

* George French Angas, *The New Zealanders Illustrated*, London, Thomas M'Lean, 1847, p 31.

Sue hung over into the box. This was her monument. Her story. I felt a moment of discomfort, waiting for the reprimand for intruding. But there was none. There was, however, a dawning realisation, bringing with it a different sort of disquiet, that Richard's cousins' farm at Mangatangi was on Waikato land that had once belonged to Sue's ancestors. A strange, uncomfortable connection between us that would stay with me.

In the meantime, while Julia and I discussed the 'Queering the Museum' workshop we had both attended, Sue breathed in her past, took photographs, came to know this tribute to her ancestor.

We had requested this visit because it was a piece in the puzzle Sue was putting together. Some months before, she had announced to me that in 1847, when George French Angas executed his exquisitely graphic representation of Te Wherowhero's monument, none of the chief's children were dead.

'Not one of his children had died,' Sue repeated. 'Isn't that weird? Do you think Angas made a mistake? Information often came by word-of-mouth, and there was a language barrier. Perhaps he misunderstood what the person told him and got it wrong?'

'That's it!' I exclaimed. My mind was racing through the possibilities. 'Perhaps it's a monument to his first wife, Hinepau! After all, the monument was erected many years before Angas painted it: he himself describes the pā site as "decaying ruins".'

Te Wherowhero's three days of waiting for Hinepau to give birth had ended with the most tragic news. His teenage wife, his first flowering of true passion, was dead. Their baby had survived: a girl who would be named Irihapeti Te Paea Hahau. Te Wherowhero was inconsolable, his heart broken by his loss. In memory of this terrible time he himself took an additional name — Pōtatau — meaning those who count the hours, to remember waiting for news of Hinepau. Names to Māori are like their moko, telling a story of their lives and their connections. Both his new name and the sight of Irihapeti as she grew reminded him of his first love and his first great loss.

Te Wherowhero's childhood had been one of comparative peace following the celebrated victory of Waikato over the Ngāti Toa at Te Mangeo, near Lake Ngāroto. His adult years, however, would see an explosion of violence fuelled by the musket. Te Wherowhero would fight numerous battles and make many contentious decisions, like the one he is reputed to have made to end the life of Marore, one of Te Rauparaha's wives. Te Wherowhero led his warriors against Ngāti Toa, Ngāpuhi and the Taranaki tribes.

Hinepau's death must have been in 1821 or the beginning of 1822. Only a year or so later, Te Wherowhero's forces fought a horrifying battle at Motunui. When his allies decided to feign a withdrawal in order to trick their adversaries, Te Wherowhero refused to join the retreat, waiting with the body of a fallen Waikato chief. When he was found by opposing Ngāti Toa and Ngāti Mutunga forces, it was suggested that he should be shot. Te Rauparaha would not see the great chief slain without being given a chance to defend himself. So instead, he proposed a challenge. That night Te Wherowhero would fight a group of chiefs in man-to-man combat, armed with only a garden hoe. The great Waikato warrior won this contest, gaining the respect of Te Rauparaha, who warned him not to take his army north, but rather to travel south to Pukerangiora and avoid the Taranaki war parties. Te Rauparaha and Te Wherowhero were linked by blood, both being descended from the *Tainui* waka. Te Rauparaha's advice saved Te Wherowhero and his men more bloody conflict.

Only months later, in a struggle of shocking ferocity, Te Wherowhero would raise 3000 warriors, then ultimately command 10,000 people gathered for protection at Mātakitaki pā. When enemy Ngāpuhi ransacked the pā armed with muskets, there was carnage. People were trampled or shot as they fled in terror. Te Wherowhero led a defence, fighting his attackers single-handedly, when at times he became separated from his followers.

After the sacking of the pā, Te Wherowhero and his warriors were divided, escaping in smaller bands of men. Ngāpuhi pursued the fugitives, determined to butcher the last of their foes. Te Wherowhero and his men moved through the forest with stealth. Every crack of a twig underfoot, every rustle in the branches above, chilled their uneasy minds. All were alert.

The forest was a warm amber-green as the last shafts of sunlight cut their way through the leafy canopy. The group could hear the rush of water before they saw the figure of an old woman kneeling by the Waipā River, cupping her hands to drink.

Te Wherowhero knew her. Like them, she was on the run from the marauding Ngāpuhi. He approached her calmly, quietly, making himself visible before he spoke. They whispered. The old woman told him she was one of a large group of Ngāti Mahuta women, seized by Ngāpuhi as they had tried to flee.

'I barely escaped with my life,' she whispered, showing him the terrible injuries to her wrists made by makeshift shackles. Te Wherowhero was instantly worried that his young daughter, Irihapeti, might be among the captives. Many women and children had taken shelter at Mātakitaki pā, thinking they would be safe.

'Be fearless. Know you will be avenged,' he told her. 'Go back and tell the women: when the morning star rises, they will be freed.' With this promise, the woman was gone.

As night transformed the dusky forest to darkness, Te Wherowhero and his men crept along the riverbank, feeling their way amongst tree roots and boulders. A half-moon rose, offering more speed, and then the outline of a Ngāpuhi sentine. He was soundlessly dispatched, held head-down in the surging water. The rest of the Ngāpuhi captors were slaughtered in their sleep. Te Wherowhero was true to his word, freeing the Ngāti Mahuta women, and his daughter, by dawn.

In 1826 and 1832, Te Wherowhero and his forces again fought Ngāpuhi, and between 1833 and 1836 he led a number of bloody battles against Taranaki tribes. By the time Te Wherowhero was in his mid-forties, he was looking for other solutions to settle territorial, personal or collective grievances. He was tired of war. His life had been peripatetic, lived in constant movement, protecting territories, attacking enemies, leading his people. In 1835, he moved with his followers to Ihumātao, on the edge of the kai-rich Manukau Harbour. This would become the site of meticulously built gardens, the walls and kūmara trenches tattooing the landscape with their presence for generations to come.

In between his campaigns, Te Wherowhero had taken four more wives: Whakaawi, Raharaha, Waiata and Ngāwaero. With them he had produced three children: a son, Tūkāroto Matutaera, who became Tāwhiao, and was born to Whakaawi at Ōrongokoekoeā in 1822; and Mākareta Te Otaota; and Tīria. He wanted more for his mokopuna than just bloodshed.

Te Wherowhero had a healthy distrust of Pākehā, but their religion suggested a new way of living without violence or utu. So he attended Anglican services in mission churches, but refused to be baptised. Te Wherowhero saw the good in Christianity's principles, but not in its protocols. He would not bow to a foreign God nor to a foreign ruler, but he would make them allies.

So when Captain Symonds arrived with a copy of the Treaty of Waitangi to sign, he would not. But he did offer the settlement of Tāmaki Makaurau, or Auckland, his protection, moving to a cottage at Pukekawa, in what is now the Auckland Domain, where matters of law were vigorously debated between Māori and Pākehā.

Te Wherowhero became a bridge between two cultures who saw the world very differently. Communicating openly between Māori and Pākehā, he always maintained a strong allegiance to the interests of his people. He vehemently protested the 1846 confiscation, when Governor George Grey dictated that all the unoccupied or uncultivated Māori land become the property of the Crown. He made a clear gesture of support for Te Rauparaha, accompanying him home on his release from government detention.

Te Wherowhero was a chief who wore his cloak wisely. He saw Pākehā as people Māori could work with, but only on the same terms. So when he was approached to take the kingship, he saw in Māori sovereignty an equalising of power structures. His sovereignty was not intended to clash with the British Crown, but to communicate and secure the interests of Māori.

Thus, a new king was placed on our Antipodean chessboard. Chief Te Wherowhero had warrior knights, alongside whom he had fought on many occasions. He had his tohunga, or bishops. For his castle he went to Ngāruawāhia, where his descendants would build the Tūrangawaewae marae. A king must also have symbols that convey his standing. He already had his master carvers, working in wood, pounamu and bone, and now two flags were developed specifically for Kīngitanga. The white cross of Christianity and the red of Māori mana were central to their message. Stars appeared in a coat of arms, which were to be placed on the doors of the meeting house at Ngāruawāhia. Other artefacts that arose from the Kīngitanga movement include carved pātaka, a carved throne, a tokotoko and a Bible. Each tells a part of the story of Te Wherowhero becoming king.

Te Wherowhero's crowning speech at Ngāruawāhia in 1858 expressed his wishes for the future. He saw himself as the 'eye of a needle through which the white, black and red threads must pass', and 'challenged his people to seek peace' and 'to hold fast to love, to the law, and to faith in God'.

CHAPTER ELEVEN

Dovedale Avenue was Paradise

Our one big task before moving house from Bishop Street to Dovedale Avenue was to re-home Billie the chinchilla, who had proven to be antisocial in more than just his sexual appetite. His other addiction was eating wood. He chewed furniture, toys, doorframes, skirting boards — everything wooden — and, predictably, he liked the hard woods best. Kauri was his weakness.

'We can't take that awful chinchilla to Dovedale Ave,' Sue announced. Once Sue laid down the law, which she didn't do very often, *that was it*. 'How are you going to get rid of it?'

'Sell him.' I had already considered the idea, as I was expecting a Billie ban at Dovedale. Sue nearly killed herself laughing.

'Sell him,' she repeated, in disbelief.

'I'm feeling lucky,' I told her. 'I sold the house, which was a miracle. I feel confident we'll sell Billie, too.' So, I rang up the local newspaper and placed an ad. The children were away holidaying with their fathers and their new partners. This meant there was no child-generated pressure to keep the furry sex-fiend. In my advertising text I called Billie a 'chinchilla', but didn't add in brackets the word 'RODENT'. As a consequence, we received many calls for chinchilla cats. One distraught response came from an elderly woman whose chinchilla cat had been run over. Luckily Sue got that one. When I heard her counselling the woman, who was in floods of tears, I breathed a sigh of relief.

'Nothing!' Sue shouted to me from the bathtub afterwards. 'We've had no real enquiries.'

But the real deal did come — in the form of a lovely lady who told me on the phone that she kept animals instead of having children. 'But if your youngsters ever wanted to visit Billie, all they have to do is ask,' she said, when she came over to see him. I was pretty sure we had a sale: I was certain when I saw Billie acting like a paragon of virtue in his dust bath.

'Would you mind if I took the cage, too?' she asked. 'It will save my husband having to build another one.'

'Most certainly, take the cage. Please do,' I responded. We helped load the chinchilla and his cage into the back of her station wagon.

'Here's my address and phone number,' she said, handing me her business card. 'Remember, the children can come anytime.' As she drove away I tore up the business card she had given us and put the pieces in the bin.

'We won't be needing that,' I said to Sue. 'I'd be too frightened she'd want to give him back. Thank God we're changing address.'

Dovedale Avenue was paradise after Bishop Street. On the ground floor was the lounge with large wood-burner, a kitchen and a utility room. Up a wide flight of stairs were the bedrooms. Ours covered the whole floor space of the internal garage and glassed workroom downstairs. The other upstairs bedrooms were a lottery. We put Jason and Jeremy together in a large, funky room with a walk-in toy cupboard. Alex got a smaller bedroom, but had his own space. While Katherine got a splendid double room with skylight, jutting Swiss roof-angles, and space enough to accommodate a large pink couch, which folded down into her sofa bed. The previous owners were camellia fanatics, so the garden and outside courtyard were full of camellias.

The children settled in very quickly. There was an enormous park over the road, and we spent hours playing touch rugby and badminton. We kept the pattern of the children staying together every second weekend, which was something we all looked forward to. The major merging issues were over meals. Sue maintained her gourmet cooking on a vastly diminished budget.

She read cookbooks like I read a good murder mystery — for pleasure. Every day we had something amazing. Like most children, ours, mine especially, preferred the dubious delights of chicken nuggets and other junk food, and so found the upgrade in cuisine a challenge. When they all stayed over, we frequently sat down to a chorus of moans about dinner.

This began to irritate me. The early 1990s was an interesting time in the history of New Zealand cooking. With waves of immigration from China and South East Asia, completely new foods were coming onto the market. At the closest supermarket to Dovedale Avenue, they began to sell chicken feet. I walked my trolley a little faster past this section because the pale, puffy feet with immaculate toenails were too graphic and evocative for me. That is, until I hatched my plan.

I am a child of Stephen King's *Carrie* generation. This was the most disturbing movie of my teens. It wasn't the vat of pig's blood emptied onto Carrie's head that terrorised me, but her claw-like hand punching through the mound of soil on top of her grave . . . to grab the arm of an unsuspecting mourner. When I saw the pile of chicken feet in the cabinet, I couldn't get *Carrie* out of my mind.

After a particularly frustrating blended weekend of food moans, I said to Sue, 'We've got to do something about this. We have to teach them a lesson.'

'How are you going to do that?' We were in the middle of a vegetarian phase, and every item on every plate screwed someone's face up.

'I've got an idea that will give them something to think about.' I told her my plan.

'You can't do that,' she announced. 'That's too mean.'

'Just watch me.' It took some convincing, but by the next time we went to the supermarket I had won her over. Instead of taking a wide berth around the chicken feet cabinet of the meat section, I went straight to the counter.

'How many feet do you get for a kilogram?' I asked the shop assistant.

'I don't know,' she replied, shuddering. 'Shall we count them out? How many are you after?' She pulled a loose fitting see-through plastic glove over her right hand.

'I'm not sure, I haven't thought about it. Let's see . . .' I did a bit of mental arithmetic. 'I'll take 14.' She watched the needle climb rapidly on the scales.

'If I throw in another, it'll round it up,' she said, hovering over the pile with one last anaemic-looking foot.

'Okay, pop it in.'

'That'll be $3.50,' she said, barely managing to disguise her disgust as she taped the bag shut. 'If you don't mind me asking, what are you going to do with them?' When I told her she was shocked. 'I don't think I should be selling them to you.' Reluctantly, however, she handed me the bag.

'They'll be fine, honestly. The kids will survive. I'll have six chicken thighs as well, please.'

'That's brilliant,' I said to Sue, as we loaded the groceries into the car. 'Stage one accomplished. Stage two and three: cooking and serving.' When we got home, we coated the feet in soya sauce and cooked them long and slow in the oven, rotating each foot in the sauce until it looked like it was coated in glossy black varnish.

Dovedale Avenue had a sweet little dining area between the kitchen and the lounge that could be shut off by Japanese sliding doors. While the children were draped over chairs and couches watching Friday-night telly, we surreptitiously slid the screen doors closed so no one could see what we were up to. Taking four Chinese rice bowls, plus a matching serving bowl, we filled each one with rice, then pushed the macabre black feet into them *Carrie*-style. In the small bowls we put two feet facing each other; on top of the central serving bowl we had a Stonehenge of seven feet in a circle. In the cooking process the feet closed down like half-clenched fists and the nails shone as if they had been polished.

'Wonderful,' I whispered, 'but I think we need some garnish.' I opened the outside door and grabbed bits of greenery from the nearest camellia bush. Four seats; four places set; the serving bowl in the middle alongside a small vase of flowers; a candle, lit: it was a picture of horror.

'Dinner's ready!' Sue called.

'Yes. Come on, kids, dinner's on the table,' I added. With that, the opaque sliding doors flew open and the children flooded in. Katherine screamed, Alex began to cry, Jeremy gleefully grabbed one of the chicken feet and made clawing motions in the air accompanied by monster noises. Only Jason sat down politely with eyes like saucers in front of his bowl.

'Okay, everyone, relax, this is not really dinner. We thought it might—' I was just about to explain the link between chicken feet and moaning about the food put in front of you when I noticed that Alex had raised the sprig of camellia bush up to his mouth and was about to eat it.

'No!' I shouted, grabbing it out of his hand. 'Don't eat that!'

'But I'm not eating those awful feet,' he replied, still crying.

'You don't have to; we've got your real dinner in the oven.'

Unfortunately, the real dinner was chicken thighs, and we had not considered how effective the feet would be at putting us all off eating anything to do with chicken. No one ate much dinner that night. Even Sue and I struggled when we came to eat ours after the children had gone to bed.

'I don't think I can face this,' I said to Sue after a few mouthfuls of thigh.

'Yes,' she replied, putting her knife and fork down, 'I don't think I can either.'

'I guess we've all learned our lesson,' I said, picking up her plate, putting it on top of mine, and carrying them out to the kitchen.

The only clear winner was the enterprising Jeremy, who asked me if he could take the chicken feet to school in his lunchbox at the end of the weekend. On Monday night, when I asked him what he had done with them, he told me he had chased girls around the playground, running the claws through their hair. Jeremy's semi-mummified feet lasted more than a term before the teacher caught a whiff of them decomposing in his school desk and confiscated the remains. Although the trick did not have quite the intended reaction, it did dramatically reduce the number of culinary complaints.

Towards the end of the year, I went to the university registry office to pick up an application form for a doctoral scholarship.

'Will you come with me?' I asked Sue. 'I need some moral support.' We met at lunchtime and made the trek up to the scholarships office on the fourth floor. When we approached the counter, we were met by a well-dressed, middle-aged woman.

'Yes?' she enquired, as if she had a million better things to do than attend to us.

'I'm here to pick up an application form for a doctoral scholarship.'

'Oh, you are, are you?' she said, looking me up and down. 'You do realise, they're only given to the university's brightest students? I wouldn't bother applying if you're not an A or A+ student.' This concluded our conversation as far as she was concerned, and she continued looking through the paperwork she had brought to the counter. When she glanced up a few seconds later, she was clearly surprised to find we were still there. Sue, who was smouldering on my behalf, addressed her in an uncharacteristically forceful manner. 'She *is* an A student, and we want an application form, *now*.'

With that, our scholarships lady moved reluctantly to the filing cabinet behind her. She pulled out a drawer, flicked through the file tabs, then extracted a form. Handing it to me, she said, 'You do realise university scholarships are intended for *young* students in financial hardship?' I gave Sue a warning nudge to stop her before she gave the woman another piece of her mind.

'Don't worry about it,' I whispered to Sue. Even though the woman was condescending, I didn't think it was a good idea to alienate her.

I went home, filled out the form, got it signed by my supervisor and department head, and took it back to the scholarships office. As she skimmed down the application form to make sure I had filled it out correctly, the scholarships lady was transformed by what she saw. It was like the rising of the sun. She asked me how my day had been, and wished me luck when I left the room. The results were not due out for some months, but in the meantime I made other trips to the scholarships office to enquire about grants and fellowships. I told her about my children and my finances, and she listened, and we became friends.

'Notification of scholarship winners will be in the post soon,' she told me on one of my visits.

'If I don't hear in the next few days, does that mean I don't have one?' She wouldn't commit, but that was the impression I got. Every day, I went to the mailbox, full of hope. Nothing was there. More days went by, and I became depressed. We so desperately needed the money. Finally, I heard from a friend that she had received a letter to say that she had a scholarship. That was the last straw. Late that afternoon, I drove to the university and went up to the scholarships office, and burst through the door.

'I'm sorry,' I shouted at the scholarships lady, 'I just have to know if I've got a scholarship. It's really important.'

'Haven't you heard yet?' she asked, mystified.

'No, not a thing — but my friend has.'

'Well, let me see,' she said, moving straight to a basket of outgoing mail sitting on the desk behind her. 'There was a bundle that missed the mail on Friday.' She picked up a pile and began sorting through them. 'Yes,' she said, 'here it is. I thought it had gone out today, but it's still here.' She walked back to the counter and handed the envelope to me.

This was a moment of pure anxiety. The sound around me shut down. I wasn't aware any more of the scholarships lady or even where I was. My future was in that manila envelope. As I ran my thumb along the inside of the flap and tore it open, my hands shook. I fumbled to pull the letter out and lay it flat. *Dear Joanne Drayton*, I read, *It is with great pleasure that—* I couldn't see anything more because I burst into tears that were accompanied by racking great sobs that shook me.

Why I broke down so completely is a mystery to me. Leaving the Church under a cloud; putting all that drama and emotion together with an affair, and a coming-out; then blending in a new relationship, family structure and house — all this may have had something to do with it. Because, at the end of all of the change, there was only one institution left in my life still intact, and that was the university. The university's money was important to our survival, but its endorsement was everything. What also meant a huge amount to me was the fact that I could go off the Domestic Purposes Benefit and support myself. Who knows how many meltdowns the scholarships lady had seen in her office, but it could have been a few because she was around the counter in a flash with a box of tissues and a hug. She shed a tear with me, and in the end we were both laughing and dabbing our eyes with wads of tissue. She would never know all my story, but she had come to realise what the scholarship meant to me, and that was enough.

V

As they reached the walrus colony, Bjorn, who was the unspoken leader of the hunt, motioned for them to halt and be silent. The last thing they wanted to do was send the herd into a panic. If that happened, the beasts would likely lumber off the rocks and into the sea. Then, only the youngest and weakest would be left, and these were of little use to them. The older, more mature males were the ones that carried the thickest, longest shafts of ivory in their tusks. Bjorn motioned to the men to divide up into groups of roughly a dozen. To each he indicated a large male.

Keeping downwind and out of sight of the colony, they positioned themselves ready to attack the walruses simultaneously from different angles. This was an experienced group: they knew not to pre-empt the assault and spook the herd. It took some time for each group to creep into place so that Bjorn could give the signal, a shrill whistling birdcall.

The attack began with a paroxysm of noise and movement, then the bloodbath began. To get at the desirable giant males the men slashed and cut at anything in their way. Upon reaching their quarry, they wounded the enormous males with arrows first, then lunged at them with spears. At the end of the slaughter, two of the three biggest male walruses lay dead, while another had slipped, severely wounded and sporting several arrows, into the sea. He would likely wash up along the coastline in the next few days, dead. All in all, their kill totalled 11, not including the suckling mothers who had stood firm to defend their young and perished. The baby walruses were then picked off for their soft skins.

This would be their biggest harvest. Now that the surviving walruses were alert to the hunters' presence they would be nervous, and quicker to dash into the sea. The rest of the day was spent skinning the beasts, and cleaning and separating the biggest heads from their bodies so the skulls and the precious ivory could be taken back intact. Finally, the best steaks of meat were hacked from the flesh and wrapped in skins so they could be carried. Everyone was loaded down with blood-drenched items.

Thorvald carried the head and tusks of one of the finest beasts on his back. Flies were beginning to buzz around the raw flesh, following the party like a cloud. Even Thorvald found this part of the process odious. They stopped several times on their way to rest and resettle loads. As he sat, Thorvald watched a large black fly crawl across the glassy eye of the head he carried, like it was dancing on a pool of iridescent oil.

Back at the camp, the skins were salted and hung out on lines to dry, and chunks of meat were smoked on racks. The tusked heads were taken well away from the campsite and buried. Nature would do much of the work for them. That long twilight night the hunters ate walrus and toasted their successful cull.

The next day the preparation of meat and skins continued while Bjorn and a small party returned to the walrus colony. He wished they had been more circumspect with killing and left less blood around, for the walruses had not returned in any sizeable number. The few they surprised were those too badly wounded to find another sanctuary, and this was the case the next day as well.

On the fourth day they found the body of the third giant male washed up along the rocks. While his struggle to escape their knives and spears had been valiant, he had not escaped the cruel wounds they inflicted. Already the seagulls had helped them. Bjorn was tempted to leave the body and come back when there was less flesh to remove, but he felt he couldn't risk losing the spectacular tusks. The ivory was probably as valuable to itinerant parties of Skraeling as it was to them. So, he began the hideous task of removing the skull and tusks. The smell was almost unbearable. When he had completed the disgusting work, he went down to the sea and washed out his clothes, cleaning both his hands and then the knives. It had been a long day and it was late by the time they carried their latest haul back to their base.

As they approached the campsite, coming out of the trees, Bjorn noted that there were no sounds, no buzz of conversation, no laughter. This was immediately disturbing. He signalled to his men, who had already drawn their swords. Fanning out and crouching, they edged forward. As they got closer, Bjorn could smell the unmistakable odour of death. The first body he came across had been struck through the heart by an arrow, and was now covered in flies. The next had been similarly dispatched, then the next, until he came to his brother, whose head had been removed and no doubt taken as a trophy. Bjorn could only identify him by his dress.

The whole camp had been attacked and slaughtered while the hunting party was away. Bjorn was devastated, and so were the men who stood beside him staring in disbelief at the decapitated body of Thorvald. The attackers were Skraeling — and they would be back. The bodies had all been stripped of jewellery and weaponry, and the drying furs and preserved skins removed from their racks. The camp must have been taken by surprise.

'Quick, quick!' Bjorn called to Ivan, the most senior member of his hunting party. 'If we are to escape alive, we must leave this place now. Let's pile the bodies up, immediately. We'll burn them before we go.

'You, Ivan, come with me — now — and bring some others,' he ordered. 'The rest of you, pack up only what you know we need, and when you've finished, drag the bodies together and we will release the souls of our dead. They must not rot in a foreign land.'

Bjorn left with his small party to unearth the tusks. They were putrid and would normally have received further cleaning, but there was no time for that. The imperative was to escape.

By the time they had carried the rancid heads back to camp, those remaining at the campsite had stacked the bodies of the slain men high and covered them with walrus oil that would quickly combust. The boat was packed.

'Start dragging the boat down to the sea,' Bjorn called to his men. 'I'll light the fire. Wait for me just beyond the breakers. I'll be there soon. We can't afford for the Skraeling to see the smoke: once I light the fire, we must flee.' He took the flint he carried with him and the tinder-dry moss he used to set the spark alight.

His hands shook as he glimpsed his brother's body there with the rest. The moss ignited, and in a sheltered space amongst the cadavers it blazed for a time, then died. Bjorn tried several more times before the oil caught and began to burn. Black smoke billowed into the air. Suddenly a multitude of arrows flew past him, lodging sickeningly in the bodies that were already alight. One, however, found a more painful target, going through Bjorn's thigh. Breaking off the tip of the arrow, he pulled the shaft out. The pain would come later.

He began limping towards the water, his shield held above his head. As he struggled through the waves, arrows thumped into the shield and splashed around him. To avoid the attack, the boat was beginning to move out to sea. The last part Bjorn would have to swim. He launched himself into the water, propelling forward for what seemed like an age before he felt the welcome arms of his fellow seamen pulling him onboard. The oars were withdrawn and the sail set.

As they got further out to sea, Bjorn stood with his men, watching in tribute as the bonfire of bodies blazed on the beach. Their ivory had come at too high a cost.

CHAPTER TWELVE
Things You Love

Although we spent three incredibly happy years at Dovedale Avenue, there were many difficult challenges for all of us there. The only daily constant from my old married life was Morris the cat. Sadly, the custody of our two cats could not be shared. Richard kept Ethel and I took Morris, who became a real companion. Changeover days for the kids' custody were especially hard. Richard had a new partner and a new baby boy within a year, and Sue's ex-husband continued his live-in relationship with his friend at work. Vendettas were played out through the children, who suffered the transient existence of shared custody that over time can divide and diminish life. But there was happiness in our getting together as a blended family that rose above the hardships. Or at least I felt it did.

Sue completed her Fine Arts degree, graduating in 1994. I continued full-time on my PhD, grabbing the relief teaching my cousin Philippa offered at Christchurch Girls' High when I could. I had not one dress in my wardrobe, which was compulsory uniform for female teachers at that school. A visit to the 'opportunity shop' soon sorted that out.

'Shouldn't you try them on?' Sue asked as I put an armful of $2 frocks on the op-shop counter.

'Nah, they'll be fine. I only have to wear them for the day.' This logic was flawed, I realised, when I attempted to run at high speed to collect my relief work from the office of the deputy principal, Sally Comer, and nearly fell on my face.

'That dress is a straitjacket!' I announced to Sue after school. 'I had to shuffle around all day like a Geisha. It'll make a good rag. No way I'm wearing that one again.'

We shared the last Christmas we had in Dovedale Avenue with a young lesbian couple in their mid-twenties whom we had become friends with through university. Nicole was completing a Master's degree in women's studies, and Kirsty was in the very last stage of a PhD in molecular biology involving frog cells. The end of her PhD was delayed when she went on a short holiday and came back to find most of her research participants — an aquarium full of frogs — dead. By the time we became friends, the end of their studies was nigh. Their plan was to move back to Germany, where Nicole was born and Kirsty hoped to do a post-doctoral fellowship.

That Christmas we took the children to hear Nicole's German choir singing Christmas carols. When we arrived home at almost midnight, Nicole had the most magical German gingerbread house waiting for them. It was enormous: big slabs of gingerbread cladding, decorated with icing, sweets, and a sprinkling of icing sugar for snow. It was Hansel and Gretel's house, and the children gaped at it in wonder. A pile of lollies sat waiting, as if they were chopped wood in a forest clearing.

'Can we have some, Mum, please?' Jeremy begged.

'You have to ask Nicole: she and Kirsty made it.'

That night everyone feasted on a little of Nicole's fantasy.

The children spent Christmas Day with their fathers and their new partners, and we picked them up on Boxing Day. Instead of going to Golden Bay as we usually did, our plan was to meet up with Nicole and Kirsty in Arrowtown. We would drive down with the four children in the back seat of Sue's white Ford Telstar. The two young ones sat in the middle scooped together in one seat belt. The bigger boys had their own belts. It was hot and sticky in the back seat, and negotiations had to be made between them to scratch a nose.

It's a six-hour trip from Christchurch to Arrowtown, and Sue managed to leave her camera on the dining-room table, so 40 minutes into the journey we turned around and came back. This was exasperating for everyone, but we were photographing gargoyles in Dunedin for an article I was writing for the *Historic Places* magazine so needed the camera. By the time we were on the road again the nor'west arch was high in the sky; and the suffocating foehn winds were blowing like they had travelled across a scorching desert.

Things were still a little tense in the car over the camera having been left at home when Jeremy made his first indiscretion. The previous day he had eaten a big, greasy Christmas dinner, and his stomach never handled fat well. His first fart sent the back row of tightly packed children into convulsions. Alex and Jason wound down the windows and stuck their heads out like puppies on the tray of a pick-up truck. As the day got hotter, Jeremy's gastro contributions to the poisonous atmosphere of the car's interior got more and more unbearable. Numerous times we pulled off the highway to let everyone out for a breather.

It was about six in the evening when we drove into the car park of the fish-and-chip shop at Twizel. Being Boxing Day, it was the only food place open for miles around. The car park was full, and the fish-and-chip shop crowded with holidaymakers. Although the heat of the day had passed, it was still a furnace in the fish-and-chip shop with its steaming vats of bubbling oil. I had taken everyone's orders, and Sue was outside looking for a wooden picnic table for us all to sit at.

I placed my order with the couple behind the counter, a man and a woman; then I spied Jeremy, who had come in with Alex and Jason and was playing with a slot machine by the wall. It was so hot and the place so packed that I gave Alex my ticket with our order number, and told him to pick up our parcel and bring it out to the table when it was ready. As I stepped out of the shop, I was passed by a mammoth-sized bikie and his female pillion passenger coming in. The bikie was a daunting man, dressed all in black leather and heavy studded boots, with missing front teeth, homemade 'tats' on his face, and wrap-around dirty-dog sunglasses. He swaggered rather than walked, and was as broad as he was tall.

'Jeepers, look at that,' I said to Sue, gesturing at the line of black and silver Harley bikes in the car park. About five minutes into our conversation at the picnic table, Alex came haring back.

'Mum, Mum!' he called out to me, hardly able to get the words out as he was nearly killing himself with laughter. 'You'll never guess what just happened! Jeremy farted in the fish-and-chip shop, and the bikie man shouted at the people behind the counter: "Jesus-fucking-Christ, where did you get your fish from? China?"' My sympathies went out to the proprietors, especially with so many people standing in the shop.

We laughed with Alex, then I told him: 'Now go back and wait for the order, we're all starving.'

While Alex was away, the bikie and his 'moll' seated themselves at a table close to us. Sue and I were so shocked by what had happened with Jeremy that we were both still gaping. Mistakenly, our leather-clad lovebirds thought we were gaping at them.

'What are you looking at, you fucking bitch?' the bikie called out to Sue. 'Take a photograph, it lasts longer.'

'Why would she bother looking at you?' I shot back.

'Fuck up, lesbo cunt!' he shouted at me, an assumption made on the basis, I presumed, of my short haircut. The interchange was about to escalate when it was interrupted by the arrival of Alex and Jason with our huge haul of fish and chips in two monster parcels wrapped in newspaper. With that, the bikie and his rudeness evaporated from our consciousness. The two young ones joined us, and we all sat in blissful silence as we ate. Sue and I were relieved, however, when we heard the roar of engines and watched the gang leave the car park in a long procession of bikes.

The promise for dessert had been chocolate-coated ice-creams, which I bought for everyone from the dairy next to the fish-and-chip shop. We weren't on the road long when Jeremy struck again. The windows in the back of the car flew down, and Alex and Jason hung out as Katie gagged, while Jeremy looked sheepish.

Suddenly there was a howl from Alex, then floods of tears.

'What's happened?' I asked Sue, unable to look around because I was driving. Poor Alex, it seemed, had lost his ice-cream. In his frenzied rush for fresh air, he had wound down the window at high speed, holding his ice-cream in one hand and the handle in the other. The wind rushing past the car swallowed everything on his stick and all that was left was a thin layer of chocolate at the centre.

After that unpromising start, the week-long stay in Arrowtown with our friends was wonderful. On the way home we stayed with my cousin Jenny and her husband at a farm in Middlemarch, and the next day drove into Dunedin to take our photographs of the Cargill Monument.

'Every time we go away there's a disaster,' I said to Sue, in tears. We had come home to find my beloved cat Morris near death. I thought his snuffling had been a reaction to his feline flu jab.

'It's either cancer or sinusitis gone out of control,' the vet told me as soon as I took the cat to see him. 'We could do a test to work out which one it is, but, either way, it's terminal. He's not eating and he's very sick. What do you want us to do?'

'No tests,' I said, 'I don't want any tests.'

'Do you want him euthanised, then? I think it's the kindest thing to do.'

'Yes,' I replied, completely shattered by the prospect.

'You can hold him while I do it,' he said. So I held my dear cat as the vet injected the violently blue liquid into his veins. As Morris relaxed, I realised his death was just a letting-go of life, a quiet transition to another state. I'd never held death in my arms before.

For days afterwards, I expected to see Morris waiting for me: in the driveway, on the window-ledge looking out. Sometimes I imagined I saw him at the corner of my eye, but when I turned my head, he wasn't there. Gradually I stopped seeing and looking for him, and I even came to see his death as a positive — for him at least, if not for me. Because things were looking like they might change again, and Morris was getting older. The move from Bishop Street to Dovedale Avenue had been difficult for him, and now there was a possibility we might be moving again to a job in Whanganui.

'I've found the perfect job for you,' Sue had announced when I arrived home from university late one April afternoon in 1996. 'It's in the *Gazette*. I copied down the details. Here,' she said, handing me the piece of paper. 'You've got to apply. We need the money.'

So I got my slim résumé together and applied for the job. Although the position at the polytechnic seemed almost too good to be true, I was overwhelmed with apprehension about what getting it would mean. How would we reconfigure our custody arrangements? Then there was leaving Christchurch, which was a place I loved. Many times I faltered and changed my mind, even after accepting the position.

It's weird what you think of when you're about to leave a place, especially one loaded with memories. We had buried Morris in a box in the garden amongst the camellia bushes. I cried so hard I could hardly see to dig the hole.

'Dig it deep,' Sue had instructed me, 'you don't want anything digging it up.' So, Morris's grave was deep, and over it we planted a miniature burgundy-red rose bush. At the time I thought we would be living in that house forever, and here we were, just a few months later, contemplating our departure.

'We'll have to leave Morris here,' I announced to Sue, who gave me the astonished look of a farmer's daughter listening to townie sentimentality.

'No, I don't mean his bones; I mean the rose. We'll have to leave his memorial rose bush.' Then I confessed to her that I *had* contemplated taking him and the bush with us: 'but they are probably better left where they are,' I conceded. Like the mother and the child buried at Purau when their tribe fled, and like the treasure hidden in the sands of the Bay of Uig, sometimes precious things have to be left. One part of me wanted to stay and hold on to what I had; the other accepted that sometimes you have to leave the things you love behind.

We exited Christchurch feeling these losses. There was grief and tension, but also the thrill of the unknown. 'Thank goodness we don't know our futures,' Sue has often said, and at this point in our lives this was so true. If, in the glass reflections of a crystal ball, I could have glimpsed life ahead, it would have frozen me. I don't think I would have had the heart to go forward.

For this decision to move to Whanganui changed everything. The need for an income and to escape with Jeremy sped us on. There was no time for premonitions or halting apprehension.

We arrived at Barbara's on that fateful night full of turmoil and secrets. First me and Jeremy on the bus, and then Sue in the Ford Telstar. Believing, as you do when you are 30-something, that all it takes to shape your destiny is determination. We were so charged with our own unfolding dramas — the drum-beat of adrenaline pounding in our ears — that we did not hear Barbara's own grief. Just a few days before we had arrived, she had buried her name-sake favourite niece, who had died tragically young of cancer. I saw the sadness in her face, but didn't understand her loss as she would come to understand ours.

I patched her pain in my mind with the thought that we might be a comfort, human company in her cold, old house. And maybe that was true. But we were also a liability. Refugees, with all the brokenness and chaos that that entails. And my primary motivation was survival. Our survival. Because everything felt dangerous, and everything was at stake.

V

Her eyes look out of the photograph frame in Russell Bishop's essay, two watery wells of blackness that resonate the past.

'She's beautiful,' Sue announces, staring back at her great-great-grandmother.

There is no better word than 'beautiful' for Irihapeti Te Paea Hahau, her dark eyes flashing with the fire of youth. She could almost be adolescent, but in her teenage years there were no cameras in Aotearoa so she must at least be in her mid-twenties.

She has a grooved moko on her chin and lips, which looks carved into her flesh, done by the painful technique of hammering the pigment-tipped chisel into the skin with a mallet. Irihapeti is a Māori woman of high rank. She wears a tasteful, elegant dress — the attire of a young Victorian — with a white collar that crosses at her neck, held together by a jewelled brooch. There is a settled confidence, but also a courageousness and a determination about her. She looks to her past for guidance, but she is also a woman of the future.

Irihapeti grew up motherless among her father's Ngāti Mahuta people. She belonged, but didn't belong, her birthright buried by bloodshed and time. Te Wherowhero, the great warrior chief, was often away fighting battles and exacting revenge. He would take more wives and produce more children. By the time it came to his investiture as King, her mother, a child-bride long dead, was left off the list of official wives. Irihapeti Te Paea Hahau — a noble woman, a rangatira — was a princess without a bloodline to the throne.

Some inheritances could not be denied her, though. She would share three things with her father: a warrior's spirit; a belief in the politics of marriage; and, ultimately, a profound faith in a monotheistic God. These were the treasures she carried with her: her taonga for life.

Irihapeti married at 16 years old. However, if the union she made with the tall, redheaded 20-year-old Scotsman John Horton McKay began as a politically strategic alliance between Māori and Pākehā, then it would end as a love match. The respect and the love were mutual. She wore Pākehā women's clothes to pass in the settler world of the 1840s for him, and he dressed in a Māori warrior's cloak and carried an ornately carved spear for her. There is a photograph of him standing proudly — if a little incongruously — a white warrior. John Horton McKay lived as a Pākehā–Māori, fluent and fluid in the way he moved between two languages and two cultures.

Like many mixed-race couples, they traded goods and supplies, opening a general store at the settlement of Putataka, which a few decades later would develop into the town of Port Waikato. Irihapeti was both entrepreneurial and astute. Their business — the business of trade between Māori and Pākehā — flourished, and so did their relationship. Their first child, Marianne, was born in 1838, when Irihapeti was 18 years old. Records show that Marianne was followed by at least 11 more children, including Annie, Catherine, John, Benjamin, Henry, Clara and Albert.

This was a bicultural marriage. Irihapeti brought her children up knowing the ways of Māori, while John Horton raised them as Scots. The McKay tartan was even adopted by Kīngitanga as an emblem of clanship and royalty.

Irihapeti would have understood all about strategic marriages, as her mother's had been, and would have been conscious her own brought two powerful peoples together, which should benefit its progeny, their children. She saw mission schools as a source of new knowledge and enrolled all of her children. Education opened opportunities, creating pathways into the Pākehā world.

Irihapeti toiled long days and nights to keep their general store open, and feed and clothe her children. Life was a cycle of pregnancies, domestic work and serving in their shop. But, like her father, she had a huge capacity for work, and she had her faith. When Bishop Selwyn visited the settlement of Putataka, she had her children baptised at once.

While she used old medicines and practised Māori lore, Irihapeti's soul belonged to a Pākehā God, and her heart to peace.

CHAPTER THIRTEEN
Barbara and Ringley

Making love at Barbara's was difficult. I wrestled with my conscience the way I imagined most red-blooded males would not. Sue and I had not discussed the nature of our relationship with Barbara. That was a problem for me; one I would never get used to. The secretiveness and the silence about our sexuality made me feel like a leper without a bell. Then the children had to be considered. We waited until they were away or in bed. But if all the conditions were perfect, then there would be—

'Yoo-hoo!'

This was Barbara, coming down the hall looking for company.

'What are you girls up to?' she would call out to us, as we dashed frantically between the beds to find our clothes.

'Nothing much, Barbara,' I would shout back, as I undid and re-buttoned my shirt properly, and flung Sue her bra from the floor by my bed. Unexpected visits played hell with our libido. Love-making was like cold fish after an awkward cup of coffee with Barbara.

Heaving two bodies onto one single bed also had its perils. We were neither of us that small, and I remember more than once an avalanche of mattress, sheets, blankets, and us both slipping to the floor. Sex in a single bed took concentration. The movement of arms, legs and heads needed to be synchronised. Love-making was like backing an articulated truck up a narrow alleyway; there was no taking your hands off the wheel. And deep down I knew it would be the end of everything if Barbara discovered us. This would be catastrophic. However, the ultimate passion-killer for me was Dorothy.

Barbara's aunt Dorothy might have been dead, but she was my conscience, and I felt she was always watching.

What I remember vividly, too, was sitting in the lawyer Kennedy Quinn's office. We needed a local legal representative to fight the custody case, and our lawyer in Christchurch had recommended her. On the first meeting she looked up at us sternly over her glasses after she'd finished reading the counsellor's report.

'Your son Alex doesn't feel comfortable living with two lesbians,' she told us. 'Did you know he was teased at school?'

Maybe I should point out that everyone involved in the legal case, even our own counsel, felt sorry for Alex. In relation to our having custody of Jeremy, it was almost impossible for people to imagine two females bringing up a male child. Women had brought up sons and daughters on their own for eons, of course. But add the magic word 'lesbian' and suddenly the project became unimaginable.

Right from the beginning, Kennedy Quinn was pessimistic about our chances of winning custody of Jeremy, or of ever seeing Alex again. She was so negative about our prospects, that I imagined she must be an imposter. A plant, working for the other side to prove to me just how insane my aspirations of motherhood as a lesbian really were. At our appointments, I felt as if I were in the dock myself, desperately parading in front of her all my high-minded middle-class notions about justice, fair play and equality for all. Which she then shot down with homophobic realities. None of these basic human rights applied to us anymore, it seemed.

'As far as the law is concerned,' she announced, 'you've stolen one son and abandoned the other. You are lucky that Jeremy hasn't been taken away from you already.' Although I knew this was true, I couldn't contain myself.

'But—' I began, ready to unleash an army of well-reasoned justifications.

'No buts,' she said, stopping me. 'Technically you've broken the law. You've taken a child. That's an offence. You've been very irresponsible, and it will be almost impossible to convince a judge otherwise.'

Kennedy Quinn told it the way it was, and underlying everything there seemed to be a note of condescension. It felt like she thought she was doing us an enormous favour defending such an out-there case. I left her office depressed and despairing. Feeling like a sexual offender out on bail.

When I wasn't having every warty aspect of my unnatural life cauterised by my hostile lawyer, I was preparing one lesson ahead on the lecture timetable to give to my students. The great thing about preparing as you go is that the material is as fresh for you as it is for them. Working very late at night in our massive lounge under a small, low-wattage light-bulb around a plastic picnic table that Barbara had let us bring in from outside, I would call out to Sue: 'Listen to this! In 1923, at an event in New York, a Dada performance artist arrived drunk and proceeded to urinate over the audience. I bet they wanted their money back after that show.'

It amazed me that such flagrantly unconventional behaviour should be lauded in the history books while our love had to be hidden. Back then I shared a fresh sense of scepticism with my students, and a feeling that the gullible, pretentious art world had been duped. But these were men, of course, and this was art with a capital 'A'.

As an academic, once a week I was eligible for a research day, which I spent on Edith at the Sarjeant Art Gallery. It thrilled me whenever the curators had one of her works up on the walls in the main gallery. It was usually a key work plucked from its family in the basement. My privilege was knowing where it fitted in her story.

'I am just in full swing now never had such a time in my life working all the time, funny old stick aren't I?' she had scribbled down on a postcard to her brother soon after her arrival in London in 1913. Edith, who had just started life-drawing classes at 27 years old, had seen her first male nude. It was a mystery to me why she never returned to England like Frances Hodgkins thought she would. Though I knew something terrible happened back in New Zealand.

During my many visits to the art gallery I got to know the staff.

'So you're living in Aunty Barbara's flat now?' asked one of them at lunch in the basement around a green-and-yellow-flecked, 1950s-style Formica table. 'You're game.' This was Barbara's hip young nephew, Craig Collier, who was an artist and did odd jobs around the gallery. He was tall, slim and good-looking, with long, black hair that he wore either pulled back in a ponytail or curling luxuriously over his shoulders.

'Do you know that it's haunted?'

'Yes, I do,' I replied through a mouthful of cheese sandwich. I swallowed. 'Have you ever seen anything there, yourself?' I had to know.

'No. Only heard the sound of footsteps in an empty corridor, and realised that things had moved while I wasn't around. But other people have seen real things. Mike, Barbara's handy-man, went into the lounge one day and the French doors burst open and shut wildly, while the net curtains billowed into the room like sails. Being a down-to-earth sort of bloke Mike went over to check it out. There was no wind, no people — nothing — to explain the doors opening and closing. Mike was freaked out and swore he'd never go inside the house alone again.'

'Right, that's it,' I said when Sue picked me up from the steps outside the front of the Sarjeant Gallery that evening. 'We're booking a hotel room next time we want to make love.' The story of the French windows poured out with just a few embellishments. Sue looked unimpressed. Even sceptical.

'I know you don't believe me, but Dorothy's watching us,' I insisted. 'I'm sure of it, and it frightens me.'

The pressure was on to find somewhere else to live.

Recalling it now, I can see the funny side. From a distance in time it has the hallmarks of comedy, but then my life felt like a gothic novel unfolding chapter by chapter. Soon after our escape from Christchurch, Richard came up to Whanganui, bringing the darkness of doubt and uncertainty with him. Like a king-player he was there to strategise and ultimately take his piece. He held one of my sons like a pawn at his side, and now he wanted the other. During our negotiations I had asked for just two-and-a-half more years with Jeremy because he was so young, but he wanted everything, and who could blame him? So did I.

Richard took a motel room down the road from Barbara's and systematically interviewed everyone. He made appointments with Jeremy's new headmaster, his new teacher and his doctor, and saw or contacted them all before he returned to Christchurch.

Then it began. When we were in bed at night the phone would ring sometimes six or eight times. I would wake suddenly, struggling to remember where I was. Then the whole frightening nightmare came back to me and I would battle through the pitch-blackness to find the phone, which hung on the kitchen wall.

When I lifted the receiver, sometimes there was the wild screeching of a fax machine. Other times there was just the hollow sound of someone listening.

'Hello,' I would say.

Nothing.

'Hello, is someone there?' I would repeat in a voice pitched slightly higher each time, as my anxiety mounted. After an eternity's wait, the receiver at the other end would click off with a jeer. The listener had finished playing with me. I would be left standing there in the cold and dark, scared, angry, in turmoil.

'Who was that?' Sue called out to me the first few times.

Then it became: 'Was it the fax machine, or the mystery caller?'

And, finally: 'Did you wait long enough to hear them hang up?'

I would try to get to sleep afterwards, knowing I had classes to teach the next morning. But my mind would churn backwards and forwards like a washing machine, hoping sleep would come. Sometimes, just as I was about to drop off, the phone would ring once more, threatening and sinister, and the cycle began again.

Eventually I decided to unplug the phone from the wall. The calls slipped seamlessly into the daytime, and more astonishingly when I was at home, as if the caller knew my whereabouts.

I rang the phone company.

'Yes, we do have an electronic log of those calls,' said the female voice at the end of the line. 'But no, madam, I'm afraid we can't divulge any information about the caller or where they're calling from. That would be a violation of their privacy according to the Privacy Act.'

'Hey, wait a minute!' I exclaimed, getting annoyed. 'Do you mean to say that someone can ring me at any time of the day or night, on my private line, that I pay for, and you won't tell me where those calls are coming from?'

'That's right, madam. We don't make the laws; we just follow them.'

'How in God's name am I going to stop it happening?' I demanded, in utter frustration.

'We can start a file,' she said, finally jumping to the fact that I needed mollifying. 'You must keep a record of every nuisance call that comes in, then ring us and we'll officially log them.'

'Ah! At last.' I called down the phone with renewed hope. 'So then you can report it to the police.'

'No, madam, we ring the number and tell them off.'

'Tell them off?' I shouted, dumbfounded. 'And what good do you think that will do?'

'Sorry, madam,' she responded, any hint of concern vanishing. 'That's all we're legally allowed to do.'

This was my only hope.

'Okay,' I said, settling myself. 'So how quickly can you ring them up?'

'Not immediately. You have to log 20 or more nuisance calls a month before we can act.'

From this time on I began recording only the daytime calls. I couldn't let the phone ring incessantly at night, so we continued to unplug it as part of our bedtime routine. Each month the number of calls fell just below the magic total. Finally, I gave up. The phone pursuit persisted for over a decade. Randomly, but regularly. The eerie listening at the end of the line continued to haunt us.

Although Barbara's study was my favourite escape, as the year progressed it became an increasingly rare one. The addition of Katherine to our family meant another child to taxi to after-school events. Jeremy's plan to terrify her with Barbara's mannequin had been only partly successful. He lurked in doorways, and around corners, watching to catch a glimpse of the innocent Katherine tripping along the dim, dark corridor, an unknowing victim about to be traumatised by the mannequin. His anticipation mounted as he waited.

The next thing I knew he was gleefully teasing her.

'I saw you jump! You got a fright, you got a fright!' he sang. But I knew it was only wishful thinking on his part because she flatly denied being scared by it at all.

'No, I didn't. Dumb things like that don't frighten me.' Yip, I thought to myself, as cool as an ice tray. That was something I admired about Katherine: no matter what came her way, she handled it.

There is something snobby about ballet classes for young children. The phrase 'ballet mothers' was not coined by accident, but by close observation of the type. On the Darwinian scale this is a highly competitive species. While one ballet mother in a set of parents is probably an asset, two was not necessarily twice as good. More to the point, among ballet mothers it was unforgivable.

Poor Katherine tipped the scales at an incomprehensible three ballet mothers, which probably put her in the *Guinness Book of Records*. Since moving to Whanganui she had lost one. This was Julia, Sue's ex-husband's new partner. But I was still one too many for Whanganui. While mothers stared at us like they had just seen a *doppelgänger*, Katherine skipped into her ballet classes as if she were a princess.

Even so, it was tough for her because she arrived in Whanganui towards the end of the year when rehearsals for the Christmas performance of *The Nutcracker* were already underway, and all the major parts had been cast.

'Of course, you'll get a part next year,' we told her by way of commiseration. 'It's sad to miss this one, but there will be others.' Even I thought this was a bad bit of spin. Especially since Katherine loved her ballet and if she had stayed in Christchurch she would certainly have had a part in the Christmas production. The previous year she had been a pixie in the Southern Ballet's *Cabbage Patch Kids*. This year she was in line for promotion to a fairy. But Katherine was philosophical about it, much more philosophical than I would have been.

Sue had been in touch with the local ballet teacher over the phone, finding out the time and place of her first lesson. Wednesday at five o'clock in the teacher's private ballet studio finally came around, and we arrived a little early, as arranged.

We had rehearsed it. Sue was her mother, and I was a friend: a close friend. Yeah, yeah, I thought, I believe you, but thousands wouldn't. She'll smell a rat for sure. But we were determined to make this a one-mother-deal, for Katherine's sake. I needed to be introduced, though, in case Sue couldn't pick her up.

The ballet teacher's studio turned out to be a magnificent wood-panelled space, sumptuous enough to make Margot Fonteyn's eyes pop out. This was unexpected in small-town Whanganui. But as it turned out, it was the ballet teacher rather than the room that had the most impact. Katherine's teacher moved across the floor with effortless grace.

Shirley McDouall was small, straight-backed and looked like at any minute she might pirouette or fling her leg onto the barre and turn herself inside out. This was quite something because she was in her sixties. Her greying hair worn up in a bun was the only real indicator of her age. The skin on her face was finer and less sun-damaged than that of her contemporaries. She was a notable fund-raiser around town; her husband chair of the Chamber of Commerce and a district councillor. There was something local and parochial as well as travelled and cosmopolitan about Shirley McDouall.

It worried me that such a conventional woman would have to come to grips with such an unconventional family. And, although I stuck to the agreement and never gave anything away, from the moment I met her I knew it would only be a matter of time before she worked me out.

'So this is Katie,' she said as she welcomed us, clipboard in hand with our enrolment papers attached. 'Is that what you'd like to be called?'

Silence.

Although Katherine was an assertive member within the family, throwing the most spectacular tantrums on occasions, she was painfully shy in front of others.

'Katie would like to be called Katherine,' I declared, knowing that if I left it to her, we'd all be staring at the floor for the foreseeable future.

Almost immediately Katie had stepped off the plane, she'd announced to her mother that the old Katie was gone and from now on she wanted to be called Katherine. Sue struggled to remember it because she was so used to us calling her Katie. But I was not so connected to the old name that I couldn't remember the upgrade.

'That's a lovely name,' said the ballet teacher. 'Unfortunately, Katherine, all the roles in *The Nutcracker* have been filled and the chorus has been rehearsing for some time, so there's nothing I can offer you. I'm sorry about that.'

Katherine, who was holding Sue's hand, and whose eyes were still glued to the floor, shrugged her shoulders and said, 'That's okay.' However, I knew with a sharp pang of guilt that it wasn't.

'Just so long as you know and aren't too disappointed,' said her teacher.

Girls, all roughly Katherine's age, but shorter, began to pour into the room accompanied by their overdressed, overanxious mothers.

'I guess we had best get started,' the teacher said, then clapped her hands over the babble of excited conversation.

'Gels,' she called, when the chatter had almost subsided, 'it's time to settle down now. We have a new girl starting today.'

'Come on, Katherine,' she said, taking her by the hand, 'come and meet the class. We finish at 6.30pm promptly,' she said, turning to us. 'Can you make sure you're back here on time, because otherwise I have to wait behind until your child is picked up.'

With that we were dismissed.

Out on the street, we stood looking at each other, wondering what we could squeeze into an hour and a half of dance class. The exact same hour and a half that I usually like to relax in with a glass of wine.

'How about we go back to Barbara's and have a cup of coffee?' Sue suggested.

'My thoughts exactly, but I was thinking of a glass of wine.'

We negotiated. This time I would drink the wine and she would drive.

Not knowing the area very well, we got horribly lost on the way home. When finally we drove down Barbara's drive we were firing insults at each other over one another's map-reading capabilities and sense of direction. Things got nasty.

By the time we reached the flat we both needed a drink. I poured two glasses of Chardonnay and we collapsed into two white plastic picnic chairs. It was my first soporific moment of a day that had been hellishly busy.

'That's good,' I said, as I relaxed.

The next bit of conversation was devoted to damage control.

'No. I didn't mean you were useless at following directions, exactly . . .' And so the reconciliations continued until Sue looked at her watch.

'My God!' she exploded. 'Katherine! Quick, we're late.' We leapt up, dashed out to the car, and made the quickest exit down Barbara's drive we safely could. We didn't get as lost going back, but we did miss the turn-off and had to double back. When we arrived, the beautiful tree-lined street that had been full of parents' cars was empty, and at the gate stood the ballet teacher and Katherine, waiting. My heart sank. We were out of the car in a flash, gushing with apologies. I wouldn't say the ballet teacher was happy about it, but she was magnanimous.

'Well, never mind — I'm sure it won't happen again,' she said. 'I've been thinking about Katherine, and I do have a role for her in *The Nutcracker*. It's a character part. Too late for her to dance, but she can be a kitchen maid. How does that sound, Katherine?'

Silence.

Even though her eyes were still glued to the ground with shyness, it wasn't hard to tell from her expression that inside Katherine was glowing with pleasure.

'Wow, a character part, Katherine!' I exclaimed, when we got back in the car. 'Isn't that kind of your teacher to do that? And we're really sorry for being late.'

Katherine *was* thrilled. She turned up to every rehearsal, watching laborious runs and re-runs through tedious dance moves, until she got her little spot of limelight. She would move across the stage making sweeping motions with an imaginary broom. It was a small footnote to the main action, but huge proof that the ballet teacher had a heart.

In the dress rehearsal, she was given a broom and a costume all of her own. It was black, but she never complained. Even at that young age she knew that scullery maids cornered the market on drab and dreary. Sue put Katherine's make-up on first, then across it smeared her badge of honour:

cinders. After the last full dress rehearsal, Katherine came home and told us her character was involved in a top-secret surprise for the audience. She was pleased to have this inside information, and even when baited and cajoled by Jeremy she remained tight-lipped.

The build-up to the big night was huge. The performance was to be staged in the spectacular opera house. Whanganui had an art gallery, an opera house and a velodrome, all suggesting hopes for a big cultural and sporting future that never quite eventuated. But on occasions, especially around Christmas, the ticket-box opened, the floodlights burst into brilliance, and the opera house came to life. The building was magnificent, with richly decorated architraves and cornices and a ceiling of starry lights set in a vault fit for a palace.

The season was three nights long. We decided to go on the middle night when the production would, we hoped, be at its best.

On the opening night, Sue escorted Katherine in through the stage door at the rear. The performers were to robe and have their make-up done in the dressing room. The ballet teacher didn't want to let anything out of the bag.

'It's a madhouse in there,' Sue told me as she ducked her head to get in the passenger's seat.

'Do you think we should have gone to every performance?' I responded, feeling bad knowing that most of the other ballet mothers would.

'Nah,' she replied, 'one's enough for both of us, and I'll go to the final night as well.' So, we drove home wondering the whole time how things would go.

'We might as well have stayed,' I said, as the three of us, Jeremy included, got back in the car three hours later to pick Katherine up. 'I've done nothing but worry about how things went.' I knew Sue had been worried, too.

She got out of the car and dived into the scrum of pastel-coloured tutus that engulfed the stage door, eventually re-emerging with Katherine, in her black.

I manoeuvred the car out of the park and inched my way along with a jam of other parents and spectators until I broke free of the congestion.

'Well, how did it go? Tell us all about it,' asked Sue.

Silence.

'Come on, tell us how it went.'

Silence.

'Come on, Katherine, we're dying to know,' I prompted.

'Okay. Mostly,' she replied.

'Mostly!' shouted Jeremy. 'You were only on stage for a few seconds.'

'The bit that I did was okay. But the rat went out of control.'

'What rat?' challenged Jeremy, taking some real interest at last.

Then the whole story came out. The ballet teacher's secret weapon was a rat that was built over the top of a remote-control racing car so it could be directed from off-stage. The effect had been marvellous in the rehearsals. It was the sooty scullery maid's job to sweep the creature spectacularly into the wings as she went about her housework. At rehearsal, the rat was one of the best performers.

On opening night, it turned from star to saboteur. As Katherine began her spring-clean, lining up her broom behind the rat's bottom so she could push it off-stage, the rat went feral. It charged wildly in the opposite direction at top speed. With her broom now in proper pursuit, Katherine dashed after it. At first the audience believed this was part of the show. But then, in an electronic frenzy, the rat sped over ballet shoes, between legs, knocked over props, and bashed into the backdrop and curtains.

Katherine and the runaway rat careered around the stage. The audience began to laugh. This was more like the *Keystone Cops* than *The Nutcracker*. Finally, in desperation, Katherine cornered the recalcitrant rodent and whacked it on the head with her broom. Pretending it was dead, she picked it up and swiftly carried it off-stage to the resounding applause of the entire audience.

The next night was much tamer. The rat behaved itself and Katherine provided us with a seamless performance. On the final night, when Sue went on her own, the robotic rodent was back to its old tricks. Once again Katherine had to kill it and haul it off, supposedly dead.

'Not again!' I exclaimed when I picked them up. 'I thought they'd fixed it up. Did the audience laugh again?'

'Yes.'

'Were you upset?'

'No.'

That was Katherine for you. She took on every challenge with a calm self-assurance. Even a deranged rat was no match for her calm, cool, eye.

The rest of the year evaporated and the Christmas custody arrangements were once more back on the table to be contested. This meant more unpleasant appointments with the lawyer to hammer out the last details. It was hard for me to hear, but Alex would not be with us at all over the summer break, and Jeremy was to spend Christmas in Christchurch with his father.

I began to realise that the chances of my seeing Alex again were slipping away. This was heart-breaking, and, on top of this, there was the ever-present fear that if I delivered Jeremy to Richard for Christmas he might never be returned. Maybe Richard felt desperate enough about things to snatch him back? I don't suppose things, in truth, were any more certain for Katherine. It would always be up to her whether she stayed with us or not, and that seemed an awful weight to put on a child's shoulders.

Our drive out to the airport was a mix of feelings. The children were out of school and off to see their fathers, and the excitement of Christmas Day was ahead. This was also a hiatus in the legal proceedings, a chance for us to be together on our own for a bit. But, in my darker moments, I knew both the peace and the pleasure were fragile. My fear was always there, lurking, following me, a constant companion. I had lost so much. Fear hosted every horror my imagination could invent. My greatest dread was losing the people I loved: Sue, Jeremy, Katherine, Alex and Jason. Like a person drowning, I clung white-knuckled to the wreckage of my life: too tight, too suffocating, too much. I wanted not to care whether I was breathing water or air, whether I floated or sank. But the survivor in me knew that it mattered.

We drove home from the airport engrossed in our own thoughts. Our flat at the back of Barbara's house echoed with a strange hollowness. For the first time in many years it had resounded with children's laughter and voices. Now it was still again.

Sue and I were driving down to Golden Bay. We had tickets booked on the Interislander ferry in a day or so. The children would join us there after Christmas. But now things were suddenly quiet; not so much us as the house. Its emptiness and its darkness returned.

The next morning, I went for a run, as I did most days. Down St John's Hill, around Victoria Lake and then back again. All my best ideas came when I ran. Somewhere, while I was sweating my way up the long sweep of the hill and down Barbara's drive, I had a brainwave. It bubbled up from nowhere, and I was eager to tell Sue. I burst into our flat calling out to her.

'Sue, Sue, I've just had the most amazing idea!' I was still running as I entered the lounge. There in the passageway between the bedrooms was Sue. But when I looked again, she'd disappeared. A bit rude, I thought. Assuming she had gone into the children's room, I began exclaiming my epiphany again. I threw the door open, expecting to regale her with my brilliance — and there was no one there. I stood in the doorway, disorientated for a moment.

How could that be? And then I realised, of course, that she must have gone into the door opposite: into our room. That's dumb, I thought, how could I get that wrong? Bounding across the passage, I pushed on the door, beginning my sentence again. As the door flung open, I launched into the room. There was no one there, and nowhere else to go. In the deepest way possible it frightened me. Like something had walked across my grave.

The burning thing I wanted to tell Sue had gone from my mind, and I can't remember what it was to this day. I finally found Sue having a bath in the bathroom area off the kitchenette.

'You won't believe what's just happened to me.' I was ashen.

'Would you mind passing me the soap? It's over there on the handbasin.'

'No. No. You've got to listen.'

'Okay. But would you mind passing the soap, first?'

So I told her about the figure of the woman I'd seen in the passageway. There for an instant, then gone. Sue looked unimpressed.

'Who do you think it was?' I finished.

'I don't know, but if I were you, I'd keep it to myself. I can just see the lawyer looking over her glasses when you tell her that one.'

'But you do believe me?'

'Look, it doesn't matter what I think, it's what they think. If you go around telling stories like that they'll think you're a nut case, for sure. You'll never see Jeremy again.'

I knew she was right, but that didn't stop the thing playing over and over in my mind. Had I seen someone in the passageway? Or was it just a flash from the plastic rim of my red glasses? The figure wasn't so much furtive as fleeting, standing outside the children's door. Was it that the children were not there and the vacuum drew something into the space? Or was it the stillness that invited her back?

Although I felt no sense of hostility or aggression from it, the experience scared me half to death.

VI

Where the Lewis ivories were carved and who carved them were of pressing interest to Frederic Madden. He needed proof of their provenance to build his case for the acquisition board when it met. For some time now the museum's interest had focused on exotic world histories — Greece, Rome, Egypt. This homely medieval army lacked the monumental drama of other things in the collection. Not knowing their pedigree would only further weaken Madden's case. Once again he headed for the Viking sagas, hoping they would help him trace their lineage.

Mostly the sagas recorded the exploits of great warriors, churchmen, earls and kings, but there were stories that also celebrated the artistry of carvers, illuminators and goldsmiths. One such record was an Icelandic story entitled *The Saga of Bishop Páll*. This mid-thirteenth-century saga tells — remarkably — of a woman carver, Margaret the Adroit, who at the time was the most skilled carver in all Iceland. The legend explains that 'Bishop Páll sent many gifts to his friends abroad, both gyrfalcons and other treasures', and that 'Margaret made everything the bishop wanted.'

Margaret, who was a rare and talented artist, lifted the crozier she was carving up to the light. The piece was not much longer than the palm of her hand, yet it was covered in a twisting, writhing bestiary of figures. The most chilling yet also captivating creature was the dragon, which was savaging a smaller beast, pinning its victim with its beak and tearing the animal's flesh with its cruel mouth. This was Hell in ivory, and the lithe snake-like dragon with its teardrop eyes was the Devil. Below the dragon-devil was a montage of damnation, with figures twisting and turning around the crozier's neck.

The crozier was Margaret's most magnificent piece yet. She twirled the creamy object in her fingers so she could see its grain. Its swirling rings were patterned like a milky-white agate. She had watched the form emerge. The walrus ivory had still carried the stench of death when she had cut this piece from the base of the tusk. Ivory is unforgiving, hard to shape, yet prone to shatter like glass. A flaw invisible to the eye could do it: something in the beast's history, in its slaughter, or the rough-hewn treatment of the primitive saw. Each day had its apprehensions, especially because this was a work to celebrate the consecration of Páll Jónsson in Trondheim. Páll had commissioned the crozier himself, and Margaret and her husband, Thorir, who was priest assistant to Páll, were to travel with him to Trondheim.

A rough chisel-mark was revealed as she held the object closer to the light. She wet her finger in a basin and picked up some fine-grained sand and rubbed the ivory with the mild abrasive until the line disappeared. Then she polished the surface with wood ash and horsetail grass. These finishing touches were only possible in strong daylight.

The sea voyage from Skálholt in Iceland to Trondheim in Norway was long and dangerous. It was late in the summer season, and the risk of an early storm would normally make her hesitate about the wisdom of such a journey. But if she chose not to go, her husband, Thorir, would be away through the long winter and for some months afterwards. This protracted separation would be cruel as there were no children, just them, and she would be alone. Trondheim was also a place of pilgrimage and wealth. Travellers from many far-flung shores met there to worship and trade. Margaret was hoping to pick up another ecclesiastical commission and carve while she was there. She also hoped to replenish her supplies of ivory; the traders had not been through Skálholt for months now.

The voyage went without incident. Settled weather held the late summer storms at bay. As they sailed up the fiord of Trondheim, Margaret felt a sense of exhilaration. The cliffs of the fiords loomed skyward. They were stark and magnificent, much higher than any cathedral. They were God's cathedrals. Margaret squeezed Thorir's hand as they approached the wharf; he returned her gesture with a smile.

Svein shifted restlessly from one area of his ivory-carving studio to another. What bothered him most was the damage to his reputation. He had a premium place amongst carvers: generally he was regarded as the greatest carver in Trondheim. What disturbed him was the work of Margaret the Adroit. The studio was working on a large commission, four chess sets for the Archbishop of Trondheim. To fulfil the order quickly, Svein had taken on Margaret's services. Now he wished he had not. Looking at her ivories was torture.

He moved over to the bench where she worked, lifting up a piece she was carving to examine the detailing. Swallowing with difficulty the lump in his throat, he looked at it. How did she do it? What techniques had she used to capture that expression on the queen's face, and the king? he thought, exchanging one piece on the bench for the other. Exquisite. Svein had watched her out of the corner of his eye. Stood behind her, quietly observing, hating her. The work was so fine. Svein worried that if the archbishop realised the quality of her carving he would never get work again. Sometimes it was all that he could do to stop himself from taking a mallet and knocking off their heads.

While it might satisfy his urge to destroy her work, it would only put them behind on their delivery date. Svein was working on a set, and so was Amundi, Thorstein and, of course, Margaret. Any delays would be disastrous. Already they were anxiously awaiting the arrival of supplies of ivory from Helluland. A ship was expected any day. Margaret's bench reflected the situation; she had carved the king and queen and some smaller pieces from a length of tusk she had brought to Trondheim with her. The rest of the ivory the workshop had supplied. Completion of the four knights demanded cutting a broad section from the base of a tusk. The consignment could only be completed once the new supplies had arrived.

This commission was as highly paid as it was risky. His carvers, including Margaret, had sworn an oath not to reveal the nature of their work. The order to produce the sets had not come from the archbishop directly, but from his special envoy, a monk known as Brother Dominic. According to the monk, the archbishop's name was never to be mentioned because the playing of chess was despised by many influential people in the Church, especially the Abbot Absalom. The carvers were being paid not just for their skill, but for their silence.

Svein jumped at a sudden rap at the door: he was on his own. The knock came again. There were rumours that the abbot might punish anyone breaking the

Church rules over chess. He quickly removed the pieces from Margaret's work area, putting them out of sight on a shallow shelf underneath the bench. The banging came again, this time more urgently. Muffled, but still audible, he could hear someone calling his name. The voice sounded angry and impatient.

'Hello... hello there,' he called back, trying to calm the person as he moved swiftly to open the door. He had barely turned the key in the lock and lifted the latch when the door pushed open. To his relief he recognised his caller. It was Bjorn.

'Where were you, man? What kind of welcome is this?'

Bjorn, he noted, looked pale and troubled. His snowy-blond hair hung into his eyes in threads damp with perspiration. He laboured under the heavy weight he carried, and was limping badly. Even though Bjorn's burden was disguised by its fabric cover, Svein knew what it was.

'Ivory!' he exclaimed in delight. 'You've brought us more ivory.' Bjorn and his brother Thorvald were the workshop's suppliers. With some difficulty he took the bundle of tusks off Bjorn and, staggering under the weight, moved over to lay them carefully on the bench.

'Where's Thorvald?'

'He's dead.'

'Dead?' Svein repeated, in disbelief. 'How?'

'He was killed by Skraeling. They cut off his head. I burned his body along with other dead kinsmen on a beach in Helluland.'

'Oh, my God,' Svein said in a rare empathetic moment, before his mind switched to the matter of supply.

'Will you be making more voyages, then?'

'I don't know,' Bjorn replied, staring at the uncovered section of ivory as if he were in a trance. 'Time will tell. I have to make a voyage to Dublin. After I return, I will think again.'

The threat to the future of his ivory supplies worried Svein far more than the loss of Thorvald's life. He hadn't even liked Thorvald, who was way too hard a bargainer for Svein's liking. He wondered whether the younger brother would be as difficult.

'So, the price?' he said, uncovering the tusks completely so he could assess their value. They were in fine condition. 'I'll offer you ten gold pieces a tusk,' he said, knowing they were worth far more.

'Ten gold coins — ten! You must think I'm mad,' Bjorn said, as he reached across the table to wrap up the ivory and go.

'No,' Svein called out, grabbing his arm to stop him, 'don't do that. How about 12?' Several more offers were rejected before a price was finally settled upon.

'You've robbed me,' Svein concluded, placing the money on the bench grudgingly.

But Bjorn was in no mood to accept such an affront. Grabbing the carver by his neckscarf, he lifted him off the ground. 'This pittance you've paid is the price of my brother's life! You should be ashamed of yourself.' With that, he dropped the terrified carver back to the floor, scooped up the coins and left.

No one was more pleased that the new ivory had arrived than Margaret the Adroit. It was excellent quality, and broad enough to easily accommodate the knight mounted on his Icelandic pony. She had observed Icelandic ponies for years, and would draw on that knowledge to bring the creature alive. Svein had already taken the best pieces of ivory for himself, but there were enough good bits left to complete her set.

She took the first piece she had hewn from the tusk and coated it in chalk. Into the chalky ground she incised the lines she would follow as a guide. They were only a beginning. Quickly they would disappear and she would work from the copybook of patterns the studio kept, and from her own instincts and experience.

Her fellow carvers crowded around her section of the workbench to admire each face as it was released from its ivory mask. Everyone, that is, except Svein, whom she regarded as a jealous, joyless man. He envied her. She could feel it. Although she had enjoyed Trondheim and working in the ivory studio, Svein was someone she would not miss. The commission was almost ready to be handed over and he would certainly take the credit for her work.

CHAPTER FOURTEEN

An Amputation

Conflict over possessions tears families apart. Living with Barbara at Ringley we encountered a fierce feud over the ownership of inherited property. Between Barbara and her nine other siblings there was an element of resentment. Barbara had inherited almost everything from the three aunts, and no one felt the injustice of this more keenly than her older sister Jean. Both were wealthy spinsters, and they loved to hate each other. Barbara's theory was that Jean bore more than a passing resemblance to Dorothy.

'Mad,' Barbara declared, 'mad as a March hare.' There was so much animosity in Barbara's descriptions of Jean that I pictured her as someone deranged. So, when I finally met her, I was pleasantly surprised.

I was researching down in the basement of the Sarjeant Art Gallery when one of the staff informed me that Jean was upstairs and hoping to meet me. The gallery was neutral territory for the sisters. Jean was rarely invited to Ringley.

I was expecting there to be a family likeness. Jean was about 10 years older than Barbara, who was the baby of the family. As Barbara was short and rotund, Jean was tall and ethereal. While one was clay-footed and connected, the other floated languidly like she had been delivered on a gust of wind. Or sometimes, I thought, perhaps by broomstick. Her hair, in opposition to Barbara's short, straight locks, stuck out in a wild frizz like a half-erected umbrella. She wore black sheer fabrics. Her make-up was applied in bursts of fitful concentration as she squinted into the mirror. Frequently her lipstick was smeared and one eye more accentuated with shadow than the other. Her voice was croaky and rough, with a pitch that drilled itself into you.

The thing that was quintessentially Jean was her fingernails. They were deeply corrugated, sharply pointed, and always had a dot of nail polish on them that never reached the edges. Like her sister, there was something of the farmer's daughter there, a rough readiness to counter her vagueness.

At our first meeting, I stood in front of her, gaping, speechless like a ventriloquist's dummy, not quite making sense of the difference between the sisters. My first utterances were nonsense comments to fill the awkward space. Fortunately, she didn't seem to notice.

'I hope you will visit me,' she said when our conversation warmed. 'You must come and see my house, which looks out over Virginia Lake.'

I didn't take up her offer at first. After mentioning the idea to a stony-faced Barbara, I decided it was impolitic to do so. But whenever we bumped into each other in town, or at the gallery, she would repeat the invitation.

'Come and see my paintings of Edie's' — which was what Jean called Edith — 'and bring that nice friend of yours, what's her name?'

'Suzanne.'

'And bring the children.'

Much to my relief the children had been safely returned to our care. I had fretted and paced until their arrival, while Sue's eyes rolled skyward at me in mock derision. While her coolness was balm to my soul, I never completely stemmed that fight-or-flight flow of adrenaline that fed my anxiety as the minutes counted down to their arrival.

'Okay, so don't let the cat out of the bag,' I said to the children when we picked them up after school. This was code for don't tell the nice lady that you have two mothers.

'Best behaviour, okay?' I finished. It never failed to amaze me how intuitive they were about the issue. Now I realise this was the survival mechanism of children in queer relationships. We were a liability for them. We opened a box of difficult secrets best kept hidden.

Just as you get to Virginia Lake, going up St John's Hill, there's a steep, overgrown drive. Sections of it — where the concrete has broken away — are rough, rutted shingle. At the top was Jean's house: a single-storeyed modernist home built in the 1960s or 1970s, with a view to die for. As soon as our car pulled up, Jean was out to greet us, croaking a welcome and smiling slyly because she had out-manoeuvred Barbara, at last.

'Come in. Come in,' she said directing us past a plot of plastic flowers that she had stuck in the ground around the front entrance. Out of the corner of my eye, I saw the children nudging each other and pointing at the plastic flowerbed. Oh, no, I thought, they are going to misbehave. It was a risky business mixing my eccentric family and professional lives together.

'Through here,' Jean called, ushering us into her spacious lounge that overlooked the lake. More eye-catching than the picture-window view, however, was an enormous sunken area in the floor full to the brim with balls of wool. Later Sue explained to me that this was a conversation pit.

'Would the children like a lemonade?' Jean had arranged a little table with long glasses for the soft drinks and wine goblets for us. There was also a plate of chocolate-coated toffee biscuits. I could see Jeremy's hand twitching.

'Would you like a chocolate biscuit, Jeremy?' Jean asked.

'Yes, please,' said Jeremy, grabbing one.

'Have as many as you like.' That was Jean, generous to a fault: indulgent of everyone, including herself.

Once the children were settled at the table with their lemonade and biscuits, she poured us a glass of wine each.

'Yes,' she said after she was seated and had taken her first mouthful, 'I'm very lucky to have this place.' Then she turned to us both and asked: 'Have you seen my lovely wool? I've been collecting these balls for years.'

I didn't quite know what to say; I'd never met a wool hoarder before.

'Awesome,' I responded, trying to sound enthusiastic: 'so many different colours. Is there a pattern to your collecting?'

'No. Just whatever catches my eye. I go for colour and what will look nice. I've got some very expensive French wool that cost me $30 a skein. Look, I'll show you.' With that Jean got up from her end of the couch and walked over to the woolly mammoth and extracted half a dozen balls.

Even I — a shopper who feels five minutes trying on clothes is four minutes too long — was impressed. They were beautiful. As I handed them back to her, I looked up to see Jeremy glancing sheepishly in our direction with a ring of chocolate around his lips.

'I hope you haven't eaten all those biscuits.' I looked at the plate. Just a token one left.

'You'll never eat your dinner, you two.'

'Aaw,' croaked Jean, 'I wouldn't worry about that. They'll be alright.'

Knowing the damage was already done and that our hostess was unperturbed, I sat back.

'So, are you planning to do anything special with the wool, Jean?' Sue asked. She was petting a couple of magnificent balls like the true shopper she is.

'It's a little business I've got on the side,' she chuckled. 'I get my ladies who live locally to knit them into jerseys for me, and I sell them to pay for my trips to the USA. I take two enormous suitcases filled to the brim with hand-knitted jerseys. I used to send them but the tax got so high, so now I just take them with me.'

'Is that legal?' I asked.

Jean laughed. 'What they don't know won't hurt them.'

'So Jean's a cardie smuggler,' said Sue under her breath after we were in the car and well away from the house.

'Looks like it. I wonder how she's going to explain 50 woolly jumpers and not another stitch of clothing in her case to the American Customs authorities when they open her bags.'

And, of course, it happened. On one of her USA visits, Jean was arrested for dealing in illicit woollies. Border control opened her bags, and a cornucopia of jerseys sprung out.

'Surely, ma'am, you are not intending to wear that many jerseys in Los Angeles in summer?'

Jean had to come clean.

'No,' she admitted, 'they are not all mine. They are gifts.' This was a worthy attempt at subterfuge, but when she was asked to list the people who were to receive them, and could only come up with a handful of names, she was nicked.

The contraband was confiscated, and Jean was given a formal warning and a hefty fine, which she had enormous difficulty paying in American dollars.

Barbara was rubbed raw by our visits to Jean and resistant to any peace-making efforts on our part, although she came begrudgingly to accept them.

Meanwhile our custody battle continued, and, in spite of Barbara's enchanted house and a property big enough to run wild in, it was a battle keeping the children with us. Richard would ring Jeremy and cry on the phone, or send him sad letters about his old life in Christchurch and how much they missed him. It was a struggle to keep making what we had to offer them look good. At any stage, the children could say 'I've had enough of this weird existence with two mothers', and they would have been whisked back to their fathers on the first plane. The counsel for the child for Jeremy was hovering in the background, seemingly itching to be kingmaker and return the stolen prince, just waiting for us to fall over. There were many days when I thought we would. Our existence as a family and even as a couple was precarious.

I worried about Jeremy at school. Whanganui was a small, tight-knit, parochial community. There were few spaces in its fabric for new arrivals, and most of them were at the bottom of the pile where life was more fluid and fragile.

It was here that Jeremy met Cody, a sweet-natured, finely built, young part-Māori boy. He was clever, agile and should always have done much better at school than he did. Jeremy and Cody became the Laurel and Hardy of the school playground. Cody was the inspiration for many of the dodgy things they did, and Jeremy the muscle. Together they were an unbeatable team.

Rumours circulated about Cody's family, but I liked his mother.

It was inevitable that Jeremy would want to go there and stay overnight, especially after the kittens were born. Cody owned the mother cat, and Sam, Cody's brother, the father cat, and neither of the cats had been de-sexed.

'Can I have the mostly white kitten?' Jeremy asked me after his first visit to see the kittens. I was keen to try to make things good for the children, to draw them in, and to secure our survival.

My answer 'No, you can't', became a 'maybe', then 'You'll have to ask Sue...'

'I can't believe you said that,' she snapped at me as soon as Jeremy got out of the car to go and play at Cody's. 'It's blackmail. If I say "no", I look like the ogre. It's not fair. And what about Katherine?'

Unfortunately, Katherine had also seen the kittens and wanted one, too. 'That's not all,' Sue continued at an ever-increasing volume. 'I wanted a purebred cat, not a mongrel!'

'Have you seen them, though? They're so sweet. Let's just take two to keep the kids happy. I've asked Barbara if it's okay. She said "yes" to one. So, we can probably squeeze in another.'

Sue looked dubious.

176 The Queen's Wife

'But even if it's okay with Barbara, are you sure we've got the money? Owning pets is expensive, and you know what happened last time. It was a complete disaster.'

She was right, and I knew it. We were haemorrhaging money with the custody case. Not only were there exorbitant lawyers' fees, but also expensive flights nearly every holiday, new schools, new uniforms, and the multiple medical appointments deemed necessary for Jeremy's good health. Often well before the end of a pay packet there was nothing left.

I knew I should refuse to have them. One day I would make one risky move too many and we would all go under; I just hoped the kittens wouldn't be it.

'I just can't say "no", Sue. We'll have to manage it somehow. The kids have had such a demanding time. It would be nice to give them something special that's theirs.'

As it transpired, although I won the toss, the game hadn't even started.

We picked up the kittens. Jeremy took possession of his little white female with tortoise-shell sprinkles, but Katherine and Sue made a late substitution.

'If you want one with lots of character,' Cody's mother said, 'take this one.' They had been scrutinising the four little long-haired orange-and-white toms and had chosen one from birth, but at the last minute they took Cody's mother's advice.

We called them Tigger and Petal. Although they were too small to be taken from their mother, they had become a burden and Cody's mum was keen to re-home them as quickly as possible. They looked very tiny even in Katherine's thin arms.

Unfortunately, some of the crucial learning regarding their development had not yet happened. They had left the litter before the lesson on grooming, and as a consequence knew nothing about that, let alone toilet training. I remember looking longingly at other cats, legs in the air consumed by their toilette, and wondering where ours went wrong. We called them 'polecats', especially Petal, who never learned anything much about personal hygiene, and often had a rangy odour.

But it was toileting that gave us grief. They had no idea at all. We started with a dirt box all pristine and full to the brim with litter. I put them in it, one by one. Made straining noises, creased my face with the effort of a phantom bowel movement, then grabbed their paws and pretended to cover it up.

'There,' I said, when I'd finished the tutorial, 'that's how you do it.' Sorted, I thought, as I went to bed on their first night with us. The next day was a scatologist's dream. Miniature poohs embellished the skirting boards and took pride of place just a foot or so from the dirt box as if to taunt us. Even at six or seven weeks old these kittens were masters in the arts of psychology. They were already adept at manipulating their human owners to cause the greatest possible disturbance.

'I think they need newspaper,' announced Sue. 'And at least there's one pooh near the box.'

'They're doing just fine without reading a newspaper,' I said, looking at the wreath of poohs dotted around the children's bedroom.

'Don't be smart,' Sue retorted. 'I just don't think they want to use the dirt box at the moment.'

My God, I thought, she's right. The sides were high and formidable. Newspaper would make things effortless.

'Okay, you go grab some newspaper and I'll clean up the misfires.'

What a saint, I thought, as I grabbed the brush and shovel and began the hideous task of wiping down the carpet. We left the kittens curled up innocently on the end of the bed, then delivered the children to school, and drove to the polytechnic. Sue had managed to pick up some hours teaching on the foundation art programme and was loving it.

It was after 5pm before we were all back at the flat again.

The smell hit us as we came through the sliding door.

'Gross, that's awful,' Katherine grimaced.

I didn't even have to look. The newspaper was in pristine condition, but there were what my brother calls 'landmines' everywhere.

'Okay, Dr Doolittle,' I demanded of Sue, 'what next?'

'They were your idea in the first place,' she responded, handing me the brush and shovel. 'Better get this lot cleaned up before Barbara sees.'

I glanced over and saw the kittens in almost exactly the same position as they had been when we'd left them in the morning; I couldn't believe how innocent they looked.

'I've got it!' I shouted after I'd been cleaning a while. 'Let's put some of the poohs on the paper, so they know that's where they belong.'

They proved to be the only poohs that made the newspaper. In fact, they stayed there on display so long that Sam the dog sneaked through the sliding door one day and devoured the lot.

When we drove south to Christchurch at Easter to prepare our house there for renting out, the kittens were too young to go to a cattery. There was no choice: we had to take them with us.

It was a very long trip, reaching a climax of misery when I stepped in the kittens' milk, spilling it all over the floor mats as I got back in to drive the car off the ferry at Picton. The children were delivered to their fathers door-to-door this time, and the plan was that Sue and I would spend the time scrubbing walls, cleaning carpets, and working in the garden of our Dovedale Avenue duplex. Our small courtyard area was full of blooming camellias. I checked to see the little rose bush I had planted between the camellias was still there, and it all looked so sumptuous and pretty that I longed to stay. But there was no chance of a job for me in Christchurch, and no return to any semblance of my old life. Now the legal contest was entrenched, the game had assumed its own dangerous momentum. There was no turning back until the contest had been lost or won.

The children were to holiday with their fathers, then spend some time with my parents in Golden Bay. After that, my parents would put them on a bus to meet up with Sue at Picton, and travel across with her on the ferry to Wellington, then drive to Whanganui. I had to fly back early to Whanganui to resume work at the polytechnic.

Even in our duplex in Christchurch the kittens proved resistant to potty training. On Sue's last night in the house before she left it for our tenants, she arrived home late from dinner with friends to find the house had been carpet-bombed by the kittens. It had to be pristine for the tenants, so there was nothing for it: the cleaning gear, which had been packed away in the car, was taken out again and the carpets cleaned. It was very late before she got to bed. Her departure was delayed again in the morning. More cleaning, then re-packing. By the time she was on the motorway heading north, she was dangerously late to meet the kids and get on the ferry.

I received the message at the end of my teaching for the day. The switchboard operator at the polytechnic had received a call. Sue had had a car accident driving from Christchurch to Picton to pick up the kids.

'What sort of an accident?' I asked.

'I'm sorry, I don't know. The call came from a motorist at the scene of the crash. He said someone would be in touch with more information, and the message was to tell you that they would ring you on Barbara's cellphone.'

Barbara had lent me her mobile, which was the missing link in the evolution of mobile phones. And a bit of a misnomer, too, as it was the size, shape and weight of a small Tardis.

'Did you get any impression of what's happened from what he said?' I asked.

'Not really, but you'd think if it had been a fatality he would have told me.'

These words were slim comfort as I paced the floor with Barbara's cellphone in my hand, waiting for it to ring. All possible scenarios went through my mind from mortal injury to death. But perhaps the craziest thought to cross my panic-stricken mind, or it seems the craziest now — but back then it was a reality — was that it would be Sue's ex-husband who would be officially notified: I had no legal rights to be with her in hospital. All I could do was pray. Although disenchanted with formal religion, I hoped nearly 12 years married to an Anglican clergyman had earned me some brownie points upstairs.

I was in the teachers' workroom when the mobile began to ring. I jumped violently. It was a reflex. Fear, adrenaline: it felt like someone had pulled a trigger. My hand shook as I pushed the button.

It was such a relief to hear Sue's voice.

'Are you okay?'

'I've crashed the car into a lamp-post and it's written-off. The front is smashed in. There's no hope for it.'

'But you — are *you* okay?'

'I'm so lucky. I've got whiplash, I think, and I'm bruised. But the man who stopped to help me said he thought I'd be dead, that no one could survive such a bad crash. He said I should go out and buy a Lotto ticket because it's a miracle I'm alive.'

'How did it happen?'

'I'm not sure. I think I fell asleep at the wheel. One minute I was driving along, and the next I'd crashed into a power pole and the whole front of the car was smashed in and the horn was blaring.'

'Where are you now?'

'On the stretch of highway just past Kaikōura. The victim support person is here already and they're going to drive me to Blenheim, where they will put me on a bus to Picton.' Picton was where we had originally arranged to meet the children.

'Right. I'll drive down and pick you up in Wellington. I'm so relieved you're okay. Are the kittens still alive?'

'Yes. Amazingly, they've survived. They must have been badly tossed around, but when I came to and looked back, they were sitting up wide-eyed in their cage and completely silent for the first time on the trip.'

I was still stressed and in shock when I left Whanganui in a borrowed car for the three-hour drive to Wellington. Close to the township of Paraparaumu, the five o'clock traffic started to get heavy. The day was still, the car stuffy and my concentration was lapsing. I'll have a coffee, I thought, a quick in-and-out from the drive-through.

It took a matter of minutes. I rested the paper cup between my legs, and with both hands firmly on the wheel, I attempted to find a gap in the oncoming traffic. For a split second there was a pause. In an explosive instant, squealing wheels, I launched into the traffic. Once across and in the far lane I accelerated one more time to match the flow.

It was probably at that point that the hot coffee balanced in my lap tipped over and the scalding liquid ran between my legs. It was excruciating. My trousers filled with boiling coffee, and, to avoid at least some of the blistering heat, I stood up, my left foot still on the accelerator. I was hurtling along with my bottom off the seat in 'thank-God-it's-Friday' home-bound traffic.

I could already feel the effects of the burning on my inner thighs. How bad was it? I wondered. And how was I going to explain it to Accident and Emergency, or face showing anyone the injury?

There was no chance of pulling over. No shoulder on my side of the road. I would just have to keep going. As the coffee-soaked fabric cooled, it acted as a compress. The sensation of burning was still intense, but there was some relief. By the time I reached a section of the road where I could pull off, I didn't. The damage was already done.

I found a park at the ferry terminal, turned off the engine, opened the driver's door and extracted myself from the car as gingerly as possible. I walked to the ladies' toilet like a novice rider after a day at pony club. The skin was scalded, but I was beginning to hope it wouldn't require a visit to the doctor. I hadn't met my Whanganui doctor yet, and didn't fancy scalded inner thighs being the reason for our introduction. Fortunately, my trousers were dark so the coffee stain was hard to see.

I left the outdoor toilet to find the arrival area. A cool wind had begun to blow off the sea. It was something I wouldn't normally welcome, but today it was bliss. The terminal was stark and industrial, dominated by a snaking luggage carousel and rows of stiff bench-seats.

I had only been there a few minutes when the conveyor belt lurched with a shudder into action. It was not long before the rubber curtain parted and the first suitcases came through in dribs and drabs. Then they began to flow in a steady but disorderly fashion. I glanced over at the large doorway where passengers were disembarking. No sign of Sue and the children yet, I thought as I watched for them. When I looked back at the section reserved for oversized luggage, I saw two dazed kittens sitting in their cage staring blankly back at me.

They looked none the worse for their ordeal, but was it my imagination that I detected a little guilt over their contribution to events? Sue, when she finally arrived with the children in tow, looked much more knocked around by the experience. The thing, though, that came off worst was our much-loved Telstar. It was towed to a garage in Kaikōura and sat outside in the wind and rain until the insurers assessed it, and the courier picked up our belongings and carried them north to Whanganui. Saying goodbye to the car, for Sue, was parting with a memory of her parents. So there was more grief in the farewell than normal.

Back in Wellington, we loaded kids, kittens and suitcases into the back of the car I'd borrowed from the polytechnic. It was pitch black, with no moon up above the snaking road that twists and turns along the Kāpiti coast. It wasn't long before everyone but me was asleep. Although my eyes were heavy and straining to see the road, I decided not to risk another take-away coffee.

VI

There is another picture of Irihapeti, in the National Library. A later photograph. Less grainy. The studio lighting amplified. The camera modernised in the decade or so that has passed between this photograph and the earlier one we had found. The date is 1860–61, and Irihapeti is dressed in black. There is fire in her character still, and a laconic smile that has witnessed the abundance and cruelty of life. Irihapeti is a widow. The man who powered her waka, John Horton McKay, is dead. McKay's watery grave was a swollen river he attempted to cross in flood.

Irihapeti's dress is mourning attire. An elegant black hat is perched fascinator-like on her greying hair. Around her neck is a necklace, the sort of costume jewellery used as a prop in photographic studios. On anyone else it might look heavy — a string of awkward black diamond shapes inset with domed circles — but on Irihapeti it looks regal.

Her expression hides the agonies behind it. There is the loss of her husband in 1859, and the grief of her father's death in 1860, but also the angst of not knowing how she will support her 12 children, the last of whom is only a few years old.

Photographs like this one of Irihapeti, taken by the Burton Brothers, were

Whakapapa: Sue's Ancestry **183**

syndicated. They were sent to other studios around the country where they were printed on postcards with facetious titles, such as 'Queen Emma of the Thames', and sold to the general public. Maybe this exploitation is the price Irihapeti paid for a copy of her image? A picture of grief, a memorial to her father and husband.

Irihapeti would find salvation for a time with another Highland clansman, a Scotsman named Samuel Joyce. The consummation of this late marriage required a move for Irihapeti from her store at Putataka to Raglan. At this time, there were 424 inhabitants there, with a Māori settlement and pā across the harbour at Horea. Raglan had just changed its name from Whāingaroa, and boasted just half a dozen houses, a tavern and a store.

The heat in this union, however, would quickly dissipate. In spite of having a further three children with Samuel Joyce, Irihapeti's marriage was neither a happy nor a productive one. Her second husband was a drinker and his ways were profligate.

Irihapeti, a devout woman, born and bred among a people who were coming to see alcohol as the scourge of their culture, lived as long as she could with Samuel Joyce, then fled. Homeless and now destitute, she went to live with her adult daughter Clara, who provided Irihapeti with a refuge, but not a permanent home of her own.

While Irihapeti could accept the tragic loss of her beloved first husband and the misfortunes of marrying Samuel Joyce, she would not accept homelessness in a land her people owned. The warrior spirit that had been her father's, that knew the value of land, and had fought in hand-to-hand combat for it, would not let her rest. She wanted what was rightfully hers. Her people had shaped the hills and valleys, creating terraced gardens and redoubts, felling trees for waka, clearing pathways and digging kūmara pits. The stories of her forebears could be read in each contour and plain.

Irihapeti's battle would be waged in the Land Courts, where, in 1874, she had to prove to a hostile authority that she was the unacknowledged first child of the late King Te Wherowhero. The land she was seeking had been confiscated by Governor Grey on the false pretext that Waikato Māori might attack Auckland. Ultimately, a tribunal was established to decide what land would be returned, and to whom. Irihapeti took her case to court along with many others: a widow, a neglected wife, fighting single-handedly for the rights of her mokopuna. She would not be intimidated. She would not be overpowered by an unsympathetic system.

Irihapeti fought courageously, and for the outcome, she would wait.

CHAPTER FIFTEEN

Whanganui, a City Divided

Our intention had always been to move out of Barbara's and into a place of our own. My encounter with the ghostly apparition added heat to a plan already boiling.

But finding good accommodation in Whanganui was difficult. It was a city of extremes, and this was reflected in the rental market. There were palatial properties at the high end, and hovels at the other. The middle ground was slim and quickly picked over. But at Barbara's I felt like I was living on a volcano. There was the imminent possibility of the outing of Sue and me. This was code red on the scale of personal disasters. The longer we stayed, the bigger the risk.

One day, against my good advice, Jeremy came home with a radical haircut. Barbara lost her cool. I had never seen her so angry as when she saw him. Jeremy, whose haircut did look very teen-trendy, was thrust up against the wall, Barbara running her fingers roughly through the long locks that hung down over the under-cut sides.

'Don't be like those dirty, filthy homos, Jeremy. You cut your hair like that and people will think you're one of them. Dirty, disgusting *animals*.' The violence of the outburst shocked us.

'Come on, Jeremy, let's go back to the flat,' I said, intervening. I had to get him away. There was no reasoning with Barbara in that mood, and I didn't want to escalate things. We left her seething, barely able to control her anger.

'What was *that* all about?' Sue demanded as soon as the sliding doors to the flat shut behind us.

'Are you okay, Jeremy?' I asked. He was visibly upset. 'I'm disappointed that you got that haircut, especially when I told you to get something ordinary, but Barbara was way out of line. She shouldn't have been so angry, and she shouldn't have said those things. We're obviously weighing on her. We need to go!'

That night when we were in bed, Sue asked me: 'Do you think she was really talking about us? You know, sort of picking things up subliminally?'

'I don't know, but it's pretty scary whatever the reason. Poor Jeremy — he thinks the world of Barbara.'

There was the ghost; there was us, in the closet; there were the kittens still popping out the occasional delight on the carpet for us or Sam the dog to clean up; and always in the background there were the lawyers battling like bishops across the board.

When the counsel for the child discovered that Jeremy and Katherine were sleeping in the same room, there was an instant fax. Sue and I were called in for a special meeting with our lawyer.

'Now, just let me get this clear: the children are sleeping together? You have a male and a female child sleeping in the same room?' our lawyer asked, stupefied.

'Yes,' I stuttered, 'but it's an enormous room and they're only young.'

'I don't care how old they are, or how big the room is: they have to have their own bedrooms. What you're doing is playing into the hands of the opposition. You can be inspected at any time, and if the children are found to be sleeping in the same room you will be ordered to provide separate bedrooms on the spot. This won't look good with the judge. You need to do something immediately.'

On the way home we picked up a property guide. We were going to have to take getting new accommodation a whole lot more seriously. The issue had become a game-changer.

School was another worry. Even with Cody as a friend, there were difficulties for Jeremy. There was the endemic problem of two mothers. How do you explain that to the children of conservative parents? Many parents were very narrow-minded and intolerant. There were exceptions, however, and one of them we hoped would be Jeremy's teacher.

Even before we met Mr Campbell, I noted that he was especially attentive to Jeremy. While I saw it as a positive, I was also suspicious. My ex-husband had already had an interview with him, and I knew he would have painted the grimmest possible picture of me and Sue. We were opponents, this was war, and Richard had made the pre-emptive strike over schooling.

Jeremy came home with encouraging comments in his exercise books, lots of stories about the teacher he began to admire greatly, and an invitation to try out for the junior boys' rugby team. Mr Campbell was the coach. Great, I thought, get Jeremy involved in sport and that will help him integrate into the community.

Meet-the-teacher evening came around just as we were beginning to find some balance to our lives.

'I better go to this one on my own,' I told Sue. 'Don't want to bring our relationship to his attention.'

'I'm not sure I'd worry about it too much. I'm sure Richard has done all the exposing he can.'

'You know, you're right. Mr Campbell will know the gory details. I'm sure that's why he's been so nice to Jeremy.'

'Yeah, let's brave it out together. There's no closet to hide in here.'

So, Sue and I went to the meet-the-teacher together as the parents of Jeremy. I remember waiting anxiously in the corridor outside Mr Campbell's room. Through the glass panel in his door, I glimpsed the parents before us seated, talking to him by his desk. St John's Hill was a wealthy suburb, and the children and their parents reflected this. The conventionally dressed couple smiled as they walked past us at the end of their appointment. Preparing myself, I breathed in deeply, wondering when these ordeals would end.

Sue and I went into the classroom and sat down uncomfortably on the two small wooden chairs.

Mr Campbell stood up, introduced himself and shook both our hands. He was a tallish, swarthy man with dark, lank hair, cut unflatteringly.

'I imagine you know about our situation,' I said, hoping to get the difficult part out of the way, first. 'You know there's a custody case involving Jeremy,' I continued.

'Yes,' he said, obviously familiar with the situation. 'I have already had a meeting with Jeremy's father.'

I knew it, I thought; he's been here already and given his side and probably cried. Tears. Why did mine always desert me when I felt embattled?

'Well, you'll realise, then, that Jeremy is in a difficult situation. We are trying to settle him into Whanganui, but it's been hard for him. Lots of change; two acrimonious parents. It hasn't been easy for any of us.'

'Yes, it does make it very hard for children,' he agreed, looking awkwardly down at the papers in front of him.

'And, of course, it makes it even tougher that Sue and I are in a relationship in such a small, highly visible community.'

He nodded his head: he knew that, too.

'I probably understand more about the situation than you think, Ms Drayton,' he said, shifting slightly. 'You see, my wife left me for a woman.'

My God, I thought, you have to be joking! Please, tell me you're joking. I looked at him. But he wasn't joking. In fact, no part of Mr Campbell was laughing. Not his body language; not the expression on his face; not his deadpan eyes. What's the reply to this? I thought, as my life flashed before me the way it does before an accident.

'Is . . . is that right,' I said, buying time to think a little longer. 'So, so . . . it must be more common than I imagined.'

'I don't know about common,' he responded. 'But, yes, it probably happens more often than people realise. It was difficult at the time, but we parted and moved on with our lives. I've remarried. We haven't been in touch much since. The separation was amicable, but there were no children involved. That made things simpler.'

'I'm sorry you had to go through that. In many ways, I wish it hadn't happened to us because it screws everybody's lives up.'

'Give it time,' he replied, 'things settle down. A couple of years and you'll feel differently.'

I didn't like to tell him that it had already been four years since our initial separation, and coming to Whanganui had only stirred animosities up again.

'Some things take a long time,' he continued, almost reading my mind. 'But Jeremy seems happy and settled enough at school. I know he's a lot more capable than his literacy levels would suggest.' We then chatted away about strategies to help Jeremy.

The teacher Jeremy had had before Mr Campbell had sat me down and said: 'I don't understand. Your son has a reading level below his age, but an oral comprehension level of an 18-year-old.' I told her that anything Jeremy could learn by osmosis he would, but forget learning any other way. Here, now, sitting in front of another teacher, I knew his results would look the same.

'He was taking remedial lessons after school in Christchurch. We'll start that again.' I knew this would go down like a lead balloon with Jeremy. He used to call the extra sessions 'kick-my-arse'. By the time we had settled on a strategy for helping Jeremy we were running over our appointment time. There were other sets of anxious parents waiting in the corridor.

'I think time's up,' Mr Campbell said, graciously not pointing out the fact that we had gone well over our allotment, and extending his hand to both of us. We exited via the French doors and across the veranda instead of braving the restive queue in the corridor.

'My God,' I said to Sue, as soon as we were out of range. 'Can you believe it? Jeremy's teacher was left by his wife for another woman. It seems too much bad luck to be true. What did we do to deserve this?'

'I bet he and your ex had lots to talk about,' replied Sue.

'Yes. They certainly have a few things in common.'

'It's such bad luck,' Sue agreed. 'It's hard to believe that kind of coincidence could happen.'

'Do you think he'll play fair? Or do you think he'll take Richard's side and agree that Jeremy should go back to Christchurch? Surely, he's sympathetic? He must know how it feels, poor chap. I wouldn't even blame him if he were angry and resentful. I probably would be myself. What a terrible situation to be in.'

'He seemed nice enough, and realistic. In fact, very down-to-earth when you come to think of it. I don't know how impressed he would be by your ex's melodramatics. He seems to have made a much better job of dealing with things with his own ex-wife. Maybe he won't sell out.'

'Hopefully not. But what do you reckon our chances are if he does?'

'You've heard the lawyer. She doesn't like your chances anyway. If Jeremy's teacher is strongly in favour of Jeremy returning, I'd say we're doomed.'

'Thanks!' I said, feeling depressed.

'Well, you asked. Things are bleak and you need to face it. The two principal men in Jeremy's life at the moment have had wives who ran away with another women. If they unite against you, your chances of winning are almost nil.'

Sue was right and I knew it. There was no sure ground. In fact, I thought, there hadn't been much sure ground since this whole helter-skelter existence began.

So, Jeremy joined Mr Campbell's junior rugby team, and I added irrationally competitive sideline-parent to my ballet-mother portfolio.

We had to get rugby gear two grades up for Jeremy. He was a lumbering Great Dane puppy when he ran onto the field beside a litter of whippets. His shorts were tight and his jersey stretched across his chest, while his teammates swam in their gear.

The ball-handling skills that didn't come naturally to Jeremy, because his brain was playing catch-up with his body, were offset by his weight and colossal strength. No one he tackled was ever left standing. He was the team's not-so-secret secret weapon.

I ran up and down the sideline, zealously urging him on and cringing whenever a player didn't get up after one of Jeremy's monumental tackles. The sight of the referee, coaches and an anxious parent standing over a crumpled figure stopped my heart until the whistle blew and play resumed again.

For away games, Mr Campbell hired a bus and everyone piled onboard, including parents and their extraneous children. These were my favourite games. The rural district around Whanganui is both beautiful and raw. Roads scythe through deep gorges, rough, bush-covered hill country and flowing sections of the Whanganui River.

When we boarded the bus early on Saturday morning, the beginning of the trip was often overcast, but the early sun would burn off the clouds to reveal a vivid, crisp day. In the background was a buzz of pre-teen, pre-game excitement, in the front of us a picture-window of rural landscape flashing past. We met the opposition on the football fields of sleepy, out-of-the-way towns where residents turned out in the hundreds to support their local teams.

It was on one of these trips that Sue and I began to refine where we wanted to move to.

'What do you reckon about this?' Sue asked, passing over a property guide. She had circled one of the ads with biro-pen. I had difficulty reading it because the back of the bus danced and jolted with every bump in the road.

'I can't read it properly. It's too hard to hold it still enough.'

'You're pathetic,' she said, wrenching it back and shouting out the details over the thrum of the engine and hysteria of children.

'It's a farmhouse,' she called, 'in the middle of a paddock. Used to be the farm manager's residence. It's got three bedrooms, a large lockable double garage, and is commuting distance from Whanganui, for just $156 per week.'

'Sounds perfect,' I shouted back. 'Let's ring them as soon as we get home. I bet it will be gone before we have a chance to look through it, though.'

'It's out of town and on a farm,' called back Sue, 'let's hope that puts people off.' The bus was slowing and Mr Campbell had called for quiet.

I can't remember whether our team won or lost. But Sue and I had a plan to get out of Barbara's. We rang up the real-estate agency the first chance we got.

'There has been a lot of interest in this property,' the woman said, at the other end of the phone. 'You'll have to be in quick. I've already shown a young family around it. Would you and your husband like to see it tomorrow morning?'

I cleared my throat. How was I going to respond to this one? Would I tell her an out-and-out lie? My husband is on a secret military mission in the Middle East. Or would I tell a wee white one? I am taking the house with a girlfriend, who's my flatmate: living is cheaper that way. The white one, I thought. They're easier to maintain. In a small community, a war-hero husband would come back to haunt me. But I didn't want to frighten the agent off. Or to have her think that some other family was more worthy than mine.

The drive out to the farmhouse the next day was one that I would have to do daily if we took the house. At the end of Barbara's driveway, you turned right and carried on up the Great North Road away from Whanganui. The outskirts of the town became market gardens, with huge fields of strawberries, then lifestyle blocks, and finally farms. In Westmere, at the end of a dark stand of tall pine trees, there is a farm-gate with a cattle-stop.

Mist still clung to the fields in vaporous swirls. The shingle road wound across a large paddock to a compact Somerset-brick home in the middle. You could just see the house from the road when you drove past. Behind the house was a deep ravine that made a stunning backdrop. There was a superb view of it from the main bedroom window, I noted, when the agent took us through the house.

'That's magnificent,' I said, looking out, and stooping to establish whether you could still see it lying in bed. You could.

'We'll take it,' I said to the agent, after a quick exchange of meaningful glances with Sue.

'Don't you want to look at the garage and the vegie garden?' the agent asked, confused. 'They're both a good size. The garage has a workshop and bench, and the vegie garden is almost big enough to be self-sufficient.'

'No, that's fine. Where do I sign?'

'Are you sure? You haven't seen around it all yet.'

This was clearly the first time the agent had struck someone keener to close the deal than she was.

'Absolutely sure.'

'You realise there's a bond that has to be paid up-front?'

'Yes, I realise that.'

'Well, then . . .' she said, as if the deal had been an anti-climax. 'I guess all that's left to do now is sign the papers. I haven't got them with me. You'll have to come by the office tomorrow.'

'That's fine.' I replied. 'We'll do that, and I'll bring my cheque book.'

'You don't think we're being too quick, do you?' Sue asked in the car on the way home. 'Should we have looked at some other places first?'

'No way: it's perfect for us. No neighbours; the cats can run wild; it has a wood-burner so we can toast ourselves stupid in winter; and a view of Heaven to wake up to.'

'But it's quite a drive to Katie's ballet classes.'

'It's Katherine,' I corrected her. 'Yeah, we'll have to wait in town until she's finished. We can make the occasional trip back into town, but basically when we're home, we're home. Think of the drive as a decompression chamber. Your parents were farmers.'

'Yes, but that's why I didn't marry a farmer.'

'It's not for long. Enjoy it while you can. We have to leave Barbara's and this is the best option I've seen advertised, and I love the feeling of the place. Not the house, the land. There's something primal about it.'

'How do you think Barbara will react?'

'I'm sure she'll be fine about it.'

How wrong could I possibly be?

Sunday nights were our shared dinner. That evening when we were sitting on her sofa, I broached the subject.

'So, it's been wonderful staying with you, Barbara, but Sue and I feel we have imposed long enough—'

'No, no,' she exclaimed, cutting across me, 'you haven't imposed. I'm enjoying having you stay. Don't go.'

'Well, there's the children's bedrooms—' I began.

'That's no problem. You can use one of the bedrooms in the house.'

'And the kittens—' I began again.

'They're okay. Sam will miss them if they go.'

'Yes, I imagine he will.'

'I didn't mean like that,' she snapped.

'And the weight of having us around. So many of us; and the kids so loud.

ABOVE: Sue and Jo before an LGBT dance party, c. 1993. **LEFT:** A drawing exercise in Sue's first year at Ilam School of Fine Arts, University of Canterbury, 1989.

ABOVE: Sue, son Jason, and mother Norma Marshall, 1984. **BELOW:** Jo and Sue at an art exhibition in Christchurch, c. 1994.

ABOVE: Sue Vincent Marshall, *Self-portrait*, charcoal, 1990.
LEFT: Sue at Ilam, 1990.

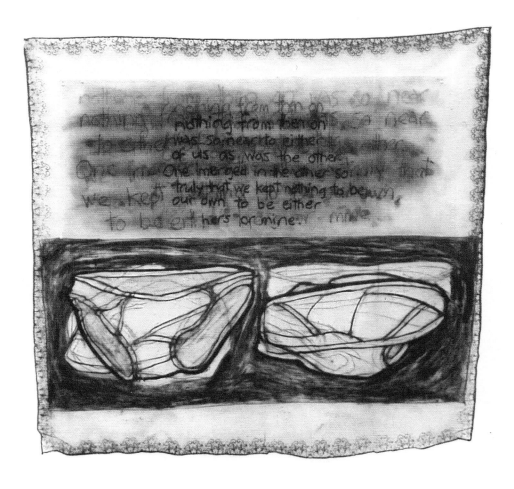

Sue Vincent Marshall, *Nothing From Then On*, 1994. 'Nothing from then on was so near to either of us as was the other. One merged in the other so truly that we kept nothing to be our own to be either hers or mine.' A charcoal and fabric work inspired by the words of self-described 'black, lesbian, mother, warrior, poet' Audre Lorde.

OPPOSITE PAGE: Chess pieces, of walrus ivory, found in an underground chamber in the parish of Uig, Lewis, in 1831: Scandinavian, mid-to-late twelfth century. **ABOVE:** King (H.NS 19) and queen (H.NS 23). **BELOW:** A selection of pieces (H.NS 19, H.NS 20, H.NS 21, H.NS 22, H.NS 23, H.NS 24, H.NS 25, H.NS 26, H.NS 27, H.NS 28, H.NS 29). ***National Museums, Scotland.***

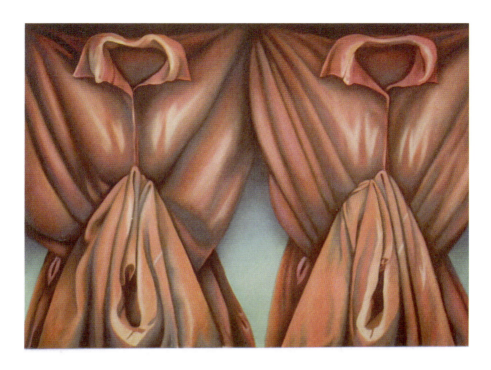

Sue Vincent Marshall, *Three Graces 1*, pastel on paper;
acrylic paint on canvas, 1998–2002.

ABOVE, LEFT: Jeremy and Katherine with birthday cake at the Bishop Street house in Christchurch, 1993. **ABOVE, RIGHT:** Katherine with Ben (one of my parents' alpacas) on Parapara Beach in Golden Bay, 1995. **BELOW:** The Drayton clan (left to right): Chrissie (sister-in-law), Pat (Mum), Malcolm (Dad), Jo and brother Guy, Parapara Beach, c. 1995.

LEFT: Birthday photograph taken by Sue at Dovedale Avenue in Christchurch, 1995. **BELOW:** Jo on a pink couch in Sue's studio at Eastdale Road, Auckland, 2000.

ABOVE: Jo and Jeremy in a roadside café, c. 1996. **RIGHT:** Jo in Sydney, Australia, c. 1998.

ABOVE: Jeremy and Sam at Ringley in Whanganui, c. 1996. **BELOW:** Barbara Stewart, Jeremy, Jo and Katherine at the bus station in Whanganui, c. 1997.

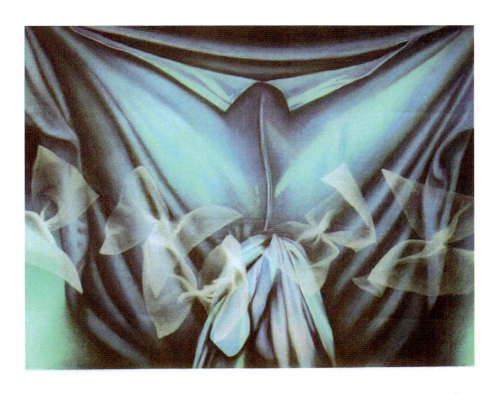

Sue Vincent Marshall, *Three Graces 2*, pastel on paper; acrylic paint on canvas, 1998–2002.

Lithograph of a watercolour by George French Angas of Waikato chief Pōtatau Te Wherowhero taken at the Marae of the Great Waikato people of the Ngāti Māhanga tribe of Te Papa o Rotu. He is drawn seated beside a log, wrapped in a blanket, observing traditional garden cultivations in 1844. First published in *The New Zealanders Illustrated*, London, Thomas McLean, 1847. **Alexander Turnbull Library, PUBL-0014-44.**

LEFT: Lithograph of a watercolour by George French Angas titled 'Monument to Te Whero's Favourite Daughter At Raroera Pah, Near Otawhao'. First published in *The New Zealanders Illustrated*, London, Thomas McLean, 1847. **Auckland War Memorial Museum Tāmaki Paenga Hira. BELOW:** Photograph of Irihapeti Te Paea, from *The whanau of Irihapeti Te Paea (Hahau): the McKay and Joy (Joyce) families*, c. 1994.

Irihapeti Te Paea, photographed by the Burton Brothers, Dunedin. *Alexander Turnbull Library, PA7-04-10.*

ABOVE: Photograph of King Tawhiao and his wife Hera, daughter of Tamati Ngapora, taken by an unknown photographer sometime between 1880 and 1894. *Family album, Ngāruawāhia.*
RIGHT: The Terry family (left to right): Cecil, Thelma, Norma, Zelma, and Lucy.

Sue Vincent Marshall, *Three Graces 3*, pastel on paper; acrylic paint on canvas, 2000–2002.

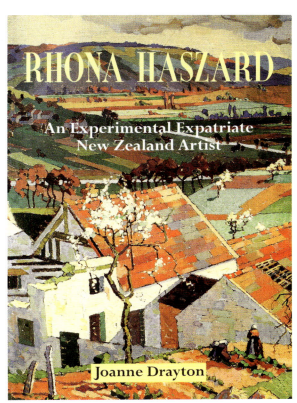

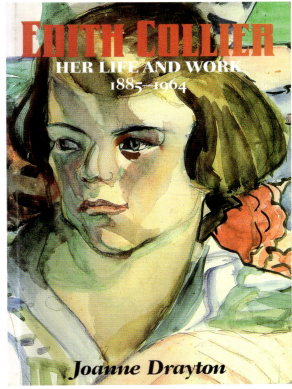

ABOVE: Book cover image of Rhona Haszard's *The Marne Valley* (1927), in *Rhona Haszard: An experimental expatriate New Zealand artist*, Joanne Drayton, Canterbury University Press, 2002. **RIGHT:** Book cover image of Edith Collier's *The Pouting Girl* (1920), in *Edith Collier: Her life and work 1885–1964*, Joanne Drayton, Canterbury University Press, 1999.

ABOVE: Jeremy, Jo, Katherine and Sue at the opening of the Rhona Haszard exhibition at the Hocken Library in Dunedin, 2002. **LEFT:** Jo in role as her alter ego Gladys Stitches on the way to a performance at the Maidment Theatre, Auckland University, c. 2003.

Sue Vincent Marshall, *Three Graces 4*, acrylic paint on canvas, 2004.

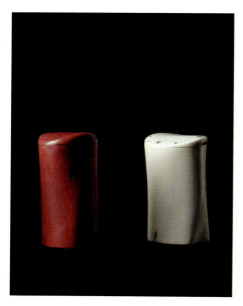 

ABOVE, LEFT: White queen *Gunnhildr*, beef bone, 2012. **ABOVE, RIGHT:** Red queen *Hinepau*, beef bone, 2022. **BELOW, LEFT:** Red and white pawns, beef bone, 2010. **BELOW, RIGHT:** White knight *Leif*, beef bone, 2013. ***Neil Finlay.***

LEFT: White king *Ragnar* and queen *Gunnhildr*, beef bone, 2011 and 2012. **CENTRE:** Back view of thrones, beef bone, 2011 and 2012. **BELOW:** White king *Ragnar*, queen *Gunnhildr*, bishops *Dominic* and *Stephen*, rooks *Thorvald* and *Bjorn*, beef bone, 2009–2012. **Neil Finlay.**

Sue Vincent Marshall, *Forever Tender: Triptych*, acrylic paint on canvas, c. 2016.

OPPOSITE PAGE
ABOVE: Red rooks *Te Pō* and *Te Ao*, beef bone, 2020. **CENTRE:** Rooks, *Bjørn* and *Thorvald* with central bishop *Dominic*, beef bone, 2009–2011. **BELOW:** Red bishops, or tohunga, *Wairaka* and *Ngātoroirangi*, beef bone, 2014–2017.
Neil Finlay.

ABOVE: Beth Hudson, *Cutting the Cake*, oil paint on canvas, 2014. **RIGHT:** Jo and Sue at Le Garde-Manger in Queen Street, c. 2013.

You remember what Sam and Jeremy did to your flowerbed. Kids do crazy things,' I continued, 'and it's a good time to go before something irreparable happens.'

I was referring to a very unfortunate incident where Jeremy and Sam dug up one of Barbara's favourite flowerbeds. She arrived home to find plants pulled out and lying on the driveway, dirt everywhere, and great furrows and holes gouged out of the bed. Barbara went ballistic.

'What did you do that for?' I shouted at Jeremy after I had placated Barbara enough to get her out the flat door.

'Sam made me,' he answered, with a quivering lip.

'What do you mean: Sam made you? How can a dog make you do something like that?'

'He started digging, and when I looked into the hole I saw a piece of broken china with a pattern on it. So I decided to help him. We found bits of old blue glass bottle and pieces of smashed pottery. I got so interested I forgot that it was Barbara's garden. Sam did most of the digging. He'd already uprooted the plants when I got there.'

From the profile I was developing of Sam, I wasn't surprised that he was the ringleader. But of course there was no convincing Barbara when I talked to her afterwards. So it was Jeremy, not Sam, who ended up in the dog-box.

'Jeremy knows better, now,' Barbara responded after a slight hesitation. 'That won't happen again, will it, Jeremy?'

'No, it won't,' he answered.

'But with young kids it's hard to predict what stupid thing they're going to do next.'

'No,' she said, 'no, you're not to sign those papers. There's no need to go and you're safer here with me.'

'Barbara's got a good point about the security,' said Sue when we returned to our flat later that night.

I accepted all Barbara had said, but was noncommittal about whether it would stop me signing. I had thought she'd be secretly relieved to see the back of us. Her resistance caught me off-guard. I didn't want to hurt her, or to diminish all that she had done for us. But I was determined to go. The custody battle depended on it. Separate rooms for the children were essential. We would be leaving ourselves open to attack if we didn't have them.

The next day as we were leaving for work, Barbara caught us in the driveway.

'I'm feeling very unwell,' she announced. 'I may need your help over the next few weeks as I'm feeling off-colour and I'm worried. This is not a good time for you to go. Especially now, when I need you most. You're not still going to sign those papers, are you?'

I had hoped to leave for work undetected. Now the gauntlet was down.

'We'll see,' I said, slipping out of the confrontation. 'The property will probably go before we get there. They don't stay on the books long. Oh, is that the time? Better go.'

'Barbara looked murderous,' Sue said when we were out of sight of the house.

'Yes. That was a close shave. I don't blame her, rattling around in that old house on her own. But how can I tell her we're not the people she thinks we are, that we're living a lie *under her roof*? Honestly, I can't keep doing it. I respect her too much for that.'

I was sad but excited to sign the papers that evening after work. It was a new beginning. We would have our independence back. I was exorcising my guilt and my ghost: or at least I thought I was.

We drove down Barbara's drive for the last time as tenants with regret, but we were free. It was only then that I told the children about the ghost. I'm not sure why. Perhaps it was by way of a confession, a purging. Sue stared grimly ahead, disapproving. She had told me not to tell anyone, not even the children, but I couldn't resist it.

'Why didn't you tell us before?' demanded Jeremy, miffed at my secrecy.

I went into a complicated explanation about my red plastic glasses frames catching the light and how I might have imagined the ghost.

'I wish you'd have told me, because the whole time I was there I felt someone was watching us.'

'Do you mean the mannequin?' I laughed, enjoying my own joke.

'No,' he replied, affronted. 'Someone else.'

'Wow,' I said, taking him seriously at last. 'Who was it?'

'I don't know, but someone.'

We made the rest of the trip out to the farm in silence. Now I was in trouble with both Sue *and* Jeremy.

Past the stand of tall pines, I pulled off Great North Road and got out to undo the chain around the gate. This would become a ritual. Once over the deep, rattling cattle-stop, I got out of the car again and pulled the heavy gate shut behind us. The drive up to the house was more of a dirt track with shingle laid on top.

Not long after we arrived, a large removal van followed us over the cattle-stop and up the drive. It had brought our possessions from Christchurch, where they had been in storage. It was hard to believe that we had been at Barbara's more than nine months, I thought, as I unpacked a box of kitchen items.

The children had a bedroom each, and we had the view. I never grew sick of it. You were in the landscape, even when you were lying in bed, and there was something elemental about the place. The house was surrounded by a low hurricane-wire fence. Beyond it the paddock dropped into a gorge that ran parallel to the house. The drop looked dangerous and deep, but it was impossible to tell how deep because the bottom was out of view from the bedroom window.

What you could see was lush, green grass, sheep trails, and trees twisted by the wind. There was a timeless silence there, broken by the occasional haunting call of a bird or faraway bleat of a sheep. Sunrises blazed across the early-morning sky, and bad weather rolled up the valley.

The long drive into town from the farm was a blow after being at Barbara's, which was so convenient.

'We'll have to leave home earlier tomorrow,' I snapped at Sue, as the four of us flew along Great North Road, arriving at school and work late on the first morning. At the other end of the day, though, it was bliss as we escaped our jobs and city lives and were enveloped by the countryside.

Sue was working on the Art and Design Foundation programme, and I was still preparing one or two classes ahead, teaching art history and theory to degree students. The Quay School of the Arts was located on the banks of the Whanganui River, after Whanganui Polytechnic had bought the old buildings there. Back in 1854, when Whanganui was being settled by the Europeans, it was tipped to be the capital of New Zealand. It was ideally situated, with a harbour close by and the Whanganui River flowing deep and wide through the hinterland to the sea. The river was a relentless volume of water capable of carrying passenger steamers and barges between the back-blocks and the ocean.

Nearly 150 years later, the Quay School of the Arts occupied the old warehouses that had originally stored wool and agricultural produce destined for other centres. The forecourt and front entrance of the art school had been redesigned with flair, the façade being whimsically askew, looking like someone had taken an empty cardboard box and pushed it sideways into a rhombus.

My office was in a heavy old brick building that sat squat and square on the other side of the road. The bright and breezy paint job on the outside camouflaged the ugly, dark, lacquered interior. I shared my office with an artist who had won a Rhodes Scholarship to study an obscure strain of Celtic poetry for his PhD, and in the process discovered what he really wanted to be was a painter. Warwick McLeod was a giant, at 6 foot 6 or 7, and good-looking, so no one ever argued with his decisions.

We arrived in Whanganui in the aftermath of the Moutoa Gardens conflict. The issue has slipped from the headlines now, but at the time it was one of the hottest disputes around. The gardens were just a few paces from my office door. It seemed to me at the time that the conflict was between radical Māori and red-necked Pākehā. Today, I would give it a more complex spin. But, however you look at it, Moutoa Gardens was a flashpoint between two cultures. The gardens were symbolic. They were sacred land to the Māori and a place of civic remembrance for the Pākehā.

Moutoa Gardens was a special place for the Māori because there had been a pā there, which was a site of neutrality where all the tribes in the area could trade safely. When the land on which Whanganui was built was sold to the Crown, Māori believed this sacred ancestral spot was not part of the sale.

As if in defiance of Māori claims, Pākehā officials made a civic park out of the piece of land, and a statue had been erected depicting the local militiaman John Ballance, who went on to become one of New Zealand's early prime ministers. Around the base of his statue was the inflammatory inscription: *To the memory of the brave [Pākehā] men who fell at Moutoa, 14 May 1864, in defence of law and order against fanaticism and barbarism [Māori].*

In February 1995, the year before we moved to Whanganui, relations between iwi and local government became national and international news. Māori ownership of Moutoa Gardens was part of a Treaty of Waitangi claim. A stand-off ensued and the iwi Te Rūnanga Pākaitore decided to occupy the land: their land. The police were drawn into the conflict, and in the struggle to regain control of the land, tents were erected and the stone statue of John Ballance beheaded. The statue had become a chess piece taken in the battle for Moutoa Gardens. But this was no game, and, with Sue's Māori and my Pākehā heritage, these divisions felt personal. Our union was about love, yet here was another force pulling us in different directions.

The thing that made us both laugh, though, was the sight of the headless statue of John Ballance topped with a decaying pumpkin, which was periodically renewed. By the time we saw him, John Ballance looked more like a Halloween horror than a civic hero.

VII

Across the wooden boards of a narrow street in medieval Trondheim ran a young monk. Even though signs of spring were everywhere, frigid winds from the frozen north still funnelled down the fiord, battering Trondheim cruelly. The monk gripped his scapular tight under his chin, and with his other hand, now almost numb with cold, pulled his cowl over his shaved head so that it hid his face.

His slim, dark figure slipped past the heavy Romanesque façade of St Gregory's Cathedral: he was moving with some urgency. Once he had completed his task, he could return to the monastery and breathe easy.

He thought it odd that no one had lit a candle or two in the carving workshop. It was even stranger when he knocked, and, instead of being greeted, the heavy wooden door swung open. This was very unexpected, as the workshop door was usually bolted. Ivory was a precious material, and often prized gems and valuable metals were kept there, too. He moved cautiously into the room with his arms outstretched in front of him. Archbishop Stephen had sent him to collect four ivory chess sets. He was to pay Svein in coins, then take them to a merchant ship waiting in the harbour. The ivory pieces were to be a tribute paid to help broker peace in Ireland. They were illicit contraband, outlawed by the Church, but this only increased their value.

'Is anyone there?' he called, as his eyes began to adjust to the gloom, and he started to make out vague shapes. At the end of the room he could see the last glow of a bed of embers.

'Are you there, Svein?' he called out again. There was still no sign of anyone. He had reached the workbench, feeling his way along it as he went. Perhaps he might find a candle. As he approached the dying embers in the grate, their faint glow revealed a figure, slumped in a chair close to him. The monk's hand ran through something wet and sticky on the bench that gave him a terrible start. Was it blood? he thought as he raised his fingers to his nose. The smell was unmistakable.

'Holy Mother of God, it CAN'T be!' the monk shouted, moving towards the figure. 'Wake up.' He shook the form, which slipped to the floor at his touch.

He needed light. The monk ran his hands along the bench in sweeping motions. Closer to the fire he found a candle in a shallow bowl. He carried it to the fire, burying the wick in its fading coals. Finally, the flame took hold and the area was illuminated.

He looked down. Sprawled at his feet was Svein, the man's eyes open but staring sightlessly. His throat was slit so violently from one side of his neck to the other that it gaped open.

The murder had happened so quickly that Svein was still clutching the ivory piece he had been working on. The terrified monk removed the object with some difficulty from Svein's stiffening fingers. The dead man's hand was cold. Taking his cross from around his neck, the young monk held it over the body and prayed that Svein's soul would find a resting place in God's eternal kingdom.

Even so, the monk was irreverently quick. He could ill-afford to be discovered. It was Sunday, and Svein was only in the workshop to receive the monk's payment and hand over the pieces. He had obviously been working on the last piece. But where were the rest of the games-men? There was no helping Svein now, and the monk had his mission to complete. He scanned every corner for the rest of the ivory figures.

There was nothing, nothing at all: just the meticulously cleaned and stacked carvers' tools of the trade — chisels, files, hand-drills and fine-bladed saws. In the area where newly or nearly finished work usually sat, there was just a neatly finished comb, ornately decorated with mythical beasts along the handle. Without a doubt the chess pieces had been taken, but not just for their value. If this had been the case, the ivory comb would have been taken, too.

He would have to go immediately to his archbishop and tell him what had happened. One last look around the room to make absolutely sure the sets were not stored out of sight. On the floor he noted two bloodied footprints. The prints were not his, so they almost certainly belonged to the murderer. He knelt down to study them. The print had distinctive diagonal ridges running down towards the heel from right-to-left. He knew the pattern. It belonged to the sole of a monk's sandal.

Careful not to leave a second set of prints as he departed the room, the monk put the chess piece Svein had still been holding in the leather bag which hung from a cord around his waist and drew the door closed behind him. He pulled his cowl well over his face and sped away as quickly as he could. It wasn't until he reached the abbey that he saw anyone — a seaman making his drunken way home from the tavern.

The archbishop's palace was a formidable structure built close to the cathedral. Its imposing forms were just discernible in the moonlight; two oil lamps burned at each corner of its doorway. The monk had no intention of making his return obvious. The servants' entrance at the back would be more discreet.

'Archbishop Stephen,' he said in a low voice, once he had reached the private rooms, 'are you awake? It's important that I speak with you.'

He put his ear to the door and could just make out the vague sound of someone moving inside. A moment or so later he heard the heavy latch draw back to reveal the archbishop.

'Come in, Brother Dominic,' he said.

The monk proceeded to tell his superior what he had found, finishing with the footprints and the fact that all the chess pieces were missing, but the highly prized ivory comb was still there.

'So you think the assassin might be a zealous cleric opposed to chess? The abbot is one of those. We cannot do anything more for Svein, however if we are quick we may be able to retrieve the pieces before they are destroyed.'

'But how can we hope to ever get them back?' the monk asked.

'I will call on the abbot in his offices first thing tomorrow. While I discuss our shared landholdings, you will search his chambers. The assassin almost certainly handed the pieces to the abbot for safekeeping until they can be destroyed without arousing any suspicions.'

This seemed a very risky venture to the young monk, but he had sworn an oath of obedience, which compelled him to do what he was instructed.

Archbishop Stephen stood up and prayed for the monk's safe return with the chess pieces, then made the sign of the cross on the monk's forehead.

'God go with you now and forever,' he finished.

CHAPTER SIXTEEN

Whanganui and the Family Court

After the Moutoa Gardens furore, Whanganui, always a place of racial tension, was a city divided. No student at the Quay School of the Arts internalised that conflict more tragically than Lionel. His Pākehā mother was a teen when she fell pregnant, and his father a fierce young Māori warrior from the Hawke's Bay who was killed in a road crash. Lionel had grown up in a Pākehā world, separated from his heritage, from the bloodline to which he was so visibly connected.

As he reached his late teenage years, the separation became so painful he began reaching out to his hapū. That process was underway when he moved to Whanganui and began his studies. Lionel was a printmaker: the intense, unforgiving distillation of printmaking suited him.

The Quay School print room had been an old wool warehouse divided by a mezzanine floor, with a flight of heavy, worn wooden steps up to it. The space was the realm of coffee plungers, rollie cigarettes, and disreputable deep-buttoned student sofas.

Lionel lived at the print room. He was a quiet, watchful young man with deep, desperate longings. While everyone liked Lionel, no one ever really knew him.

Marty, the tutor, set Lionel's class a project to produce a print each day until the end of term. The prints were to be an unfolding story, which could be a personal narrative or something purely abstract. The aim of the exercise was to show development, and to foster a daily commitment to the medium.

No one put together the pieces in Lionel's print story until it was too late. He made his final etching on the last day of the term, which ironically was Friday the thirteenth. Lionel had been private, almost secretive, about his prints. He finished his final print, left it in his studio space and went with a group of students to a Black Friday party.

The art school was a tight-knit community, an enclave of misfits in a polarised and parochial town. The students were viewed with suspicion. They were a remnant, the progeny of Woodstock in the provinces. Like most art students, they smoked cannabis and partied. Their student flats were a debauchery of grubbiness: every mother's nightmare. One student rented a space so small he had to sleep standing upright. He stored his gear there, and if he wanted to do more than slump against the wall, he couch-surfed with friends or slept on one of the many tatty sofas dotted around the studios.

The Black Friday party was one to remember. The atmosphere was heavy with cannabis fumes, and students got 'wasted' on alcohol. So no one exactly knew when Lionel left the party. A group of his friends went looking for him in the early hours of the morning, but figured he must have gone home with someone else, or got so drunk he never made it home.

It wasn't even light when Warwick, my giant-sized colleague, made his way down to the print room the next morning. It was unusual for him to be up that early, especially on a Saturday, but he had an exhibition he was working on and the opening was not far away. The term now being over, he got more done when there were no students around, and this was his first opportunity since the beginning of the year to focus.

He let himself into the print room with his master key and discovered Lionel's lifeless body: he had hung himself from the mezzanine banister rail. Perhaps it was the shock, or maybe just his instinct, but Warwick sat there on the sofa with Lionel and watched the sunrise.

'Okay, Jeremy. You don't have to sleep with Lionel tonight. If you and Katherine don't want to sleep with him in the meeting house, you can go to bed on the bus.'

I knew taking the children to Lionel's tangi would be a mistake, but my colleagues had persuaded me it was a good idea. But as soon as I mentioned the fact that we would be sleeping with Lionel's body, all hell broke loose with the kids. Jeremy kept badgering me about it on the bus.

I tried bribery, guaranteeing them both a mattress in the meeting house *by the door*. Jeremy and Katherine conferred. No way were they sleeping with a dead body, even if they could make a quick exit. Finally, I suggested sleeping on the bus. The next issue was which of us would sleep with them. We had just begun this next phase of negotiation when we pulled off the road and into a car park close to a magnificently carved wharenui. The students flooded off the bus, which had been hired by the polytechnic to take us all to the last night of Lionel's tangi.

His open coffin was at the far end of the wharenui, and around it, wailing and weeping, were the kuia of Lionel's tribe. Sue and I were swept along with the crowd, the children between us. I didn't even have time to consider Jeremy's sensibilities about dead people before we were there, standing directly in front of Lionel in his coffin. Jeremy took my hand, but more to comfort me. You couldn't help but cry in this confluence of grief. I wept for the loss of my own son Alex, and for Lionel's mother's loss: I had experienced similar pain, and my heart cried out for her and this tragic waste of youth.

Lionel's Māori family, who had been with him now for two days, were joined by his teachers, friends and fellow students. We spent the rest of the day talking about him, about his passion for printmaking, and about his life. No one could make proper sense of what he had done, and many of those closest to him were angry. They felt cheated. Why hadn't he confided in them? But the wailing and the tears at Lionel's tangi helped wash away much of the anger and confusion, so what was left was an overwhelming sense that one of the world's beautiful souls had passed from this place to another.

'Mum, Mum . . . Mum!' said Jeremy, tugging my sleeve.

'Yes, Jeremy,' I said, 'what is it?' I felt we had exhausted the topic of dead bodies for the moment.

'It's okay. We'll sleep with Lionel,' he said. 'We're not worried now.' After all the agonising, this surprised me.

'So you're not afraid?'

'No,' he replied. 'Lionel's just a person who's not alive.'

'That's great, Jeremy. I think you'll be much more comfortable sleeping in the meeting house.'

Jeremy did say, however, that he and Katherine would take up the offer of mattresses by the door, just in case.

So, everyone, the kids included, slept with Lionel on his last night on the marae. If anything, the wailing got louder and more plaintive in the early hours. The truest friends remained awake with him, singing to him, telling him stories, and chanting his soul away. Jeremy snored through the whole thing. I noted with some amusement the next morning that the students sleeping close to him had abandoned their mattresses to escape the noise.

Right to the very end, and even after the undertakers had slipped the lid over the coffin and screwed it down, the women wailed. When the hearse drove away, we had breakfast in the marae kitchen, packed up our sleeping bags and boarded the bus for the Presbyterian church service in Hastings. But maybe everything that needed to be said and done had happened on the marae, and Lionel was already home.

My research on Edith Collier was like going on a treasure hunt without a map. Interviewing people and chasing up paintings and threads of information often revealed unexpected gems lost to time or neglect. My investigations had taken me back to Whanganui's special research library. Attempted murder and homosexuality, I thought, as I picked up my photocopies, stacked them neatly and evenly in a pile, then put them in my folder and bolted for the door. I had a lecture to give and would be late if I pushed the photocopier button one more time. Sue was picking me up after class: the kids were spending the weekend with friends, as I was giving a paper at a post-graduate conference in Wellington and Sue was coming with me. However, I couldn't wait to read what I had photocopied.

I had had a tip-off from the director of the Sarjeant Art Gallery, Bill Milbank.

'Come and look at this,' he'd said on one of my many visits. He had taken me to the gallery entrance and out through the heavy doors, guiding me down the front steps and around the side of them, to the memorial foundation stone. On it were listed the notables and the visionaries responsible for erecting this glorious edifice.

'What do you notice about the stone?' he asked, directing me to a section of it with his hand.

'It looks like a chunk has been cut out, then repaired.'

'That,' he said, 'is where Mayor Mackay's name was removed.'

'Why did they do that?' I asked, intrigued.

What he told me had sent me rushing to the periodical section of the reference library, this time to research the antics of a scurrilous mayor. I had photocopied every single newspaper article I could find on the subject.

By the time I got to class that day, the lecture theatre was already full and there was the usual expectant buzz of conversation. I knew time would be tight, so I had packed my lecture notes on top of the folder of papers in my bag. It never failed to amaze me how I could give a lecture that seemed to purge my soul, while I was distracted by something else. The custody case had taught me to leave my own tragedies at the door. But this time it was the photocopies that were burning a hole in my brain. The snippets I'd read as I'd pushed the copy button had only fanned the flames. The final slide of my lecture flicked up onto the screen and I was free.

Sue and I had timed our departure from Whanganui for the Wellington conference down to the last minute. She was waiting outside the lecture theatre in the car ready to pick me up. She had already moved into the passenger seat, thinking I would be taking the wheel.

'No, no, I can't drive,' I called to her, holding up the folder to the window. 'I've got to read these.'

I stood beside the door until she reluctantly got out. I knew she'd be disgruntled. It was 3.15pm. We would be pushing it to make the pre-conference drinks at 6.30pm, but I would get through what I wanted to read in the car.

'As soon as I finish, you can pull off the road and I'll take over.'

'Okay,' she said, more or less appeased, 'but read them out loud. After the day I've had, all I want to do is collapse. If you bury your head in those things, I'll go to sleep again and drive off the road.'

'No problem. I won't be able to *stop* myself reading them to you.'

I skimmed across the first photocopied newspaper to find the beginning of the article.

'Ah! Here it is. Oh, my goodness! You won't believe this.'

'*What?*' Sue shouted in frustration, dying for me to read it to her.

So, as we sped across the countryside I began to piece the story together, threading through sensational headlines and scandalous news copy that must have seen newspapers fly off the shop shelves in their day. Mayor Mackay had been one of the great instigators of the Sarjeant Art Gallery. He was a cultured man, but also young and charismatic enough to inspire the founding fathers to dig deep to fund this ambitious project, a stellar art museum in the provinces.

There was a competition to design the building, and submissions came in from all over the world. Plans were proudly put on display, but only one entry could win. A compact but still ostentatious neo-classical design with a stunningly lit central dome won the day. Building began just before the First World War, but was suspended when the war barons called for austerity, and Whanganui's little extravagance looked unpatriotic. If war was the only issue, there might have been a way around it, but in truth the council was broke. As the bombs rained down in Europe, building costs skyrocketed at home.

It was Mayor Mackay who picked up the project when it faltered and ensured that it was completed. Concessions were made, plans altered, and the council and the community dug even deeper into their pockets. Mayor Mackay emerged from the difficult process as Whanganui's young hero. His name was emblazoned on the foundation stone, and the building was opened in 1919, with all the pomp and ceremony of a town brimming over with joy and belief that the Great War had been the war to end all wars, forever.

Into town came the returning soldiers. One of these was a good-looking young man called D'Arcy Cresswell. D'Arcy had family in Whanganui and was there to convalesce: he had been injured in the fighting in Europe and was struggling to recover. There was something magnetic about D'Arcy that attracted both men and women. He was enchanting — young, beautiful and steeped in an English bohemian culture. While resident for long periods of time in London, he mixed with the Bloomsbury literati, writing letters to Lady Ottoline Morrell, who became a dalliance and his amour. During his first visit to London he enlisted, was injured, and then repatriated to New Zealand.

D'Arcy Cresswell was homosexual, and this must have been evident enough to Mayor Mackay to arrange an encounter. On the face of it, Mackay seemed in every way to be a conventional man. After all, he had married into a socially élite family and was the father of several daughters. But all was not as it seemed. And when he arranged to meet Cresswell after opening hours at the Sarjeant Art Gallery, he was risking everything. As well as the proposed tryst between the two, Mackay promised Cresswell that he would show him his collection of lewd pictures. It was after dark when they met.

Cresswell was brutal and confronting from the beginning. Although he knew what the implications of their meeting were, he feigned innocence and threatened to expose the mayor's homosexuality publicly if he did not pay him £1000. The next day Mackay shot Cresswell in a futile attempt to silence his blackmailer. He staged the shooting to look like there had been a struggle and he had killed Cresswell in self-defence. But Cresswell survived, and when he regained consciousness he gave a very different account.

At Mackay's trial, the story of his homosexual advances was revealed, and his collection of pornographic photographs, of women mostly, was confiscated and used as evidence against him. He went to prison in 1920 and was released after serving six years of his 15-year sentence. The Mackay family was mortified by the revelations. His wife and daughters changed their surname in a futile effort to escape the public shame. The ex-mayor's children never saw their father again.

The luckless Mackay, who was rarely, it seems, in the right place at the right time, was killed in Germany in 1929. After being released from prison in 1926, he escaped to London, where he took up a position as a foreign correspondent for the BBC. He was accidentally shot and killed when reporting on a political rally in Nazi Germany. Among my folder of photocopies, I even had his death notice. In the context of the escalating conflict in Europe, his death barely raised a banner headline. For Mackay's family, his end was healing, but not closure. His wife and daughters remained fugitives for the rest of their lives. We were in Paraparaumu before I'd finished piecing together the story.

'Why don't you pull over the next place you can, and I'll drive? Sorry this has taken so long.'

'No problems,' said Sue, as she indicated to pull into a layby area. 'It was fascinating. Poor man, though. You can't help feeling sorry for him. It's hard to believe they thought that rubbing his name off the foundation stone would remove the scandal from the history books.'

'Yes,' I replied, as I lowered myself into the driver's seat. 'I bet that's a story that will never rest.'

'I'm sure there's people around who still think about it today. I wonder if that's why Barbara's so paranoid about homosexuals?'

It was then that I understood the extra layers of disapproval I had felt in Whanganui: being homosexual in the minds of locals was tied with blackmail, attempted murder, scandal and disgrace. We didn't have a hope.

Room rental was relatively cheap in Whanganui's central business district, so Sue took a studio in town, above our lawyer's offices. Teaching at the polytechnic part-time meant she still had the opportunity to do her own work. So, when she could, she would nip up to her studio and draw, paint and sculpt. To stand back from her work and see whether what was in front of her fitted with what she had in her mind's eye gave her the greatest pleasure. She was happiest when she was lost in concentration. Her theme at the time was bras and undies — our bras and undies. She was exploring the issues of a new relationship. I enjoyed her playful explorations of our sexuality in her art, and I loved the fact that she was so happy doing it.

Going through the main entrance of the building where she had her studio was a mix of emotions for me. To the right was the office of our lawyer Kennedy Quinn, and just passing it was a stressful reminder of the seemingly insoluble custody battle. But up the grand staircase with its carved wooden balustrade was the excitement of Sue's studio, which reminded me of a cross between a mad inventor's cave and the props department of a progressive Russian ballet company. Sue was casting fabrics in resin, and coating various materials in varnish, including our underwear, and mounting them on grained sheets of marine ply and pristine white gesso surfaces.

Her studio was a clutter of bundles of Dacron, stacks of hardboard, pots of half-used gesso made out of rabbit-skin glue, bags of plaster, bottles of turpentine, and tubes of paint. Equipment was everywhere. Sue created art the way she cooked. When she was in the zone, it looked like someone had wildly stirred the ingredients with a ladle: and every lid was off, and every bag open. While the clean-up was horrendous, the results were magical.

As the custody case became dire, and the pressure to mark polytechnic work intensified, Sue got to her studio less and less often. Sometimes I would turn up unexpectedly to collect her.

'Quick, quick,' I would call from the doorway of her studio. 'I've just got this terrible fax, and we have to respond immediately. What do you think I should say?' I would ask, thrusting the fax in her face. There were many awful messages. As in a game of chess, each side took turns moving piece after piece to take the other player off the board.

It was cruel, but I was also a drama queen, and Sue indulged me. Unbelievably. She would drop everything and come, and we would sit in the Red Eye student café and work out our next move.

The most unexpected thing was the change in Kennedy Quinn, our lawyer. It happened gradually: like the melting of the polar ice sheets, she warmed. I started to realise, as if waking out of a dream, that I was no longer on trial, that she was no longer playing devil's advocate. She had frightened me when I had felt she was against me; now she was on my side, I felt the opposition should be frightened.

Not long before going to the Mediation Court, she called us into her office for a meeting of warlords before battle. The day was hot, or maybe it just felt hot because her corporate maroon and grey office was filled with enormous blowflies. It was odd to see so many blowflies in one room, like Heathrow airport with multiple take-offs and landings.

Kennedy Quinn was disturbed by them, too.

'I don't know where these blowflies are coming from,' she said, swatting one away with a wad of file notes. 'Marie has sprayed the room twice today, but they just keep coming back.' I could hear buzzing around me, a death-throes buzz. I glanced down, and upside-down on the floor was a spray victim thrashing away its last moments.

'Don't worry, Kennedy,' I said, looking up from the plush carpet. 'We have them out at the farm all the time. When they manure the paddocks, or there's a dead sheep close to the house, we have to shut all the windows, or the kitchen ceiling goes black with blowflies.' This piece of information seemed to offer her little comfort. After another whack, Kennedy Quinn left the room, calling to her office administrator as she strode out the door.

Sue was strangely quiet. I had tried to catch her eye a couple of times. Immediately the door closed behind Kennedy Quinn, she turned to me with a look of panic.

'I think I know what it is,' she hissed.

'What? What is? What do you know?'

'The rabbit-skin glue,' she said between her teeth. 'It's gone off.'

'What do you mean?' I was still blank.

'It's gone off. The rabbit-skin glue, upstairs, it's *rotten*.'

'Do you mean to say that these blowflies have come down from your studio?'

'Exactly! I boiled up a pot of rabbit-skin glue to make my gesso. It's been so long since I've been up there. It's probably gone off.'

'No, surely not—' I was just about to explain why, when Kennedy Quinn thrust open the door again, this time with Marie in pursuit, brandishing a can of fly spray and cutting a swathe through the aerial display above our heads. I shot Sue an agonised look.

'Oh, don't worry. This is just a regular household spray,' Kennedy Quinn reassured us, misunderstanding my look of mortification. I could see why Sue had made the connection, and I had an awful feeling she was right.

'Marie, I want you to phone the landlord right now and let him know. This is impossible. They must be coming from somewhere.'

'I've already rung him. He's not there at the moment, but I'll keep trying.'

'Well, where were we?' Kennedy Quinn said as the door closed behind Marie, and she flicked a buzzing body off her desk. 'I apologise for all this disturbance. We've gone through everything. Looked high and low for whatever is attracting them.'

Not quite high enough, I thought, as I pictured Sue's studio upstairs.

'My mother has problems with rats. They sometimes eat poison bait and die in the roof or the walls,' I offered.

'Yes, Marie swears she can smell something nasty upstairs.' I flashed Sue a worried look. Now I was certain her rabbit-glue was the culprit. So, our meeting continued against the sound effects of dying flies.

The meeting was a role-play session. What would happen when I went to mediation? What were they likely to say? And how would I respond? But while we went through all the various permutations in painstaking detail, she made one thing clear: ultimately almost everything depended on the judge. If they were a 'hanging judge' we could sing the 'Hallelujah Chorus' and still end up looking like She-Devils. If Kennedy Quinn had seen the state of Sue's studio when we sneaked back after office hours to clean it out, she would have been convinced we were. The pot of rabbit-skin glue was there, decomposing, and the room smelt like the armpits of Hell.

A few days later, I took a flight down to Christchurch on my own. Sue was looking after the children and Kennedy Quinn couldn't represent me in court. She sent the legal papers to my old firm in Christchurch, and I was to be escorted to mediation by a legal representative. It was endgame time. Richard and I must face each other in front of the judge, who had read our lawyers' submissions in advance. It was the judge we needed to convince. He was the adjudicator: he would ask the questions.

The day before mediation I met with my legal team.

'Have you got something more feminine to wear?' my Christchurch legal representative had asked, looking me up and down. 'And I'd get rid of that dark red lipstick,' she advised.

'Do you think it's a bit strong?' I asked.

'It looks like you've been sucking someone's neck. The last thing you want to do is look like a vampire.'

Now there was a challenge, I thought: to find something more feminine. I went through my suitcase of dinner jackets and wing-collared shirts. Nothing suitable. So I borrowed a pair of tights and a skirt from my sister-in-law, Chrissie. I turned up at my next meeting with my legal representative looking like I was on the way to a Quaker prayer meeting. I wasn't convinced that baggy stockings and a matronly skirt cut the right image, but I would give anything a shot.

On the morning of mediation, the legal representative looked at me, very pleased at the transformation. I wore my mother's electric-pink lipstick, which was all the rage in the 1960s, and made me look like an amorous goldfish. When I stood in front of the judge in my frumpy ensemble, nothing about me was real except the aching desire to keep my sons. Although they called it mediation, it had all the trappings of a real court.

Judge Somerville walked in, and we rose. The judge was seated at a raised desk, and Richard and I sat with our counsel at either end of a bench facing him. Nerves are a strange thing because they take away your memory, probably to save you the agony. What I do recall is the way the judge included Sue in the list of people involved, which he read out.

'*Miss Marshall*,' he said, as if she were someone to emphasise. The fact that he seemed to want to draw everyone's attention to it was an ominous sign, I thought, and it rattled me.

Then it followed. Question after question; answer after answer; move and counter-move. There was no let-up. I felt like I was fighting for my life, and I did so to the bitter end. I had no sense of either of us winning, or of being more persuasive. The result appeared to fall between us. I would have hated the judge's job, but his summary comments seemed to go in our favour. He believed me that Jeremy would be okay, perhaps even better off, with us for a time. Richard could take his case to the Family Court if he wanted to, he told him, but that was expensive and likely to have a similar outcome.

I couldn't believe it. After all this time, we had won. For now. But Alex was beyond my reach. Taken, perhaps, forever. This would be one of the resounding tragedies that would echo through my life. The absence. The milestones I would never see. The events I could not attend. Thoughts like this make me sick. Don't believe that grief isn't scarring and that people don't die of broken hearts. But this day was a victory, and the prize was time with my youngest son. This was my checkmate.

VII

In the Kelly family album at Ngāruawāhia there is a remarkable photograph of Irihapeti Te Paea Hahau's half-brother Tāwhiao, also named Tūkāroto Matutaera. The feeling when you see it is odd. A wrench. There among the memories of wedding groups, baby showers, baptisms, Christmas gatherings and tea parties, it stands out — incongruous — but also where it should be. To me it feels like an important museum piece; to Sue it is family.

For her it is a personal encounter with a great-great-half-uncle. Seeing it is an uncovering of a message from the past, carved in light on glass, and delivered on paper to the generations to come. Tāwhiao is hers, trapped in her gaze.

Strangely intimate, yet also posed, it is a studio photograph of Tāwhiao and his principal wife Hera. Tāwhiao sits in a chair looking fractionally to his right, away from the lens. He is strong and defiant. Hera stands beside him. There is a tenderness in the way her hand rests on his shoulder. She is dependent on this great man, but not demure. Hera looks out at the viewer directly, less comfortable, or perhaps less familiar, with her circumstances, but she is not afraid.

Tāwhiao is middle-aged, or older, and worn. He is a husband here, more than he is a warrior or a king. This is not a domestic scene, but it is about a private not a public relationship.

Unlike his father, the second king was the subject of many images. Tāwhiao sat for three paintings by Gottfried Lindauer, a chief proudly holding his mere in readiness, the kiwi feathers of his cloak rich and dark around him. He became the poster-boy of the studio photographer eager to preserve the purest essence of Māoritanga. For Tāwhiao's face, forbidding yet compassionate, carries the carving of his ancestors. Like his half-sister, he is the past and the future of his people.

His clothing is a quirky mix of Māori and Pākehā dress. Tāwhiao wears a fashionably tall top hat, riding boots and a dapper tartan jacket. The jacket fabric is comfortable and soft, but well-tailored. Around his neck is not a tie or cravat, but a pendant, and around his waist a piupiu, or flax skirt. The mix of cultures and formalities is fabulous. Images of Tāwhiao are coveted, not just because of his photogenic qualities, but because he is king.

Tāwhiao's succession to the throne, though, was far from guaranteed. Te Wherowhero's death at Ngāruawāhia, in June 1860, left a cavernous gap in the power balance that Kīngitanga was intended to address. Te Wherowhero had been loved and feared by the rangatira of the Waikato confederation. His tangi brought life to a stand-still. Everyone grieved — friends and enemies — for his death marked the end of greatness established before the coming of the Pākehā. His generation of warrior leaders was the end of an age.

His body was placed in a marble mausoleum inside a rectangular wooden structure, which had distinctive bargeboards and pediments but was uncarved, nothing like the detailed memorial to Hinepau. Its style was perhaps a forerunner of the new architecture that was to develop at Parihaka and with the Rātana Church and other such anti-government movements. The mausoleum was also the subject of a painting, but this time a modest little watercolour sketch by the topographical painter William Fox. His tomb was guarded by warrior sentinels during the Land Wars.

No one felt the weight of Te Wherowhero's passing more heavily than those who were tasked to choose his successor. The question was: who would it be? If Kīngitanga followed the strictures of the British monarchy, then Te Wherowhero should be followed by his son Tūkāroto Matutaera Pōtatau, but there were contenders from other tribes, such as Wiremu Tāmihana, and Māori did not automatically exclude women from power.

In fact, Tūkāroto Matutaera's sister Te Paea Tīaho Pōtatau (half-sister of

Irihapeti Te Paea Hahau) had established herself as a worthy opponent in the Kīngitanga power struggle. She was a leader like her father, living at Māngere under his instructions and encouraging peace between Māori and Pākehā. She was well respected by the confederation of Waikato tribes for her vision and quick-thinking intelligence. She was a prospect as much as Tūkāroto Matutaera was, and without his drawbacks. Tūkāroto Matutaera was not as magnificent or magnetic as his father had been. Nor did he appear to have the same potential.

At the end of various campaigns and confederation consultations, just two factions and their two contenders were left: one supporting a daughter of Te Wherowhero and the other a son. Even John Gorst, magistrate and inspector of native schools, became caught up in the contest. Siding with Te Paea Tīaho, he saw Tūkāroto Matutaera as unworthy, with abilities 'too slender' to fill the office. He wrote in his record of events at the time that Te Paea Tīaho had inherited 'more of the courage and virtue of her warrior-father than his weak and effeminate son'.

Speculation between opposing parties ended when Wiremu Tāmihana sided with Tūkāroto Matutaera. Te Paea Tīaho withdrew from the contest and Tūkāroto Matutaera was installed as king. At the investiture, he took on a new name. The second Māori King would be known as Tāwhiao Tūkāroto Matutaera Pōtatau Te Wherowhero.

His father had led the Waikato federation two years before his death. Tāwhiao was only on the throne for two more years before chaos rather than Kīngitanga reigned. Nothing Tāwhiao could have done would have changed the situation. He was always intended to be a centralising voice for his people, but, with the confiscation of Waikato lands, that voice was largely silenced.

Governor Grey's ultimatum that the people of the Waikato either pledge allegiance to the Queen or leave the land between Auckland and the Waikato, meant thousands of Māori were forced to flee the region and remain homeless. This act of geographical genocide would begin the bloodiest of conflicts between Pākehā and Māori.

Confronted with fighting on an unprecedented scale, Tāwhiao became less of a warrior king and more of a Messiah. Ravaged, dispossessed and depleted, Tāwhiao's people looked to him not for military leadership, but for spiritual guidance. His words of encouragement were healing; his hope for the future, prophecy.

King Tāwhiao's presence among his people was powerful in its consolation and promise of a better time to come for Māori. He was a devout Christian, and in the lost and wandering tribes of the Bible he saw the experience of Māori; in Pākehā control of Aotearoa, Rome's occupation of Jerusalem. God's covenant of deliverance for the Jews offered similar hope for dispossessed and disillusioned Māori. Tāwhiao was a peacemaker, not a warrior king. His impotence and his incapacities were shaped by the dictates of his time. His decision to lead his people, regardless of this, was his own.

He and his followers lived from 1864 to 1881 in a state of spiritual seclusion away from the turmoil of war. His charismatic presence and pacifist ideals were not unlike those of Mahatma Gandhi's against the British in the following century.

He travelled intermittently to sustain his people, and played games of cat-and-mouse with Governor Grey. Grey's play was always for Pākehā advantage. When in 1878 he offered to the Māori King confiscated and unsold territory around the Waipua and Waikato Rivers, and at Ngāruawāhia, plus financial assistance, and rights over the roads in the region, Tāwhiao refused. The *quid pro quo* was easement and safe passage of a railway line through this contentious whenua that would link Auckland and Wellington. Tāwhiao saw the trap, and countered Grey's incursions by calling for the honouring of the very document his father had refused to sign, the Treaty of Waitangi.

He called the settler government to account for lapses of the treaty agreement, and in the late 1880s established his own parliament at Maungakawa. His invitation to join Te Kauhanganui, and establish a parallel parliamentary body representing all Māori, was not universally accepted. The principle may have appealed, but the idea that Tāwhiao would be its reigning monarch did not. Although Tāwhiao had the respect of his chiefly peers, his political sway became more and more limited. His personal conduct was also contentious. He was a heavy drinker, and as well as being a holy man he was a peacock. At over 6 feet tall, with an impressive moko, he was spectacular whether dressed in Māori or Pākehā finery. He spanned both worlds and often dressed dramatically between them.

When he sailed to England in 1884 to put a petition before Queen Victoria, he looked awe-inspiring. In Sydney, Australia, on his first stop, he was ridiculed by the press. But his startling appearance sent another message. By the time Tāwhiao and his entourage reached Melbourne, his celebrity status was established. Outfitted in magnificent blue frock coats, with shiny silk hats and buttonholes bulging with large bouquets, the visiting party stunned crowds at the Victoria International Exhibition. Indeed, Tāwhiao and his entourage were later forced to abandon their hotel in an attempt to avoid the press.

Tāwhiao's time in London was a blazing buzz of tourist sights and sounds. He took head-turning strolls along the Strand, ate out at the Gaiety Restaurant, explored the West End, Covent Garden, Madame Tussauds, and the London Zoo. Tāwhiao's visit to the British Museum proved to be his most disturbing experience. At the heart of this great temple to Empire were the rooms housing the treasures of ancient Egypt. He had perused other parts of the museum with mixed interest. But when it was explained to him that the sarcophagi contained the dead bodies of ancient Egyptian rangatira, the room took on an entirely different aspect. Instead of being an exhibition of antiquities, it became a desecration. A graveyard of spoils. A defilement. The room's unquiet spirits overwhelmed him and he was terrified. Gasping for air, and grabbing the arm of his attendant, he demanded to be removed, immediately. He was visibly shaken by the time he reached the street, with its throngs of pedestrians and acrid smell of coal fires and horse manure.

In spite of the strong sensory overload and many temptations of London, Tāwhiao was a paragon of ginger-beer-drinking temperance. His unaccustomed sobriety was a deliberate strategy, supported almost forcefully by Governor Grey and Tāwhiao's tour-minders. For Tāwhiao's trip had a much more important mission than just seeing the sights.

Tāwhiao had suspended his life in Aotearoa and travelled halfway around the world to speak for his subjugated people. If he wasn't a ruler according to the protocols of traditional kingship, or a representative of all Māoridom, he was an indigenous ambassador, speaking for a confederation of tribes living in exile, betrayed by a treaty with the Crown that should have protected them.

The last part of Tāwhiao's petition stated:

We your Māori people continue to hold fast to the Treaty of Waitangi and its principles together with its mana . . . [we] request an audience with the queen so that we can renew the words of that treaty and so that neither the New Zealand government nor any action of it is able to undermine the Treaty.

Tāwhiao's request for an audience with Queen Victoria was declined.

CHAPTER SEVENTEEN
The Vengeful Victory

Our farmhouse on the outskirts of Whanganui was a sanctuary. Beautiful and calm or raging and wild, whatever the weather it was magnificent. I felt a sense of awe there that I have never experienced before or since. I wish I could honestly say that things got much easier after mediation, but we were never short of a nightmare or two. Some of the old pressures remained, especially for Jeremy, who continued to receive tearful phone calls from his father, and to be interrogated over whether he was happy with the judge's decision; and of course there was the sadness of Alex. It is hard to express how raw this felt, a tearing away of something intrinsic. I craved the wholeness that I had had when both my children were a part of my life. The king had won a victory. But Sue and I had to play on together, and either I coped or we would be destroyed.

Our first spring there was a country idyll of newborn lambs frolicking in the sunset. The house was located in the middle of what must have been the farm's busiest maternity paddock. We righted cast sheep, and rang the farmer when ewes were in trouble lambing, or when we spotted an orphan. I loved the evening rush-hour traffic of young lambs that wore a track around the house chasing each other, and our isolation from other people.

Sue and I could relax again. Drop the jolly-hockey-sticks, 'we're just good friends' routine, and be natural. The nearest neighbours were on the far side of the enormous stand of black pines. We became acquainted as you do in the countryside. Abundantly kind, they were the most withered old couple I had ever met. Small, browned by the sun and bony, they looked like ancient specimens in an entomologist's cabinet. We met the husband first. He came over with a white plastic shopping bag full to the brim with vegetables from his market garden.

'Come over and fill a bag, pick whatever you like. Any time at all,' he said with unexpected intensity. 'The wife and I are on our own and we like people dropping in.'

'That's very generous of you, but really you shouldn't have.' I took the sack from his sun-baked hand and looked inside. New potatoes, carrots, cabbage, there was even a head of broccoli.

'I'd wash that well,' he said, when he saw what I was looking at. 'The green caterpillars are rife this year. If you eat them accidentally they can give you a nasty stomach ache.'

That was it for a while. We were too reserved to go over and help ourselves. He made several more visits to us before we were game enough to venture onto his property.

One blazing late summer Saturday afternoon when the cicadas were shrill and the distant hills shimmered with heat, we finally visited our neighbours. The market gardener was hoeing a long stretch of beetroots. His wife, whose name I never knew, was pushing a wheelbarrow full of produce. She was every bit as frail-looking as her husband. But for her long steel-grey tresses and large hooked nose, she could have been his twin. They had a fairy-tale quality to them that was just missing a moral to end the story.

The children were given plastic bags and instructions to harvest all the silverbeet they could collect. Sue and I followed the gardener and his wife, who smiled relentlessly at us, while he picked the best, plumpest vegetables from his expansive garden. We could hardly carry everything home.

As winter approached, I began thinking about how we were going to keep warm. Wind swept across the fields with unrelenting fury at times. In the same way that spring was more alive and summer more intense there, winter would be colder and more exposed.

'Get a cord of wood delivered from the local timber company,' Mike, the technician at the polytechnic, suggested. 'It's as cheap as chips if you cut it up yourself. You can borrow the circular saw from the woodshop — I'll show you how to use it.'

I ordered a cord of wood.

We arrived home from work a few days later to find in our drive a massive bundle of long, thin, tree-length off-cuts from the timber yard. The bundle sat there for some days before dropping temperatures, and wind and rain, spurred me to take the project on. We picked up the polytechnic's circular saw and workbench, loading them into the back of our newly acquired Ford Sierra station wagon.

Now I understand why timber workers are often missing a digit or two. No matter how careful I was, the blade seemed hungry for my fingers. Time and again the ferocious teeth caught on a knot or twist of bark and leapt dangerously towards them. I did feel a certain pride, though, when I carried basketsful of dirt-cheap, dry wood inside, which we burned with reckless abandon. The wind howled in the bitter blackness outdoors, as we sat short-sleeved in a Sahara of stifling heat. While I, with the worst circulation in the world, felt like I had achieved a state of near nirvana, the rest of the family cooked.

When the refrigerator was bare and we went visiting the kindly gardeners next door, I couldn't help bragging. I told the husband about the mighty cord of wood that I'd cut up all on my own.

'Yes, I know about that,' he said. 'I watched you cut it up each day.'

'How could you do that?' I asked, startled.

'Through my binoculars, of course,' he said, as if he were David Attenborough dispensing birdwatching advice to school children. 'I see everything,' he said. 'I can even see you inside your house.'

Suddenly, my whole perception of this thin, bony little man changed. Clearly, when he wasn't market gardening, he was a voyeur. I couldn't help feeling a rush of revulsion. What had he seen? How often had Sue and I kissed or hugged by a window?

'I watch the hawks, too,' he added, as if that somehow justified him training his binoculars on us.

Nowadays I think I would challenge him, but at the time his guiltless ease about the whole thing left me speechless until we were walking down the drive.

'Did you hear that?' I said to Sue, between clenched teeth, just in case Mr Neighbourhood Watch was staring down his binoculars and reading my lips right then.

'Yes. I can hardly believe it. What a creepy thing to do, and he didn't even seem to worry about it.'

After that, the blinds at our place were pulled across at odd times of the day, and nothing much ever happened on the side of the house closest to the black pines. When my mother came to stay with us, wanting to give her the complete country experience, I took her over to meet our neighbours.

'We haven't seen much of you lately,' the gardener said as I introduced him and his wife to my mother.

You'd be right there, I thought. 'This is my mother, Pat Drayton.'

'How do you do?' he responded, extending his thin hand. 'I'm afraid there isn't much in the garden at the moment.' But he and his wife still skirted along the rows and managed to fill yet another bag to overflowing.

'They're lovely neighbours,' I explained to my mother on our way back home, 'but we've had a few problems with the husband.' I was just about to tell her about the binoculars when my mother cut across my political correctness.

'Never mind him,' she said. 'I just want to know where his wife parks her broomstick.' A few days later Mum left on hers and normality was resumed.

Children should carry a health warning. Something like 'Toxic: handle with extreme care' or 'Personal protection equipment such as respirators, gloves and goggles should be worn at all times'. My lurgy-magnet toddler Jeremy became in his pre-teens a collector and communicator of viruses.

For years after he himself was cured, Sue and I would play happy hosts to his especially virulent verruca virus.

'Mum, Mum — would you have a look at the bottom of my foot,' Jeremy said, one Sunday night, lying on the floor and waving one of his massive fleshy feet in my face. 'My teacher said I've got warts.'

'I doubt it, Jeremy. Where would you get warts from?' But of course I looked and to my horror his foot was covered in a multitude of tiny holes. At the bottom of each hole was a verruca.

'Oh, crap, Jeremy, I think she's right. Hold the other one up.' If possible, it was worse. How could I not have noticed? This was not just a few warts, it was an infestation. We haunted the doctor's waiting room like unquiet souls, coming back and back for creams, oils, acids, pills . . . and then a breakthrough.

My mother, who is intensely superstitious and believes whole-heartedly in pagan cures and ancient rituals, buried a piece of steak in her backyard, said a few spellbinding words, and the warts disappeared overnight. The problem with the intermittent use of black magic is that it can backfire, and backfire it did.

At the same time as Jeremy's feet emerged pristine, ours became blighted. The demon, cast out, had found two new pairs of soles to inhabit. I can now testify to the fact that verrucas like vintage feet way more than near-new. This I know because the virus travelled across our feet like a wind-fanned fire. When things got so bad that I began to hobble, I thought it was time to visit the doctor myself.

I sat nervously in her waiting room, wondering whether I could afford the time off work. Things were piling up. I sat there and wondered how I had ever managed to fight a custody battle with the number of things I had on the go.

The large white clinical clock on the other side of the room ticked away. The waiting room was empty now the elderly woman sitting opposite in the heavy camel-coloured coat had been ushered in. The room usually thronged with people, but this was mid-morning on a weekday. For me, it was supposedly a quick appointment between classes.

After what seemed an interminable wait, the door opened and the old lady emerged.

'If you aren't feeling 100 per cent better on those new pills, make sure you come back.'

'I will, Doctor,' she said, shuffling off with a prescription sheet clutched in her hand.

'Joanne,' the doctor said, turning to me, 'come on in.' She and I had bonded during Jeremy's verruca treatment, and were now on a first-name basis. As I had never told her about the meat my mother had buried in the backyard, she was under the impression that we had defeated the virus together.

'This won't take a minute, Bridget,' I said, embarrassed that I had such a trivial childhood ailment to show her.

I sat down in the seat she indicated and hummed like an electric pylon. Not through my mouth, but through my whole body. My hands moved compulsively, shifting and straightening things; doing up and undoing buttons. My toes tapped the ground, while I twisted uneasily in the chair.

'So, how are you?' asked Bridget after a short pause.

'Fine, fine, busy, busy,' I blurted, still buzzing with electricity.

'What do you mean "busy", exactly?'

All I wanted to do was to take off my sock, show her my verruca, and get back to work. But as I started to tell her why I felt busy, I got swept up in the story, giving her my full repertoire of anecdotes and embellishments. I had effectively lost a son; survived a custody battle (so far); was teaching full-time at the polytechnic; finishing off my PhD; curating a nationally touring exhibition of Edith Collier's work; and had a contract to write a book for Canterbury University Press.

'Hmmm,' she murmured. 'I think I'll take your blood pressure.' I was still itching to take my sock off, so rolling my sleeve up was an anti-climax. She wound the inflatable strap around my arm, then pumped it up and let the air out slowly, taking the reading.

'That's got to be a mistake,' she said, perplexed. 'I sometimes get odd readings. I'll do it again.' She repeated the process, pumping furiously. There was still something wrong.

She tried a replacement machine.

'I'm afraid this is quite serious,' she said.

I know, I thought, because you haven't even looked at my verruca yet.

'I'm sorry if this is a shock, but your blood pressure is 168/90,' she said.

These were just numbers to me: I was unimpressed.

'What does it mean?' I asked. 'I don't know much about blood pressure.'

'Unfortunately, this means you've got the blood pressure of a 75-year-old!'

Now, that *was* a shock. I thought of the elderly lady in the waiting room that morning, and wondered whether she was doing better or worse than me. I was 39 years old and a long-distance runner. How could this be?

My verruca worries evaporated.

'The top figure is worryingly high,' she explained. 'It's the number that's affected by stress.'

The doctor grabbed a pad of forms from a shelf beside her.

'Now,' she announced, as she picked up her pen and began to fill out a form. 'I'm writing you a medical certificate for time off work.'

I was mortified.

'I can't afford to take time off work. In fact, I shouldn't even be here now — I've got far too much to do,' I said, looking at my watch.

'You can't afford not to,' she responded. 'With blood pressure as high as yours, you could drop dead at any minute.'

'Dead?'

'A heart attack, stroke. Take your pick.'

I was gobsmacked.

'But there must be something I can take?'

'Not when it's stress. You need to treat the cause. My advice is to go home, put your feet up and relax for a while.'

'*Relax?*' I repeated the word like it needed translating.

'You must take time off. Doctor's orders.' And that was her final word on the subject.

I went to see my doctor with a verruca (which I must add was never treated), and came out with a medical certificate for six weeks' paid sick leave. I went back to work, dropped my bombshell and drove home.

Now, as anyone who has spent any time with me will confirm, the word 'rest' doesn't exist in my vocabulary. Like the wind, I am never still. Perhaps that's why my father, when he registered my birth, spelt my middle name 'Gale', instead of 'Gail' as instructed. My sick leave, however, was a chance to enjoy time on the farm with Sue and the children, and when they departed for work and school in the morning, it was time to reflect.

What it gave me was a chance to review all the material I had collected for my PhD: the multitude of photographs Sue had taken of Edith Collier's work and the vast collection of notes compiled.

There was one event I needed more information on: the bonfire. Barbara's sister Jean was the key to it. I decided to interview her. No children, no distractions this time. I rang her up and arranged a meeting on our own.

'I don't know whether I'll be much help,' she said, as she opened the front door. This was followed by one of her creaky chuckles. I can hear the odd pitch of her voice with its slightly nasal twang, even now. She ushered me into the lounge with its lake view and wool-pit. Waiting on one of her Italianate tables was afternoon tea.

'Milk? Sugar?' she asked, as she poured the rich, dark liquid into a Royal Doulton teacup from an ornate silver teapot.

'Just milk, thanks,' I said, as I fumbled in my bag for the tape-recorder.

Jean looked alarmed as I placed the machine on the table between us.

'I hope you don't mind me getting started,' I said, as I made sure for the umpteenth time that the tape was the right way around and we were beginning on side A. There were only two buttons, ON and RECORD, and in those days remembering to push both simultaneously felt like scaling a mountain. I was all focus that day, though, because I knew this was an important interview.

'How about I ask you a few questions while we're having tea? Is that okay? Just relaxed, no pressure.' I added this last bit because Jean was looking more nervous still. Like she might do a runner, and I didn't want that.

Better launch in, before she bolts, I thought.

'So, how old were you when it happened? I've been trying to work out the maths and it doesn't seem to add up.'

'I was about five,' she croaked. 'Or was it four? No, I'm sure I was five years old. I remember the brand-new patent-leather shoes I was wearing. I can remember them now: covered in dew and glinting in the early-morning sunlight. Edie had gone off in the car shopping.'

'So what year was this, Jean?' I interjected.

'Well, I was five years old, so it must have been 1926.'

For a start this was fascinating because the burning was generally thought to have taken place in 1922, immediately after Edith Collier's arrival home from her nine-year stint in the United Kingdom.

'Okay, so tell me what happened.' Great, I thought, as I glanced down at the little plastic window in my recorder and saw the tape whirring around picking up every word.

It seems that Jean was staying with her grandparents and her maiden aunts at Ringley, and her grandfather Henry Collier was angry with his daughter: Jean's Aunt Edith. He was stewing, in fact.

'Disgusting, disgusting,' he kept repeating over and over again to himself. As soon as Edith had disappeared down the drive in the car, he grabbed Jean by the hand and took her outside to Edith's studio, which was a farm building on the property, a short distance from the back of the house. Jean said that, even at five years old, she knew something ominous was about to happen.

'Come and help Grandpa,' Henry instructed.

They went hand-in-hand to Edith's studio, Henry once more repeatedly muttering 'disgusting' along the way.

'You wait here,' he ordered, as he entered the building and began sorting through Edith's paintings. They were stacked in piles against the wall. It looked like a random arrangement, but it wouldn't have been because Edith loved her work. She held on to it like a parent clutches their child, unwilling to allow them independence. Edith gave little of her work away and sold even less. Her studio was a visual diary of a time in her life that meant more to her than any other.

Henry was rifling through nine years of paintings, prints and drawings. He scooped up what he could see that was 'offensive'. It was her nudes that upset him most, but there was also her very modern work. This rankled with him, too. He selected a pile of these canvases and carried them with some difficulty to the door.

'Here,' he said, handing some of the smaller ones to Jean.

'No, G'andpa, these are Aunty Edie's,' the child said to him.

Without a word, he gestured her off. Their destination was a large bonfire at the back of the property where they burned their rubbish. He piled the canvases up, some in frames and others on stretchers, and lit a match. It was not long before the precious canvases were burning fiercely. Jean remembered the flames like she did her shoes, only she saw these through her tears rather than the drops of morning dew.

Henry made several more trips from Edith's studio across the long grass to the bonfire. Each time he carried a bundle of paintings.

Jean estimates that more than a dozen of Edith's best works went up in flames that day.

'Aunty Edie will be angry,' she told her grandfather.

That afternoon when Edith returned, Henry said nothing, so Jean went and told her what they had done. Edith was beside herself. Furious, she marched down the corridor to tackle her father. They had a cataclysmic row.

'What did you have to go and do that for?' Henry demanded of his young grandchild, when the tears and anger of their argument abated.

'What did he think?' Jean asked, turning to me when she got to this point in her story. 'That Edie wouldn't notice? She loved those paintings. They were everything to her, and he destroyed them. *Of course* she'd notice.'

'So, do you think this event had much of an impact on her career?' I asked, answering her question with another.

'Yes, it did. Definitely. She was so deeply hurt by what he did that she went away with her friend Eulalie who lived close by and painted at Kāwhia. They were away for months. She painted at the pā at Kāwhia. Mostly old Māori women.'

I remembered seeing those works in the gallery basement. This was a pity, because in a way they reflected something of what had happened to her. They were so much less innovative and modern. The spark that fired the work she did in the UK, especially her later work there, had been extinguished.

'Why do you think she painted women?' I asked.

'Because she found them more interesting. But then she was also very shy of men. She had a suitor once, a nice young man, who used to come to the house, and every time he came to the door, Edie would rush away and hide.'

This reminded me of a letter I had recently received from Jean's older cousin, Patricia Lonsdale. While we were on the subject, this was the perfect time to ask.

'Patricia wrote me a letter the other day, and in it she said that Edith hated two things: men and tomcats. Is that true?'

'Oh, no,' Jean replied. 'No, no, that's definitely not true.'

I had always thought of Edith as demure. She appeared very female-centred to me. But what Jean seemed to be saying made my imagination run wild. A scarlet woman, I thought, casual relationships with men, affairs, a child born out of wedlock. Suddenly my PhD turned 50 shades greyer.

'*No,*' Jean said, one final time, 'Edith didn't have anything against tomcats. Absolutely not; in fact, she had four neutered males.'

There went my image of Edith, 'the dark horse', up in smoke.

I had finished my notetaking for the evening when Sue asked me, out of the blue: 'So what made Henry Collier burn the paintings, do you think?'

'Well, there were several reasons. Here, look at this,' I said, passing her a photocopy from one of my many piles on the dining room table. It was an art review from the *Wanganui Chronicle*.

'Edith arrived home in 1922, but it wasn't until 1926 that she showed her work in a very high-profile exhibition. Her painting was rubbished. The critic hated it. I think Henry was so annoyed with the response that he went out and burned her paintings. They were too modern . . . And then there was the scandal over the mayor.'

'What do you mean?'

'You know. The homosexual Mayor Mackay fiasco and his attempted murder of D'Arcy Cresswell. It hit the headlines with such an impact in 1920, and was so closely linked to the Sarjeant Art Gallery that they delayed the big opening exhibition that was planned. It wasn't until 1926 that they were game enough to revisit the idea. The big exhibition that included Edith's work was intended to showcase the gallery to the world.'

'So why were Edith's paintings such a problem for Henry? The works the critic moans about, here,' Sue said, reading the review, 'are portraits and seascapes. It's the modern elements he doesn't like.'

'Yes, but Henry knew there were more controversial paintings in Edith's studio. Pictures of nude women. They offended his sensibilities, and maybe there was a hint there for him of homosexuality: a woman painting another woman nude. Who knows what ripped his ration book? Maybe it was just that he had supported her overseas for nine years and she came back with a foreign painting style he detested.'

'I wonder how she felt,' Sue said, 'coming home and finding them burned.'

'According to Jean, she was devastated, and, apart from a painting trip to Kāwhia, she never found the same desire to work again. Edith painted sporadically, producing the occasional canvas that she was never completely happy with. I know this from talking to Barbara, who I'm interviewing again tomorrow, by the way.'

I could never get away with talking to one sister and not the other. Somehow they would always manage to get wind of my 'treachery' and become sulky and distant, like I had breached some natural law. But there were things I needed to know, anyway. I was still on leave, so the next morning I drove Sue to work, and the children to school, dropping them off like it was a country milk run. Then I took the car up St John's Hill to Barbara's.

We still dropped in once a week, at least, for dinner, so the long drive up to the house wasn't loaded with nostalgia, as it would later become. This morning it was just Barbara, the tape-recorder and me. By now she had settled down and stopped being frosty about our departure. She even had new tenants in the back flat. We weren't quite as close as we had been when we were living there, though. This was sad because I loved Barbara, and still do. She gave us shelter when we needed it. She comforted us. Barbara was greater than a good Samaritan; she was our saviour.

I parked the car to one side of the garage, so the tenants could still get in and out.

'Hi, Barbara,' I called as I climbed out of the car. She was already standing on the doorstep, while Sam, who had launched himself outside, was barking furiously at me. 'How are you?'

'Not bad: I've been better, though,' she replied. Since we'd left, Barbara had developed a battery of ills. Mostly she used patent medicines and weirdo treatments. The consequence was that she never got any better. She would go to Palmy, which is what she called Palmerston North, and have her aura measured, her crystals read, or her electro-magnetic field realigned.

'Maybe if you don't get better this time you might try going to the doctor,' I suggested.

'No. I don't trust doctors,' she replied. Barbara was stubborn and, like Edith, wary of strange men; in her mind doctors were all male.

She had just come back from a series of weirdo treatments.

'So, do you think it's worked?'

'It's too early to tell, but I did feel this delightful sense of well-being.' Was that before or after she paid the bill? I wondered. Probably before: because the cost was always astronomical.

'Come in here,' she called, ushering me through the kitchen and into the conservatory. You would have sworn Barbara and Jean had swapped notes. Barbara's table was ornate metal painted white in the same Italianate style as her sister's. Once again refreshments were waiting, but this time it was coffee latte with frothed milk served in delicate white china coffee cups. She

226 The Queen's Wife

had cheese on crackers, enough to feed a rugby team, shortbread to burn and a pile of chocolate mint biscuits. I groaned inside when I saw how much food she had put out. If I had just crossed the Sahara on foot I might have done it justice.

The annoying thing was that Barbara would invariably announce that she was looking after her figure and she wouldn't be able to eat much.

'This is amazing, Barbara! You shouldn't have gone to so much trouble. I've not long had breakfast.' I dropped this in as a get-out-of-jail-free card, warming her up to the idea that I would only put a small dent in this miracle morning tea that would feed the five thousand.

'I'll just go and froth the milk,' she said, as she disappeared back into the kitchen. My coffee was already done. 'I won't be long,' she shouted over the noise of the frothing machine, gurgling and hissing away.

She returned a few minutes later, holding a slender bone-china coffee cup topped with snowy white milk.

'Help yourself,' she said, grabbing the smallest cheese-topped cracker and putting it on her plate.

'I have already,' I replied, through a mouthful of shortbread. 'This is delicious.' Barbara was always fussy about the food she bought. While we ate shop-bought biscuits, or Sue's home baking when we were especially lucky, Barbara bought the very best bakery produce.

I wiped my fingers on the dazzlingly patterned paper napkin she had put out for me, and, as I had the day before, I reached down and fossicked in my bag for the tape-recorder. As I picked it up my hand accidentally pressed down on the PLAY button, and there was Jean's gravelly voice. I hit the OFF button instantly, but even that was too much Jean for Barbara's liking.

'Hope you're not listening to her,' she announced. 'Jean has a vivid imagination. She thinks she was the aunts' favourite, but that's not true. I was their favourite niece. The aunts put up with Jean because they had no choice.'

'We didn't talk much about the aunts,' I replied, changing the subject. 'We spoke mostly about Henry burning the paintings.' I knew that would move her on. Barbara wasn't born when they were burned, so whatever thoughts she had on the subject they would never be as valid as her sister's.

'What I wanted to talk to you about today is Edith's time following her arrival back from Kāwhia after Henry had burned her paintings. You were living here at Ringley with your grandparents and aunts at that time, is that right?'

'Yes,' she responded, promptly forgetting Jean as she cast her mind back.

'I was one of the youngest of 10 children, and my mother needed a break. She had crumpled under the strain, so the aunts took me in. It wasn't until I was older that I went back to my parents, and it was a huge shock. My mother and I were strangers. I'd seen her regularly, but that was very different from going home to live.'

'So how did Edith cope with life at Ringley, do you think, after years of living on her own in London?'

Barbara didn't hesitate over this one.

'I think she found it hard. She never moaned about it. But you could tell. For years she kept up with what was happening on the art scene in London.'

'How did she do that?' I asked, thinking this might be rather difficult from small-town Whanganui in the 1930s and 1940s.

'She subscribed to English art magazines. I don't remember the names. She ordered the latest art books from catalogues, and each day would race everyone to the mailbox, hungry for letters from friends overseas. Right to the very end of her life she bought paints and canvases. When I came to help my aunts Dorothy and Thea sort out her things after her death in 1963, there were trunk-loads of art equipment in her art studio, most of it unopened and untouched.'

'What did you do with it all?'

'We gave most of it away to nieces and nephews who she had encouraged to take an interest in art. Anything that had dried up or been chewed by silverfish we threw out. It took us days to go through everything. What was there must have cost a fortune.'

'Obviously, she never gave up the desire to paint.'

'No, she never did.'

'It's really sad that she didn't carry on painting and experimenting with her work. It was so important to her as a young woman. Do you think she had difficulties giving it up? Did she ever discuss it with you? Not when you were young, but when you were older.'

'Not directly. But when she was much older she bought a cottage at Castle Cliff beach. It was here that she planned to live away from Dorothy and paint.'

'Why "away from Dorothy"?' I asked, my curiosity piqued. 'Were they at logger-heads?'

Barbara laughed, repeating my words, 'logger-heads', as she reached across the table for another cheese cracker. She held the cracker suspended.

'Dorothy was at logger-heads with everyone,' she said.

'So, she didn't get on with either Edith or her other sister, Thea? I guess by that time their parents were gone.'

'Definitely gone,' Barbara said, raising her cracker for a bite. 'Henry, Edith's father, died in 1935, and her mother, Eliza, in 1946 . . . I think that's right.'

'So the sisters had lived all those years together at Ringley?'

'Yes, and it was far from amicable. Edith and Thea were close, and Dorothy was the outsider. She just got madder and madder as the years went by.'

'I imagine it was pretty frustrating for them all. It reminds me of that film. What was the title now? . . . That's right . . . *Whatever Happened to Baby Jane?* Bette Davis torturing her bed-ridden sister. Do you remember it?'

'I think I do, I'm not sure.'

'Maybe you'll remember the scene where Bette Davis serves her sister a meal in bed, and when Bette lifts the lid of the dish there's her sister's dead parrot cooked and served up on the plate,' I explained gleefully. Now I have a filmic fascination for the macabre, but, back then, when I saw the movie as a child on television, it haunted me.

I picked up another piece of shortbread, and waited for her reply.

'Things did get violent at times,' she reflected. 'There was even physical violence. In fact, I have a theory that one of Dorothy's beatings actually brought about Edith's death.'

'You're joking.'

'No. I'm not joking at all,' Barbara said. 'The day Edith died was the day the *Woman's Weekly* was delivered — or maybe she collected it — I can't remember. Anyway, Dorothy got annoyed about something and took to Edith, hitting her hard with the rolled-up *Woman's Weekly*. She went into a fury. Couldn't stop. I can remember Edith with her hands up over her head trying to protect herself.'

While the picture taking shape in my mind was mildly slapstick, the look on Barbara's face was far from amused. This was no time for levity.

'So you think that contributed to what happened?'

'You can't help wondering because she died that night: 1963 it was. Out of the blue, she had a brain aneurism and died.'

'Do you think Dorothy felt any responsibility?'

'I doubt it, but I told her at the time that she shouldn't have done it, and there would be trouble for her if I caught her doing it again. I didn't know then that it was already too late.'

'But do you think it killed Edie? I mean, really?'

'I don't know. Dorothy was angry and she hit hard. Maybe that day she went a step too far.'

I heard the tape-recorder click. We were at the end.

'An apt place to finish,' I announced as I ejected the tape and put it back in its case. 'I could go on forever, but I think that will do for now. I'll let you get on with your day.'

I will miss these sessions with Barbara and Jean, I thought, as I drove down Barbara's drive then turned right onto Great North Road heading north to the farm.

'Murder,' Sue repeated, when I told her the story that night over a glass of wine. 'Surely not?'

'No,' I said, though reluctant to step back from my sensational words. 'Maybe it would be better described as "assault with a deadly *Woman's Weekly*".'

VIII

By the time the monk left the archbishop's rooms it was well after midnight. He would have just a few hours' sleep before it was time to rise again for morning prayers. He slept in his robes. His plan was to attend prayers with the other monks as usual, then slip away.

Through the whole of Matins, which began well before dawn, he was distracted. He tried to concentrate wholly on his prayers to God, but his mind kept wandering off, either in planning his heist or in fits of terrible imaginings over being caught.

After breaking his fast, he crossed the quadrangle, pulling his cowl over his head so he would be indistinguishable from any other monk. The abbey was on the far side of the cathedral. It was an impressive building, as the abbot was a powerful man. It would be difficult to break in. The windows were barred and shuttered. His best plan was to pass himself off as one of the numerous monks in the abbot's service.

Instead of stopping at the abbey, he went past it down a crowded thoroughfare to the market square. Along one of the rows he saw the baker's stand, loaves of coarse-grained bread stacked one on top of the other.

'I'll take a dozen large loaves,' he said, indicating the pile at the front, which had obviously been placed there to tempt buyers. 'And can I buy the basket over there to carry them?' It was an expensive purchase, but one that gave him a cover to enter the abbot's kitchen.

Purchases complete, and loaves stowed, the monk made his way back to the palace, standing discreetly in a doorway to await the arrival of Archbishop Stephen. He was there some time before he saw the archbishop and his entourage approach the front entrance of the abbot's residence.

With his cowl still up, the young monk carried the loaves around to the kitchen door and walked in as if he were delivering an order. No one stopped him. In fact, although he heard someone moving around in what was probably the pantry, there was nobody in the cooking area itself. He took the loaves out of the basket, stacking them carefully on the table. This done, he moved along the corridor towards the formal rooms at the front of the abbey. He passed humble, rough-hewn doors that led to store rooms, servants' quarters, and, as he got further from the kitchen, visitors' rooms and monks' cells.

At this point he encountered two well-dressed clerics engrossed in conversation. They barely noticed his lowly existence; his empty basket making it look like he was attending to some domestic task. The abbot's rooms were upstairs, and the servants' much less grand back staircase went up steeply to his left. Things are going well, he thought, but is it too well? Might the abbot's assassin be lurking nearby?

His body tensed as he reached the top of the staircase. Still no one, but he had an eerie feeling that danger was not far away. A little way down the passage was a door covered by a large velvet curtain. The door was ajar and the curtain pulled slightly back. He must be quick. Noiselessly he crept to the door, and, after establishing that there was no one in the first chamber, he began searching. What he was looking for required a good-sized storage space. There was no sign of the chess pieces in the abbot's bedroom. He looked in the wardrobe, under the wash-stand, running his hands along the wood-panelled walls and his feet across the floorboards to check for secret panels to hidden closets and man-holes. Nothing.

The only space left was the small anteroom next door, which was clearly the abbot's private office, set with a desk covered by inks and fine sheets of vellum. A large shelf held a number of books. There was nowhere obvious to store the chess pieces. Undoubtedly, they would be well hidden. The monk could see no changes in the level of any of the floorboards, but when he ran his fingers along the back wall, he felt a ridge where the wooden panels were very slightly raised.

Just then he heard voices coming up the stairs.

'God save me,' he whispered, the words escaping before he had a chance to stop himself. He scrambled frantically to see what he could find to open the secret door. The closest thing was the bookshelf. He pulled a couple of heavy volumes out. There was nothing behind these, but behind the next two volumes he found it: a lever that released a latch inside the wall, allowing a hidden door to swing open. He bent down, and in an instant squeezed into the cramped closet and closed the panel behind him.

The voices were much closer now; he barely dared breathe. The conversation belonged not to the abbot, but to monks moving around his chamber, probably straightening the bed, replacing his water jug, and collecting his linen. From the sound of things, one monk was standing in the office doorway, talking over his shoulder.

'The ink pot's nearly full,' the man called to his companion, 'it will last the week.' After this, the sound of their movements receded down the corridor. How much time did he have until another monk, or even the abbot, came along? How long would Archbishop Stephen be able to stall him?

It was almost impossible to see in the dark of the closet. He felt around for the door mechanism, releasing it so that the panel popped open, suffusing the small space with a dull light. Not far from where he crouched was a large object that could be a sack. He reached over and pulled it towards him. Even under the grip of one hand it felt promising. Untying the leather thong at the top, he plunged his hand into the bag, retrieving a chess piece and looking at it in delight.

Depositing the sack into the breadbasket, he moved as soundlessly as a cat, out of the hiding place and through to the bedroom. By the basin he found a towel. If he was stopped, he could say that he was taking the abbot's laundry away. He laid the towel across the top of the bag. He felt more hopeful as he rapidly descended the staircase. As he approached the kitchen, he again heard voices. This would be harder. He pulled his cowl down over his face, lowered his head and proceeded purposefully into the room, shifting the weight of the basket. He was on the doorstep before one of the monks in the room looked up from their work around the kitchen table and saw him.

'Hey, you!' he called. 'Where are you going with that?'

Quick as lightning Dominic was out the door and off. Subterfuge was pointless now. Once they looked in the basket he was finished. He flew down the alley and onto the main thoroughfare. If he could make it to the marketplace, he would be able to disappear into the crowds. He could hear someone calling after him to stop.

It was urgent now that he hand over his bounty to the captain who was to carry the chessmen to Ireland. The wharves were not far from the marketplace. With a sense of desperation, Brother Dominic scanned the wharf, eager to get rid of his contraband. He hesitated just a second or two, taking in the scene before he settled on a direction.

Suddenly, an arm grabbed him around the neck from behind. The assassin, he thought as he twisted, swinging the basket to hit his assailant in the chest. His attacker was momentarily winded, letting go of his headlock and doubling over for a second. The next thing the monk saw was a flash of sunlight on metal as his attacker thrust a knife at him. He moved away just in time. The thrust was so vehement that it tipped his opponent off-balance. At that point, a towering giant of a man rushed towards them, and Dominic knew he had no hope of escaping now. That was until the giant hit the assassin heavily on the back of the head with a wooden oar.

'He won't be giving you any more trouble,' he said to the monk, who bent down to look more closely at the body. The assassin was most certainly dead. The monk knelt beside his body and prayed for his soul.

'I believe you've got something for me to take to Dublin. I am Bjorn Erikson,' his saviour said, as the monk rose to his feet. 'My men will take care of this,' he said, gesturing to the corpse.

CHAPTER EIGHTEEN

Life's Strange Little Detours

My blood pressure gradually returned to normal, and, although my sick leave from Whanganui Polytechnic felt like it went by in a flash, it was a very productive time because it gave me the space to assemble the most comprehensive picture I would ever have of this elusive woman, Edith Collier. When my PhD was completed, I extracted a book from the bones of my research, which I wrote and refined over a few months, working with Mike Bradstock at Canterbury University Press. But the crowning glory was a touring exhibition of Edith's work.

Well, it was more than just Edith's work: it also included paintings and prints by Frances Hodgkins, another Kiwi compatriot who had taught Edith when they were in St Ives, and two other early Australian modernists, Margaret Preston and Gladys Reynell. Edith had worked with the two Australians in Ireland in 1914 and 1915, and at Bibury, in the Cotswolds, in 1916.

I had a devil of a job borrowing work from Australian galleries for the show. If New Zealand's major public collections didn't rate for the big Australian galleries, which they didn't, then Whanganui was equivalent to a boil on the backside of a gnat. Not fully comprehending our diminutive proportions on the scale of global art-gallery loans, I sent letters of introduction, describing the project and soliciting them to lend some of their prized paintings. I sent both a faxed copy and a hard copy by snail-mail, then waited.

Nothing came. For the first few days I watched the fax machine at work, expecting it to lurch into life at any moment. As the days passed, I switched my attention to the mailbox. Still nothing. To the next series of letters and faxes I added an email address — which was still a rather new technology at that time. The cycle began again, with the addition of an email in-box to scrutinise pensively. Still no word.

Time was ticking by. I had already sold the exhibition to galleries all over New Zealand for the colossal price, in those days, of $3000 per gallery, and I had called it *Edith Collier and the Women of Her Circle*. So far we had Edith, but no circle. How were we going to explain this to the galleries that had purchased the exhibition? Would they ask for their money back? And would the critics pan the show because it promised more than it delivered?

My blood pressure began to rise again. I could tell. I had started to pace the floor, and strum, and fidget.

'Why don't you just ring them up?' Sue asked, interrupting one of my diatribes on the evils of Australian galleries.

'That's a great idea!' I said, as if I had just been handed a solution to the Cuban missile crisis. 'But do you think I'll get through?'

'You won't know if you don't try. Why don't you check their website? See if you can get a phone number and ring them.'

Now, that was an idea I was only just getting used to. A website, I thought, as if contemplating the exploration of Africa.

'I'll do it,' I said. 'I'll give it a shot.'

There was no chance of me doing it that night, though. I would have to mentally prepare myself. So I went to bed early.

I finished lecturing at 3pm the next day. Back in my office across the road, I sat staring at my phone. I had looked up the first gallery site, and, after countless checks and cross-checks, had a phone number written on the pad in front of me. Looking between my pad and the phone, then back again, I felt like Amelia Earhart about to launch into the blue.

'I want to put a long-distance call through to a Sydney number,' I told the operator of the switchboard at the polytechnic, and then I gave her the number.

'Certainly, I'll put you through now,' a woman's voice responded. I could feel beads of sweat running down my back. It wasn't an anxiety attack exactly, but I was anxious. The phone at the other end rang and rang, and I was just about to put the receiver down when someone picked it up.

I introduced myself stutteringly, saying I'd been trying for months now to make contact to borrow some works from their collection.

'Where did yew say yew were calling from?' the man at the other end asked in a broad Seedney accent.

'Whanganui,' I said.

'Where's that exactlee?' he asked. After a convoluted description of where he might find Whanganui on the map, he admitted he had received my letters and faxes.

'Yees,' he said, 'yees, I've been meeaning to get around to that. Where deed yew say yew were ringing from, again?'

'Whanganui,' I repeated, trying not to lose my temper.

'And when do you want these works?'

'The show opens on the fourteenth of August.'

'You haven't left us much time,' he said.

If I had said what I wanted to say, the conversation would have ended there and then, but I wanted the works more. I toned it down.

'If you'd responded to my first approach, we'd be a lot further ahead by now.'

'Yees, possiblee,' he said. 'Now, Wonganuee, you say. Does it have an art galleree?'

'Yes,' I replied. 'You can see a picture of it on the letter-heads I've been sending.'

There was silence at the other end.

He was obviously consulting a pile of my correspondence. I had had a picture of my various messages spewing out of the fax machine directly into the rubbish bin. But this had not been the case.

'We can only loan work for the first four shows on your itineraree, and that's on the basis that the galleree passes our streengent 20-page condition report. We find smaller gallerees usually don't come up to standard,' he finished.

'Perhaps you can fax the report document to me, and we can fill it out and get it to you as soon as possible?' I gave him my work number, put down the phone, and it wasn't long afterwards that I heard the fax machine whirring away in the office and a Dead Sea Scroll of fax paper spilled onto the floor.

Damn, I thought, looking at the vast number of boxes that needed ticking before we could even think about bringing the works over to New Zealand.

Depressed, I trimmed the scroll into A4 lengths and went to see the head curator, Paul Raynor.

He scanned the document.

'Definitely stringent,' he said, taking in a breath, 'but pretty standard. I think we'll manage it; a few dehumidifiers in the right places should get the figures right. As long as the cost isn't too high, I don't see any problems.'

The accounts for crate building and shipping came in from the Gallery of New South Wales, and also from the Gallery of South Australia, which had similar hoops to jump through, and although they did cost an arm and a leg, the Sarjeant Gallery decided to go ahead. The exhibition was a massive undertaking. We borrowed works from private collectors, family members, and from galleries around New Zealand, including Te Papa and the Hocken Library. The exhibition opening and the launch of my book — with the catchy title *Edith Collier: Her Life and Work (1885–1963)* — was to be a huge civic function.

I went about promoting the event with shameless zeal.

We had been living in the farmhouse for just over 15 months when we received the sad news that it was about to be sold. This would have been tragic if the previous winter had not been so wet and humid, creating ideal conditions for ovine facial eczema. Our country idyll of newborn lambs tripping happily around the house became a horror of dead and dying sheep. Some stood in silent suffering, others were cast on the ground in some awful position that made death a certainty. I remember stopping the car in the driveway and getting out to put a sheep back on its feet. After a mammoth struggle I realised it was too weak to stand. Our pleasant pasture of hope and regeneration had become a killing field.

So it came almost as a relief to hear that we *had* to move. I found shifting such an ordeal; I would probably have sat there, an unwilling witness to heartbreak, if it had been left to me.

'We've got no choice, we can't stay,' I announced to Sue when I got off the phone after talking to the farmer.

'Sounds fine to me,' she responded, 'but let's get something nicer and closer to town.'

I knew what she meant. The farmhouse was primitive, especially in comparison with its garage, which had workbenches and storage space to burn. Blokes' priorities: the kitchen had an oven that looked as if it came out of the ark, while the garage was flash enough to build one in.

'Okay, but I'm way too busy to go around looking at rentals, so whatever you want is fine with me. Just give me a final look through it, and I'll sign along the dotted line with you.' So that's how we left it. Sue indulged her interest in real estate and interior design by looking at properties, and I kept my head down working on the exhibition, lecturing, and hoping she would need me as little as possible. Already we were collecting cardboard boxes and newspaper to wrap things.

The exhibition preparations were moving ahead. I had loan request papers returned from all of the lenders of private works, and by moving the dehumidifiers around the gallery we had achieved all the mandatory temperature and humidity levels to approve the loans from public galleries. My book was almost ready to go to the publisher.

Then a major headache came from an unexpected quarter. When I was in the United Kingdom researching Edith Collier for my PhD, I had visited Bonmahon. It is a small — correction, *tiny* — village in Southern Ireland where Edith had painted. I'm not sure what we were hoping to find after 80 years. But, miraculously, the first person I spoke to, Jim Cullinan, knew who I was talking about because his mother had been Edith's child model while she lived in the village.

It was a wonderful reunion: New Zealanders in Bonmahon again for the first time in 80 years. We were given the royal treatment. Jim, who was introduced to us as the local historian, and Mary Galvin, the campsite owner, drove us all over the district identifying the sights and ferreting out the places where Edith painted. Finally, he took us to where she had her studio in a quaint little row of two-up-two-down houses.

'My mother,' Jim told us, 'used to stare out of the cottage window looking across the valley to Edith's studio: "I wonder if she ever became a famous New Zealand painter" she would say to herself.' His mother named his sister after Edith, to remember the woman who had lived and worked there so memorably in the opening years of the First World War. I wrote to Jim and the owner of the camping ground after we left Bonmahon. When we moved to Whanganui, I told Barbara and Jean about my contacts there, and Jean became an enthusiastic correspondent, too.

One day Jean appeared at the gallery demanding to speak with me. I was down in the basement with Richard Wotton, the photographer, looking at the last-minute set of new negatives he had taken of some of Edith's paintings for the book.

I cringed. Jean was a pyromaniac when it came to arrangements. One of those people who meddles, without seeing consequences, and by the time you wake up to it, everything is ablaze. I had a premonition, the abruptness of the visit, the summons. She was up to something.

'I've got some terrific news,' she announced. 'I've taken the liberty of inviting a representative to come over from Bonmahon for the opening of Edie's exhibition. Jim Cullinan can't come and neither can Mary Galvin, so they have deputised a young art student who is studying art at Cork to come on their behalf.' She was breathless with excitement. 'I've promised him a place to stay. I don't suppose we've got a bit of spare cash to pay for his ticket?'

I was speechless. Jean had invited some random art student over from Ireland to Whanganui for the exhibition, and promised him a free ticket, accommodation, and probably more. Once I had recovered enough to move my lips, my first strategy was to pour cold water on the whole thing.

'That's a great idea, Jean,' I pretended, 'but since Jim and Mary can't come, I think it's pointless proceeding. Why would a young man want to come all the way out to New Zealand for an exhibition he had nothing to do with? I'm sure he'll find it very dull.'

'But he *is* interested,' she said, 'because he's already committed to coming. Mary tells me he can't wait. His tickets are booked. He's staying with you for three weeks. It's all organised.'

'With *me*,' I repeated. OMG, I don't believe it, I thought. 'But he won't be able to stay with us because we're itinerant. We haven't even got a place to live ourselves at the moment.'

'Oh well, perhaps he can stay with me for a while.' That sounded just the thing: a barely post-pubescent male staying with the sometimes mad-as-a-snake Jean. How incongruous could you get? But Jean was still looking dangerously enthusiastic about the idea.

'Look, you don't think there's any chance of him cancelling the tickets, do you?' I asked, grasping at straws. 'Has he paid for them yet? If he was hoping to get some cash from us, maybe his payment hasn't gone through. He can save his money and we can send photographs instead.'

'I don't think we can do that,' she croaked, shaking her head, 'no. He wants to be an ambassador. That's what they've told him: he's to be the ambassador from Bonmahon.'

Keith Fitzgerald arrived from Ireland in the eye of my storm. I felt terrible because I wanted to do much more for him, but it was too hard. At home we were in the middle of shifting. Sue had found a gorgeous place for us in Aramoho. It was almost brand-new, with a view from the kitchen and dining area that looked out over the township of East Whanganui and across the Whanganui River to the hills on the far side of the river valley. On the other side, the property backed onto a lifestyle block where the owner kept the tiniest miniature horses. They were as big as a medium-sized dog. The first time Sue and the children and I saw the property all together, the wee horses ran chasing each other down a hill that followed along our boundary fence. After the facial eczema of the farm, it was like moving from a death camp to Disney.

'This seems too good to be true,' I said to Sue, as I locked the car and walked up the drive to view the property.

'Well, it's a big jump in rent,' Sue reminded me.

'Yes, but you get so much more for another $80 a week rent. Why would anyone want to leave such a beautiful place? And why risk renting it in Whanganui?' All these questions would be answered soon, but, in the meantime, we felt like royalty with a dishwasher and an architecturally designed house.

Our friendly technician from the polytechnic, Mike, helped us ferry our trailer-loads of possessions. With the extremely heavy things like the fridge and the washing machine, he carried them inside for us. In between short bursts of unpacking, I gave lectures and tutorials, and went up to the art gallery to check progress and help with the layout of Edith's show. All my life seemed to be about boxes. At home they were cardboard; at the gallery they were huge wooden crates arriving from Australia and all over New Zealand.

It was while Paul Raynor, Celia Thompson and I were opening a particularly massive crate that Jean arrived with Keith. She had just picked him up from the airport. He was tall, dark-haired and pencil-thin, wearing wedge-tight black jeans and a black sweater. He looked jet-lagged and shell-shocked. I estimated him to be about 19 years old, and probably way too young to get much pleasure out of the company he was about to keep for the next week or so.

I had tried to involve Barbara in the hosting project. I thought she might have given him a bed for a few nights, but as soon as she found out Jean was the instigator her mouth flat-lined in defiance, and all signs of interest died.

'I suppose he can come over for lunch or dinner one day,' she conceded.

'That's great, Barbara, thanks,' I lied. 'I'm sure he'll appreciate it. So you don't think you'll be able to have him to stay even for a night or two?' Thinking, I would have one last shot.

'No,' she responded. 'I refuse to bail Jean out this time. She invited him, she can have him to stay.'

There was no arguing with that one. I felt the same way myself. But as I stood looking into the eyes of this spotty lean-teen, I couldn't help feeling compassion laced with lots of guilt. He was like a possum frozen in the headlights. Fear, confusion, I couldn't be sure what it was.

'Lovely to meet you, Keith,' I said, holding out my hand to shake his.

'I'm sure you'll have a wonderful stay at Jean's place,' I called out, as they departed, more prayerful than optimistic.

So the unlikely pair disappeared from my days leading up to the exhibition, but not from my troubled thoughts.

It was both a massive and a magnificent show of work by Edith Collier and the great female experimenters who worked with her in the opening decades of the twentieth century. As I had been researching and writing on the subject for nearly six years, it was a moving experience to see the distillation of the best of Edith's paintings on the white walls of the Whanganui art gallery. Seeing it for the first time with the crates, equipment trolleys, ladders, bubble-wrap and spirit-levels gone, and the signage up was remarkable.

My parents were in the United Kingdom, so they couldn't make it to the opening, but Roger Sowry, an old friend from my time as an American Field Service (AFS) scholar, did. We had spent our year away in the Midwest of America together. Since his year as an exchange student, he had been elected a Member of Parliament, advancing to become a Cabinet minister and part of the Brat Pack, a tight group of National Party young-bloods. Although a strident Labour Party supporter, I was always won over by personality. I liked Roger, and on a purely selfish level it looked better on the invitations to have 'the Right Honorable', rather than a 'no-name', opening the show. Roger had got thicker around the middle and thinner on top than I remembered, but I was delighted to see him again.

As a prospective AFS student waiting to go away, I had given up looking longingly at photographs of other exchange students' host families. I resigned myself to the fact that my host parents were old and morbidly obese, and that I had no host brothers and sisters at home. Hosting an exchange student was a futile attempt on their part to fill the family nest when Becky, the last of their children, left for college.

My host mother stared back at me from the black-and-white photograph they had sent, like the serial killer Aileen Wuornos in a mug shot. She was stern and sour-looking, while my host father stood beside her, beaming approachably.

We had our orientation at Stanford University in San Francisco, and on the long bus trip halfway across America I got to know fellow scholar Roger Sowry. He was a pale-skinned, fair-haired youth who wore the biggest brimmed hat I had ever seen. It was July and the days were as long, hot and exhilarating as our futures, which seemed to stretch out forever.

AFS flew us to Chicago, then booked us seats on old Greyhound buses that shuddered and shook their way across the country. It was there that we parted. New friends: now best friends. Roger heading to Minneapolis and me down through the Midwest. Periodically, we would lose a student as they were delivered to their host parents. The seats were bone-shattering and the air conditioning non-existent. I was among the last to be delivered. My bus halted finally at a station in Kansas City, where the last of us separated.

My host mother proved to be every bit as truculent as her picture had suggested, and my host father, Joe, as tactile as a squid. Their personalities were polarised like night and day. Ruth was cool and critical, and I was desperate to please. She pushed my needy button. I felt okay about my relationship with Joe, but the more distant and withdrawn Ruth became, the more I wanted her to like me. The harder I tried, the further she drew back.

Maybe if I'd had a host brother or sister this would have counted as collateral damage — 'you can't get along with everyone' — that sort of thing. But often Joe was out at work, or a meeting, or his club, and there was just Ruth and me staring at each other across the kitchen table in silence; frosty one side, supplicating the other. The time until school began dragged. It was like crossing off the days in solitary confinement.

One morning at breakfast, the atmosphere was especially toxic. This made no sense to me as I was trying extra hard to please her. In my desperation, I had taken to trying to read her mind. What was she thinking? Was there something I should be doing? What would melt those frozen features into a smile? Other people made her laugh, why couldn't I?

I was pondering this problem as I played with the last of the Raisin Oatie Clusters in the bottom of my cereal bowl.

'There's something very serious I want to talk to you about.' The words were Ruth's, and they cut right through my distracted speculations. There was an edge to her voice that was so cold it was a polar plunge.

She had my complete attention.

'I want you to stop your affair with my husband. RIGHT NOW! And if you don't stop listening into our phone conversations I'll have you sent home.' The word 'stupefied' would only begin to cover the way I felt. I had no idea what she was talking about. My first response was to laugh. Hysterically. I hoped she was being funny. But there was no flicker of humour there.

'How can you believe that?' I responded. 'I'm 17 years old. Why on earth would I want to have an affair with a man three times my age? It doesn't make sense. I like Joe. We get along, but he's my host father. This is ridiculous.' My defence, mixed with self-righteous indignation, poured out. 'What's more, I would *never, ever* listen in to anyone else's phone conversations. Where on earth did you get that idea from?'

'I've watched you,' she said, unmoved by any of my protestations. 'Jumping up to do things. Offering to help me bag ice after Joe and I have been talking about it on the phone. Either you're a mind-reader or you've been listening in.'

That was the moment when the injustice of it all struck me full-force. Not only was an affair with her husband the biggest irony ever, but, after trying so hard to anticipate *her* needs, I was now being accused of eavesdropping. I argued my case valiantly, but nothing I said shifted her. Ruth continued to believe that Joe and I had deceived her and that I was fundamentally bad.

When I spoke to my AFS counsellor a week or so later, she said if I left Joe and Ruth's place I would have to leave town. Centralia was too small a community to leave a prominent family for a new placement. People would talk, she explained. It would make things difficult for AFS and for me. In the end I decided to stay.

I'm glad I stayed because many years later we made up. Joe and Ruth came out to New Zealand to visit for a month, 10 days after Jeremy was born. She apologised to me for her strange, paranoid behaviour, which I thought was very brave and gracious of her, since so much time had passed and there was no need. I learned then that relationships that you work at are often more meaningful than ones easily gained. In the struggle to connect, you learn things. Ruthie taught me that forgiveness is an essential ingredient of every friendship. Sometimes you offer forgiveness, and sometimes you receive it.

There was one more relationship that year that taught me something. My farewell to Missouri was a weeklong stint as a leader at summer camp for Girl Scouts in the Lake of the Ozarks. My role there was ambiguous, as I would be leaving camp before the Girl Scouts arrived. This was orientation week for the camp leaders, and I was there to provide a flavour of Antipodean 'exotic'. We had a wild time camping in cabins in the woods that fringed Lake Ozark. I was finally free of moody, menopausal Ruth, and about to return to Christchurch and resume my old life. The year had been a frightening and fabulous suspension of reality, and now I was going home.

The first night at camp, my bag was raided by raccoons, who unzipped the zipper, with their tiny feral hands, and plundered my stash of cheese crackers, chocolate cookies, Reese's Peanut Butter Cups and chewing gum. They unwrapped each item, took a bite, and either carried it away into the woods or left it littering the cabin floor. Initially, I wondered if it might have been a Girl Scout leader gone rogue, then I spotted the raccoon pooh in the bottom of my bag.

The second night I fell in love, as you do in these crazy states of suspension between worlds where there's no gravity; I was drawn to Jane, as I had not been to anyone before. I knew she was different — for a start she was four years older and at university. But there was something else, something that pulled me towards another possibility . . . But loving a woman was an aberration, I told myself: I just didn't want to believe it.

Jane and I were inseparable for that week; yet we never talked about our attraction, and we never did anything about it. Still, the intensity of my feelings frightened me. After I left the Girl Scout camp, I thought about Jane a lot. She dropped a gift off for me at Joe and Ruth's house in Centralia — a pair of army fatigue trousers and Antoine de Saint-Exupéry's *The Little Prince*, both all the rage in the 1970s. But I was not at home when she called by. This was fate, I decided. A clear sign that our passion was never meant to be. We wrote numerous letters after my return to New Zealand, but stopped once I married. Life has these strange little detours, I told myself, and nothing happened anyway.

But time changes everything. Twenty-two years later, I was listening to Roger Sowry, who was opening my exhibition with all the spin of a slick politician. After the opening speeches and the musical items, the most memorable of which was a cello piece by Chopin, I signed books. This was my first book, of which I was inordinately proud. It was then that I realised my calling at last. I was an author.

I signed and signed, until I was at the end of the queue, and finally there was just Sue, me and the kids in the car driving home late at night to the tail-end of our unpacking. The children had had a great time playing with their young friends.

After bustling the children off quickly to bed, Sue and I collapsed into a chair with a mug of tea.

'Well, that's over,' I said, kicking off my shoes, sitting back and closing my eyes. 'I'm stuffed.'

'Yeah, me too,' Sue agreed, looking like she might nod off over her drink.

'There were so many people there,' I continued, a little louder so that my voice jolted her awake. 'Did you see what happened to Keith? I caught an occasional glimpse of him, always with a drink in his hand, and towards the end of the evening looking decidedly disorientated.'

'Drunk as a skunk,' Sue declared, roused from her near-slumber. 'He went from one end of the drinks table to the other, consuming everything. He's going to have a bad headache tomorrow.'

'He's probably drinking himself into oblivion to forget that he's living at Jean's.' This comment wasn't meant to be mean. I was just flaying myself again.

'When are you moving him over here to stay?' Sue asked, as she glanced at a pile of cartons filled with stuff yet to find a home.

'Shall we give ourselves a day's grace? I'll ring Jean and let her know that we'll pick him up the day after tomorrow.'

The handover was in front of the Sarjeant Art Gallery steps. Jean was already there and waiting with her charge when I pulled up. They exchanged what appeared to be a poignant farewell, after which I loaded his suitcase into the boot of our car. As I did up my seat belt, I felt a sense of apprehension. I had no idea whether he would feel hostile or happy; whether he blamed me or not.

Initially I had trouble understanding his heavy Irish accent. Gradually my ear became attuned. It seemed that his time with Jean had been as eccentric as I feared.

'So did . . . did you have a good time?'

'Yes,' he said, after some internal deliberation, 'I did.'

'Really? You're not just saying that?'

'I enjoyed myself, honestly, but . . . but . . . Jean is a little odd if you don't mind me saying.'

'No, no, that's fine. But you were okay?'

'Yes,' he affirmed again. What a relief, I thought.

'What do you mean by "odd", then?'

'Jean never cooks.'

'You mean you didn't ever get a meal there?'

'No. Never.'

'So what have you eaten?' I demanded, concerned. I looked up and down his scrawny body. His legs were like chopsticks anyway, so it was impossible to tell whether 10 days' fasting had left them any worse off.

'I don't mean I didn't eat anything. I meant Jean didn't cook at home. We ate every main meal at a restaurant called Shangri-La overlooking Victoria Lake.'

'You're kidding me!'

'No, I'm not.'

'It must have cost her a fortune. How can she possibly afford it?' This was a rhetorical question, but I *was* wondering.

'She has a tab with the restaurant, which she pays monthly.'

'You mean she eats there regularly herself?'

'I mean she never eats at home.' Today, this fact may not seem as impossible as it did then.

'Why doesn't she eat at home, do you think?'

'It's the oven,' he said, with a visible shudder. 'It's disgusting.'

My mind raced. I pictured it dripping with splatters and thick, congealed fat covered with a generous coating of dust and disease.

'Was it filthy with fat?' I asked, visualising the dreadfulness.

'No,' he said, his eyes wide open, 'with spider's webs. They were thick over everything. The first morning I got up and went to the kitchen to fix myself a piece of toast. She'd said, "Help yourself to anything." I was just trying to save her the trouble. I opened the oven door and inside was a spider's nest. Her kitchen was draped in cobwebs.'

'Sounds a bit like Miss Havisham's wedding breakfast.'

'Exactly,' he announced. 'But without the rats. For a start, I thought she must have done it as a joke. Then I realised they were real.'

The shock of Jean's kitchen was offset by regular meals out. Jean bought Keith anything he wanted to drink, making regular trips to the liquor store to keep him in dark ale and expensive whiskey. He was much older than his years: a young Irishman, moody, philosophical and already ponderous and questioning about the world. The unextinguished embers of Jean's youth drew air from this friendship and burned bright momentarily. They had laughed and talked together, while I fretted and worried that I had abandoned them both.

VIII

There is no existing photograph of Te Paea Tīaho Pōtatau, the sister of Irihapeti and Tāwhiao. But in the pages of John Gorst's book *The Māori King* you can catch glimpses of her. She is an elusive figure, revealed vividly, fleetingly, against the context of major historical events, then disappearing, and reappearing again to welcome Governor George Grey to the Waikato or negotiate peace at a moment of crisis.

Sue first discovered Te Paea Tīaho in Gorst's book when she picked it up from a trestle table of give-away books. Sue was browsing, flicking through the spines of books, reading out the titles to me.

'This one looks interesting. It's about the Māori King.' She was saying this because I had already advised her not to bother looking. I had an instinct to keep well away from trestle tables in churches. Having known too many church fairs and their tableaux of horror — fingered cookbooks, blind dolls, broken games, matted blankets, things worthy and worn — I was sceptical. Sue handed me the book as proof that treasure can still be found on a trestle table, and a treasure it was.

The dust jacket featured a tukutuku pattern; the feel of the book design was 1950s.

'This was written by Gorst at the height of the Kīngitanga movement and published in 1864, then reprinted in 1959,' Sue explained, running her finger down the book's imprint page.

'Wow,' I responded, reassessing my opinion of trestle tables. 'That's quite a find.'

'Shall I keep it?' she asked, still influenced by my initial cynicism.

'Of course you should. This is your family.' I checked the handwritten sign again to make sure it was free, and then we took it home.

The book sat for a while unread, its foxed pulpy pages not suggesting its hidden wealth. Gorst would prove a fascinating commentator on his times, unravelling the stories of both Māori and Pākehā.

Sue went to Gorst initially to find out about Irihapeti Te Paea Hahau. For a long time she hoped and imagined that the heroic Te Paea of Gorst's story was her great-great-grandmother. But after much consultation it turned out to be Te Paea Tīaho Pōtatau, Irihapeti's half-sister.

'Don't be disappointed,' I said when the verdict came through, 'she's still your distant aunt. You should be pleased to have an aunt like that,' I added with more than just a tinge of 'princess envy'.

Te Paea Tīaho was known among Pākehā as Princess Sophia. Sophia, Greek in origin, meaning wisdom. Gorst would have had her as the queenly replacement for Te Wherowhero: a wise woman, the fitting replacement for a wise king.

She was 35 years old and in her prime when she first met Gorst, and he, 10 years younger and married with children. But during Gorst's time in the Waikato from 1860 to 1863, there was something between them: a bond of respect, a friendship.

Te Paea Tīaho, probably a full sister of Tāwhiao, established herself as a leader of her people when she was sent by her father Te Wherowhero on a bid for peace. To avoid tension escalating to all-out war between the Hawke's Bay and Waikato, Te Wherowhero sent his daughter and two other young women as hostages to underwrite his pledge of peace. The three women may well have lost their lives before they had even had a chance to explain the purpose of their visit, but the Hawke's Bay tribe, thinking the vessel they were travelling on was a whaling ship, permitted them to land. Te Paea Tīaho delivered Te Wherowhero's plea at a council of chiefs, and was so convincing that a guarantee of goodwill was extended and the three young women freed to return to the Waikato.

After that Te Paea Tīaho was often used by the chief as an emissary for peaceful co-existence with Pākehā. When lawlessness stirred again in the buffer zone beyond Auckland and the Waikato, Te Wherowhero sent her to live at Māngere and keep the peace. She was his trusted representative, a spokesperson for his beliefs. She was a committed Christian, whose life was one of service, lived in honour of her father and for the good of her people.

When Te Wherowhero died, she was still in Māngere, kept away from his deathbed by duty. Te Paea Tīaho remained independent. She would never marry or have children. She was powerful in her own right; a woman like Wairaka, Toroa's daughter, who plunged the paddle into the sea and 'acted as a man!'.

In Gorst's book, Te Paea Tīaho is there as a candidate for kingship, and when again living close to Raglan, she took the dramatic step of pulling out Wiremu Nēra Te Awa-i-taia's marker pegs from the ground. He planned to build a road from Raglan to the Waipa River, which would open up a transportation route with the potential to move government troops into the Waikato to attack. The King's supporters saw this as dangerous, and the pegs that marked its passage were removed.

Again, at Te Awamutu, Te Paea Tīaho was there keeping the delicate balance of peace between Pākehā and Māori. Problems had arisen over a planned school to train young Māori men as government servants. This initiative, as well as the building of a bulletproof steamer to transport goods and troops along the Waikato River, were regarded with great suspicion by Kīngitanga. In retaliation, they stole all the sawn timber intended for the school building. Gorst, who was magistrate and inspector of native schools at this time, and was personally affected by this, appealed to Te Paea Tīaho. She sent out word among her people that the timber was hers and must be returned. Being a woman of high rank, it was impossible to ignore her wishes, and the timber was surrendered. 'Now,' she said, 'I shall give the timber to Mr Gorst.' She wrote urging him to fetch his timber, adding a postscript: 'One thing, I have forgotten; please give me a little tobacco.'

She was there also to welcome Governor George Grey when he made a surprise visit to Ngāruawāhia in January 1863. As King Tāwhiao was away, it was his sister who greeted the governor. She joked with him, asking him why he 'hadn't made the surprise complete by cutting down the King's flagstaff because, as a guest, "she would refuse him nothing"'. Te Paea Tīaho was on easy terms with powerful people, both Māori and Pākehā.

When things became increasingly unsettled around Te Awamutu, she told Rewi Maniapoto that the mission station and missionaries were there under her personal protection, and that they were not to be attacked. Initially, he respected her wishes. Later, when Te Awamutu again came under threat, Te Paea Tīaho interrupted a rūnunga of chiefs at Ngāruawāhia. She was upset and tearful, begging them to defend the mission station at Te Awamutu against Ngāti Maniapoto, and stop the war that would inevitably result. Her words of peace were carried away on winds of escalating turbulence.

When it was clear to Te Paea Tīaho that things were becoming increasingly hazardous, she rushed to Te Awamutu to tell Gorst's wife and children to flee. Acting on his own sense of imminent danger, Gorst had already sent his family back to Auckland. The Land Wars marked the end of Gorst's time in Aotearoa and his friendship with Te Paea Tīaho. He and his family would return to England and Te Paea Tīaho would disappear. She was now a princess without a peace to fight for, a woman in a man's world of war.

She was about 50 years old when she died in 1874. Her death notice reports an enormous tangihanga of people gathered at Tāwhiao's home at Waitomo to farewell their much loved Princess Sophia. She was buried in the sacred grave site of her ancestors at Taupiri.

Tāwhiao would outlive his sister by nearly 20 years, dying in 1894 and being buried at Taupiri, also. Their half-sister Irihapeti won her battle in the Land Court, and in January 1874 received Lot 470 in the Parish of Taupiri. She was buried on Taupiri mountain with her siblings in 1900, this strong woman having lived to the ripe age of 80.

If Te Paea Tīaho was the peacemaker of this illustrious brood, then Irihapeti made its progeny: two marriages and 15 children, who were both Māori and Pākehā, people who internalised a land and culture struggle and would have to find their own peace.

CHAPTER NINETEEN

A Clean Start in Auckland

We were only six weeks living in 'My Little Pony Mansion' in Aramoho, Whanganui, when the real-estate agent came to deliver us the gut-wrenching news that we had just over a month to vacate the premises. It was a body blow. We were just settling down with a glass of wine one evening when we heard a knock. I opened the front door, invited the real-estate agent in and offered him a drink. He said 'No thank you', and stood there looking awkward. I knew there was something coming.

'I'm afraid the owners of this house, who now live in Australia, have decided to sell.'

'But . . . but, you said this was a long-term let. You guaranteed us at least six months here. We only took it because of that.'

'I'm sorry, madam,' he responded, his manner stiffening, 'but that's the law. We've given you notice and you have 40 days to vacate the property.' Quite frankly, I was glad he didn't take my offer of a drink because I would have had to resist the temptation not to grab the glass back and throw the contents in his face.

Finally, we'd found some peace. Keith had gone home to Ireland, the exhibition had moved on to the first venue of its tour, my book was already into its second reprint, and my PhD was pending confirmation after the addition of some extra paragraphs. The monstrous pressure I had been under was easing — and now we were facing another shift.

The idea of moving was one that inspired nothing but fear in my heart. Since marrying Richard, I had moved nine times. My life was in a state of perpetual flux: my cabinet had none of the luxury of fastidiousness or sense of permanence of my mother's. I felt like the few treasures I had collected were constantly swaddled in tissue paper or bubble wrap, either awaiting a shift or being unpacked. Each move was expensive and difficult, and the prospect of another left me traumatised.

I was moaning about it at work the next day when Molly Morton, one of my colleagues in the Computer Graphics department, informed me that a verbal promise was pretty much the same as a contract.

'If he guaranteed you a six-month stay, then you can take him to the Tenancy Tribunal. It doesn't cost much, and if you've got a witness they'll probably lose.'

'Great! Thanks, Molly, that's amazing. I'll ring them right away.' So I did. I made an appointment, and the same real-estate agent visited at the same time the next evening. He was on his way home, he explained.

'I got your message that you wanted to see me. Here's the list of things you need to do before we can give you your bond back,' he said. I could sense his feeling of victory over us. I suspected he was delighted at the devastation his news had caused.

'There's just one thing I'd like to say before you go,' I said, leaning over to take the long list of bond-repayment requirements. 'You promised we could stay at least six months in this house. Your promise is a contract. If you make us leave before that we will take your firm to the Tenancy Tribunal. You made a commitment: you are breaking the law if you don't abide by it.' My hand was shaking as I delivered him my ultimatum. It was as much a bluff as anything.

His firm had rented the property knowing it was likely to go on the market at anytime. The look on his face said it all: the threat of going to court; his utter distaste for me — a lowly *lesbian* (which was obvious from our living arrangements). He was affronted by my audacity, but had to be compliant.

'If you feel that strongly about it, I'll go back to the owners and try and convince them to delay their plans. But if you stay here, you'll have people coming through for viewings.'

'If that's the case, then I want a discounted rent.'

'I'll get back to you about that,' he said, barely concealing his contempt.

The outcome was that we stayed on. We paid a little less, but once the property was listed we had a constant stream of people coming through. After a while it felt more like living in a zoo exhibit than a home.

Knowing that we had to move again was unsettling. We began to feel, too, an undercurrent of resistance to our relationship. Whanganui was a small town, with small ideas: the ghost of D'Arcy Cresswell still hovered. While the discrimination wasn't overt, nor was our relationship. We only revealed it where we had to, or where we felt safe, especially after our experience with the tyre man . . .

On the way home from work one evening, Sue had told me about a helpful, mild-mannered biker who ran a tyre repair and sales yard. He had been badly injured in a motorbike crash and now dragged a foot when he walked. One arm was paralysed, also. He had offered Sue some unbelievably cheap tyres to replace the ones on our car that he said were no good. She went in for a puncture repair and came out with a quote for four new tyres.

'I'll have to check with my friend,' Sue said, taking the piece of paper. They continued talking, and, when it emerged that I was female, he confronted her: 'So, are you and your friend a couple?'

'Yes,' she responded, caught off-guard by his shrewd reading of our relationship and his directness.

Sue and I discussed the purchase that night, and we delivered the car together the next day to have the tyres fitted. The tyre man was very attentive. Under the blackened leathers and workshop grime, I could see he was disabled. We were both impressed by the way he had left the bike gang behind and built up a business.

That evening the phone rang. My first thought was that it might be our phantom caller again, or perhaps the real-estate man. I hesitated. Then, thinking better of it, I picked up the receiver.

'Hello,' I said, with the trepidation I now felt when I answered the phone. It was the tyre man. I relaxed. We chatted away pleasantly for a while. Was I happy with the new tyres? Did I feel the car drove better with them balanced? Great follow-up service, I thought as I moved to conclude the conversation.

'You seem like nice girls,' he said, changing the subject. 'We got along well together, didn't we?'

'Yes,' I said, 'and thank you again for the deal on the tyres.'

'I was wondering,' he continued, 'whether you would be interested in a threesome. I'd give you girls a good time,' he said, with a sleazy tone to his voice. He then began a lengthy description of his physical assets, and his broad-mindedness about our sexuality. He didn't have anything against lesbians, and we were to feel free to behave in any way that came naturally. He was launching into a list of girl-on-girl sexual activities that he thought we might try when I sliced through his string of fantasies. He seemed surprised that I had a problem with his proposal. At that point I gave him a piece of my mind and hung up.

'Who was that?' Sue asked, when I got off the phone looking red-faced and angry. I told her everything.

'Dirty bastard,' she responded. 'What a creep.'

'Yeah, half the population hates us, and the other half wants to go to bed with us.'

The first of our new tyres exploded when we were travelling at high speed on the open road. I just managed to control the car as I slowed and brought it to a halt on the side of the road. We took it to a new tyre-repair place, with a revised plan. Only Sue would go into the shop, and she would drop into the conversation a story or two about her husband. It turned out that all the tyres were bad: cheap, dangerous imports that were potential killers.

'We need to get out of here. This place is too parochial,' I said to Sue. The episode with the tyre man blew a shrill warning for me.

By that time, the Red Eye café was our regular haunt, and Sue and I met there for a cup of coffee sometimes before we picked up the children. It was adult time and we loved it. One Wednesday the newspaper was sitting on the table, as usual well and truly read by the many students and staff from the polytechnic who went there. I was in full flight, whinging to Sue about the fact that we needed to move to a bigger centre, when glancing down at a random page of the paper she spotted a tiny advertisement in the Situations Vacant section. She read it out to me. It was another polytechnic lecturing position, only this time in Auckland.

'That's my job,' I said to her, after reading the ad, absolutely certain it fitted perfectly.

I remember the day I heard back about the position. It was one of my vacuum-cleaner moments, only this time I was hanging out washing. Sue brought the phone to me outside. It was Douglas Lloyd-Jenkins, design historian and head of my interview panel for the vacancy at Unitec. He sounded hesitant on the end of the phone, and I was convinced he was ringing to tell me bad news. I had felt certain it was my job, but the interview didn't seem to go well. It was therefore a sublime moment when Douglas told me I had the position. I remember kneeling down and giving thanks, probably to the laundry goddess, for a clean start and a ticket out of there.

Telling the children was hard. It had taken time for them to settle. In the three-and-a-half years that we had been in Whanganui they had made friends and moved schools. Jeremy had gone from primary through intermediate, to secondary school, where he had completed his first year. High school had been another drama. Neither he nor Cody had got into the popular co-educational school, and we were left with little choice. The pressure came on us for Jeremy to go back to something flasher in Christchurch. Emails flowed backwards and forwards until in a dazzling demonstration of lateral thinking we got Jeremy into St Augustine's College, an integrated Catholic boys' school. The game of chess between Richard and I had not, as I had hoped, ended. It was still move and counter-move, in spite of our Family Court mediation. Every unguarded change in our arrangements opened an opportunity for an attack.

A shift to Auckland would turn everything on its head again for Jeremy, but Katherine was just about to start high school, so the move was better timed for her. Still, it took some fast talking to bring them both around to the idea.

While Whanganui, and Barbara especially, had given us so much, it was also the site of a battlefield for me. I had fought for a child, and I had lost one there. It was a place of heart-rending victories and losses. I had sent letters to Alex that were never responded to, and had gifts and cards returned. At one point Richard sent me a helpful list of designer brands that they felt were acceptable, along with a warning that any cheap imitations would be returned. This was brutal. When I tried to pursue things over Alex through the counsel for the child, he refused. The custody case was over and it hadn't gone the counsel's way, and he wasn't going to go beyond his brief to assist me.

Leaving Whanganui, then, was more than just a departure: it was an end. I lost much of what it was to be a parent, in the way I imagine it feels when you lose a limb. When a child, a part of you, is taken from you, everything you try to replace it with feels fake. Selfishly I believed I had grieved long enough for Alex, and I naïvely wanted the torment to stop, but of course it never does.

It was the breathlessness of Auckland that struck me. As a child of the wind, born in the blustery chill of Southland and raised under Canterbury's hot nor'west arch, wind had been a prevailing force in my life. So Auckland in sultry January was disturbingly still. When I looked out of the kitchen window at the banana palms that separated our flat from the next-door neighbours' place, every lush leaf was motionless in the heat and humidity.

Accommodation was hard to find in Auckland, so Sue and I had pounced on the first halfway decent place we looked at. The house was in zone for Avondale College, where we hoped the children would attend school, and was down a long drive, well away from the road for the cats. We were to discover it was a slum property that a landlord had literally white-washed over. The walls, ceilings, kitchen benches, and even the filthy linoleum floor had all been given a quick lick of white undercoat, which meant cupboard doors jammed, windows were painted shut, and every time you crossed the kitchen floor you stuck to it, leaving tacky grey footprints.

'There's that strange insect again,' I called out to Sue, but by the time she looked around a split second later, each time it had scuttled into the workings of a jug, behind the washing machine, or under the fridge. I began to wonder if I were imagining things. Ultimately, we discovered they were the straying members of a massive cockroach infestation, which we then inadvertently moved to our next house.

The plumbing knocked and banged like the percussion section of a pre-school orchestra, and the place smelt dirty and dank. From April onwards a black film of mildew formed in swirling patterns like a Judy Millar painting on the ceiling. The epicentre of the nightmare was our double wardrobe, where we discovered our clothes had become liberally sprinkled with welting outcrops of mildew. As the temperatures cooled, I went to pull out one of my heavier black jackets only to find it spotted like a Dalmatian.

Although our dry-cleaning bill went through the roof and all our clothes had to be repeatedly washed, the bigger plan worked brilliantly. The children were allowed to enrol at Avondale College, and the cats had a safe and happy transition. Nothing about our awful living conditions mattered because the city of Auckland was at the end of our driveway. It was an enchanted city, full of wonder and promise. After more than three years in sleepy Whanganui, we had woken up. All five senses were switched on and vivid. The city was our drug.

Not long after school began, we took the children to New Lynn mall, a warren of hallways lined with dazzling shop-fronts. The crowd that day, unnaturally large even for a mall, was pressing along the corridor to an open space in the centre of the complex. I could see a stage.

'Let's find out what's happening,' Sue called to me over the crescendo of excited noise. She took Katherine's hand and I grabbed Jeremy's, and her arm, and we surged forward, packed together like clothes in a carry-on bag.

'Are you sure we should be doing this?' I asked, feeling increasingly claustrophobic. I eyed the exits in case of a stampede.

At that point, a slickly dressed young man with a microphone launched himself onto the stage. The sound system screeched then rumbled into submission. He blurted on indecipherably. Then I thought I heard a familiar name. I looked at Sue, shocked.

'Did he say Anastacia?'

'Yes, I think he did,' she responded. We were astonished, because Anastacia is an American singer-songwriter who we admire. At the time she had an international hit album.

It was one of those divine moments. Just as the significance of the stage signage began to sink in, the timbre of Anastacia's tremendous mezzo-soprano voice immersed us all in the opening strains of her hit song 'Not That Kind'. She electrified the crowd. She was an Amazon with a voice that delivered every effortless note with dexterity. In the flesh, which was amply revealed in her bikini bra and tight trousers, she was a stunner. I struggled to see her through my tears, which were shed more for me than for her. For the first time in years, I felt connected to the world.

My workplace had literally been a lunatic asylum. Unitec was located in the expansive grounds of what had been Oakley Mental Hospital. I could walk there from our house, across the verdant campus. While the land was lush and productive with its own vegetable plots, landscaped lawns and flower gardens, the buildings were a gothic horror. Built before patients were 'clients' or 'consumers', and when mental health was incarceration rather than 'care', every brick was laid to keep the 'lunatics' in and away from everyone else.

When you walked across the threshold of Building One, it was there: the fear and the foreboding. Rumours had it that there had been a suicide in every one of the many stairwells. Like an Escher print, a labyrinth of connecting corridors and staircases endlessly met but never connected up. This was the architecture of insanity. Years later, I was still discovering new staircases and passageways.

However, in February 2000, Building One provided respite of another sort — from the sweltering heat and sapping humidity. The ceilings were high, the walls thick, and the windows narrow and penitentiary-like. The only beauty was the magnificent Victorian tile floor in the foyer, a flamboyant extravagance in the context of meanness and madness.

My first day I raced headlong through a door that I thought led to the student café, only to find that I was in what had hitherto been a time-out space, which was not much bigger in width and breadth than a coffin. It was a sobering moment, when my exhilaration collapsed under the weight of the building's history. I wondered how many inmates had stood there, angry and weeping. Mortified at the thought of someone seeing me, I slunk away like our cat Tigger did after he had been caught on the kitchen bench.

My office was on the second floor, in a wing off the main body of the building towards the end of a grim series of cell-like rooms. The corridor terminated with a large, open space that I imagine had once been a dormitory or communal lounge. My workplace, a corner room slightly bigger than the others, was filthy and littered with the remnants of past inhabitants, including a filing cabinet with records dating back to its days as an asylum.

My first day was shared with a young academic. I was 41 years old and she in her mid-twenties and madly in love, it seemed, with a young man she had left behind in Australia. The age difference between us was like the Rift Valley. The generation gap that had never seemed to be an issue at Whanganui Polytechnic was glaring at Unitec. Over 35, you were finished as far as many of the young staff members were concerned. But Sonia was too distracted by her own issues to be conscious of any difference between us.

As soon as she walked over the threshold, she wanted to leave. I could see her point. The building disgusted me, too. I loved the way she handed in her notice with such flourish just days after her arrival. I vicariously enjoyed the insult, the assertion that the offices at Unitec were barbaric and the conditions cruel. But I'm not sure how much she made of this in her exit interview, if there ever was one.

Unfortunately, my life was not that simple. I had children and a mortgage: I was locked in a job. But Unitec had a bigger budget than Whanganui, and this spelt opportunity. So, although I was physically incarcerated in a madhouse, my mind travelled to new projects and places. The prompt for this came one day when Douglas Lloyd-Jenkins, my boss, crossed paths with me in the corridor.

'Have you put an application in for research funding?' he asked, coming to a halt mid-stride. His question caught me off-guard. I had forgotten about it. For several weeks I had waited for my phone and internet to be connected. By the time it was, my in-box bulged with messages. I had only made a dent in them by the time the funding applications were about to close. There was too much to do, so I had dismissed it as an idea. Douglas's reminder now galvanised me.

'Don't miss out,' he warned. 'I'll resend you the application form.' I had never received much funding before, so I was sceptical.

'I don't have the time at the moment, and I probably won't get anything, anyway.'

'I'm the chairperson,' he replied. 'You'll probably get something, if you've got a worthwhile project.' A worthwhile project, I thought to myself, well, I've certainly got that.

Rhona Haszard had risen from my dull pile of art reading like a phoenix from the ashes. While most art historians fixate on art objects, I am captivated by the artist's life. Rhona's life left me gobsmacked. She fell from a four-storey tower in Alexandria, Egypt, at the tender age of 30 years old. Although her death was undeniably tragic, in her three brief decades on Earth she had managed to acquire two husbands, conduct a raging affair, and establish an international painting career. And all that was before you even got to the tantalising speculation about how she fell.

The coroner's official verdict was accidental death; that she had fallen from the tower while sketching. Privately, rumours told a different story. The most enticing theory was that she had been pushed by her second husband, Leslie Greener. There wasn't any concrete evidence to support that scenario, but it had nevertheless ignited imaginations at the time and continued to smoulder as the years went by. The other idea also dispersed widely was that in a desperate mental state she had taken her own life by jumping to her death.

All of this was churning over in my mind as I looked at Douglas, trying to work out whether he was being realistic about my prospects of getting any money. I didn't have time to chase fantasies.

'If you get a proposal to me by first thing in the morning, I'll read it through and give you some feedback,' he said, smiling. So that night after the children had gone to bed, I sat down to write my proposal. Rhona Haszard was mentioned teasingly in a couple of survey books, but apart from that there was nothing substantial. I didn't have much to go on except that she was a brilliant painter who came to a mysterious end. For me that was enough, but I wasn't sure that was going to convince the funding committee.

I slaved away on my application until the early hours of the morning. I treasured this time to work. There was the silence to help you think, and the magical feeling that you were the only person in the world still awake. The funding application was submitted on time.

IX

Perhaps the last riddle for Frederic Madden to solve was how the ivories were transported from their carving studio in Trondheim to their hiding place on the Isle of Lewis. This line of research suggested a slightly different story to the others already proposed for how the chess pieces arrived on Lewis. The history of the Vikings' far-reaching maritime empire explained a lot. In fact, the stretch of Irish Sea that connects to the Atlantic Ocean via the North Channel was practically a transit corridor for Norse vessels, and the Hebrides — which included the Isle of Lewis — and Skye, on the west coast of Scotland, were the gateway to Europe.

These were savage seas, and Viking ships travelled close to the coast for fear of turbulent waters and lashing storms. But like the fragile bird that dances on the crocodile's back and falters, vessels were often smashed to pieces on jagged rocks and perished. According to Madden's investigations, one such *knörr* was carrying a consignment of chess sets made in Trondheim and destined for the palace of a king or bishop in Ireland.

Bjorn Erikson was one of many traders who used this seaway. Sailing from Norway to Ireland and back to Greenland, where he came from, was a regular route. On this particular day, he and his crew had anxiously watched an approaching black bank of cloud moving at frighteningly fast speed towards them. Bjorn called his crew to their oars in the hope that they might outrun it and find shelter in a cove along the coast. But suddenly thunder rolled, lightning cracked, rain beat down; the sound was deafening. White-capped phantoms swelled to huge heights in the dying light of the day. The ship pitched, dangerously close to capsizing.

Bjorn's knuckles were white with strain as he held on to the one thing he must save. The leather bag he gripped was saturated and its cargo heavy. He would never be able to swim with it. He reached down into the blackness and whirl of water that was shin-deep in the bottom of the boat and wedged the bag under his seat.

The waves were so big now that they were washing men off the boat: those who were too exhausted and frozen to hold on. The battle to survive was as much inside as out. Bjorn wanted to see his homeland again, and his family. Over the maelstrom, he heard the soulful rending of timbers: rocks. The ship shuddered. There was a hiatus, then the next terrifying wave emptied men, cargo, everything into the sea. Bjorn knew he would not survive long in the frigid water. His limbs were heavy and his body shaking uncontrollably. He had to move quickly, had to find a piece of wreckage buoyant enough to lift him out of the water. In the darkness he could make out a crate. The effort to swim to it and haul himself onto it exhausted him.

It was dawn when he woke. The crate that had carried him through the night was disintegrating in the surf on the shore. Collapsing onto the sand, Bjorn lay stiff and badly battered, but alive.

He must see if there were any other survivors. His first steps were faltering, but soon he was moving steadily along the beach, scanning it to see what had come ashore. At the very end of the bay, he could see the wreckage of the ship cast on its side like a beached whale. Dotted along the stretch before it were bits of debris and bodies, lifeless and unmoving. The day was still and clear, which made the destruction he was witnessing even harder to comprehend. He turned over the first body. It was a slave-hand, but among the others were men he knew well. Bjorn wept.

As he neared the shattered hull, he thought of the bag he had secured under the bench and wondered whether it would still be there. The timbers were so badly damaged, it was difficult to work out where it would be. But, picking his way over, he reached into the hull — and there was the bag.

Bjorn looked up and down the beach to see if anyone was watching. Shipwrecks attracted salvagers. Anyone seeing the wreck might loot its bounty, and he would not have the strength to stop them. He must get the bag away from the boat and hide it. He sunk under its weight as he heaved it onto his back. Ironically, even though he suspected some of the pieces may have been lost to the waves, the bag felt heavier now than when he had taken possession of it in Trondheim.

He planned to deposit his hoard in the sand dunes, and leave it there until he knew it was safe to come back and carry it away. As he clambered back over the wreck, his eyes were set on a bank of dunes well away from the ship. Speed was imperative. How long did he have before the wreck of his ship was discovered?

He shifted the bag higher up his back, repositioned his hands to secure their grasp and headed for the dunes. The initial rush of gratitude he had felt at surviving the wreck now deserted him. The destruction of his ship, the death of his men crashed on him in waves of despair. His body ached, while a burning thirst seared his throat. Only the thought that he must hide his hoard kept him going.

Far away, he thought he could just make out a tiny speck moving against the distant hills. He couldn't be sure, but a sudden rush of fear rose up like bile in his throat. Scavengers were attracted to wrecks like carrion to a dying beast. How long would it take that distant speck to become a person, then a band of marauders picking over the bones of his ship? His only hope was to disappear amongst the sand dunes and hide his loot.

CHAPTER TWENTY
Around-the-World Ticket

Katherine found her feet in Auckland, while Jeremy struggled to establish himself. Setting them free in a cosmopolitan city was for Jeremy less about liberation than it was about uprooting. He missed his friends and never found a match for Cody in his new classmates. When Jeremy joined his Year 10 class, his fellow classmates had already been together a year. I watched with a growing sense of unease as he tried to fit in. Katherine began school in a new top-band Year 9 class. Her friends were rambunctious, hormonal and academically bright, while Jeremy's were lumbering and spotty, with more interest in lunch than lessons. I hoped things would settle down for him, that he would find his equilibrium, but I knew deep down he was in trouble, and, therefore, so was I.

Katherine picked up her ballet again, though nothing could ever replace the magnificent Shirley McDouall. The closest dance class was above a fabric store in New Lynn. There was no tree-lined street, no superb studio, and no charismatic teacher with exotic connections to the Royal Ballet Company in London. The trip there at 5pm was a congested drive along Great North Road at the speed of a funeral procession if the car was lucky enough to be moving at all. In summer it was hot and sticky, and in winter dark and often raining.

While we were there, I don't think I had realised how much we had got out of the benevolent Barbara and the eccentric Jean — and Whanganui — and the intimacy of familiar faces and people knowing your business. I had longed for anonymity, for people not knowing secrets, especially ours. Yet now I missed these people. The positive of leaving them behind was that we didn't have to be as shutdown about our sexuality.

Apart from Jeremy, the other person who bore the brunt of the shift was Sue. She lost her lovely job at the polytechnic, which meant she was out of work again in her mid-forties. Her position in Whanganui teaching tertiary students had been a dream job, and now there was almost no chance of her getting another one. The loss of her income made a big difference, too. So we sat down together one day and began to bash out a CV that she could take around the local high schools. Relief teaching, while being intermittent, was our best option. She worked at a number of schools before Kelston Girls' became her favourite.

We established a comfortable pattern of life, although even in our mildewed tenancy we continued to receive our mystery phone calls. Sue had already given our real-estate agent in Christchurch instructions to sell our duplex, and we were looking for a place to buy in Auckland. Living in our own home after four years in rentals seemed like an unimaginable luxury.

We began traipsing around the properties we could afford. The 1990s had been a boom decade of building in Auckland. It was also a period of corner-cutting and expansion, when anything was possible. Sue's cousin, Gus, a builder, looked at properties with us.

'These walls are made out of polystyrene,' he said, slapping the side of a house we were viewing with him.

'Polystyrene?' I repeated, unable to quite comprehend what I was hearing.

'Yes, polystyrene: they say it's 100 per cent reliable — as long as you don't damage the plaster coating.'

'Who'd have thought they'd be making houses out of polystyrene? Would you buy a polystyrene house, then?'

'No fear,' he said laughing. 'I wouldn't touch the stuff with a 10-foot bargepole. What are the chances of the surface never being damaged? Zero.' So, courtesy of Gus, Sue and I were a little bit more alert than most to the leaky-building crisis that was about to engulf the new-build housing market and send people rushing back to the solid old weatherboard state house.

This meant we were looking for something in the school zone for the children, *and* made out of a sturdier material than the packaging around a new TV set.

We found it in Waterview: in a brick-and-cedar house with four bedrooms, and a study, three toilets and a swimming pool. It was an enormous building on a tiny section. The house was so big in relationship to the land that the only sense the previous owners could make of the extremely modest backyard was a swimming pool. From the lounge it was one leap and you were in it—providing you remembered to open the sliding doors. The children fell in love with the pool, and that cinched it.

At the time we were negotiating the deal we were so cash-strapped that when solar heating for the pool for an extra $5000 was offered by the owners, I said 'No'. Sue wanted to throw caution to the wind and purchase the heating as well as the property, but I was too mean. Which I can hardly believe now because it sealed our fate. From the moment of the first plunge into the pool it was a dice with death in the form of a cardiac arrest.

We settled on 21 July, Katherine's birthday, while I was down in Dunedin overseeing the hanging of the Edith Collier exhibition at the Hocken Library. Sue and I had met Linda Tyler, the gallery director, at a conference the year before.

'She's a dynamo,' Sue had said to me after our first encounter. 'I'd make friends with her if I were you.'

But, as it turned out, it was hard to be anything else. Linda is a whirlwind of positive energy, who gathers friends like my mother collected objects for display. Linda's rare gift is making everyone believe they are in her precious cabinet. While I was in Whanganui negotiating the Collier show travelling to the Hocken Library, she was unreservedly enthusiastic. Now that it was down there and we were walking around the gallery space, nothing had diminished.

Linda has a zest for life. Her behaviour is compulsive. I have always felt she must be haunted by something. Perhaps it was her father's howls of despair when her mother died of cancer, very young. Or her own scoliosis, which she told me, flippantly, was the worst case the specialist had ever seen. Whatever propels her is so strong that I would sit back in awe, watching this blonde firebrand with fingernails as tough as a parrot's claw dash about with unfailing efficiency, doing things.

There are some people in life who you learn things from, and Linda is one of these for me. Her compulsion to fill every moment; the way she merges life and work so no opportunity is lost; and the fact that she never holds on to anything more firmly than the pursuit of her great project, which is living life to the full. It was exhausting watching her, but it did shift me up a gear.

While I was in Dunedin, I also talked to Linda about Rhona Haszard. Her eyes lit up immediately.

'Fascinating,' she said, with intensity as she sorted a pile of papers on her desk, the phone pinned to her ear by her shoulder waiting to be put through to the operator. 'Fabulous artist, but what about her scandalous life . . . Hello?' she said into the phone, but the pause was only temporary and the elevator music continued. 'Damn call-waiting . . .' she said to herself. Then to me, as she binned a pile of superfluous printouts: 'We have her magnificent *Isle of Brecqhou, Sark* in the Dunedin Public Art Gallery collection. We've also got a couple of her minor works here at the Hocken, and one by her first husband. Rhona Haszard's life reads like the script of a soap opera, doesn't it? As well as her untimely death there's that first marriage to fellow artist Ronald McKenzie, then her elopement, in 1926, with Leslie Greener.'

'Yes,' I said, smiling to myself. 'That scandal would have rocked teacups and shocked the grand dames of Christchurch.' In the 1920s, Christchurch was a conservative place, not unlike the Christchurch Sue and I had encountered. Rhona Haszard was a bohemian flapper whose contemporaries were wilder than those who came before and after them. She and her generation belonged to the inter-war decades. Pumped by positivity at the end of the First World War, and oblivious to the signs of the next, their mission was to set the codes and conventions of their parents on fire. Rhona Haszard was one of the more adventurous souls who flew into the flames and burned.

Linda seemed keen to sponsor an exhibition of Haszard's work, so that was enough for me to feel the old sense of adventure again. I was on a mission to find out how Rhona Haszard died; why she died; and to exhibit her work. The last time it was shown was in 1934, when her second husband, Leslie Greener, brought a posthumous exhibition of her paintings and prints back to tour New Zealand. His intention was to sell them so her work could stay in public and private collections in the country of her birth. He was well remunerated for his efforts, which only added weight to the murder theory for those who believed that behind this magnanimous gesture was a callous killer cashing in. But this had meant most of her important work was repatriated. So I left Linda with the seed of an idea for an exhibition hosted by the Hocken Library.

My proposal for research funding arrived back in my pigeonhole at Unitec with a disheartening number of changes to make. For a start, I had to supply a travel budget.

'How much does it cost to go to Egypt?' I asked the young travel agent at our local mall.

'Is it just Egypt that you want to go to?' she asked me, grabbing a pen and writing EGYPT in large childish letters at the top of the page.

'No, but I thought I would price the most preposterous place first.'

'Where else do you want to go, because we've got these around-the-world tickets that might work for you?'

'Around-the-world?' I repeated, mesmerised. 'How can an around-the-world ticket be cheaper than going there and back?'

'I don't know,' she said, 'but the rules are that as long as you never go backwards you can go anywhere you like.'

So Sue and I had the travel agent jot down on her pad all of the places where Rhona Haszard had painted, then our travel dates and names. She began clacking the information into the computer. We sat with bated breath, wondering whether she could configure our itinerary so we never retraced our steps.

'Got it!' she said at last. 'You'll be going via Asia, first to London, then Paris, Brittany, Egypt, and home via the USA.'

'Well, that won't happen,' I said to Sue under my breath as we walked out the door, a few minutes later.

'What do you mean, "that won't happen"?'

'Just that,' I hissed, 'and keep your voice down. It won't happen because we won't get enough money to cover the trip. Look at how much it's going to cost,' I said, passing her the piece of paper with our itinerary jotted down, at the bottom of which was the price of an around-the-world ticket. 'If work doesn't give us the money for at least one whole ticket, we'll never afford it. Even then, it's a risk with the mortgage to pay. It'll never happen,' I repeated, feeling more depressed than I had when I went in because now I knew what I was missing out on.

That night I sat down at the kitchen table and typed out the budget. I added on the extra train tickets, a few incidental costs, and emailed it to Douglas. For a while it played on my mind. The next morning I checked my incoming emails incessantly, then gradually gave the concept away. It was a week or so later, in the corridor again, that I bumped into Douglas. He was on his way to see me. I noted he was carrying my research application.

'I'm afraid . . .' he began. Here we go, I thought, another rejection. 'We can't give you all you've asked for. As much as this is a worthwhile project, funds are limited and have to be shared around. But we've covered the cost of your flight and a train ticket or two.'

'You're kidding me.'

'No, no.' He added, 'We thought it was justified. If you are prepared to cover your accommodation, I can give you the cost codes, and as long as you spend the money this academic year, you can go. Congratulations,' he said, as he handed me my application and strode off. I looked in shock at the list of destinations. This is going to be some adventure, I thought.

'But how are we going to afford to pay for another ticket?' Sue demanded that evening. 'You'll have to go on your own.'

Trust Sue the pragmatist to bring everything crashing down to reality, I thought.

'There's no way I'm going on my own. You know that's out of the question. If you can't come, then I'll have to can it.'

'You can't do that,' she responded, horrified. 'How often do you get an around-the-world trip paid for?'

'Exactly — and for me to be able to use it, we both have to go.'

'Maybe, but things are going to be tight. There won't be any spare money.'

'A shoestring,' I reassured her, excited. 'That's what we'll travel on. You know we can do it.' This was a plausible argument because we'd been living on one ever since we'd got together.

'We need to investigate things. Don't you have to have shots to go to Egypt? I bet you do.'

'Yeah, probably. Why don't you ring the doctor if you're home tomorrow and find out?'

The next day the phone rang in my office.

'Bad news, I'm afraid.' It was Sue. 'I've just got off the phone to the doctor's nurse. It's going to cost $900 each for the shots, and you have to have them three months apart over nine months. That's an extra $1800. So the trip is out of the question.' This was devastating news after spending the day relishing the idea of a trip.

'We won't even have time to have the whole course of injections before we go away,' she added.

'That's the solution, then.'

'What solution?'

'We won't bother having them. If we can't even finish the course, let's

Around-the-World Ticket **269**

not start it. We're only going to Egypt for a week. What can happen in that time?'

'Quite a bit.'

'Well, ring the doctor's nurse back and ask her if people go without being immunised. Go on, ring, before we make the decision to flag it. See if we absolutely have to have them, then call me back.'

I hung up the phone and pushed aside the art books I'd been reading. What a rollercoaster ride. If we weren't going, there wasn't much point pursuing the project. I looked out the window. My summer and autumn were dominated by the large green leaves of an enormous tree outside my room, which filled the window. They gave the space an uncanny livid green tinge. In winter and early spring, the branches were bare black fingers and the light through the narrow window a dismal grey. It seemed that there was never a season when my artificial strip-light was not on.

The phone rang again, and I pounced on it.

'Hello, is that you, Sue?'

'Yes. The doctor's nurse says the shots aren't mandatory. But she thinks it's a huge risk going without them.'

'Just as I thought. We don't need them, so let's buy the tickets, now.'

Teaching at Unitec was a busy baptism of fire. After the small boutique-sized classes of Whanganui, this was mass-education on a grand scale. Each class I would encounter 208 students, all sitting in the darkness. They mobbed out at the end of each lecture, and I recognised no one. I missed knowing my students as individuals.

Each morning I stared at my garments in despair. For the first time in my life, I had a walk-in wardrobe, but my clothes were the tatty, tired remnants of life as a curate's wife, then as a defendant in a legal suit.

My wardrobe was one big second-hand SaveMart.

'You're going to have to buy some new clothes,' Sue said to me one morning, as I stood before her in my third mix-n-match crap-couture combination. 'That looks terrible.'

'But this is my best jacket. I think it's an excellent distraction from the trousers, which I admit are a bit tired.'

'Tired — tired!' shouted Sue. 'You look like a bag-lady!'

'That's a bit harsh.' But when I walked over to the mirror, I could see what she meant. My dismal attire put a new spin on the phrase 'streetwear'.

'But I can't afford anything new.'

'Doesn't matter. You can't go around looking like that. Have you seen the beautiful clothes your students wear?'

'Well . . . yes,' I agreed. I had to admit that Auckland students were a different breed. There was nothing alternative about them. Not even a hint of the old hippie. She was right. I was out of step. My students were the children of baby-boomers. Their rebellion was to go corporate. They drank orange juice at art openings as they coolly checked their mobile phones.

'Okay, I'll have to spend some money.' But where to start? Underpants? Bras? I thought. No. What they can't see won't hurt them.

'I'll help,' Sue offered.

I had never been a big clothes shopper. There were vague recollections of a time when my dress sense mattered, but it was less a case of reviving these memories than contacting them by séance.

'You're on,' I responded. 'This weekend. Let's do it.'

I flinched when the shop assistant swiped my plastic card through the EFTPOS machine. Parting with money for clothes was hard for me. We had gone to the most expensive shop first.

'Bloody hell, these trousers are over $100!'

'Yes, that's right. That's what normal people pay for a pair of trousers.'

'But it's outrageous. It's only a bit of material. How much do you reckon the material costs?'

'You're impossible. It's not about cost; it's about the label.'

'Well, the label doesn't look like it's worth $100 either,' I replied, peering inside the waistband.

'Not that label, you idiot, the shop's label.'

'If I have to pay that much for a pair of trousers because of the label, I'll be wearing them inside out so everyone can see it.'

'Are you all right in there?' came a voice from behind the curtain. 'Have you got the right size? Do you want me to get you another colour?'

'No, we're alright thanks,' I called out, pulling on the next pair of trousers quickly just in case she whisked the curtain back.

'She thinks we're shoplifting,' I whispered to Sue when I thought the shop assistant had gone away.

'No, she doesn't. Don't be ridiculous,' Sue said; the signs of frustration were showing.

'Why is she hanging around, then?'

'Because she's trying to sell you a pair of trousers.'

My experience of clothes shopping was limited. As a rule, I held things up to my chin or waist and guessed. If there was a mirror to check the colour, that was a bonus. The one time I tried on a maternity bra that my mother-in-law had offered to pay for, the shop assistant, demonstrating its versatility, whipped down the two trapdoors at the front to reveal my bosoms. This mortification cured me of any remnant of curiosity for trying on clothes.

'Well, whatever she's doing, I don't like it. It's creepy having someone hanging around outside. And why is she so friendly?'

As soon as we entered the shop, she had gushed over us like we were old friends. How had our day been? What was the weather like outside? Two pairs of trousers: $200. Now as I looked in my plastic bag, this novice shopper realised the friendliness was just a ploy.

Our purchases weren't going to transform my appearance, but I was done with shopping. It took so much longer when you had to try everything on, and we'd been in there way longer than five minutes.

'Let's get home, quick,' I said, bumping into someone as I made a dash in the direction of our car. My escape was halted. Sue grabbed my arm with an iron grip.

'Not so fast: we haven't been to Glassons yet.'

'But they've gone young,' I responded, hoping to put her off. 'Look,' I said pointing to their shop window.

'Never mind. There's bound to be something you can dress those trousers up with.'

'We'd better be quick. I've got a pile of marking to do.'

Sue began swishing through the racks of clothes, rubbing some of the fabrics between her fingers, then pulling the occasional item out.

'Is this your colour?' she asked, holding a garment up. 'It's winter.' She had the winter bit right, I thought: the whole thing left me cold. I was now slumped in the chair by the counter, sullen and pouting.

'Get up!' Sue snapped. 'If you don't participate, I'm off. You're lucky I care enough to help.'

Realising I'd pushed my luck, I threw myself with gusto into the closest rack of clothes and feigned interest. Stroking synthetic trousers until the sparks flew, like I cared.

'We're here to look at tops,' Sue called from her rack. 'What do you think of this?' she said, holding up an item.

'Great,' I said, well aware that I was skating on thin ice. 'Shall I try it on?' By that stage she had collected quite a bundle. No good looking hangdog and risking a scene, I thought.

'Can we try these on?' Sue asked turning to yet another beaming shop assistant.

'Yes, certainly,' the young woman replied. 'How many items do you have?'

'I'm not sure.' Sue began counting. 'Eleven,' she said finally, having reached the end of the armload.

'That's fine,' the attendant said. 'There's a cubicle free at the end of the row on the left-hand side.'

'If I'm to try all of these on you're going to have to hang around and tell me what looks okay. Don't just bugger off.'

'I'll stand outside,' replied Sue. 'Now get in there and get on with it.'

Reluctantly, I took off my coat, jersey, shirt and singlet and began trying on Sue's knit cotton tops. Red ones, long- and short-sleeved tops with matching vest: black ones, the same deal. It was endless. Some of them I had to try on twice because Sue had forgotten what the first combination looked like.

'I don't believe it!' I exclaimed. 'I've only just tried that combination on.'

'Tough. I can't remember.'

'Well, pay attention this time.'

'Look, I'm doing you a favour here . . .'

After I tried on the last two combinations in quick succession, Sue admitted she couldn't decide.

'Can't decide!' I repeated, looking at the mounting jumble of clothes on the cubicle floor.

'I know!' Sue exclaimed. 'I'll go and ask that nice shop assistant to come and help us.' She was gone before I had a chance to stop her. I was half in one combination when Sue whisked back the curtain.

'What do you think?' she said to the girl, then barked at me: 'You've got it on inside-out. Put it on properly.' So, in front of the young woman, I took it off, then put it on again, around the right way, then tried on the other option.

'What do you think?' Sue asked, looking at the assistant.

'It comes down to sleeves,' she replied, looking at me. 'Do you like long or short sleeves?'

'I'll take both,' I exclaimed, delighted that I could solve the problem so easily.

'Here,' I said picking the items off the floor and passing them to the assistant. 'Sorry about the shambles, but I've had to buy these new clothes, because I've just got a lecturing position at Unitec,' I added self-importantly.

'I know,' she replied, smiling, 'you're *my* lecturer.'

'Oh my God, *I'm not?!*' I said in horror, grabbing a garment back and clutching it in front of my shabby bra.

The year sped by like no other. In April I had graduated, the first person across the stage to have their PhD conferred in the Arts in the new millennium. June and July slipped from one semester to the next. I got used to the bigger classes, and began to enjoy the buzz of a lecture theatre that seated over 200 people. The marking, however, was horrendous because my colleagues cruelly convinced me that my predecessor had done all the marking and that I must follow suit. It was a year of 18-hour-long marking sessions before I figured out the ruse and made them shoulder some of their own responsibility. By the end of the year, I was nearly brought down by it. I could write the book on how to get economy-class syndrome, without leaving the office.

Sue and I left for the United Kingdom as soon as school was let out at the end of the year. In fact, Jeremy and Katherine flew down to their fathers a day or so early to catch the cheap fare. Jeremy had promised to set me up with a Yahoo account, because in those days there was no accessing your work email from abroad. Everything was a rush, and setting up a personal email account was the very last thing on my list. I'd been up all night packing. The kids were going off for the summer holidays, and we were ready for a five-week around-the-world trip.

On the way to the airport, we stopped off at my office to get the email sorted. Just Jeremy and I went inside: Sue and Katherine sat in the car waiting. We mucked around filling in website fields and scrolling down lengthy drop-boxes until I looked at my watch.

'Oh my God!' I shouted. 'Quick, push enter and let's get out of here. We're going to miss the plane.' We ran back to the car like we were being harried by the hounds of Hell.

'Are you crazy!' Sue screamed at me as I turned the key, threw the car into reverse gear and shot backwards out of the car park. 'We'll never get there in time. It's impossible.'

'Sorry, sorry,' I repeated, knowing there was nothing for it but to apologise. And drive. By this time, we were out on the street, running amber lights and barrelling along as fast as I could safely go. When I wasn't glancing down at the speedo, I was checking my watch. Sue was right, there wasn't enough time to get there. At the airport I shouted to everyone to run ahead.

'I'll catch up,' I called, as I grabbed the kids' bags out of the boot and locked the car doors, then ran as fast as I could after them. I caught up just as they were walking down the corridor to the boarding gate. I looked at my watch. We were too late. The plane had gone. But as we turned the corner, I could see that the boarding area was still full of people.

'I don't believe it,' I gasped between breaths, 'I think the plane's been delayed.' The last passengers were just boarding as we arrived.

'Okay, sweetheart,' I said to Jeremy, as I handed him his bag. 'Have a wonderful time. I'll send you lots of postcards and bring you something nice back.'

'Bye, Mum,' he said, giving me a big hug.

'Merry Christmas!' I called, as I blew him a kiss.

'Merry Christmas to you, too, Katherine!' I shouted, blowing her a kiss and waving frantically as they both disappeared through the doorway.

'I'm really sorry about that,' I said, turning to Sue, as soon as they were gone. 'I mucked up badly. I feel terrible. We didn't even get to say goodbye properly. It was so rushed, and it's all my fault.'

Sue is the most forgiving soul when it comes to something significantly bad. I should have been publicly flogged for causing so much stress, but she was philosophical.

'Well, you won't make that mistake again.'

'I certainly won't.'

It was always a strange feeling whenever the kids left. Although there was the relief of not having to deal with their daily needs, there was also that painful sense of loss. Like a part of me had been removed again. I also had the added pressure of wondering whether Jeremy would come back. My trepidation had lessened with successive exchanges, but I always knew that Richard had it in him to try to keep Jeremy. To make an endgame move that would leave me devastated.

This was what he thought I deserved. So freedom from parenting was always bitter-sweet for me, and even more bitter this time because we had separated in such a rushed manner.

At home the place was silent. I went around the bedrooms, Katherine's upstairs and Jeremy's on the ground floor, taking the sheets off the beds and collecting the laundry. Although we had asked them to tidy up, it still looked as though they had gutted their wardrobes and taken out their drawers and shaken the contents onto the floor.

'Well, what do you expect?' Sue demanded as I stood at the entrance to

Jeremy's room, dismayed. 'They've got us for role models. We never put anything away, either.'

'I don't think we're quite that bad.' But I knew she had a point.

The next day our friends, Neil and André, dropped us off at the airport. My separation anxiety was gradually being overtaken by a new emotion: wanderlust. As I sat in the departure lounge, I realised that it had been four years since my last great adventure to the UK, when I was researching Edith Collier. I had come back to Christchurch to escape with Jeremy, and ultimately to lose Alex. Perhaps this is why parting from Jeremy this time had such an ominous feeling to it.

But things are different now after the custody case has been resolved, I told myself — calmer, more settled. Although we still got phone calls from our stalker, they were intermittent and at longer intervals. Sometimes there was a cluster, but these were only occasional. I neutralised my doubts as best I could. The departure lounge is a no-man's-land of space to think backwards and forwards in time. Even though Jeremy's return to us after the holidays worried me, I decided to focus on the immediate future.

IX

Sue was shocked when she learned that her great-grandmother Maria Louisa Stubbing was buried at Waikumete Cemetery in Auckland. She had always assumed that Maria would have been buried at Ngāruawāhia with her whānau. Perhaps even on Taupiri mountain. But when the circumstances of her great-grandmother's death are considered, the reason is obvious.

'Waikumete Cemetery's so close,' I told Sue in my best don't-mess-with-me voice. 'We have to go and see it.' I was surprised when my idea wasn't immediately embraced.

'I can't go this weekend, Katherine's coming over and I have to cook dinner.'

'But this is your great-grandmother's grave,' I replied. 'Get a takeaway.' Then I added what I knew would be a winner: 'If you're too busy, I'll go on my own.'

It's funny how those big family deaths in the past disappear under the details of the ever-present, which always seems more compelling.

But I had planted the idea, and by the time we got in the car one blustery spring morning in September 2021, Sue was more excited than I was. She had found Maria's plot online, and was giving me directions as we drove down

Great North Road, which was strangely quiet and sparse of traffic because of another Covid-19 lockdown. Before we left the house, we had debated about whether we were allowed to visit Maria's grave at alert level 4. Sue searched online, too. 'We are permitted to go to the cemetery for exercise, or to visit a grave: socially distanced,' she told me.

Maria's burial site was along Glenview Road. Over the years the one thing that had exponentially improved Sue's and my relationship was Siri. If I had known what a marriage guidance counsellor she was, I would have employed her sooner.

But before Siri got a word in, Sue shouted out: 'Stop, it's here! Park behind that van.'

The wind was cool and crisp as we got out of the car, and the sky a revolving shadow-lantern of billowing white and grey clouds.

'We'll never find her grave,' Sue determined before we had even crossed the road and entered the cemetery through a gap in the hedge. 'It's just a plot number. There's no headstone. Here's a photograph of the spot.'

'Oh,' I replied, staring at the image on her phone screen of an anonymous-looking square of grass. 'That could be anywhere.'

Between the paths we found an open patch of tilted ground dotted with white wildflowers — small, star-shaped and delicate. Sue held her phone up with its green square against the grass.

'It was taken looking up the rise, not down,' I pointed out to her. Then Sue opened the photograph up to show the top of the image. There along the skyline was a distinctive tree and an oddly shaped telegraph pole. We moved along the plots, passing headstones until we stood in front of a space of long grass, with that exact view behind it.

'This is it!' Sue exclaimed, delighted to find Maria's grave. 'Division A, Row 4, Plot 62!'

But in that piece of ground there was not one grave, but two. If there had been a headstone, it would have read:

Maria Louisa Stubbing born 25 December 1854 —
died 18 November 1918

and her much-loved son

Harold Bowie Stubbing born 23 August 1876 —
died 7 November 1918

Both mother and son had died in the influenza epidemic of 1918. Sixty-four-year-old Maria had rushed up to Auckland to nurse her ill son. Harold died not long after her arrival, and Maria, just over a week later. Ironically, her two soldier sons had returned home safely after serving overseas during the First World War, while Harold, who had stayed home, died.

The influenza epidemic, which possibly began in Kansas at Camp Funston, then swept through Europe and Asia before the end of the war, brought its own scourge. It would kill more people than the bloodiest human conflict ever known. Globally, somewhere between 20 million and 40 million people lost their lives.

In Aotearoa, 9000 people died. Hospitals and healthcare professionals struggled with the acute demands of the pandemic. Systems slumped under the vast number of deaths and bodies needing to be buried. Whole households were slaughtered by this invisible enemy, especially in Auckland in poorer areas where people were packed closely together. For every one Pākehā who died, Māori counted eight more.

Bodies were gathered together in a makeshift morgue where Victoria Park is now. From there they were transported by train to Waikumete to be interred in mass graves, which were sited closest to the railway line to minimise the potential spread of infection. At the cemetery 1100 victims of the influenza epidemic were buried, 400 of them with only one headstone.

Maria died as she had lived, selflessly. She was one of Irihapeti's younger children, born at Waikato Heads, but was just young when her father John Horton Mackay was drowned and her mother moved to Raglan with Samuel Joyce.

She married Scotsman Benjamin Stubbing in Whakatāne and settled at Taupiri, near Ngāruawāhia. They were drawn to the area, it seems, to be near to the Māori King and her other relatives. And close to land that her mother had fought for, and to Irihapeti's burial place on Taupiri. Ultimately, they would lease a mission property at Hopuhopu and farm it until Maria died. Benjamin Stubbing supplemented their income by working as an overseer of road construction in the central North Island. The couple had 12 children. Maria became a midwife in her local community, often staying overnight and preparing a meal for a family that had welcomed a new life into the world. She was renowned for her cooking and hospitality.

Maria's death at Vermont Street Hospital, in Ponsonby — a school requisitioned and refitted for nursing the sick and dying — was just one more among many.

For her family living away from Auckland, unable to attend the interment or memorialise her passing, this was personal, and a double tragedy.

In an unmarked grave in the Nonconformist section of Waikumete Cemetery, they had lost both a mother and her son.

CHAPTER TWENTY-ONE

The Spirit of My Ancestors

The train from Heathrow airport to London charged through leafy railway sidings heavy with winter rain, then brick-walled backyards, and finally chimney pots that seemed to whizz past at high speed. Flashes of people's lives flickered like a strobe light in my consciousness. Sue and I looked on intrigued, whereas the local Londoners just let it fly by unobserved. I longed to be that wearied by it. Instead, I was as transfixed as my grandmother and the rest of New Zealand gazing at flickering newsreels of England, until our train sank down below the city. Station platforms became light-filled caverns carved out of the underground.

It was a struggle with our bags. Every time the tube lurched forward, the bag that I thought was so sensibly packed bashed against my knee like a sledgehammer until I shifted the awkward weight slightly to one side.

Stepping out onto the platform was an enormous struggle. People squeezed into and off the train through doors that snapped shut in an instant. It was hair-raising trying to do that plus wield our huge bags. The final straw was the grim flight of steps up to the street. If it wasn't for the kind young man who offered to help us, we would likely have remained defeated at the bottom.

'I'm never, ever going to pack this much again,' I snarled as we battled our way through the throng of Oxford Street shoppers. There was no logic to the way people came at you.

'Famous last words. You said that last time,' Sue jeered.

'True,' I conceded. That was my resolution every time I went anywhere with a suitcase. Even after they came with wheels like ours did now.

'It'll be different next time,' I said, gritting my teeth, as yet another person walked up the back of my heel. 'Don't get too far ahead. If I lose sight of you in this lot, I'll never find you again.' I was starting to panic. Occasionally a gap in the crowd would allow Sue to move ahead, and she had the map. It was that primal fear of losing someone.

'I think this is our street,' she shouted finally, pointing so I could just see her hand.

'Yes, that rings a bell,' I called back. It was difficult extricating our bags from the press of people.

'Good to be out of that lot,' I said, after running over the foot of a particularly aggressive pedestrian with sadistic delight. We had navigated side streets with odd, disconnected stretches of footpath, which in some places disappeared altogether. We were exhausted. The wind felt doubly bitter after the lovely summer we had just left. But this and twenty-six-and-a-half hours' long-haul flying could not dampen my sense of elation. We were in London again.

'Follow me, please,' said the young male attendant at the youth hostel, whose heavy European accent I struggled to understand. 'Vee hav got you a verry goot room unt za ground floor.' He stepped out of his office, locking the door behind him with a key selected from an enormous bunch.

'I'm afraid zah only room left has a double. No single beds,' he said looking compassionately at both of us. 'I could drop zah price a little . . . a free breakfast also, perhaps?' So each morning for the next three weeks we were compensated with a continental breakfast for the inconvenience of sleeping together.

'It's not often being a lesbian works in your favour,' I said, propped up in bed hungrily polishing off my pottle of yoghurt.

'There's so much here,' Sue replied, 'I think I'll keep the rest of mine for lunch.' So that became the pattern for the day.

The youth hostel proved to be colourful accommodation. We soon learned to wear our sturdiest shoes on party nights, which were generally Friday and Saturday. The toilets were places of carnage. Faeces, blood, vomit, stray underpants and the occasional used condom were all there. If you weren't careful, going to the lavatory was a baptism in bodily fluids.

'My mother would be horrified,' I complained to Sue, after my first encounter. 'Out of here like a robber's dog, she'd be. Free breakfast or no free breakfast.'

But party night was not the only fright.

'Oh my God!' Sue called as she barged through our door. 'You're never going to believe the shower.'

'Was it good? What's the water pressure like?'

'It's not the pressure you're going to find hard!'

'What do you mean?'

'Well, there was so much hair in the drain it looks like someone has killed a cat and tried to flush it down the plug-hole. I got rid of some of it with a paper towel, but it just kept coming up. I reckon if I'd carried on I might have fished up hairs belonging to Henry VIII.'

'Gross. I'll wear my jandals.'

'Jandals!' Sue laughed. 'Jandals,' she repeated, nearly killing herself. 'Try wading boots!'

I went to the shower room well prepared. Along with a towel, hair shampoo and conditioner, I took three plastic bags and an ice-block stick from the kitchen. So armed, I went into battle with the British plumbing system. Locking the shower-room door, I undressed, put a plastic bag over each of my jandals, and the third, smaller bag over the hand that flourished the ice-block stick and went to work on the plug-hole. But it was a battle I could not win.

When I had removed as much hair as I could, I turned the water on and stepped in. It wasn't long before the shower box as well as my plastic bags filled up with water. In the end I gave up, de-bagged my feet and thought of England.

London was cold. Evenings bedazzled with Christmas lights were some compensation, but we still froze. The wind blew bitter, while days dawned slow and sodden with rain. Occasionally, a silver orb would appear in the sky. The weather would have weighed more heavily upon us had the city not been so enchanting, with its ancient buildings, monuments, parks and endless history.

Even sitting outside in the rain under our umbrellas on the steps of the

Victoria and Albert Museum drinking our flask of coffee and eating leftover breakfast did not dampen our enthusiasm. There was nowhere to eat inside except the cafeteria, and we couldn't afford a cup of coffee: not every day, anyway. We visited the Tate gallery, too, but I spent most of my time in the research library at the V&A.

Walking into its book-lined reception area was a trip back in time. Aging volumes with heavy leather-bound bindings ran floor-to-ceiling. The topmost shelves were accessible only by a long, narrow ladder that slipped sideways along an ingenious rail. I had to record my entry and exit in a book, and there was a rigorous procedure to be gone through before I was allowed into the reading room. I had had to send a letter of introduction from my boss in New Zealand, in advance. And now I needed to apply for a temporary reader's card.

I was exhausted and still jet-lagged by the time I finally sat nodding off over the catalogues containing information about Rhona Haszard. For the next few weeks I read through *Studio* and *Colour* magazines; articles on Claude Flight, the experimental printmaker Rhona had exhibited with in the 1920s; and books on the English post-impressionist Camden Town Group, who were her models. While I read and took notes, Sue either drew from sculptures in the exhibition halls, visited shows or window-shopped. Most lunchtimes, she joined me on the steps in the wind and the rain; we must have looked a destitute pair, but in fact we felt as if we were on top of the world.

The highlight of my final few days in London was a visit to the British Museum to see the Lewis chess pieces again. Standing before them now that I knew so much more did nothing to detract from their mystique. I still had a compelling sense that I wanted to own them. To possess these objects that were a thread through time that connected my ancient Scandinavian ancestors to me. Then, I had an idea. I decided to carve my own version of the Lewis chess pieces in bone. Bone was a material that I had fashioned into items I'd given away for years. Now I was going to make something for me. I wanted to carve them by hand, to give them the value of time and allow the potential for them to carry a trace — in the way that Māori believe a taonga or treasured object carries traces — of the wairua of their ancestors. I was going to carve the objects I wanted to keep in my cabinet.

'I thought it was a ferry,' I said, white-knuckled from holding onto the arm of my seat. Terrified by the idea that I was on a train *under the sea!*

'How could you get it so wrong?' Sue responded, amused.

'The Eurostar. Look,' I said, waving the boarding passes in front of her face. 'That sounds like a boat to me.'

'But weren't you a bit suspicious when the itinerary said we had to catch a train at King's Cross St Pancras Station?'

'No,' I said. 'I thought a train trip to Dover to catch the ferry might have been included in the ticket. It was expensive enough,' I added.

'Well, there's no escaping now. What can happen, anyway?'

My mind was bulging with disaster-movie possibilities. I shut up. There was no point in tempting fate by explaining them to Sue. So I sat back, closed my eyes and tried to convince myself that I was somewhere else. Anywhere else. Fortunately, the movement of the train was soporific, and it seemed no time before I was jolted awake by a voice over the intercom.

'Bonjour . . .'

Oh crap, I thought, as I went through the backpack that was wedged between my legs rather than in the overhead luggage rack because it was so stuffed full of books and research notes that it wouldn't fit. That's dumb. My *Lonely Planet* travellers' guide to French was still in my suitcase.

'Is she saying something about a station?' I asked Sue. 'Did she say "Gare"?'

'How would I know?'

'You were listening, weren't you?'

'So were you.'

'Yes, but I can't understand her accent.'

'That's not an accent. It's French.'

'But she speaks it so fast and runs it all together.' The one comforting thought was that we didn't have to get off the train before it reached its terminus in Paris.

Sue worked miracles with the French *métro* map. She sorted out the colour-coded numbering system, and the fact that the word *port* on many of the signs wasn't where ships docked. It was early evening by the time we reached the youth hostel, which was a compact, modernist building that had five levels, including the basement where a complimentary breakfast of coffee, bread and pastries was served.

Between the concierge's broken English and my rubbish French, we managed to get our breakfast vouchers and a room key. The room we were given had six bunk-beds, but for that night we had it to ourselves. Getting into the room, however, was the problem. We couldn't get our key to work in the lock. In the UK it was the plumbing; in France it was the door locks, which existed in their own unique paradigm.

We went downstairs and with difficulty communicated our problem to the concierge. The key was faulty, I told him, because it wouldn't open the door. He left his desk reluctantly, demonstrating with a flourish, when he got to our room, what we had struggled so long to do.

'*Voilà!*' he exclaimed, with lots of supporting hand gestures.

'*Très bien. Merci beaucoup,*' I said in my best French accent — which was a mistake, because he then poured forth a torrent of incomprehensible conversation. I would soon learn that if your accent sounded as poor as your French vocabulary, people might take pity on you and speak English.

'Did you understand any of that?' Sue asked me after he had left.

'Not a word,' I admitted, even though I had nodded my head knowledgeably the whole way through. After that it was hit-or-miss whether we got into our room.

That night when I went to the toilet, I left a pair of socks in the door so it wouldn't snap shut.

'Sue, Sue,' I called out across the darkness when I got back. 'You won't believe it.'

'What?'

'They're shooting up in the toilets.'

'Do you mean drugs?'

'Yeah. They were sitting all over the floor in the women's toilet injecting themselves. Tourniquets, syringes: the lot. Bold as anything. Right out in the open.'

'Good thing we're not staying long.'

'You can say that again.'

While we were in Paris, we visited the Louvre and the Musée d'Orsay. The Louvre, especially, left me speechless. We got lost in its cavernous corridors, all 12 miles of them containing 300,000 works of art. After a four-hour 'wonder blast' of art and archaeology, we ran out of steam.

'I can't walk another step,' Sue said, stopping in her tracks.

'I need to sit down.' I put on a brave face, but was not far off complete collapse myself.

'I need a cup of coffee — now.'

'Over there,' I said, pointing to one of the museum's cafés. As we approached, I could see the prices listed on the sign above the counter.

'Bloody hell! Look at the cost.'

'Yep,' replied, Sue, 'and you have to pay more to sit down.'

'Rubbish.' But she was right, I found, as I got closer and could see the small print. 'These cups of coffee are going to cost us NZ$21!' But there was no choice. My feet were blocks of concrete and my lower back felt like it had been trampled by a herd of migrating bison. I joined the queue, which snaked out the door, while Sue scoured the tables for two spare seats. I practised my coffee request all the way to the counter, then was struck down by performance anxiety. I'm not sure what I ordered in the end, but it was the worst cup of coffee for $21 that I have ever tasted.

We visited the magnificent Gothic Notre Dame cathedral, took a boat ride on the River Seine, and discovered the lustre of the city's lights on its shimmering waters at night. Paris was as beguiling as it was foreign to me.

The next day we took the train south from Gare du Nord through a series of connections to Finistère, a region of Brittany on the west coast of France. We arrived at the train station in Quimper without a place to stay. In those days, there was no internet and also no chance we could afford the tariff of anywhere our travel agent could book in advance. After looking at a list of accommodation available on a noticeboard in the train station, we took a wild stab, ending up outside a large boarding house with our monster bags.

'You stay here,' I said to Sue at the bottom of the steep flight of steps. 'I'll see if there's anything available.' Quimper was provincial; there were no English-speakers here; and French was spoken with its own particular dialect. I stumbled through my introduction, and then asked if there was a room available for two. The proprietor was a tiny, sallow-skinned woman who ran the business on her own except for the help of her ancient dog, who was blind.

The little Scottie dog was white and wire-haired, with misty blue eyes that looked like you were viewing the sea through the bottom of a green glass jar. The dog followed his mistress, as if acting in some official capacity. To get to me, he walked around the edge of the room with his shoulder running gently along the wall until he got close to where I stood, and then he launched into the blackness, literally following his nose. I patted him. We were friends.

The *pension* owner said the only room she had left was a double room with a double bed. This was communicated in words spoken loudly and slowly, and gestures that were wild and erratic. I loved it. My mother's family were Huguenots, and the woman's extravagant mime reminded me of some of my own.

'She's a bit eccentric,' I told Sue, as I grabbed my bag and began lugging it up the steps. 'I'm afraid there's only one double bed left, so it looks like we're going to have to sleep together again.'

'You'll just have to stay over your side,' she shot back, and we both laughed. I filled out the paperwork, showed the *pension* owner our passports, and she took us upstairs to our room. We struggled with our bags up the narrow staircase.

'*Ne mangez pas dans la chambre,*' she said, before shutting the door behind us. The room was dark, with embossed brocade curtains and furniture fabrics, and a rich burgundy bedspread. It felt as if we had travelled back to some ancient time.

'We can't afford to eat out, so we'll *have* to bring food back to the room,' Sue said when our proprietor was safely out of earshot.

'Yes, but we'll have to be careful, we can't leave anything around. I reckon she'd be a bit of a handful if she caught us.'

'Well,' said Sue, looking at the receipt for our four-night stay, 'we're paying enough for the room. There shouldn't be any restrictions at all.'

Before we lost the light that afternoon, we went out to the local market, which was a collection of stalls with the most remarkable food I had ever seen. The cheeses, breads and pastries alone made anything I had ever eaten before seem over-processed and anaemic. What wasn't swimming or crawling on the fish stalls was exotic-looking. Animals complete with fur, feathers, and heads with sightless eyes hung in profusion. It was a historic market only slightly changed from the days of its earliest beginning.

Sue and I stood stock-still and stared like we had been struck by thunder. I hovered for ages before finding the courage to begin negotiations. I learned quickly that they were more interested in your money than your pronunciation. As long as you pointed accurately and held up the right number of fingers there was a good chance you would get what you wanted. The cheese selection was our downfall. They all looked magnificent, and Sue's strategy was to watch and buy what the locals bought. So we observed for a while, and when the runny cheese in a round like a giant Camembert emerged as a favourite, I ordered a chunk. It would become something of a millstone, as the longer it lasted in our care the more stinking it got.

'Jeepers, one whiff of that and the landlady's going to think we're hiding a dead body,' Sue said, when I handed her the package to put in our shopping bag.

'Yes, we'll have to eat it fast.'

Unfortunately, the cheese vendor and I had failed to communicate quantities adequately, and he had lopped off a much bigger piece than I had asked for. The cheese took too much of our food allowance to throw it out. The Scottie dog, whose portfolio I now realised was sniffing out contraband, was onto us from the beginning. I could see in his sea-misted eyes that he knew.

'Quick, up the stairs!' I said as he began his long walk around the walls of the room to get to us. I concluded from his large tummy and ambling gait that he was more of a foodie than a trained sniffer dog on border patrol. Nevertheless, we were upstairs and in our room before it became an issue. He had missed us.

I like strong cheese, but that one smelt as though it were rotting. We weren't eating our bread and cheese long before there was an odd rattling at the door.

'Quick, put the food away,' I said to Sue under my breath.

'That won't help. It stinks in here.'

'I've got an idea' — and with that I raced over to my bag, grabbed my perfume, shot a couple of squirts into the room and sniffed to see if there was an improvement. The door rattled again. I bolted over to avoid a suspicious delay, expecting to see the proprietor ready to evict us. First, I looked ahead, then along the corridor, then down . . . to see her second-in-command (2IC) staring sightlessly up into my face.

'It's only the dog,' I called to Sue over my shoulder, 'relax.'

'Go back to your *maman*,' I said to the dog, pointing to the stairs.

'What good is that going to do?' Sue pointed out, irritably, having spent a furious few seconds packing everything away. 'He only understands French and he's blind.'

'Well, we can't have him scratching the door.'

'Here,' she said, handing me a small piece of cheese on bread, 'give him this, then tell him *au revoir*.' So I did, and as the treat approached his nose, he very gently took it from my fingers.

'*Au revoir*,' I said, and he was gone. Each night when the strong cheese came out, he scratched at the door for his kickback and never dobbed us in to his *maman*.

We did, however, pay a price for our sins. First Sue became violently ill with what must have been a cousin once removed from the Spanish flu. She lay groaning with a high fever, barely able to get out of bed. I was left to sightsee and do the daily bread shopping alone.

The coastline of Finistère and the tiny coastal settlement of Camaret-sur-Mer was where Rhona Haszard had painted. On my solitary excursions, I discovered that even in winter there was a bus to Camaret-sur-Mer, just two hours apart one day a week over the New Year period. I booked tickets for the day it travelled, in the hope that Sue would be well enough to go, then promptly got the flu myself.

I was sitting at the desk in our *pension* room, tapping away at the laptop I had borrowed from work, when beads of perspiration began to form on my forehead in such profusion that they ran into my eyes. First, I boiled, then I froze. I had not been sympathetic enough to Sue. Almost delirious with the pain in my neck and head, I failed even to register the dog's evening visit. With Sue off her food, and now me, the cheese had grown even more vile; we were almost grateful for Scottie's visits. I was desperate to get well enough to visit Camaret-sur-Mer. The body-aches were followed by a heavy cold, then a severe chest infection. Fortunately, as I got worse, Sue got better.

Until the very day of the trip to Camaret-sur-Mer, I was not sure whether I would make it. Sue was worried my chest infection would become pneumonia. She wouldn't let me out of the room until I was dressed in almost everything I had in my suitcase. I grabbed the biggest handkerchief I could find, my money, passport and camera. We went downstairs, and were heading across the reception area, when we were assailed by the wiry little *pension* owner. She was gesturing wildly.

'*Non, non!*' she was shouting, then something I couldn't understand. I was just about to make a full confession to our eating in our room, when I realised what she had in her hand was the paperwork we had filled out when we first arrived.

'Non pay! Non pay!' she shouted. '*Vous n'avez pas payé!*'

'But we have paid you,' I interjected. '*Nous vous avons payé.*'

By this stage she was almost hysterical.

While we had stayed additional nights because we were sick and needed to wait for the one day that the bus went to Camaret-sur-Mer, I knew we had paid for everything. Our *pension* owner was pointing at the dates of our original stay, forgetting we had given her money for the extra nights. I had kept the receipts, but they were in our room.

'Bus,' I said. 'We are late... *en retard*,' I repeated, pointing emphatically at my watch. 'We will be back soon... *bientôt... On se parle bientôt.*' But by this time she had thrown herself dramatically across the door, arms outstretched to stop us leaving. I dashed a look at Sue: 'I'll have to go and find the receipts.' I left poor Sue, and our hostess and her dog, who was just finishing his circuit of the room. Upstairs, I pulled my suitcase apart before I found the receipts neatly tucked in the outside pocket. Sure enough, we had paid.

When I came down and showed her, the landlady was a profusion of apologies, gushing, hugging and kissing. But all we wanted to do was to make our escape.

'We'll never make it!' Sue shouted to me as we raced down the street. I was still feeling very unwell, and the last bit I had to walk in order to catch my breath. The bus had just gone by the time we got there. The next one was a two-and-a-half-hour wait, meaning we would be in Camaret-sur-Mer for a mere 15 minutes before the only returning bus to Quimper left to come back. The atmosphere around me was scorched with fire and brimstone.

'That crazy old bag!' I exploded at Sue. 'She made us miss our bus!' Righteous anger was followed by despair. 'What do you think: is it worth a six-hour bus ride for 15 minutes in Camaret-sur-Mer?'

'Of course it is,' Sue responded. 'But are you sure you're well enough to go?'

'No,' I replied, 'but if you're prepared to go, so am I.'

Sue and I sheltered in a café nearby with another awful cup of coffee until the next bus left. We were early boarding and got seats at the front of the bus. It was an inclement day, cold and wet, with sudden squalls of rain that beat down hard. The elevated view from the front of the bus was expansive, though. For a long time we looped through fields of grass and fallow paddocks, dark and brooding, waiting for spring. Once we hit the coastline, our travel was transformed by breath-taking seascapes of jagged black rocks and aquamarine seas. I could see why it had captured Rhona Haszard's imagination. When she was there in the mid-1920s, she painted the fleets of tiny fishing boats that dotted the inlets, their maroon sails vivid against an emerald sea. She painted in summer at the passionate beginning of her second marriage, to Leslie Greener.

I was looking at the same timeless views, but in winter when steel skies added a grey hue to Nature's palette. I still felt ill, but the experience was uplifting. Even our 15 minutes in Camaret-sur-Mer felt well worth the trip. We saw the old, upturned wreck on the coast, and the roofs and chimney pots that both she and Leslie Greener had painted. The settlement was quaint, the houses traditional Breton cottages, and the view across the rooftops to the sea, bewitching. We slept on the trip back. Darkness quickly overtook the day, until the lights of the villages we drove through became a soporific blur, then nothingness. We were not sorry to say *au revoir* to our landlady, but I would miss the visits of her 2IC, Monsieur Scottie.

In Paris we stayed overnight in the same youth hostel, this time in a dormitory accommodating four people. The room was well designed, with massive windows that looked out over the snow that was now settling in the streets. When we went to bed there was just us, and we hoped it would stay that way. But before midnight we heard a key turn in the lock, and into the room came a young Russian woman in a Cossack hat, heavy full-length fur coat and high-heeled leather boots. Her striking face, statuesque figure and long, blonde hair made quite an impact.

She greeted us in her few words of English, pushed her bag under the bunk, and got ready for bed. Before I was conscious of her doing much more, I was asleep. It was a fitful sleep, disturbed by my anxiety over travelling to Egypt in such poor health. Sue's worried voice mixed in with my own night terrors for a while before I woke, and realised she was calling me.

'Jody, Jody, wake up! Quick! Wake up!'

'What's wrong?' I responded in a whisper. But as soon as I gathered my wits about me I could tell. The temperature in the room was arctic, and the large window by my head was tilted so far open it looked as if it might drop off its hinges into the street.

'Shut the window, quick! It's freezing — you'll die in this temperature.' The culprit was our Russian roommate, who must have come from the steppes of Siberia and had a sudden attack of homesickness. The next morning my chest infection was worse, and I was even more concerned.

We took the Eurostar to London, and then the tube to Heathrow. At the airport I converted our euros to Egyptian pounds. In a very exaggerated way, the woman at the counter put on rubber gloves to count the Egyptian money out. I found it bizarre, but obviously the whole notion of handling the money revolted her. I tucked it away in my passport holder, which was under my shirt, noting as I did so that the paper money was soft and worn.

'We can still back out,' Sue said, when I returned to where she was sitting. 'You don't have to go. If you're feeling sick, you shouldn't go, because it's dangerous.'

'I want to go, I'm pretty sure I'll be okay. We've come this far; we can't give up now.'

It was late at night when we boarded the plane, and in the early hours of the morning when we arrived at Alexandria airport. The desert has a peculiar musty smell. In the blackness it was unmistakable. As much as anything, it is the smell of absence, of nothing but an expanse of sand and dirt. I wanted to feel exhilarated, but instead I felt a bleakness that was chilling.

We walked in the darkness from the plane to the airport building. There is a civilian airport close to Alexandria, but in 2001 all flights were going through a military airbase about 60 kilometres from the city. The military airport was brutal in its finish and facilities, and its staff looked like Mexican bandits. They wore dishevelled woollen military uniforms that were wrinkled, with buttons missing and in need of repair. They were heavily armed with rifles and guns.

Immigration was a man at a makeshift desk with an oversized stamp, which he banged down with enormous force. Standing around him was an armed guard of tatty-looking soldiers. We were well up the Immigration queue to get our passports stamped, but, by the time we finished going through the bag search, Sue and I were the last foreigners to leave the airport. The Customs officers had unpacked and unravelled everything in our suitcases, lewdly laughing and nudging each other as they did so. We were disconcerted, but failed to see the ruse for what it was.

'I look after you, ladies,' said the senior officer, as he helped us close up our suitcases. 'I will make sure you get a good taxi. Bad taxi drivers take advantage of lovely ladies. I take care of you.'

'No thanks, we'll be fine,' I said, feeling overpowered by the man.

'Yes, yes, I insist,' he exclaimed, grabbing our bags and corralling us out the door into the swarm of taxi drivers touting for a fare. The next minute, I looked around.

'Our bags have gone,' I called to Sue, stricken with fear, and so had the man who had been holding them.

'It'll be okay,' she said. At that point I distinguished a voice from the furore.

'You ladies taking taxi to Alexandria?' a man shouted. 'I have your bags.' And sure enough, strapped to the roof of a beaten-up taxi not far away were both our bags. Instantly suspicious, I asked him to give them back, but he refused.

'You pay, you pay, it costs £60!' he shouted in my face. '£60!' He opened the car door for Sue and me, still shouting '£60 . . . £60' as we did up our seat belts and he got in the front passenger seat by the driver. They spoke together in Arabic. This conversation was less heated than ours, and occasionally they laughed.

The taxi pulled out of the hurly-burly of people on to a wide, largely empty highway. As soon as we were underway, the driver turned off the car's headlights. By the pallid light of the moon we rocketed along at a terrifying speed. I grabbed hold of Sue's hand in the darkness. There was no way I felt able to stop them or to control things. We were captive, and the ransom was going up.

'You pay £100!' our assailant turned around and shouted at me. 'It's long way to Alexandria, you pay £100, not £60.'

'But I haven't got £100,' I said. I had my £80 Egyptian from Heathrow, and that was all.

'You pay £100, or else!' he screamed, repeating it with escalating aggression. 'We take you to ATM. You get more.' I squeezed Sue's hand; that sounded dangerous, and I knew she would be thinking the same thing.

'A hundred pounds is too much,' I called to him above the engine noise. 'I'll give you £80.' My defiance sent him into a rage.

'If you want to get to your hotel, lady, you pay,' he spat at me. The word 'ATM' terminated our conversation.

The driver had a weird way of speeding up, then taking his foot off the accelerator and slowing down, which put my nerves on edge. I held on to Sue's hand like it was a lifeline. We whispered together. Only one of us could get out of the car at the ATM. If we both got out, they would most certainly be off with our bags.

'I don't think I can face it,' I admitted to Sue. 'You know what I'm like at getting money out. Under pressure I'll muck it up. The last thing I want to do is get my credit card eaten up.'

'I don't mind going,' Sue replied. 'You wait in the car.'

'Are you sure?'

'Yes, I'm sure.'

For most of the journey we travelled through featureless darkness, but as we neared Alexandria there were flashes of suburban settlements, highlighted by street-lamps, floodlit compounds or the occasional neon sign. More than once I saw a solitary robed figure watching us speed by. It was to a silent street in one of these suburban areas that they took us.

'ATM!' our aggressor screamed at us as the car pulled off the road.

Reluctantly, I let go of Sue's hand.

'I'll be back in a minute,' she said.

With her back to us, I could not make out what was happening. Seconds ticked by like hours. Eventually she was back in the car.

'Did you get it?' I asked anxiously, because not every ATM was compatible.

'Yes,' she said, 'I've got it.'

'Thank God,' I responded, the relief almost bringing me to tears. She handed me the £200 we had agreed to get out. I hid most of it away in my money-belt, and the remainder I kept clenched in my fist.

When domestic houses gave way to high-rise buildings, I began to believe we might get there. It was still pitch-black when we pulled up outside our hotel.

'Stay in the car until he takes the bags off the roof,' I whispered to Sue.

Our persecutor was on the pavement with his hand in my face, before I was out of the car.

'A hundred pounds,' he said, pushing his hand towards me, 'and £50 to get your bags back.'

'You're crazy. You've kidnapped us, now you are holding our bags ransom? We agreed to £60, which is still too much. This is outrageous.'

'A hundred pounds for the taxi ride, lady. Extra for the bags.'

I looked around for some assistance, but there was no one. If we wanted to get our bags back, we would have to pay.

X

There was no time. If Bjorn lingered any longer, chances were that the speck of human life down the beach, if indeed it was human, would see him. With that thought and the urgency that flooded in behind it, he gripped the sack, fiercely moving it, once more, high onto his back and using the weight of his powerful body to propel himself forward.

By the time he reached that faraway point on the beach that he believed he had been looking at, the terrain had changed quite dramatically. Soft sand had given way to rolling dunes and marram grass, with rocks strewn around. He walked a little further before he stopped.

This seemed like a promising spot. Looking around, he spied a large piece of driftwood, ideal to help dig. His would use the rocks around him to line the hole to protect the ivory from the coarse sand and the tiny creatures that fed on the flesh and bone of fish stranded on the shore. He thought of his dead companions in a spasm of grief, washed up, and now worm-meat. How would he explain to their families what had happened? When he came back to recover the pieces, he would get his money, he thought, and give the families he knew some assistance.

He stood up and surveyed his work. The sand certainly looked disturbed, but soon the evidence would be gone, as the wind and the rain reshaped its surface. Although he was utterly fatigued, he felt lighter. This valuable bounty would have made him a target. Now it was hidden.

He needed to get his bearings; remember the landmarks and the shape of the hills. Moving cautiously towards the beach again, he planned to take one last look over the wreck before he headed inland. The dunes were like rolling waves at sea, just high enough so that his clear view was only as far as the one in front of him. Thus they provided cover for the three bandits lying in wait behind one of these swelling pyramids of sand. They had plundered what they could from the dead bodies — rings, wristlets, knives, scabbards and leather goods, objects that had up to then signified identity, vocation and status. The wreck and its fatalities had been surprisingly rewarding.

Bjorn stumbled into their line of sight like a mouse in front of a cat. The leader put his hand up to stop the other two. They watched Bjorn struggle past. As he moved ahead, they fell in behind.

The only thing Bjorn remembered hearing was the dull thud of a heavy weapon on the back of his head. When he came to, he was being dragged roughly across the sand towards his ship by two brutes whose iron grip was nearly tearing his arms from their sockets. It wasn't until they were close to the wreck that they released him, dropping him face-down in the sand.

He had watched the lives of manacled slaves, caged on land and chained into ships to labour their last days at sea. The hope was escape, or return from captivity as a slave for those few from prominent families who could afford to pay a king's ransom. Bjorn believed he would escape. The thing that burdened him the most was that if he was forced to leave this unknown place, how would he ever find the chess pieces again?

CHAPTER TWENTY-TWO
Alexandria, Egypt

Our hotel in Alexandria, Egypt, was listed in the *Lonely Planet* as being on the fifth floor. As we went up past the other levels in the ancient lift with walls made of chicken wire, I noted each was a disused chaos of dirt and filth. In the dim light of the lift-shaft I could see ceilings fallen in, furniture upturned and leaves littering the floor where broken windows had allowed the wind to carry them in. Frail and faltering, the lift shuddered disturbingly under the weight of Sue and me and our suitcases. I was relieved when we could unhook the concertinaed mesh door and step onto the landing.

We were not expecting much. Our shoestring didn't stretch far. The décor in the lobby was tired and the surfaces worn, but it felt like a sanctuary after our taxi ride. We had no accommodation booked, however, and that made for an anxious moment or two while the man behind the desk checked their reservations. A room was available, he confirmed, but we would have to pay in advance to secure it. I paid him most of the rest of the cash Sue had withdrawn from the ATM. There was just enough left to buy breakfast. He handed me our room key, and in no time we were ensconced. It was a plain space with beaten-up cream-coloured walls and Persian-patterned bedspreads. The bedspreads wrestled with my eyeballs, which were already suffering after 36 hours on the road.

'I'm stuffed,' I said, as I collapsed on the single bed closest to the windows.

'I'm not even going to bother getting into my pyjamas,' Sue replied as she fell into the bed that ran along the adjoining wall.

'Oh, for a few hours' sleep.' Instead of getting under the covers, I pulled up the coarse wool blanket folded at the end of the bed. Perhaps I should have made a bigger commitment to sleeping because as it turned out I could not sleep at all. Our adrenaline-packed night had left me exhausted, but alert. Occasionally I would drift off, only to find myself re-enacting a disconcerting sequence of the evening's events.

'Are you awake?' I called to Sue as soon as a steady shaft of daylight came through the gap in the curtains.

'Yes,' a disembodied voice answered me from the dimness.

'Did you sleep?'

'No,' she answered. 'Not at all.'

I got out of bed and went to the window, pulling the heavy drapes back so that daylight flooded in. The view across a busy road, along the corniche and out to the Mediterranean Sea was riveting. The vivid aquamarine of the water, the juxtaposition in the street below of a donkey pulling a cart and driver mixed with the hustle and bustle of modern traffic made it tantalising. Two worlds collided in this instant, and that I would learn was Alexandria, founded by the Macedonian Alexander the Great. Worlds had been colliding there forever. It was the meeting place of ancient cultures. The Egyptians built their tombs and buried their dead here; the Romans had come, conquered and gone, leaving an amphitheatre, bathhouses and temples; the Christians had found a foothold in the catacombs, surviving as Coptics; and even the Vikings probably made it this far.

Like the lure of a star in a far-off galaxy, civilisations had sent their emissaries, missions and armies here to meet in war and peace. It had been a battleground, a satellite state, a cosmopolitan hub of wealth and thought, and a marketplace. This antique city had been all things to all people, I thought, as I stepped through the sliding door onto the balcony, but what had it meant to Rhona Haszard, and why had she so tragically ended her life here? I sat down on one of the two chairs at a tiny table looking out to sea. It was an odd feeling being in Alexandria at last.

The book project had begun badly. After I learned that there were papers belonging to Rhona Haszard in the archive at Te Papa, I had taken the overnight train down to Wellington to consult them. I took a pile of first-year marking with me, and when I began nodding off over the scripts, I curled up across two cramped seats with my long coat over me and tried to sleep. From the train station, I delivered my bag to the Bunny Street backpackers, and then walked to the archive. I was there waiting for it to open. The archivist knew who I was, and greeted me personally, because we had exchanged emails. A box was waiting for me on the archivist's desk.

My perusal of the papers started bizarrely with a letter from Leslie Greener directed to me, or at least the reader of the archive. As I began to comprehend the immaculate handwriting in red pencil, I understood why the letters had been collected together. Leslie Greener had intended to write a biography of his late wife himself, but as time passed the project became less central to him, and was finally abandoned. This file was the resource he had planned to use, and his annotations and prompts to memory were all through it. I had just settled on a fascinating letter about a crush Rhona had had on her female English teacher at Southland Girls' High School when the archivist appeared from nowhere and snapped the folder shut.

'I'm terribly sorry,' he said, as I gaped in horror, 'but you can't read that file without the permission of Rhona Haszard's legal heir.'

'I can't believe it! Why didn't you tell me this before?' I demanded.

'I didn't see it on the access requirements, sorry. I should have checked more thoroughly.'

'Do you mean to say I've come all this way and can't consult them?'

'I'm afraid that's the case.' I was dumbfounded by his oversight, but still determined to push ahead.

'Well, where does her heir live?'

'Our last address for her is in Titirangi.'

'Damn!' I exploded, 'That's where I've just come from.' This had little impact, so I left promising that I would be in touch as soon as I had tracked her down. Sherry Smith, I thought, looking at the name and address on a piece of paper the archivist had given me — not very distinctive. I walked out onto the street in something of a fugue, too tired by the overnight train trip and too shocked by my sudden eviction to register where I was heading. It wasn't until I was walking down Lambton Quay that it came to me.

That evening I rang Sue from a payphone at the backpackers.

'Sweetheart, you won't believe it, but I'm not allowed to read the Rhona Haszard file unless I have permission from her trustee. There's an embargo.'

'Why on earth didn't they tell you?'

'That's what I asked. I was furious, but no permission, no archive.'

'Where does her executor live?'

'She lives in Titirangi, would you believe?'

'Do you want me to see if I can go around and talk to her?'

'Would you? That would be fantastic. I'd really appreciate it.'

'Ring me back around 9pm and I'll let you know how I get on.'

With that, poor Sue drove out on a nasty winter evening to Titirangi. The house was down a long, bush-lined drive, which she had to navigate in the blackness and the rain. Sherry Smith, it turned out, had shifted to another address in Glen Eden, but by a stroke of luck the woman in Titirangi still had her forwarding details.

Sherry Smith was extremely cautious when Sue finally knocked on her door. She had already threatened to sue *More* magazine over a salacious article they had published on her aunt, and this late-night introduction did nothing to fill her with confidence. Sue did, however, get a phone number out of her and promised I would ring. A very wet Sue, just back from Glen Eden, gave me Sherry's phone number, and I rang her directly. With the music from the pub next door blaring in the background, I struggled to hear her. But in spite of the terrible din, I managed to talk her around. She agreed to ring the archivist first thing in the morning and give her verbal permission, and then follow it up with a letter.

The next morning I was back, waiting for the archive to open. I had lost valuable time and would have only the rest of that day before I was back on the train that evening. This was the first of a number of visits to read the file.

In that time I came to know Leslie Greener as a freethinking yet very controlling man, who directed my attention and thinking with his handwritten words in the margins of the letters. I also came to know the vivacious, passionate, yet unstable Rhona, who had died so tragically young in Alexandria.

What I hoped to find in Alexandria after 70 years I wasn't sure, but just being there was invaluable.

'I'm hungry,' I heard Sue call from the room. 'The shower's free now; get in there, quick, and let's get going.'

'Come and have a look at the view from the balcony,' I said, sticking my head around the curtain. 'It's a crime not to.'

In less than half an hour we were out on the street. I had already spotted a McDonald's restaurant. It seemed sacrilegious eating at an American chain when we were in the Middle East, but that had been the sage advice of the

Lonely Planet, which was our holy grail of travel. In Egypt, their advice was to either eat at a five-star restaurant or an American chain, or risk contracting food poisoning, parasites or some nasty bacterial infection.

'I don't think I can eat McDonald's for a week,' I said to Sue, after I had polished off my bacon and egg McMuffin.

'Tough,' Sue responded. 'It was your decision to come without the proper shots. Stop moaning.' Actually, I have to confess I'd done quite a bit of moaning. I was still stewing over the terrifying taxi ride, and when I tried to get some money out of an ATM on the way to McDonald's it spat my credit card back at me without a cent. But this was thin ice, and I would have to take a more positive attitude or I risked a full-blown lecture from Sue.

Our plan was to spend the day sightseeing, but, before we did another thing, we needed money. The rest of the morning was spent chasing ATMs, none of which discharged anything. It quickly ceased being annoying and became a serious concern. By the end of the day, we had tried every card we had in every bank machine we'd found and still got nothing. Back at the hotel that night we had to face the fact that we had no money and no way of getting any in the foreseeable future.

'If we can't buy food, we'll have to eat the chocolate,' I announced to Sue. Fortunately, we had bought some Toblerone for the children duty-free. 'I reckon one piece for breakfast and lunch and two pieces for dinner.' With that, I broke off a couple of triangular segments.

'Eat them slowly,' I said, handing Sue her evening ration, 'that's got to last you until the morning.'

Egypt flicked my switch. I worried about Jeremy and Katherine. Would they be safely returned? My unanswered question made me shiver with anxiety. Also there was Alex, the chronic loss that I was learning to live with. I couldn't rest; I couldn't sleep. My rhythms became stuck in fight-or-flight mode, and I was still very sick, coughing violently. Typing was one of the few things that gave me solace. When I wasn't pacing the floor, I was incessantly banging away at my computer, turning my handwritten notes into digital files. It drove the long-suffering Sue insane. In the early hours of the morning she would call me to bed, but I never went and she never complained. The last pencil notes I typed out were the ones I had taken at the British Library.

X

The huge capacity for work that shaped Maria Stubbing's life can also be seen in those of her children. Their upbringing at Ngāruawāhia, close to the Kīngitanga marae, taught them customary knowledge. Kīngitanga had a tradition of fostering great traders and business people, and this is the gift Maria's children were given: they developed an entrepreneurial spirit that turned risk into opportunity.

Sue remembers her nana Lucy Terry (*née* Stubbing) towards the end of her life, when, to a pre-teen, she looked small, frail and fretful after a series of small TIA strokes that removed a little of self and confidence each time. But a more accurate portrayal of Lucy and her life is given in a fabulous family photograph, which is arranged like Edgar Degas' *The Bellelli Family* painting (1858–1867), but without the marital conflict. At one end of a long family dining room table sits Lucy, and at the other, her husband; standing between them are their daughters.

Lucy married Aotearoa-born Cecil Terry, 10 years her junior, the year her mother Maria died in Auckland. She had already established her independence by travelling to Australia in her late teens to work as a waitress. When she married, she paid for the wedding herself. With Cecil, she had three girls: the eldest Thelma, then Sue's mum Norma in the middle, and Zelma, known as Ted, at the end. Lucy owned a dairy at Longburn, and, while Cecil worked at the freezing works, she cooked meals for the shift-workers.

When Cecil's elderly mother died at the beginning of the Depression, and his younger brother was in danger of losing their dairy farm at Linton, Lucy paid the debts and took over its running. Once Cecil's congenital heart condition meant he couldn't keep working on the farm, she leased the property, moving the family to another dairy and grocery store in Palmerston North, and buying a taxi. Sadly, Cecil would die a short time later, at just 41 years old, when the taxi he was driving along Fitzherbert Avenue hit a tree.

Lucy would bring up her teenage daughters alone, choosing never to remarry. In older age, she converted part of her house into a flat, living off the rent and the proceeds of a life of enormous enterprise.

Norma, Sue's mum, was the intellectual and committed feminist of the family. She was so enthusiastic to go to school when her older sister turned five that she packed herself a bag in the hope that she could enrol, too. As a child she was an avid reader, often chastised for idle hours lost in a book. As a punishment one day, Cecil (nicknamed 'Boss') grabbed the book she was reading and threw it in the fire. He was more contrite when he learned that the book belonged to a friend and not her.

Conscious of her Māori heritage, Norma involved herself in cultural groups, weaving the tāniko bodices worn by kapa haka friends. Her Māori background also gave her opportunities. She told Sue she could have gone to university, or taken the position she was offered at a museum, but instead she went primary-school teaching.

Norma wanted to help young Māori when she took a sole-charge teaching position at a tiny rural school at Bell's Junction, close to Raetihi. Little did she know that her life would change forever when she met Vince (nicknamed 'Lofty') from the nearby Waiouru Camp where he was in military training.

The students at Bell's Junction arrived barefoot on horseback to a toasty fire that Norma prepared each morning. With little equipment and few resources, she taught them to read using comics, something almost unheard of in the 1930s and 1940s. Pictures and text together; a story young people might relish reading: these were the things that captured children's imaginations.

Stories of Norma's early days of country teaching became part of her repertoire. She spoke of young Māori who struggled across rugged country in the snow to get to school, but also of a group of Collier children. Their parents were farming nearby. Bell's Junction was the closest school. Sue grew up hearing about the talented Collier infants. When Norma went back years later to a school reunion, the Colliers welcomed her like a member of the family.

'I know Mum used to teach Collier children at Bell's Junction,' Sue announced to me, when I first mentioned driving up to Whanganui to begin my research on Edith Collier.

'No? It can't be the same people.'

'Well, the family farms are very close to Bell's Junction. I bet that's them.'

And Sue was right. These were some of Edith Collier's nieces and nephews. There were 32 in total, including Barbara and Jean. It often struck us as remarkable that Norma had been there and met these people before us. Sadly, I never met Norma; she died some years before I arrived on the scene. Sue and I often speculated about how her mother would respond to our relationship, especially when we were living at Barbara's. Norma, a devout Anglican, a Māori–Pākehā, a rangatira, would have struggled.

'We will always be here for you, whatever happens,' she had promised Sue. But one day when she and her mum were talking, Norma also told her that 'being a lesbian was a difficult life and she wouldn't wish it on anyone'.

'So,' Sue said to me, 'I'm not sure what she would have thought of *us* or *you*, but she would have loved your mind.'

And that was good enough for me.

CHAPTER TWENTY-THREE
A Tower and a Death

Two days eating Toblerone rations and two days of failed attempts to find the British Egyptian Bank did nothing to settle my nerves. The streets of Alexandria proved narrow and convoluted. Intended originally for foot and cart traffic, the smaller roads around our hotel criss-crossed in a maze of confusion, a feeling that was compounded with all the signage being in Arabic.

Finally, Sue had the inspired idea of following the corniche instead of getting lost in the labyrinth of intervening streets. Once we had gone far enough along the coast, we would head back into the warren of alleyways and hopefully hit our target. After most of a day walking, we found the British Egyptian Bank — hallelujah — and when Sue tried her EFTPOS card in the ATM, we heard that magical mechanical whirring sound of money being counted.

'Serves you right for moaning about McDonald's,' Sue said, after we had sat in blissful silence eating our chicken burgers and fries and sucking violently at the last drop of a strawberry shake.

'Yes. Lesson learned, that's the end of the complaints from me.'

The next day, we visited the Alexandria Museum, which turned out to hold the not-so-spectacular remnants of the city's plundered relics. Security at the museum was on high alert after a bus-load of tourists had been gunned down at Luxor. Our passports were inspected, and our bags checked at gunpoint. We were relieved to get away from the security and into the museum, which was largely empty of people. Just a few brave, mostly German, tourists were exploring the long, dim corridors of exhibits.

I was just beginning to relax when one of the guards began shouting at us.

'Ladies, ladies!'

'Shit. What now?' I whispered to Sue. I flinched, waiting for the next onslaught.

'Come here.' I could only vaguely make out the words, but could see he was gesturing us over. As we got closer, I could hear exactly what he was saying.

'Come and see our mummy, it's this way. A very special mummy,' he added. 'It is the pride of the museum.' I was relieved. He was not acting in his capacity as a guard, but as a guide. His enthusiasm to show us the star exhibit carried us along the transverse corridor and into an atrium area at the end. There was the giant mummy in stellar position on a raised dais. It was such an anti-climax: I was speechless for a few awkward seconds. Finally, the gush came.

'That's amazing,' I exclaimed, trying to act impressed. 'I've never seen a mummy to match it.' This was true, because instead of it being the remains of some romantic pharaoh or high-ranking aristocrat, it was a mummified crocodile. The guard beamed at me in delight.

'Very ancient crocodile,' he said, looking lovingly at it.

'It's remarkable,' I said, nudging Sue. 'Isn't it?'

'Yes.'

'Thank you so much for showing us this treasure. It's the highlight of our visit' (which in some ways was true). With that acclaim, our elated guard moved off.

'You weren't much help,' I said to Sue once he was out of earshot.

'I couldn't think of anything else to say.'

After the museum, we visited Roman ruins, the catacombs, and, on our second-to-last day, Victory College, the school where Rhona Haszard and Leslie Greener had lived and worked. We decided to risk another taxi ride. Traffic flowed like a river in flood along the main arterial roads, with horns and sirens blaring and almost no controlled intersections. Many cars were old and dilapidated, but even most of the modern ones were covered in dents. This time we were safely deposited on the college steps. This felt like something of a miracle.

The fenced campus of Victory College covered a sizeable inner-city plot. There was no archive to discover here. I had already written and asked, and the college replied to the effect that they had no archives dating back to the 1920s. Sue and I had come to take photographs, and I hoped we might climb the tower from which Rhona Haszard fell.

We went through the front entrance of the main administration building. My intention was to ask the receptionist if we could take photographs of the school. It was recess and there were no children to be seen. The P.A. to the principal, who was our reception committee behind the front desk, was cautious about us photographing the school.

'I'm afraid I will have to check with the principal; fortunately, he's in today and can probably see you now. Just a minute, I'll see.' She vanished into the room behind, and reappeared a minute or so later to usher us into the principal's office.

He was a short, overweight, middle-aged man with dark rings around his eyes, sallow skin and a moustache.

'Welcome,' he said, standing up and reaching over the desk to shake my hand. 'So, you are the person researching a former staff member, I remember your letter . . . Dr Drayton?' There were two other women in the room with him who appeared to be assisting, one taking dictation and the other in the corner filing.

'Yes, I am, and this is my photographer, Sue Marshall.'

'Very nice to meet you,' he said, shaking her hand. To the two ladies in the room he said something loudly in Arabic, then laughed heartily. The women looked embarrassed. We talked briefly about my research, and periodically he would turn to the women and say something more in Arabic and laugh in a salacious manner. I watched the women's faces to gauge their reactions. They looked progressively uncomfortable. I was beginning to suspect the man was a bit of a sleaze, but I was happy to be laughed at as long as I got my photographs. In this regard he was very helpful. He even offered a guide to give us a tour and take us to the tower where Rhona fell. Towards the end of our interview, he instructed one of the women to take us to our guide. We said our farewells and the woman showed us out of the room.

I was so intrigued by what had gone on with the principal that I couldn't resist asking her what he had said.

'You don't want to know,' she replied. 'It was very naughty.' Although I had suspected as much, this confirmation still came as a shock. We had had trouble before. Some Egyptian men saw Western women unaccompanied by men as a target, others as tarts. My bottom had been rubbed so thoroughly my trousers were almost shiny. After walking along the corniche at dusk one evening, I had gathered such a persistent band of pursuers that we had to shelter in a restaurant with a coffee to shake them off. Interestingly, it was bottoms rather than boobs that attracted attention, so Sue was left largely alone.

Our guide, however, who turned out to be one of the school's biology teachers, was a paragon of sweetness. He took us around the college, then with immense pride showed us his science laboratory. I felt a twinge of sympathy when he showed us the human skeleton, so reduced by schoolboy pranks that only the leg bones were left. Or when he waved his hand along shelves of murky jars to show us unlabelled specimens paled to anaemic white after decades in pickling brine. But the room nevertheless had that timeless sense of discovery, which was bigger than bones or specimens and more about the mystery of life itself.

The biology teacher was a strategic choice of guide on the part of the principal because his room was close to the tower.

'I'm sorry,' he said, standing by a window in the laboratory that was wedged open by a block of wood. 'The internal staircase has collapsed and is being repaired, so the only way to the tower is across the roof.' It did feel a little odd as we climbed onto a wooden box and stepped over the window ledge.

The tower, another two storeys up, was a short walk across the tar rooftop.

'How do we climb it?' I asked. The biology teacher pointed to a series of iron bars, fixed to the wall like staples. They were rusted through, but still very solid, so initially I thought they would be quite safe. But when I grabbed one of the lower ones it moved under the pressure of my hand. The concrete wall, which fixed the bars, was cracked and crumbling. Any ascent up this ruin of a ladder could be dangerous.

'This is where I stop,' the biology teacher said to me. 'I'm not going any further, I've got a wife and children.'

I looked at Sue. 'You're on your own,' she said. 'I've got kids, too!' I understood. This was my deal. Why should they take the risk?

So I began to climb. The metal bars flexed in the wall as I tested my weight. Reaching the top with much relief, I gingerly climbed inside the tower through a window. There I discovered yet another obstacle. Inside was a second wooden ladder and another climb to the topmost level. The ladder was propped against a heavy beam. Originally the ladder had provided access to a wooden floor, which had decayed and disappeared except for the remnants of floorboards close to the window. If I wanted to see the window from where Rhona fell I would have to climb the ladder, then crawl across the beam to the surviving mezzanine of floorboards. Stupidly, I still had my pack on my back, which suddenly felt like a liability.

The drop on either side of the beam was considerable — 7 metres, perhaps more. The floor below was littered with rubble and collapsed masonry. If I fell, it would most certainly have resulted in severe injury, possibly death. What flashed tauntingly into my mind was the headline: *Art historian dies in fall from the same tower as her subject*. To keep my nerve, as I put one hand in front of the other and shifted my knees awkwardly along the beam, I kept my eyes strictly fixed on the remains of the floorboards ahead.

By the time I reached my target, I was perspiring profusely. Grabbing hold of the narrow shelf, I swung one leg, then the other over, until I was kneeling on it. Moving carefully at first to make sure it would hold my weight, I gripped the concrete wall as I pulled myself upright. Then, clinging to the wall, I crawled to the window. When I stood in front of it and looked out over the campus, I realised the window was not something a person could accidentally fall from. It was tall and very narrow, and the windowsill was high: well above my hip. Equally, it would have been difficult even for a strong person to toss a body from it.

There were more windows on that level, but each one was identical to the one I looked out of. It was a chilling thing to realise in the heat of the now midday sun that Rhona had most likely jumped. Even climbing up and checking the windows in the tower could not make that definitive. But I knew from the archive at Te Papa that Rhona's mental state was fragile. Seeking treatment in London for a bad back injury, she had left Leslie Greener in Alexandria to finish his term's teaching at Victoria College, as it was then called. When the term ended, instead of joining Rhona in London, he had visited his parents on Little Sark in the Channel Islands.

In the time they were apart, Rhona met an Australian expatriate and fell in love. They began an affair. When Leslie did finally visit her, he had misgivings about the Australian and the nature of their relationship. After he returned to Egypt, there was a torrid series of letters in which Rhona confessed the relationship to Leslie, and then made the difficult decision to return to him. She was only back in Alexandria with Leslie a matter of a month or so before she fell from the tower. In the morning, she wrote a letter to a friend outlining her plans for an upcoming visit to Cairo; in the afternoon, she was dead.

What irritated me was that Leslie Greener had taken such pains to point all this out in his red pencil annotations through the archive. He had kept all the letters pertaining to Rhona's poor mental health, especially those discussing her psychotherapy with quack chiropractor, Lewis Doel. It all seemed too neat somehow, like he was presenting a case. But standing in front of that window helped confirm one thing: she could never have stepped back from her easel, as one commentary contended, and accidentally fallen. I stood there looking for a while, watching a group of boys, maybe boarders who had not gone home for term break, playing soccer in a red-dirt compound: slim young adolescents shouting and calling to one another to pass the ball.

As I turned away from the window, I did wonder whether, without the adrenaline of the chase, I would survive the reverse trip down the perilous tower. After wobbling dangerously across the beam again, I climbed down the internal ladder, then the external ladder. It was with an enormous sense of relief I saw Sue still waiting for me. Our guide, the biology teacher, had long ago departed, but the window to his classroom was still open and the box in place to step on. Then it was just a matter of remembering the twists and turns of the corridors and we were outside the building looking up. It was hard to believe it had been the site of such a horrific accident.

'I never thought being an art historian could be so dangerous,' I said to Sue.

'Well, you will pick these troubled subjects,' she replied, as she ducked her head to get in the taxi.

The trip to the airport in the early hours of the next morning was our last ordeal in Egypt. We had ordered our taxi for 5.30am, which would have put us out at the airport in plenty of time to catch our flight. I was up and packing long before my alarm went off. The idea of missing the plane out of there was unthinkable. It was fortunate for us that we were ready so much ahead of time, because an hour before the taxi was due there was a heavy rapping at the door.

'Taxi! . . . Taxi!' the voice called from the other side. I cast an anxious look at Sue. The impatient, almost angry tone brought back memories of our first taxi ride.

'What do I do?' I whispered to Sue.

'Let him in,' she whispered back, rushing to fill the outside pockets of her suitcase with last-minute things. 'I'm almost ready. Have you got the tickets?'

'Yes,' I responded, as I checked for the umpteenth time that they were safely stowed in my backpack. I opened the door. On the other side was a slim man, not tall, with dark hair.

'Hurry,' he said to me, 'we go to the airport.'

'But you're an hour early,' I told him, trying to slow down our departure. The thought of us being rushed out the door and leaving something important behind irked me.

I don't know why I didn't tell him to come back later. The language thing, probably — his English was basic — and the fear that he might not return. My tactics did little to slow our progress.

'Hurry, madam,' he said as he rushed us into the lift, then into his taxi on the street. I put my hand inside my trouser pocket to check again that I had the fare.

'Now this ride to the airport will be no more than £60,' I said to him, as he went to shut my door.

'Yes, madam, certainly, madam,' he replied. Once we were out of the city, we sped through the darkness as we had the first time, and, in spite of his assurances, the cost was similarly inflated at the other end. The taxi driver stood belligerently by the boot of his car with his hand out, threatening that he would keep our bags if we didn't pay extra. This didn't faze me as much as it had before. After the usual debate, I went into my top-up pocket and got the extra money out. When he went for more, I told him that there was no more. He must have known it was the truth because with bad grace he left us standing with our bags in the blackness outside the front of the airport. There was just a single light inside. It appeared that the taxi driver had delivered us there before opening hours.

'Come on,' I said to Sue, grabbing my suitcase, 'let's see if we can get in.' The heavy glass doors at the front entrance pushed open at our touch. Directly in front of us was a security screen with a conveyor belt for luggage. Close to the door where we came in was a row of black leather and chrome seats. The area was in darkness except for an orange nightlight that cast just enough light to vaguely illuminate things. We sat down in two of the chairs.

I was throbbing with nervous energy, while Sue relaxed into her chair, shutting her eyes. My fears soon proved well-founded when, from the dark recesses behind the conveyor belt, six heavily armed military honchos appeared. They stood watching us for a while talking and laughing in Arabic. I tried to act casually, but each time I looked up they had moved a little closer, until finally one of them was toying with the luggage label on my suitcase with his gun butt.

'Would you mind passing me my book?' I heard Sue's voice say.

'For God's sake, Sue, wake up! *Look*,' I hissed.

She sat up and registered our predicament as soon as she opened her eyes.

'Don't worry about the book,' she responded under her breath.

'Pay attention,' I said to her, through clenched teeth. 'It's important. This is dangerous.' I had no idea what was going to happen, but if we had to act rapidly, we needed to do it together.

Just as another soldier began playing with Sue's bag tag there was a miraculous transformation. Suddenly, the overhead lights came on and the luggage belt juddered into action. With the abrupt burst of light, our soldiers disappeared as if into thin air. Before I could comprehend the changed situation, an airport official stood in front of us.

'I hope you ladies haven't been waiting long,' said the young Egyptian man with a British Airways badge on his suit jacket. 'Luckily I had things to catch up on, so I came into work early. Airport security will be here soon, but in the meantime it's much nicer sitting here in the light.'

'Thank you, that's great,' I replied with more gusto than probably made sense to him. 'We really appreciate it.' With that he smiled broadly at us and left.

We sat in stunned silence, still distressed by our ordeal, until security arrived to check our bags.

'What do you think was going to happen back there?' Sue asked as she lifted her bag with difficulty onto the black rubber belt that whined and clanged along.

'I don't know, but it scared me. Intimidating us . . . Something sexual maybe . . . Thank goodness that guy came along so we'll never know.'

'Next time you want to go somewhere exotic: forget it,' Sue announced to me. 'I'll never do this again.'

Even our flight home was not without its dramas. After checking in our bags, we sat waiting for the boarding announcement. Long before the plane was due to leave, a message flashed up on the screen to say our departure would be delayed. This rekindled my anxiety. As the early-morning sunlight began to fill the airport, and passengers started to flood in, I watched two British businessmen arrive. As it turned out, they were engineers installing security doors and panic rooms for wealthy Egyptians.

'Those guys might be able to help us,' I said, turning to Sue.

'Go over and ask if they'd mind us joining them,' she said, immediately getting my drift. I left Sue to look after the bags and walked over to where they were standing.

'Excuse me,' I said, 'you don't know me, but my companion and I would like to be your friends for the day.' They looked startled to begin with, but then I explained. I told them about our experiences with Egyptian taxi drivers; with getting money out of the bank; and about walks along the corniche. Finally, I finished my rant: 'and if my bottom is rubbed one more time, a genie will pop out'. At that point both men laughed.

'Please do join us,' one of them said, extending his hand to shake mine. 'I'm sure we'll have some fun. Do you know, you're the first woman I've ever met who's mentioned their bottom before they've introduced themselves?' It was my turn to laugh.

'I'm Jo,' I responded as I released his hand. 'Sorry for skipping the introduction, but I was just so stressed. We're sitting over there,' I said, pointing to Sue. 'We'll just follow you. You won't even know we're there.'

'Nonsense,' the other man said. 'We'll come and get you when we've checked in our bags. Are you a New Zealander? My wife's a New Zealander.' That was enough to get everyone talking.

Our plane was delayed all day. Mid-morning, we were informed that a bus was waiting outside to take us to a luxury hotel on the Mediterranean coast.

I have never seen a more dazzling blue sea, edged by green-and-white striped umbrellas for guests to sit under along the beach. This was an Egypt I had not seen yet: rich, indulgent and stolen by tourists. Our new friends were as good as their word. They sat behind us on the bus and spent the afternoon with us in the hotel lounge drinking beer.

It was dusk by the time the bus came back to take us to the airport. Our conversation on the bus was interrupted by a mobile phone call in the seat in front. A Dutch man recently working in the Gaza Strip was talking to a man who was holed up in a building, under fire. The political conflict there had escalated a few days before.

'Is there anything I can do?' I heard the Dutchman ask. 'Anyone I should call? . . . Are you going to be alright?' These snatches of questions were a grim reminder of how fragile the peace was in this region. I felt something of a fraud, alighting there for the shortest time, sucking what I needed out of the country and leaving. Sadly, this is what the West has been doing to Egypt forever.

We flew into Heathrow airport and, after an eight-hour layover, boarded a long-haul flight to New Zealand. The rule of the around-the-world ticket is that you can travel backwards to make a connecting flight, but you can't leave the airport, and your journey from there had to be onwards.

By the time we arrived home, we were exhausted. I had the research information I wanted and we didn't need our expensive injections, but it was one of the most demanding experiences I had ever had. For the first few days we could hardly get out of our chairs, we were so numb with tiredness.

Sue and I had arranged our trip so we got back less than a week before the children arrived. I was already thinking about their new school year, wondering whether I would survive the onslaught of 'pick-ups' and 'drop-offs', lectures and marking, plus, of course, the book on Rhona Haszard, which I was about to begin writing.

It was a day that began like any other. Our bodies were still working to an Egyptian clock. We had woken in the early hours, alert as if we were about to compete in a *Mastermind* competition. Nothing seemed to send us back to sleep, not even my faithful glass of wine. But when we stopped trying, we drifted off into a restless oblivion. Late morning, we rose and sat comatose for a while before getting on with the day, finishing the unpacking, and doing a mile of dirty washing. That day I sat in the lounge in my armchair wondering if I didn't detect a slight improvement, just a little more energy to get on with things.

I decided to go and check the mailbox, a ritual that signalled the beginning of my day. The postie had delivered some letters, which I lifted out of the box. Just a bank statement, then a power bill, I thought, looking through them, shuffling one behind the other. When I got to the last, my hand shook and my breath became constricted. Even before I opened it, I knew. I tore across the back of the envelope, hoping and praying that I was wrong. I only had to read the beginning sentence or two. My mouth went dry; my world silent. I stood there in peace. Not the kind that is about serenity or solace, but the stillness of despair.

'It's finally happened,' I said to Sue, laying the letter down on the dining table for her to read.

'What's happened?' she asked, realising there was something wrong. I collapsed into my lounge chair, my head in my hands.

'The letter over there, read it,' I replied. She picked it up and read it.

'But he can't do this.'

'He already has.' There was no pacing the floor, no energy in movement, just a quiet dying inside. Even tears felt trivial beside my lake of sorrow.

I rang the counsel for the child, but predictably his office would not intervene on my behalf, explaining that this was Jeremy's choice. He was coming up to 16, and when he was 16 years old he would be able to go back to Richard's anyway. Even though his birthday was still 11 months off, the counsel for the child refused to interfere. They felt he was ready to spend time with his father, and perhaps deep down I knew this was true. But there was no flexibility, no real listening to my appeals. Even though their position was legally flawed, the door closed in my face.

For me it was the ultimate loss, the end of my parenting, the last of my children out of my life, and perhaps, like Alex, completely. Katherine returned to Auckland ready for her new school year only to find that Jeremy had gone. It was wonderful to see her, but for a time her presence only added to my suffering. To watch Sue and Katherine interacting was to see the gap in my own life more painfully revealed, and to know what I was missing.

I went back to work at Unitec with an overwhelming sense of sadness. I struggled to concentrate, went through the motions; I was unable to explain to my colleagues what this grief meant. There was no service of remembrance, no gravestone to mark the loss, but for me it was a death. While reading Rhona's letters, I had come to understand how black thoughts might take you over the edge. But Rhona jumped — if that is how she died — and I didn't.

It wasn't love that stopped me, although Sue and Katherine were my greatest support. People live for love, but they also die for it. What kept me going was curiosity. I wanted to play on, with or without the pawns that I had strategised and fought so hard to keep: I had to know how the game would end.

CHAPTER TWENTY-FOUR

Rhona Haszard's Daughter

The Rhona Haszard exhibition wavered in and out of viability because Linda Tyler and I struggled to get enough works for the show. Although this affected me, I didn't ride the rollercoaster of emotion the way I had before. It was a matter of perspective. Whether Rhona was saved from oblivion mattered less to me than it had. Nothing, it seemed, would be as big anymore as the loss of my children. I did think of the many lesbian mothers who had had to leave their children and never see them again. I thought also of the many in mental institutions as late as the 1970s receiving shock treatment for their homosexual tendencies. It is the way of the world that two queens together are quietly punished for breaking the rules. I was lucky to have had those few more years with Jeremy: lucky to find a judge in the Family Court in Christchurch able to see past the homophobia embedded in our institutions and the games we play.

Time to think was in short supply, however, and maybe that was a good thing. An appeal over the radio uncovered more of Rhona's paintings in private collections. Loan requests had to go out to the owners, and insurance premiums had gone through the roof because, nine months after our return from Egypt, on 11 September 2001, two commuter planes were flown into the Twin Towers of the World Trade Center in New York. One of the pilots was an Egyptian. As I watched on television the black specks of bodies fall those many, many storeys down to their death, I thought of Egypt and the deep disaffection that we had felt there for the West. It seemed to me that the true origin for this apocalyptic revenge was not personal or religious, but political and historic. The horror stunned us as it did almost everyone, but the anger behind it was no surprise. Sue and I had experienced some of it.

After 9/11 the world ceased to trust. We had entered an era where everyone was a potential terrorist, and people travelling through airports and security checks were screened as if they were. In the sinister way that corporations are linked, the Twin Towers went down in New York, and in New Zealand the cost of the insurance for our exhibition went up. Overnight everyone everywhere was paying for this global escalation of risk. For us this meant a hike in the price for hosting the show on its tour. As a result, some galleries pulled out.

So, after all the ups and downs, it almost caught me off-guard when the whole tenuous scheme came to fruition. The show's first venue was the Hocken Library in Dunedin. The Hocken Library was in an old dairy company building that had been refurbished to house the library's archives, reading rooms and art galleries. My book — with another gripping title, *Rhona Haszard: An Experimental Expatriate New Zealand Artist* — was launched at Unitec in Auckland, after which I prepared to fly down to Dunedin to help Linda with the hanging of the Rhona Haszard show.

'We can't afford to pay you a curator's fee,' Linda told me over the phone. 'We're over budget already. I might be able to squeeze something out of the travel budget.'

'That would be great. I'd love Sue and Katherine to come, but we can't really afford it. If some money could be found to pay for that, it would be helpful.'

We left it there. Linda would look into it, and Sue and I would keep our fingers crossed. The irony was that at this point in my life I was the poorest I had been for years. In spite of the fact that Richard had just inherited his family fortune, he was now claiming child support for both Alex and Jeremy. Things had got so difficult that I was putting basic payments like the power bill on the credit card. I began to wonder when, if ever, this vicious little game would end between us.

'I've got the tickets booked,' Linda said, at the beginning of our next phone call. 'There's a slight hitch, though. I'm sure there won't be any problems, but I've put Sue down as Rhona Haszard's daughter. It's only a technicality, but it will guarantee the funding.'

'Rhona Haszard's *daughter!*' I repeated at three times the normal volume. 'But she didn't have a daughter. They'll only have to read my book to know she didn't have a daughter.'

'I wouldn't worry. They'll never bother reading your book. It'll be fine. Just tell Sue she has to channel the spirit of Rhona Haszard's daughter.'

When I told Sue about it that night, we both killed ourselves laughing. Linda was a steamrolling force for good, but this did seem rather dubious.

I flew down to Dunedin early to help hang the show. There were Rhona's key works on loan from the Auckland Art Gallery, the most iconic being *Spring in the Marne Valley*, but also her striking paintings made on Sark in the Channel Islands, and the paintings and prints from the Hocken Collection. The majority of the other items came from private collectors, the principal one being Rhona's niece, Sherry Smith, but also Elizabeth Orr, Judith Nicholls and others, many of whom were related to the artist in some way. It was a tricky show to put up. Because of the scarcity of works, we had had to hang everything extant that Rhona had produced. At one end of her short life were her student 'daubs', and, at the other, monumental paintings fractured in post-impressionist facets of paint like a magnificent stained-glass window. Reconciling this exponential shift in a gallery space was not without its challenges.

Sue and Katherine arrived in preparation for the grand opening with more than 200 expected guests. Jeremy and my brother, Guy, and sister-in-law, Chrissie, came down from Christchurch, and my parents and Uncle Paul drove down from Golden Bay. By then my father had developed the signs of early-onset Alzheimer's, so there was a sense that this might be one of our last family get-togethers while Dad was still well. We stayed together in motel units.

'Now remember, you're Rhona Haszard's daughter if anyone asks,' I said to Sue as we were getting dressed before leaving for the opening. We both laughed uncomfortably again. It did seem hilarious, but only because the whole concept was preposterous.

'Have you warned Katherine?' I added as an afterthought. 'I'm sure it'll be fine,' I said, repeating Linda's assurances.

We met the rest of my family in the car park, squeezed everyone into two cars and drove in convoy to the opening. The Hocken Library was already filling with guests when we arrived.

My heart was racing. I had a speech to give after the head librarian delivered his address to kick off the event. I felt around in my bag to make sure my speech was still there. I pulled it out and re-read the opening paragraph a couple of times. A good start was crucial. As long as I knew that part well. I put it carefully back in its plastic sleeve.

'Should I have something to drink?' I asked Sue, as I closed my leather bag and looked longingly at the drinks table.

'No. You have to speak in a few minutes, so you need your wits about you.' But seeing my desperate look, she relented. 'Okay, you win, but just one.'

I grabbed a glass quickly, just in case she changed her mind. I glanced at my watch. The foyer was packed with people chatting. I could just make out my family, spotting Jeremy first. In the months that he had been in Christchurch he had shot up like a giant kauri. Squeezing through the crowd, Katherine came over to join Sue, who was not far from where I stood close to the lectern. Linda, who was master of ceremonies for the evening, stepped up to the portable podium. The plan was to have drinks, nibbles and speeches downstairs in the vast industrial-styled, cream-coloured foyer. Then after the show was officially opened, people would be invited to mount the stairs or take the lift to the second-floor galleries. From my vantage point, it was quite a sight; people in their finery listening now in hushed expectation. I opened my bag, propped between my feet, and took out my speech.

My hands shook with tension as I held on to it. Conscious again of what was being said: Linda had introduced the head librarian. He welcomed notable guests, enthused about the exhibition upstairs, then paused before revealing, with all the drama of a magician showing his pretty assistant sawn in half, that the evening had one final climactic surprise.

'We are very proud to announce, Rhona Haszard's daughter has flown down from Auckland to be with us tonight!' Then he smiled glowingly in Sue's direction. The audience followed his benign glance. A murmur went through the crowd, a mix of amazement and consternation. I was waiting for someone to shout out 'But Rhona Haszard didn't have a daughter!' . . . Nothing happened. I looked at Sue. She was flush-faced and wishing no doubt that the ground would open up. I could see Katherine nudge her, and they exchanged a stunned look.

After delivering the evening's triumph, the head librarian turned to me, next in line to give my speech. My legs almost failed me. I could hardly walk over to the rostrum. After I put my notes down, I paused. Nothing came out of my mouth for what seemed like an eternity. I faltered at the beginning, but gathered momentum. My mind was oddly detached from what I was saying: instead, it was imagining what I was going to say to Rhona's niece, Sherry. How would I explain this long-lost child to her family? I heard the clapping before it sunk in that I had finished.

As soon as the head librarian officially opened the show, I moved over to Sue.

'Quick, mingle before someone questions you,' I whispered, barely moving my lips. With that, Rhona Haszard's daughter vanished as mysteriously as she had materialised.

When I caught up with Linda later, she just laughed. 'Serves him right for not reading your book.' At the end of the evening, I did have to deal with a delegation of confused Rhona relations who accosted me in the kitchen while I was stacking plates in the dishwasher.

'What did he mean, "Rhona Haszard's daughter"? There's no mention of a daughter in your book.'

'No,' I responded, 'he obviously hasn't read it. He's near retirement and maybe a bit confused,' I said, and changed the subject as swiftly as I could.

Seeing Jeremy again in Dunedin was reassuring. I had worried feverishly that things would end the same way they had with Alex. Our phone calls since he had left Auckland had been awkward; stilted, even. I couldn't help feeling betrayed, and he was resolute about his decision to shift back to Christchurch. As it turned out, he lived with Richard for not much more than a year before he went flatting at 16 years old (which I would never have allowed him to do).

Our meeting in Dunedin was closure, an end in a way to my hopeless longings. I loved him and wanted more of him than he could give me. Separations so often force children to choose, to take sides in the game. Jeremy left both our homes to take himself out of the struggle. He would live his life and I would pursue mine, independently but together as mother and son. The instinct to frantically hold on had to be resisted. He was not a curiosity in my cabinet, and nor would he be a pawn — at this point, he had marched right off the board.

All my life my mother had been a keeper of things, a hoarder, whereas my life seemed to be one of moving on and letting go. My childhood made it hard not to see my lack of acquisitiveness as a failure. But as a friend of mine observed to me, relationships and experiences are the precious things I have collected in life, and this book is my cabinet of curiosities.

POSTSCRIPT

It took me a number of years after Jeremy's departure to begin carving. The idea was brewing in my mind all that time, especially after the research I had completed on the Lewis chess pieces. Bones are the things we leave behind, I thought. The final evidence that we walked on Earth and have returned to it. There is, therefore, something infinitely beautiful about bones. I know this sounds macabre, but I remember sitting looking at my purchase from the supermarket and wondering whether I should start carving the flat shin or the rounded cannon bones. There were three on the meat tray to choose from.

This was my tentative beginning. Eventually I would go upmarket and only use bones sourced from the Superior Meat butcher on Ponsonby Road. He must have thought I was insane coming into the shop with my precise measurements and specifications for what to him were leftovers only fit for dogs. I loved the thought that I was spinning worthless dog tucker into white gold. Even then I knew the material make-up of these large beef bones was almost indistinguishable from ivory.

I began by carving the two rooks, believing their execution would be easier. They were less auspicious, and more elementary figures. Initially I thought of them as a simple flat piece of bone carved in low relief like a pendant. Then, I figured out if I closed in the marrow cavity at the top, they could be carved in the round.

There is something magical about the process of turning dead bones into beautiful objects — or at least objects that carry the spirit of time and intention. The diaspora of my ancestors in travelling to New Zealand, their movement across the world by sailing ship, had left me separated from the treasures of my ancestors. Making the chess set was a means of bringing them back. Of making them mine in a country that was my home. By carving the past, by making it material in my world, I could possess it.

Carving is a slow process. You have time to think. I have long seen chess as a metaphor for life, with a set of shared understandings or rules that protect the players and the game. They make chess a fair contest. When you break the rules by having two queens — as we did — you relinquish their protection. The familiar and acceptable moves, the army of reassuring defenders — the rooks, the knights, the bishops — are gone. You are together on the board, but also alone.

Then there are the institutions you must fight. The intolerant Church that hated chess when it first arrived in Europe and still discriminates against homosexuality today. The lawyers, the courts, the counsel for the child, the education system, your employers, your funders: inscrutable bastions of convention structured to reward straight players. Even more cataclysmic is the struggle to keep what you had, the inevitable losses, the leaving behind of things you love, and finally the lessons learned — that families should not become battlegrounds and children pawns.

It took me five years to work my way through the eight intricate figure pieces. One of the last ones I carved was the queen. Ultimately, there would be two queens — one white and one red. Long before I completed the white queen and her courtly entourage, my new boss at Unitec, David Hawkins, challenged me.

He asked: 'Why don't you carve a Māori side?' It seemed so simple that I wondered why I hadn't thought of it myself. After all, the tradition of bone carving was just as significant in Aotearoa among Māori as it was for Scandinavian Vikings. But I nevertheless felt a reluctance to trespass on territory that was not culturally my own. I saw the issues in a very different way to my parents. But, in the end, it seemed more honest and true for me to represent both parts of who we were on the chessboard.

'We are going to research your family,' I came home and announced to Sue that evening. 'I'm going to carve them. Why should we have just my ancestors on the board?' She was excited by the idea.

Being an art historian, I had learned to read the symbols and language of Western art. But toi whakairo, mahi toi and everything within the basket of knowledge known as kete aronui were things I had viewed only from the outside. Now, it was Sue's heritage; now it was personal.

As is so often the case, Sue's thread of ancestral investigation would prove even more enthralling than my own. Her cabinet of curious stories has now been told, and her pieces carved. And on our chessboard are two peoples, two families, two queens.

AUTHOR'S NOTE

Te Wherowhero saw himself as the 'eye of a needle through which the white, black and red threads must pass'.

Perhaps appropriately, this book is composed of three threads woven together. One is a love story, and the other two are a search for whakapapa and identity. The imagined sections in the different typeface have been extensively researched, and what is believed to be factual, speculative or unknown is as follows.

The Lewis chess pieces thread is based on Frederic Madden's research, but also on current theories that the ivory came from Iceland and the north-eastern seaboard of North America, that the carving was done in Trondheim, that Margaret the Adroit was carving at the time the sets were executed and could have been one of their creators, and that some speculate that the sets were en route to Ireland. The various explanations for how the hoard came to be hidden on the Isle of Lewis were first mooted by Madden, then investigated extensively by subsequent commentators. Questions still remain around this, their unearthing, and how at least 11 pieces became separated from the original hoard of one belt buckle, 14 plain draughtsmen and 78 chessmen, and still remain in Scotland. Then, there is the overarching mystery of the four major pieces and many pawns missing from the original find.

Conflict has raged over who owns the chess pieces. Museum experts and academics have argued hotly over who should write about them. The Lewis hoard is contested territory, and there are many unanswered questions still. Objects tell us so much about themselves, but they also conceal secrets. Perhaps it is their mysteries that keep them alive in our imaginations and everlastingly intriguing. Some secrets, though, have been buried by shame and it is important to uncover them, be it shame over playing a chess game, over your sexual preference or over a Māori bloodline.

Sue's thread seems more personal, but it is also part of a public history that is disputed. This thread is based on the research of Russell and Gavin Bishop, and the art and writing of George Angas and John Gorst, respectively. Beyond these key commentators are many others who sometimes hold different and even conflicting views. Hinepau, and her unrecognised position as a young wife of chief Te Wherowhero, is just one of this thread's many controversies. Events surrounding the migration of the great waka are remembered differently. How Hinepau was captured and presented to Te Wherowhero is a matter for speculation. Whether Te Wherowhero's monument was erected for a daughter or a wife is debatable. Even what is recorded as fact shifts. The number of children Irihapeti had varies between sources, as does the spelling of her married names of 'McKay' or 'Mackay', and 'Joy' or 'Joyce'. There are issues involving the interpretation of translations made between Māori and English. There are family stories that embrace ambiguity, and history that has generated dissension. Some facts can be ascertained given *time*, while others will remain forever in flux because of it.

KEY TEXTS

The following is a selection of key texts.

VIKING THREAD

MADDEN, Frederic, 'Historical Remarks on the introduction of the game of Chess into Europe, and on the ancient Chess-men discovered in the Isle of Lewis; by Frederic Madden, Esq. F. R. S. in a Letter addressed to Henry Ellis, Esq. F. R. S., Secretary. Read 16th February, 1832', *Archaeologia* XXIV, (January 1832): 203–291.

MURRAY, H. J. R., *A History of Chess*. Oxford: Oxford University Press, 1913.

OLIVER, Neil, *Vikings*. London: Weidenfeld & Nicolson, 2012.

ROBINSON, James, *The Lewis Chessmen: British Museum Objects in Focus*. London: British Museum Press, 2004.

ROGERS, T. D., *Sir Frederic Madden at Cambridge*. Published for the Cambridge Bibliographical Society by Cambridge University Library, Cambridge, 1980.

SEKULES, Veronica, *Medieval Art: Oxford History of Art*. Oxford: Oxford University Press, 2001.

STEWART, Susan, *On Longing: Narratives of the miniature, the gigantic, the souvenir, the collection*. Durham: Duke University Press, 1993.

STRATFORD, Neil, *The Lewis Chessmen and the enigma of the hoard*. London: British Museum Press, 1997.

TAYLOR, Michael, *The Lewis Chessmen*. London: British Museum Press, 1995.

WILLIAMSON, Paul, *Medieval Ivory Carving*. London: Victoria & Albert Museum, 1982.

MĀORI THREAD

ANGAS, George F., *The New Zealanders Illustrated*. London: Thomas M'Lean, 1847.

BALLARA, Angela, 'Te Paea Tīaho', *Dictionary of New Zealand Biography*, first published in 1993. *Te Ara — the Encyclopedia of New Zealand*, https://teara.govt.nz/en/biographies/2t24/te-paea-tiaho (accessed 22 August 2021).

BARCLAY-KERR, Hoturoa, 'Waka — canoes', *Te Ara — the Encyclopedia of New Zealand*, http://www.TeAra.govt.nz/en/waka-canoes/print (accessed 9 January 2022).

BELGRAVE, Michael, 'The Monday Extract: Tāwhiao, the second Māori King, goes to London to see the Queen', *The Spinoff*, 26 February 2018.

BISHOP, Russell, 'The Family of Irihapeti/Te Paea'. In: *The whanau of Irihapeti Te Paea (Hahau): the McKay and Joy (Joyce) families* (compiled by Rex and Adriene Evans). Auckland: Evagean Publishing, c. 1994.

BUCK, Peter (Te Rangi Hīora), *Vikings of the Sunrise*. Christchurch: Whitcombe and Tombs, 1954 (originally published 1938).

GORST, John, *The Maori King* (edited and introduction by Keith Sinclair). Hamilton: Paul's Book Arcade, 1959 (original work 1864).

HAAMI, Bradford, 'Mataatua and Ngati Pukeko'. In: *The whanau of Irihapeti Te Paea (Hahau): the McKay and Joy (Joyce) families* (compiled by Rex and Adriene Evans). Auckland: Evagean Publishing, c. 1994.

MAHUTA, R. T., 'Tāwhiao, Tūkāroto Matutaera Pōtatau Te Wherowhero', *Dictionary of New Zealand Biography*, first published in 1993, updated July 2011. *Te Ara — the Encyclopedia of New Zealand*, https://teara.govt.nz/en/biographies/2t14/tawhiao-tukaroto-matutaera-potatau-te-wherowhero (accessed 22 August 2021).

MEAD, S. M., *Traditional Maori Clothing: A study of technological and functional change*. Wellington: A. H. & A. W. Reed, 1969.

NIXON, Marie, 'Credibility and Validation through Syntheses of Customary and Contemporary Knowledge.' PhD thesis, Massey University, Wellington, 2007.

OLIVER, Steven, 'Te Wherowhero, Pōtatau', *Dictionary of New Zealand Biography*, first published in 1990. *Te Ara — the Encyclopedia of New Zealand*, https://teara.govt.nz/en/biographies/1t88/te-wherowhero-potatau (accessed 22 August 2021).

O'MALLEY, Vincent, *The Great War for New Zealand: Waikato, 1800–2000*. Wellington: Bridget Williams Books, 2016.

SIMPSON, Ariana, 'Puhi: Memories and experiences in their ceremonial role in traditional and contemporary Māori worlds', *MAI Review*, 2006, Intern Research Report 9, http://www.review.mai.ac.nz/mrindex/MR/article/download/18/18-18-1-PB.pdf (accessed 9 January 2022).

ACKNOWLEDGEMENTS

When I began this book, I had just lost my job at Unitec in one of those *faux* restructures which turns your life upside-down. In the chaos of the 'who am I now?' and 'where am I going?' thoughts, my revelation was that I loved writing and that was *me* and *my way forward*.

The question was — after writing non-fiction for years under the strictures of academia — what was I going to write? The answer? The book I had always wanted to write. Ironically, even as I began it, I wasn't sure what that was.

When I set out on a walk from Waterview to the Auckland War Memorial Museum on All Hallows' Eve in 2014, I penned the Prelude on a small pad that sat in the palm of my hand. I didn't know what shape the book would take or that this was its beginning. But I liked the way it made me feel, and I knew I wanted to go on. Writing became cathartic. A sigh, an exhaling of breath that exorcised ghosts, and satisfied as well as saddened. The book would become the breath of my life and of Sue's, and the life-lines of the people whose stories it tells.

The belief that material about yourself is easy to write because it's yours is a myth. So I would like to thank the many people who have helped shape this book. Some are here standing solidly on *terra firma* and some are with us in spirit. Our tūpuna we acknowledge and remember in these pages.

The following is a heartfelt thank-you to those who journey on with us, and have helped make this odyssey of the soul happen. We would like to thank friends and colleagues who have read the manuscript and offered suggestions and insightful advice, especially Dr Rebecca Hayward, Fr John Walker, Jane Croessmann, Katherine Side, Mark Kramer, Meg Davis, Claire Houliston, Meghan Davidson, Jan Browne, Tanya Aspel, Aorewa McLeod, Nicola Lunt, Karen McLeod, Charmaine Pountney and Karen Craig.

We are deeply grateful to the tuhanga of Irihapeti Te Paea, especially Gavin and Russell Bishop, Marcia and Tahu Stirling, Paula Legal, Marie Nixon-Benton, Bradford Haami, Allanah Church, Lyn Wallace, Owen Kendall, and Bishop Sir David Moxom and Vicar Julie Guest of the Parish of St John's, Te Awamutu. We are indebted also to our Drayton, Marshall, Kendall and Robertson whānau, especially to my mother Pat Drayton, brother Guy and sister-in-law Chrissie, Uncle Paul, and to our wonderful children and life-changing grandchildren.

A special and sincere thank-you to those friends who helped make this story happen, especially Linda Tyler, Stuart Bednall, Celia Thompson, Jocelyn Cuming, Marilyn and Geoffrey Shekell, Neil Finlay, David Hawkins, Charles Grinter, Frantisek Riha-Scott, Warwick Mcleod, Siren Deluxe, Julia Waite, Barry Loe, Josephine Mason, Lois Anderson, Carol Beu and my AFS sister Patti Gurekian.

Of the groups that have supported this book, we would like to say a special thank-you to Jonathan Logan, John Paine and the Logan Fellowship, which funded my magical time living at the Carey Institute in Rensselaerville in upstate New York. It was there that I first read out a section from the manuscript that would become *The Queen's Wife*. I want to thank my colleagues at Avondale College, particularly my amazing friends in the Friday Coffee Club; Sue's classmates from Ilam School of Fine Arts; our colleagues and students from the Whanganui School of Design (UCOL); the Sarjeant Gallery Te Whare o Rehua Whanganui; Pulse Art Group; also SMILES, SMART and our lovely friends at St Matthew-in-the-City, and the fabulous Same Same But Different Board. But above all other organisations towers Penguin Random House which has made this project possible. A huge thank-you to Claire Murdoch and Harriet Allan who accepted my manuscript for publication, and to Harriet for 'straightening' its eccentricities. Thank you also to the book's copy-editor Kate Stone, project editor Louisa Kasza, and to the designer Cat Taylor.

Because of the culling and disappearing of LGBTQ and Māori lives, there are gaps, voids and silences. We are profoundly grateful to all who have given this story its voice.

INDEX

A

Alexandria   260, 292–94, 298–302, 306–11
al-Mus'udi   52
Angas, George French   129, 130
Aratāwhao   86
Archaeologia   51
Ard Mhór   94, 95
Auckland   39, 63, 128, 132, 184, 213, 214, 250, 251, 252, 255–57, 264, 265, 270, 277, 279–80, 303, 316, 318–21
Auckland Art Gallery   128, 319
Auckland War Memorial Museum   63

B

Baile-na-Cille   94
Ballance, John   196
Bay of Plenty   66
Bernini, Gian   56
Bishop, Gavin   64
Bishop, Russell   63, 64, 151
Black Nuns   54
Bradstock, Mike   235

British Museum   20, 50, 51–52, 55, 74, 78, 214, 284
Burton Brothers   183

C

Calum Mór   94, 97
Camaret-sur-Mer   290–91
Camden Town Group   284
Cape Runaway   66
Collier, Craig   156
Collier, Dorothy   32–34, 155, 157, 172, 228–29
Collier, Edith   21, 27–34, 36, 156, 173, 203, 221–30, 235–39, 241–42, 266, 276, 305
Collier, Eliza   229
Collier, Henry   28, 35, 223–29
Collier, Jean   172–75, 222–30, 239–41, 246–47, 265, 305
Collier, Thea   32, 33, 228–29
Cresswell, D'Arcy   205, 225, 254
Cullinan, Jim   239–40

D

Damiano, Pietro, Cardinal Bishop of Ostia 54
Doel, Lewis 311
Drayton, Malcolm 16, 80–81, 83–84, 123, 124, 222, 319
Drayton, Pat 15–16, 18, 35, 38, 42–43, 48, 67, 83–84, 123, 124, 219, 220, 253, 283, 287, 321
Drayton, Philippa 110, 145

E

Egypt 215, 260, 268–69, 298–302, 310–16, 318
Erik the Red 117–18
Erikson, Bjorn 119–20, 141–44, 170–71, 234, 262–63, 296–97
Erikson, Leif 118
Erikson, Thorvald 118–20, 142–43, 170

F

Finistère 287, 290
Fitzgerald, Keith 240–42, 246–47, 253
Flight, Claude 284
Forrest, Mr 74, 78
Fox, William 212

G

Galvin, Mary 239–40
Gillie, Ruadh, redheaded 95
Golden Bay 36, 45, 80, 122, 123, 146, 165, 179, 319
Gorst, John 213, 248–51, 327
Greener, Leslie 260, 267, 291, 300–1, 307, 310–11
Greenland 117–18, 262
Grey, Sir George 132, 248, 250

H

Hahau 107
Haszard, Rhona 260, 267–68, 284, 290–91, 299, 300, 307–8, 315, 317–20

Hawaiki 17, 86–87, 107
Hawkins, David 323
Helluland 118, 169–70
Hera, principal wife of Tāwhiao 211
Hinepau 64, 107–8, 130–31, 212, 327
Hoaki 86
Hocken Library 238, 266–67, 318–19
Hodgkins, Frances 30, 156, 235
Horea 184
Hovell, Selwyn Te Moananui 16, 17
Hunt, Holman 104

I

Ihumātao 132
Ingrum, Joe 243–45
Ingrum, Ruth 243–45
Irakewa 86
Ireland 198, 233, 235, 239, 240, 253, 261–62, 326
Irihapeti Te Paea *see* Te Wherowhero, Irihapeti Te Paea (Hahau, Mackay/McKay, Joy/Joyce)
Isle of Lewis 14, 53, 74, 94, 97, 261, 326

J

Joy, Samuel *see* Joyce, Samuel
Joyce, Samuel 184, 279

K

Kakahoroa 85
Kaputerangi 86
Kāwhia 66, 224, 225, 227
Kendall, Terry 62
Kihi 107
King, Stephen 136
Kīngitanga 133, 152, 212–13, 249–50, 303
Kupe 65
Kurawhakaata 85–86, 107

L

Labrador 118

Lindauer, Gottfried   212
Lloyd-Jenkins, Douglas   255, 259
Lonsdale, Patricia   224

M
Mackay, John Horton (McKay)   64
Mackay, Mayor Charles   204–6, 225
MacKenzie, A.J. Reverend Colonel   94
Macleod, Malcolm   74, 94
Madden, Frederic   51–55, 74, 78, 117–18, 167, 261, 326
Mākareta Te Otaota *see* Te Wherowhero, Mākareta Te Otaota
Maketū Bay   66
Mangatangi   47, 130
Māngere   213, 250
Maniapoto, Rewi   250
Margaret the Adroit   167, 169, 171, 326
Markland   118
Marore   131
Marshall, Vince   63, 304
Mātaatua   65, 86
Matirerau   87
Maungakawa   214
McDouall, Shirley   160, 264
McDuff, Alison   110
McKay, Benjamin   64
McKenzie, Ronald   267
McLeod, Warwick   196
Milbank, Bill   203
Morrell, Lady Ottoline   205
Morton, Molly   253
Moutoa Gardens   196, 200

N
Nan Sprot, Calum   74
Newfoundland   118
Ngahuruhuru   129
Ngāpuhi   131–32
Ngāruawāhia   63, 133, 211–12, 214, 250, 277, 279, 303
Ngāti Awa   106

Ngāti Mahuta   85, 108, 131–32, 152
Ngāti Maniapoto   251
Ngāti Mutunga   131
Ngāti Pūkeko   87, 106–7
Ngāti Toa   130–31
Ngātoroirangi   65–66, 85
Nicholls, Judith   319
North America   118, 326
Norway   118, 168, 262

O
Orr, Elizabeth   319

P
Parapara beach   80, 123
Parihaka   212
Parker-Hulme murder   67
Penny Donald (Calum nan Sprot)   74
Perry, Anne (Juliet Hulme)   68
Philidor, François-André Danican   25
Port Waikato   64, 152
Pōtatau *see* Te Wherowhero, Pōtatau
Preston, Margaret   235
Pukekawa   132
Pūkeko   87
Purau   16, 20, 37, 128, 150
Putataka   152–53, 184

Q
Quay School of the Arts   35, 195, 200

R
Ra'iatea   65
Raglan   184, 250, 279
Raroera   129
Rātana Church   212
Raynor, Paul   238, 241
Reynell, Gladys   235
Rongomaiwhiti   107
Royal Museum, Edinburgh   55, 78
Ryrie, Captain Roderick   75, 77–78

S

Sarjeant Gallery 28, 30, 156, 157, 172, 203–5, 225, 238, 246
Scott, Sir Walter 52–55
Selwyn, Bishop 153
Skraeling 118–20, 142–43, 170
Smith, Sherry 300, 301, 319, 321
Society of Antiquities of Scotland 78
Sophia, Princess *see* Te Wherowhero, Te Paea Tīaho Pōtatau
Sowry, Roger 242–43, 245
Stewart, Barbara 27–36, 150, 154–55, 172–76, 179, 185–86, 192–94, 226–30, 239, 241, 256, 265, 305
Stewart, Jean 172–75, 222–25, 226–27, 239–42, 246–47, 305
Strachey, Lytton 13
Stubbing, Benjamin 279
Stubbing, Harold Bowie 278
Stubbing, Lucy (Terry) 303
Stubbing, Maria Louisa 277–79, 303
Symonds, Captain 132

T

Taimitimiti 107
Tainui 65
Tainui 65–66, 85, 131
Tamakihikurangi 86
Tāmihana, Wiremu 212–13
Tāneatua 86
Taranaki tribes 131–32
Taukata 86
Taupiri mountain 251, 277
Tāwhiao *see* Te Wherowhero, Tāwhiao, Tūkāroto Matutaera Pōtatau
Te Arawa 65, 85
Te Awa-i-taia, Wiremu Nēra 250
Te Awamutu 250–51
Te Kauhanganui 214
Te Paea Tīaho Pōtatau *see* Te Wherowhero, Te Paea Tīaho Pōtatau
Te Rauparaha 131, 133
Terry, Cecil 303–4
Terry, Lucy (*née* Stubbing) 303–4
Terry, Norma 304–5
Terry, Patricia 304
Terry, Zelma 62, 304
Te Rūnanga Pākaitore 196
Te Waro 129
Te Wherohero, Irihapeti Te Paea (Hahau, Mackay/McKay, Joy/Joyce) 63–64, 130–31, 151–52, 183–84, 211, 213, 248–49, 251, 279, 327
Te Wherowhero, Mākareta Te Otaota 132
Te Wherowhero, Ngāwaero (*née* Tukorehu) 132
Te Wherowhero, Pōtatau 62, 63, 108, 129–33, 152, 184, 212–13, 249–50, 326, 327
Te Wherowhero, Raharaha 132
Te Wherowhero, Tāwhiao Tūkāroto Matutaera Pōtatau 132, 211–15, 248–51
Te Wherowhero, Te Paea Tīaho Pōtatau 212–13, 248–51
Te Wherowhero, Tīria 132
Te Wherowhero, Waiata (*née* Tukorehu) 132
Te Wherowhero, Whakaawi (*née* Mahuta) 132
The Saga of Bishop Páll 167
Thompson, Celia 30, 31, 241
Thorir 168–69
Tīria *see* Te Wherowhero, Tīria
Toi 65
Toroa 86–87, 250
Treaty of Waitangi 132, 196, 214–15
Trondheim 54, 117, 168–71, 197, 261, 263, 326
Tūrangawaewae marae 133
Tyler, Linda 266–67, 317–21

U
Uig   53, 94, 150
Unitec   255, 258–59, 268, 270, 273, 316, 318, 323

V
Van der Rohe, Mies   15
Vinland   118

W
Wairaka   250
Waite, Julia   128–30
Waitematā Harbour   66
Whāingaroa   184
Whakaari   85–86, 107–8
Whakatāne   85, 87, 106–8, 279
Whanganui Polytechnic   35, 195, 235, 259
Whangaparāoa   66
Wotton, Richard   239